W9-CHM-040

THE ADVENTURES OF A
BED SALESMAN

THE ADVENTURES OF A
BED SALESMAN

Michael Kumpfmüller

Translated from the German by Anthea Bell

Picador
New York

www.picadorusa.com

Picador® is a U.S. registered trademark and is used by St. Martin's Press under license from Pan Books Limited.

For information on Picador Reading Group Guides, as well as ordering, please contact the Trade Marketing department at St. Martin's Press.
Phone: 1-800-221-7945 extension 763
Fax: 212-677-7456
E-mail: trademarketing@stmartins.com

Library of Congress Cataloging-in-Publication Data

Kumpfmüller, Michael.
    [Hampels Fluchten. English]
    The adventures of a bed salesman / Michael Kumpfmüller ; translated from the German by Anthea Bell.
        p. cm.
    ISBN 0-312-28748-8 (hc)
    ISBN 0-312-42336-5 (pbk)
    I. Bell, Anthea. II. Title.

PT2671.U454H3613 2003
833'.92—dc21   2002193113

First published in Germany under the title Hampels Fluchten by Kiepenheuer & Witsch Koeln

First Picador Paperback Edition: March 2004

10 9 8 7 6 5 4 3 2 1

THE ADVENTURES OF A
BED SALESMAN

1

Heinrich crossed the border at Herleshausen-Wartha on a Tuesday in March. On the face of it, it seems unlikely for a man of thirty to have been crossing that border in the spring of 1962 with nothing but a rucksack full of underwear and a bottle of whisky, not sparing a thought for his wife and children, explaining that he wanted to be a citizen of the thirteen-year-old German Democratic Republic, no need for anyone to know his reasons in detail just yet.

He had no precise plan in mind when he set out for the border that day, drove the new Citroën to Fulda railway station, then went on by train to just outside Herleshausen by way of Bebra, with the smell of his mistress still on his hands. He will have been thinking mainly of her as he walked the last two or three kilometres, turning off the main road and passing through fields, meadows and woodland, or then again perhaps he had forgotten her already, and was simply listening to his footsteps on the damp ground, reacting nervously when a passer-by came towards him, beginning to sweat slightly in his suit, waistcoat and hat, and the white shoes in which he must have cut a curious figure in these rural surroundings, so he returned no friendly greeting when he was spoken to, but just kept his eyes fixed on the next couple of metres ahead of him. At last he stopped to rest in a bus shelter, knowing that he must make his decision here, at this bus stop on the way into Herleshausen.

At first his mind had been in a state of great confusion: the smell of his mistress (her name was Marga), his fear of his creditors, his relief at escaping them, the thought of Rosa whom he had deceived, Rosa left behind with the two children, all this clamoured and flickered through his head. He sat at that bus stop for at least an hour, thinking about his life, the women in his past and the women yet to come, the beds he'd shared with them, the beginning and end of his business career, his journeys, his boozing, those years in the Soviet Union, his father's illness, his mother's early death, and yet again his mistresses who, in alphabetical order, were Anna, Bella, Dora, Gerda, Lyusya, Marga, Rosa and Wanda. He told them apart by the songs they sang, and the birthmarks he saw on them in various places when they were lying beside him.

So he sat there for an hour, waiting, and when the storm inside his head had died down, and he felt drained and determined, he got up and crossed the street from the bus stop to a café, where a young waitress served him. As a farewell gesture he ordered a big breakfast, having eaten nothing at Marga's early that morning.

Since the waitress wasn't very busy she asked if he was from hereabouts, and had he seen all those new structures that had gone up on the border, but he said no, he was just passing through, he'd only seen those new structures that had gone up on the border on TV. It was just terrible, said the waitress, she personally wouldn't want to live over there one little bit, she'd sooner hang herself.

Well, suppose he told her he's going to cross the border himself in the next few hours and stay there for good, because he won't have to hang himself over there, but here in the West he would?

He really shouldn't crack jokes at the expense of those poor things in the East, said the waitress, they didn't have any choice in the matter, and although she cast him a number of surreptitious glances after that, keeping an eye on him sitting there at the table in his white shoes and his suit, she seemed to have taken serious offence at his remark. My father had a house in Thuringia years ago, I'd like to live there, said Heinrich when she brought him his bill a little later, and she stopped short for a moment and looked at him as if to apologize, but Heinrich rose and left, making for the border.

The evening before, standing for the second time outside the door of the building where Marga lived, he had hesitated. He was still a few minutes early. He saw the light in her second-floor window, and when he tried to remember her clearly what struck him was how slender and how cautious she had been. She was probably still ashamed of that episode back in the shop with him, which would be why she had asked him on the phone to give her two hours, he couldn't come and see her until those two hours were up.

Although he had meant to wait a little longer than the appointed time, it was eight on the dot when he called again from a telephone kiosk in her street, and as her voice now suddenly sounded very welcoming he went upstairs, or rather ran upstairs to the second floor, saw her standing there, and shook hands as if they were strangers. Hello there, said Heinrich, letting her guide him through her sparsely furnished flat and immediately spotting traces of another man in the bathroom, on the coffee-table and in the bedroom, but fortunately the other man wasn't at home, or perhaps he just sometimes stayed overnight, perhaps he knew where her sharp bony places were and had learnt not to bump into them.

Marga hadn't changed much since last time, their first. He remembered her eyes when he saw her in front of him, and yet again they seemed to him very narrow and unusually small, she had cut her hair short and was wearing a dark-blue dress with an above-the-knee hemline, possibly in order to attract him. If she hasn't been alone here these last two hours, thought Heinrich, at least she isn't giving anything away, or alternatively she's covered her tracks but left the pipe and shaving brush and pyjamas lying about on purpose, as a warning. She had made something for supper and laid the table for two in the kitchen where they sat talking, perhaps she had a brother who came to town on business now and again and could stay with his sister for free – such thoughts passed through his mind, and after all he could hardly ask whether she was living alone now or with some other man.

I'm at the end of my tether, Heinrich told her, but I'm glad to be at the end of my tether, and Marga just nodded, looked at his dirty shoes and crumpled suit, didn't want to hear about it, it was probably far too late for good advice. What about Rosa? asked Marga, and Heinrich said he didn't want to talk about Rosa just now but he'd like to stay the night, and tomorrow morning he was going to the East to start a new life. He must have asked her, as soon as they finished supper, whether she minded if he spent his last night in the West with her, and in the end things went the same as usual, except that he'd never had to ask any favours before. In her own way, Marga probably liked it that he had to ask, so she just nodded again, washed the supper dishes, disappeared into the bathroom for half an hour, cleared away the pyjamas, pipe and shaving brush and a few other little things belonging to her lover or her brother, as the case might be, sat down beside Heinrich at the oval coffee table, and said he wasn't to think she didn't remember, and would he please get out of his head any idea that she'd ever been ashamed of it. So much for that.

She made him wait a little longer before they got around to it, and then nothing much happened, or rather he felt very affectionate towards her but he simply couldn't make it as a lover that night, and when Marga tried to comfort him he said he was okay, and he hoped she was okay too, he was very affectionate all of a sudden, very selfless in the art of love, and after all, he knew how someone who had failed as a lover could still give a woman a good time, didn't he?

Some time in the course of that night Marga must have told him she could see why he was going to the East, although it was still something of a mystery to her, even though she was a Communist. Heinrich was surprised to hear Marga call herself a Communist and tell him that she knew people with whom she discussed the prospects for Communism in West Germany, they'd meet in someone's flat, always a different one, talking until late into the night about the possibility of founding a Party, and sometimes, when they were all very tired and the last bus had gone, a couple of the comrades stayed overnight and left their pyjamas behind.

Write and tell me your address when you're over there, she asked when everything had been said, and he promised, because he knew everything had been said, not that I know if she'll ever answer my letters, he thought. Then they slept for a while in her West German Communist bed, which was rather narrow for two people but soft and warm and comfortable, and next morning he kissed her on the mouth, said goodbye, went to the station and bought a ticket to Herleshausen.

The West German border officials merely shook their heads when Heinrich arrived just after one o'clock, showed his travel permit and said he wanted to go to the East and had nothing but a rucksack with him, and since he was secretly afraid the police might already be after him because of the bankruptcy, to get him summarily arrested as a swindler going East with debts worth quarter of a million, he did everything very slowly and deliberately for the benefit of the border officials, said a few words about his father's home and his East German origins, carefully made a pile of his underwear, socks, shirts and trousers, opened the box containing the letters and photos, cracked a joke about the opened bottle of whisky which he would have drunk if Marga hadn't been at home, cracked another joke about his unsuitable white shoes, took care not to overdo the jokes, and waited for the officials to give their verdict. He was told he could keep everything except the sports section of

Monday's *Süddeutsche Zeitung*, just to avoid unnecessary trouble, and anyway he'd have the sports section of *Neues Deutschland* to read in future. Had Herr Hampel really thought hard about returning to his native central Germany? Yes, he had. Was he sure? Yes, he was sure. So there was nothing more the officials could say, Herr Hampel was a free citizen in a free country, the territory of the German Democratic Republic began just a few paces further on, okay, goodbye.

Heinrich was so relieved to have got over this first hurdle successfully that he felt like taking the opened bottle of whisky out of his rucksack, but then he decided a man should be able to show he felt cheerful without whisky, for after all the people over there would be watching him, and they might just possibly think he wasn't serious about starting a new life in a new and better Germany, did he think a man needed Dutch courage to go the last few metres, was that the kind of state he thought the GDR was? To avoid giving anyone the wrong impression Heinrich walked towards the checkpoint with a particularly firm tread, even whistling, and looked to left and right of the tall grating in the metal fence which marked the border here, a border over which no creditor or bailiff would pass so easily in the spring of 1962, perhaps not even a wife.

Only as he went the very last few metres did it occur to him that he had no idea what he was going to say to the people over there about his reasons. Perhaps they'd be glad to see someone like him and consequently wouldn't ask too many questions about any reasons a man had, whether good or bad, for taking such a step, just so long as he didn't want to go back to the West, and since he was escaping from the West he certainly didn't want to do that. Heinrich wanted to be treated as a welcome arrival in the new Workers' and Peasants' State, he wanted to leave everything behind, make a new beginning himself in this land of new beginnings, at the age of thirty he wanted to be a blank sheet again, a blank sheet on which anyone who liked could write.

Even as the border guard soldiers were asking to see his papers, the unsuspecting Heinrich still couldn't imagine getting anything but a friendly, hearty welcome. He was only surprised that they immediately took away his bottle, and on their second search they also confiscated the box containing his lovers' letters and photographs, although he would have been only too willing to tell the border guard soldiers all about them: their particular characteristics, their skills, his first and last times with them and the times in between – there were plenty of those – his final rifts with them; who came before them and who came after them; why none of them was in the least like Rosa (oh, they were all like Rosa), but how there was at least one tiny, familiar, special little detail about every single one of them.

He was rather taken aback by his initial reception, when they just left him alone in the company of a young soldier who didn't say a word. He could see the others making phone calls of some kind inside the checkpoint building and studying his passport one by one: born Jena, 25 August 1931, distinguishing marks, none.

After about half an hour they began asking questions. They wanted to know whether he was wanted by the police in the West (no), did he have family in the GDR (unfortunately not), what did he know about the structure of Socialism and the progress it was making (not a lot). He did know a woman in Fulda who was a Communist, said Heinrich, and he'd spoken fluent Russian since he was fifteen; that at least interested them. They asked would Heinrich please follow the Comrade Lieutenant into a small waiting-room, where he could rest for a while and drink a glass of tea, thus initiating him in his very first minutes in the East into the art of waiting: a difficult art, and he didn't have much practice in it yet.

Shortly before reaching Fulda he had run into a heavy fall of wet snow, and while the storm raged outside, making it impossible for anyone to see more than a couple of metres ahead, he tried to remember which city she had written from when she sent him the postcard back then, was it really Fulda or somewhere else with a similar name, what made him think of Fulda? Did she come from Fulda, or had she just moved there at the time, or was she passing through? She seemed to travel around a good deal, Marga the connoisseur of beds, and one day there she was in his shop asking questions and lingering, but she was only one of many, and as one of many she left no distinct trace behind. All he remembered was her voice, which was hoarse and deep and full of promise (as he put it), and since her voice was like music it could not, unfortunately, be described in words.

In the photograph she sent him years later she looked rather nondescript: a thin, pale face giving little away, rather too long a nose, he would never have taken any notice of her in the street. Summer 1968, it said on the back of the photograph, long live the German Communist Party, remember me? Love, M.

They had just let him out of jail for the first time when she sent him this photo without any accompanying letter, and although in the years that followed she visited him a couple of times on Party business of some kind in the East, when he was right at the end of his tether she too forgot him very quickly, sensitive little Communist that she was, a woman from the West with one of those mouths that always look as if they're begging or pleading for something, very softly and discreetly, and once, years ago, he had kissed that mouth with its thin, pursed lips. He can't really have been expecting her to make excuses or stipulations back then in March 1962, for he had never before known a woman, a lover, turn him away on the telephone, telling him that his visit was very inconvenient just at that moment but she'd be happy to see him a little later.

He was in a telephone kiosk at the station when she gave him this information, and not really knowing what to do with himself over the next two hours he wandered around the station concourse for a while, stood drinking a cup of coffee, and finally fetched his bag from the car and went to her flat well in advance of the appointed time. He could see from the lighted windows on the second floor of the austere new building that she was at home.

He waited, wondering about her reasons: perhaps she had another lover (well, she probably did) and wasn't through with him yet, or perhaps she was just fondly waving him goodbye, perhaps she was tarting herself up for Heinrich (no, ridiculous), perhaps she had important work to do (she was a teacher, wasn't she?), or perhaps she was just sitting in her flat toying with the thought of going out somewhere for the evening, not expecting to come home and find Heinrich still standing down in the street, waiting for her to put in an appearance and ask him up to her flat – any of these notions, he thought, might be correct.

Heinrich waited for almost two hours, thinking that just about anything was possible, dismissing such ideas, then entertaining them again, and so the time passed. As seven o'clock approached he thought briefly of going to a nearby hotel and forgetting about Marga, but then he struck a curious kind of bargain with himself and her, realizing how ridiculous it was that the terms of this bargain depended on the words and gestures with which she received him, wondering whether she wanted anything to do with him as a friend or indeed a lover, and if so what. Since he got cold if he just stood around for too long, looking up at her window and waiting for a shadow to appear, or two shadows, he walked round the old cemetery a couple of times, a place where no one had been buried for years, deciphering the names of dead strangers on the weathered stones, quite a laborious task when so little light was cast on them from the street, but there was no dead woman called Marga there.

After about an hour a border guard brought him a long questionnaire to fill in, asking him to enter the names and dates of birth of every member of his family, together with their professions and any political parties, trades unions or other associations to which they belonged, how on earth was he supposed to know all that? After a good half hour he had dealt with the six pages of the questionnaire (it was now two-thirty), then they took it away (it was now three p.m.), then came more patient waiting, they were obviously leaving him to sit and stew a few more minutes for every unanswered question. Around three-thirty an older man appeared, a civilian in a plain grey suit and check shirt, and apologized. Unfortunately, he said, Heinrich wasn't the only one wanting to cross the border into the German Democratic Republic today, would he please be patient a little longer, another half an hour and they could carry on, he'd have to say who he was again, where he came from and how much Western money he had with him, the exchange rate was one to one until evening, well, they weren't being actively unfriendly.

The two soldiers who searched his bag must have been locals, because although they were not very talkative they said enough for him to recognize their Thuringian dialect, and for a moment he felt at home, just like that. You must be from Jena or somewhere near, he said, suddenly speaking in an accent he hadn't used for years himself, and they seemed momentarily pleased, but immediately turned formal again and went on investigating his bag. When they had finished with it they searched his clothes, found a few Western pfennigs he had forgotten in his waistcoat pocket, and made it very clear how suspicious they thought such little details were, but since Heinrich spoke their own dialect they weren't about to kick up a great fuss, wait outside while we go and report, would you, and by now it was nearly four.

The next person Heinrich saw was an older officer from Saxony, there were a few more questions they had to ask about his personal details. What was to become of the wife and children he was leaving behind, were there any plans for them to follow him later? He was afraid he didn't really think so, said Heinrich, we never discussed it, but he'd like to know what was going to happen to him personally next, he wanted to go on to Jena today, he'd grown up in Jena, his father's house was there, he was known in Jena.

You mustn't think it's that easy, said the officer, in a way that made Heinrich begin to realize how inaccurate his ideas of the border guards had been, and why his flight – or his return – presented them with problems, why every question they asked him was part of a test which would decide whether they let him in or sent him back to the West. After all, said the officer, the German Democratic Republic can't let every ruined businessman or what-have-you into the country who wants to come, without any kind of inquiry, and he added something to the effect that the German Workers' and Peasants' State was not a place where social misfits could be offloaded. So let's hear your story, but keep it short, please, after all, you're not the first to turn up with some kind of tale in the fond belief that we haven't heard it before, whereas we know such stories inside out. Oh, we've had all sorts here, said the officer, all manner of unemployed we've seen and even more deserters, plenty of adventurers too, deserted wives, cuckolded husbands, the homeless family from the Ruhr, the bankrupt packaging manufacturer from Hamburg, the pickpocket from Kiel: oh yes, they've all been here. You don't need to explain what it's like in general in the capitalist West, what happens before a man packs his bag and sets his sights on the GDR, and as for all the people who once left full of illusions, and come back again disappointed and disenchanted, we can leave them right out of it.

So what had Heinrich's line of business been?

Beds and bedding.

Well, this was a new one, they hadn't had anyone in the

beds and bedding line before, but it would have been the banks that ruined him.

Oh yes, it was the banks, said Heinrich, greatly relieved that the man knew all about it and didn't insist on further details, since mentioning some of those details would have been awkward.

Then they had a brief conversation about Heinrich's Russian years and also, just in passing, about his contacts with West German Communists, a man like Heinrich, said the officer from Saxony, would undoubtedly get along well in the first German Workers' and Peasants' State, so the first step is to take you to our pleasant reception centre in Eisenach, he'd get his box of letters and photographs back when he left for Eisenach at the latest.

In retrospect, it was difficult for Heinrich himself to say when and where the idea of going to the East had first come to him, or how it felt when he ridiculed his brother while Rosa stood between them, looking desperate, and he heard his elder brother say: Go on, then, you'd better go to the East, you don't have any alternative, do you?

Of course Theodor hadn't seriously thought Heinrich might go to the East, and Heinrich himself hadn't been thinking of it just then, he simply wanted to get away, and Rosa hadn't the slightest idea, she didn't even guess at his impending ruin yet. But she sensed that by now he was capable of doing anything, and she wanted, although it was useless, to restrain him, prevent him from getting into the blue Citroën before her eyes and driving off for heaven knew how long. But where are you going, for God's sake, she cried as he left, and when he took one last look back in the driving mirror he saw Theodor spitting scornfully on the ground and putting his arm round Rosa, so now she'd have to see how she got along without her unfaithful husband Heinrich, he supposed it wouldn't be easy for her.

For the first thirty kilometres, until he reached the

Frankfurt-Hoechst motorway junction, Heinrich was incapable of any clear thought at all, but then he gradually calmed down, drove north past Homburg and Bad Nauheim, and after Giessen he went on east towards Bad Hersfeld. Somewhere along the way the thought must have occurred to him: the East. That's the last thing any of them will think of, they won't expect a man like me to cross the border and be gone for good, never to return.

Tired after his nocturnal arguments with Rosa, he stopped for a break in a roadside café just outside Bad Hersfeld, mulled the idea over – and what kind of an idea was it, this notion which had just occurred to him for the first time? – well, his brother Theodor wouldn't be able to understand it, that was for sure. He liked the idea that his brother wouldn't understand it, he liked the idea that his friends, acquaintances and business associates wouldn't understand it either, so he went back to his car, saw a road sign for Fulda a few kilometres further on, was briefly taken aback, suddenly remembering that little affair last winter, was pleased to find that he immediately remembered the name attached to the affair (Marga, that was it), so he thought of visiting her in her home town of Fulda, swapping a few reminiscences with her, a little time for reflection could certainly do no harm.

He was still on the way to the station when he remembered that there had been an unpleasant incident over this Marga last winter, that is to say the unpleasant incident had been after she left, just as he was about to go home, when Rosa turned up in the shop all of a sudden, and of course she immediately saw the bed where he had been making love to Marga half an hour earlier. He had rather enjoyed Marga's love-making and her manner in general, if he remembered correctly, and Rosa made one of those scenes which had become more and more frequent in recent years, and in which she used fewer and fewer words to express her contempt for Heinrich and all those afternoons spent with any chance-met female who happened to come his way.

So now you're even doing it here in the shop, Rosa had said, and as usual Heinrich did not reply, although the fact was that Marga had turned up in his shop quite by accident, and as for what became of her afterwards: no idea. She had just written him that single insignificant postcard from her home town of Fulda one day, and although at the time she too had seemed to him entirely insignificant now, months later, she put the most outlandish ideas into his head, and he decided that he must go and see her and make everything the same as it had been back in the shop that afternoon, even if it was only for the one night before he either went over to the East or decided – perhaps because of that one night with Marga – to think better of his decision.

You make me sick, Rosa had told him at the time, and from the way she said it he felt fairly sure she had actually seen nothing but the untidy bed, having arrived too late for anything else, or so he hoped. She never came to see him in the shop again (nor did Marga), but after this he felt she was watching him. She still hadn't given up on him back then in January 1962, seven weeks ago: good heavens, was it only seven weeks? It seemed to Heinrich an eternity.

Later on, he would say only the bare minimum about his days in the camp at Eisenach. If the questions were particularly persistent, or if he liked a woman, he would reveal that it was dark on his arrival and he had been taken to one of the wooden huts, which were still quite new, but unfortunately it was too late for supper. There must have been several hundred people in the camp at the time, eight to a hut, with three woollen blankets each and sheets to sleep in, mess kit and a bag, that was it at the start.

He didn't stop to think too much about this start, or perhaps he was too tired to do so, or he thought he could still go back on his decision if, for instance, he didn't like the other men in the hut, who were taciturn or pretending to be asleep, and wanted him to be quiet and keep his mouth shut at this time of night, imagine bringing someone into the camp at such an hour.

All things considered, it was probably only in Bautzen that he realized his decision had been irrevocable, and he was wrong if he had thought it was just a temporary measure, if it doesn't work out we can do something else, or go on from where we left off – for he did indeed see it in such simple terms. Afterwards he said: I stumbled into it, I simply stumbled into it, and later on there were some things I liked all right and some things I liked less, but I never really made any decision. What was it he always used to say? Let's wait and see what happens, something's sure to happen, and that was how he came to end up there in the East. Let's see what happens if I drive towards Herleshausen, let's see what happens if Marga takes me in, let's see what happens if I go on to the border next morning – and once the first days in the camp are over and I have a new place to live and a new job, it won't be as bad as all that (and it wasn't). Better than in the West, anyway.

He will have been thinking along such lines on that first evening in Eisenach, when the others were asleep and no one wanted to know about him, yes, he felt very optimistic, and there was a big breakfast next morning, and the five young fellows in his hut weren't so bad at all, they came from the Göttingen area and were talking their heads off and ready for adventure, looking to the future, they were going out as soon as possible to explore the place, but Heinrich had to stay in camp for a twenty-four-hour quarantine period.

There was a strange atmosphere in the camp. It was surprisingly quiet, although the huts were full of all kinds of people mixed up together, people who didn't like talking about themselves and their past, or exactly why they had come and with what hopes, they preferred to keep all that to themselves out of distrust or prudence, or perhaps on instructions. Tom was the only one with whom Heinrich had a lot of conversation from the first. Tom was just twenty and still took life easy, as something unimportant, and when he came up against difficulties (he had several times misappropriated sizeable sums of money, and had been on the run for months), when he came up against difficulties he cleared out and settled somewhere else, wherever he liked.

Heinrich met him over lunch, and shortly before lunch a man from the internal security service, the Staatssicherheitsdienst, introduced himself, sounded very friendly and forthcoming and even gave Heinrich a cigarette. His questions were few and easily answered: did Heinrich have any relations or siblings in the Federal Army, the Federal Border Police or the ordinary police force? Any knowledge of military installations? He said no. Had he settled down in the camp – thanks for the kind enquiry – and then Heinrich was allowed to go. Lunch came next and his first conversation with Tom, and then, in the afternoon, a discussion with the cultural director in the television room. A plainly dressed man in his fifties, the cultural director delivered a short speech on Western bugging systems and how everyone in the camp had a number, but you'd get used to that, thought Heinrich, the way you'd get used to the early supper, and after all the tea, sausage, cheese, butter and bread didn't taste so very different from their counterparts at home.

Going to the evening lecture? asked Tom after supper, rolling his eyes to heaven in a way which immediately told Heinrich that the lecture was nothing wonderful but one might as well go all the same, there was nothing else to do. Most of the inmates of the other huts were also there: a first lieutenant in the Volkspolizei, the People's Police, spoke on espionage, sabotage, militarists and capitalists, but Heinrich wasn't really listening, and what he did hear sounded like some new foreign language (Bonn imperialism), only a few words of which were familiar at first and had roughly the same meaning as he attached to them in the West.

There wasn't much else to do after the lecture. He exchanged a few more remarks with Tom on the way back to the hut, went to bed early like the rest of them and couldn't sleep, tried to think of Marga and how he hadn't wanted her to masturbate him, but now he was doing it to himself, moving quietly under the thin bedclothes, and the only pictures he could conjure up were of Rosa. For a moment he was surprised at himself, for it had been years since he had frankly pleasured himself while unable to think of anyone but the faithful Rosa, and afterwards, in fact, he felt tired and content and fell into a carefree sleep.

Rosa hadn't really taken him seriously back at the beginning of March when everything was balanced on a knife-edge, so little idea did she have of what was going on, and she refused to believe in his imminent ruin. All right, so you can't see any way out of it today, she had said, well, why don't we go and see Theodor and talk it all over with him, I mean, he's your brother, and I know you're not all that fond of each other, but in times of trouble blood's thicker than water, and next day you can go to Frankfurt and negotiate credit with this Offermann (a name invented by himself), and everything will work out.

You really think so?

Yes, I do. (Rosa's finest hour.) Haven't we put other things behind us, with a little give and take?

I suppose so. (All he could think of was the business of Susanna.)

They told their daughter: We're all off to Wiesbaden for a couple of days, but when we come back you mustn't tell anyone where we've been, and they put her in the back of the new Citroën and drove off; it was less than four hours door to door.

For God's sake, what's got into you two? asked Theodor, who hated surprise visits, and his wife Ilse, who couldn't stand Theodor's younger brother, asked why for goodness' sake they always had to arrive unannounced, time and again it was always the same old story. Well, it's about the firm, said

Heinrich, the first year's always the most difficult, he began cautiously. To which Theodor replied, distrustfully: Have you really been running that business of yours for a year already?

It was exactly a year in February.

How time flies.

And then Theodor left him dangling. *How time flies.* Was that all he could find to say? How time flies? Only someone who had never been up to his neck in it could talk like that, obviously, someone who always had his business affairs in apple-pie order in good time for the benefit of his nearest and dearest, shunning risks the way the devil shuns holy water (as Rosa would have said), someone who had grown prosperous solely through his own hard work, industry and prudent life-style. Heinrich sensed that his elder brother always shrank from these meetings or confrontations, but he also sensed that a change was on the way, he sensed the forthcoming triumph of the slow but sure over the unscrupulous, impatient character he himself had always been, and now, all of a sudden, he was being fobbed off with assorted empty phrases, just to keep him from coming straight out with it and broaching the tiresome subject of money once again, oh, please, pull yourself together and wait until the children are in bed, can't you?

My lawyer says there are certain clauses which mean at the best I'll be jailed for a few years, and at the worst I'll be slaving away for my creditors all my life.

I'm not responsible for your mistakes.

You're my brother.

Not my brother's keeper.

That was all they said about it that evening, and when the two women brought a meal in from the kitchen it was like any ordinary family visit, and neither Theodor nor Heinrich mentioned the matter again. But Rosa did once in her own way, long after midnight, and Theodor thought it rather inappropriate for her to start carrying on about Heinrich's difficulties at this time of night, bringing up the question of how far he had just had bad luck or how far he had failed, and the way one of those things can turn to the other, are some people failures from birth or do they simply get made into failures, these were the questions on her mind at the moment, and Heinrich, over near the door, couldn't help listening to the pair of them.

Later, he thought Rosa had sounded very gentle but determined, he only wished he knew the way her mind worked, and how she could suddenly change it completely from one minute to the next, and then she would lean over to him as she did now and whisper a couple of words in his ear, and when he heard what it was she was whispering he was glad. They were really just a couple of words spoken several thousand times before, but still he was glad.

After breakfast on the Thursday Tom said: Well, you're through with the twenty-four-hours quarantine now but they won't be letting you out of camp yet, not for some time, they have to give you a medical examination before they let you out of camp, then we can go and have lunch, and the next trick they think up quite often begins with a cigarette and ends with Lord knows what kind of complications, commitments even. That's just by way of a bit of advice, Heinrich, old fellow, you're still new here and yesterday's cigarette was only the start, by the third day at the latest you won't get off so lightly.

It took the young doctor who examined or rather questioned Heinrich no more than a couple of minutes to know all about him: he was young and strong, looked you straight in the eye, seemed fit for any kind of work. Was he looking forward to getting out of the camp, the doctor asked, and then came the questions: Do we suffer or have we ever suffered from any infectious diseases? Any contact with persons of either the male or female sex who suffer or have ever suffered from any infectious disease? Right, thanks.

Heinrich didn't even have to strip to the waist or let the doctor look down his trousers to check up on what he had said, nothing like that. Heinrich was sound as a bell and perfectly capable of working, that was obvious, for instance we need people to work on the land, people who aren't afraid of hard labour and will lend a hand when manpower's needed, they may have been bed salesmen like Heinrich, or whatever, but anyone who's ready to help build the Socialist structure is welcome here. (So now he knew.)

The friendly Stasi officer offered Heinrich a cigarette, just as he had the day before, but this time Heinrich refused it, and the friendly Stasi officer was surprised and seemed to be making notes in his head, perhaps Heinrich was the sort who could come in really useful one way or another after all, he personally had had nothing but good experiences with whisky drinkers.

So Heinrich's whisky was brought into play again, they'd kept it for him, it tasted of the old days, they offered it to him. Didn't expect to see your whisky again, I bet, said the officer, and not like this either, and Heinrich said no, he didn't expect to see it again, so they clinked glasses and sipped the liquor, for Tom hadn't said anything about the inadvisability of drinking whisky with the Stasi, and for the time being everything was innocuous. Heinrich was asked for the story of the years he had spent in the Soviet Union from 1946 to 1951, and Harms the Stasi officer (just call me Herr Harms) told the tale of his own travels through the ruins of Thuringia as a Young Communist recruiting people to the cause of progress, it was in the autumn of 1946, six months after the founding of the Sozialistische Einheitspartei Deutschlands, the Socialist Unity Party of Germany or SED, that he began believing in Socialism on German soil, a narrative he recounted between the third and fourth glasses of whisky: all perfectly innocuous.

Over an hour later not a word had yet been said about Heinrich's future, or else Heinrich just hadn't been listening properly when his future was discussed, and as Herr Harms seemed to feel at ease in Heinrich's company, Heinrich began to feel at ease himself, after all, it was his whisky they were drinking, and if they kept going at this rate it wouldn't last long.

Had Herr Harms done him a favour, or was it the other way around, or had each of them done the other a favour?

Heinrich decided that in any case he ought not to lag behind in the exchange of these little courtesies, so he flattered the Stasi man by calling the GDR a land of hope, adding that if it was permitted he'd write to his wife Rosa this very day and say so, and perhaps she could soon convince herself of the fact with her own eyes.

Well, that would be quite something, said Herr Harms.

Yes, indeed it would, said Heinrich, but I don't know if I can hope for that. In fact, he reflected, he had only dragged Rosa into it for Herr Harms's benefit, wondering whether a man like Harms had a family of his own, and went home on an evening like this to tell his wife about his latest conquests on the field of ideological battle: Oh, and I tackled a man called Heinrich, I like him, don't really know why.

Well, said Harms, saying goodbye early that evening, we can discuss it again another day, you'll have had leisure to think it all over by then, you'd better write to your family, oh, and you should gather a few first impressions of life outside the camp, there's no hurry.

Later Heinrich had some difficulty in reconstructing that afternoon with Harms in every detail (he tried only because Tom wanted to know about it), and he asked himself why the Stasi man set such store on his not forgetting Rosa, and what exactly he was supposed to think over at his leisure. However, by no means everything had occurred to him that should have occurred to him, according to Tom: Let's hope you haven't signed anything. He hadn't.

On that last evening with Rosa Heinrich hadn't begun

drinking until late in the afternoon, so he went easy on her and her suggestion of going to Wiesbaden and didn't refuse, yet Theodor was the very last person from whom he could expect help in his present situation. However, Heinrich was at least anxious to get out of town, so he invented Offermann in Frankfurt for Rosa's benefit, he'd met men like that as he trawled through pubs and bars.

There, you see, said Rosa, and she too went easy on him, and was friendly and didn't give him an earful. Heinrich almost felt that she was glad he had business problems and didn't know where to turn (for indeed there was nowhere they could turn), because that way at least he didn't get stupid ideas in his head, he was the same man he'd been four or five years ago: slightly unreliable but ambitious, and even in his unfaithfulness he was faithful to her in his fashion, which was just how she'd always imagined the man in her life. She had not been dissatisfied with Heinrich at first, and as for the few girlfriends he'd had before her (she really didn't by any means know all of it), well, they'd taught him this, that and the other.

They had both put on a bit of weight over the last few years, the lavish evening meals she cooked him and a glass or so too many of whisky had left their traces, but she was fond of the Heinrich of 1962 and still saw in him the Heinrich of 1952, that self-confident character who'd been laying bets on her with his brother, saying he'd find a chance to sweet-talk her and tell her he'd like to take her to the Fischerwiesen open-air swimming baths so as to study her in every detail.

It was in June 1952 he was betting on her, and he sweet-talked her in the street early in the afternoon, and Rosa listened to him and couldn't help doing as he wanted. Oh, all right, she said, and her friend Marie, left behind, watched in amazement as Rosa unhesitatingly got on his borrowed bicycle (he had nothing much of his own) and clung to his waist, and let him take her to the open-air swimming baths on the other side of the river, luckily he liked her new bathing costume, and there was nothing to interest him that summer in the other bathing costumes on display and the girls inside them.

Over the next few weeks she found she had to protest a bit, telling him off for the various liberties he took, but usually he knew just when and where she was going to draw the line, and when he did once go too far (his warm, dry hands finding their way under her bathing costume), it was not an unpleasant experience. After all, everyone envied her because of her Heinrich with his white silk scarf, his snappy sayings and his invitations issued from the borrowed bicycle, why, even the lovely Marie envied her, because after all it was Rosa who shared a thin towel with him at the swimming pool and let him kiss her, steam rising gently from her under his kisses, or so she hoped, it was Rosa who punished her envious friends by occasionally hinting at this or that detail of his careful but bold explorations. At this the friends always fell silent, or acted very haughty and experienced, for all their lack of experience, because in their early twenties most of them had not got far with the acquisition of anything deserving that name, so Rosa had a whole summer to enjoy seeing her women friends secretly casting glances at her Heinrich, unable to take their eyes off him, she felt it was a feather in her cap.

Years later she told Marie, the woman friend who still remained to her from that summer at the open-air swimming baths: I must have been mad to get engaged to him after less than four months, but I'm glad I was so crazy, I'm glad he took me, even though all I had was a fine pair of eyes and a body with curves enough for two. You certainly do have to be crazy to fall for that line, Marie had said, but Rosa just dismissed it, oh, don't start on about that, please, I mean, who cares about his affairs when he always comes back to me and takes me and holds me as if it were the very first time and for ever, that's life, and I wouldn't find a better man, or do *you* have a better man? Well, there you are!

She liked remembering those early days, and then there was his professional success and all the money it brought into their home over the first seven years, those were the fat years, and if seven lean years followed, well, she was ready to adjust to them.

I don't want to talk about it, Heinrich had said on their last evening together in Regensburg, the memory of his uncle's threats and reproaches still weighing on him. So what do we care if your uncle doesn't see his money again, suppose the worst comes to the worst (this was typical Rosa again), I mean, he's got plenty, and personally I don't believe, and I never will, that when the best beds and bedding salesman south of the river Main sets up on his own things can go badly wrong. (Oh Rosa, if only you knew.)

We could find a smaller flat if that would help for now, Rosa had said, and the beginning is always the worst time, I could economize on the housekeeping, or we could sell the new TV set, but Heinrich wouldn't hear of any of that. Just pack me a few things for Frankfurt, he had said, and then he sat in the TV room until long after midnight, getting drunk, with no idea what to do.

The letter to Rosa was difficult. He'd have liked to ask Harms for advice, Harms must have experience of such letters, but unfortunately Harms wasn't at the evening lecture, and Heinrich didn't want to wait until next day. He still had no plan as he began writing. He wanted her to think he was concerned for her but did not seriously expect her to follow him, so he wrote: Eisenach, 16 March 1962. My dear ones, I couldn't do anything else! I don't know how I saw it through, but I do think there are opportunities for the future here. I left my car in Fulda, at the railway station. I think of you all the time. Please write to the following address: H. H., Eisenach Reception Centre, GDR. Love to the children. Letter to follow.

After that he struck up a brief conversation with the lads

24

from Göttingen to find out what their first impressions had been, for of course he was eager to know what things were like outside the camp, and he had no idea whether it was really completely different from the ideas entertained of it in the West. The lads from Göttingen didn't seem to have thought about it very much either, all that mattered to them was the presence of a nearby town (a grey and gloomy town) in which they walked through the pouring rain, unable to find a café where they could sit and get warm. Ten years: was that a long time or a short time for a country to exist? Then again, what did he really know about this country and its people, its politics since the time when his family had moved to the West within just a few months of each other, the two brothers going over the green border at Sonneberg in the summer of 1951, and finally, after much hesitation, their father and mother and their younger siblings that autumn, by way of East Berlin, so they'd been going back and forth over borders every few years.

He did know the town of Eisenach slightly, from a visit there with a girl in the summer of fifty-one, she was the daughter of the SED second District Secretary in Jena, and had temporarily made Heinrich into a member of the Free German Youth movement, the Freie Deutsche Jugend or FDJ, for she was keen on that organization and wouldn't touch a young man like Heinrich until he'd proved he was on the right side in the class struggle.

Heinrich remembered this occasion when he left the camp for three hours next morning. The two soldiers on guard duty were not exactly friendly, but he didn't have to bother about that: he was outside.

Back then, in the summer of fifty-one, he hadn't really taken much notice of the town, he always had an eye open for small, private places where, given the right circumstances, he might make some kind of progress with that progressively minded girl, but the second secretary's idealistic daughter (Dora was her name) had nothing in her head but the FDJ and the wording of the slogans on the facades of buildings (Help Build Socialism Now!), and went on about the way she felt standing in a square named after the greatest friend and admirer of the German people, Josef Vissarionovich Stalin: wonderful, oh, it was just wonderful.

Heinrich was afraid he wouldn't find his way around the town he had once known after all these years, but when he started out he found that most of it was just the same: the market-place, the castle, the two big churches, the Bach House and the Luther House, the old park; yes, it was all there. And how much livelier and fresher it looked, with scarcely a trace left of the devastation of the last days of the war. But no square, no street was now named after that friend and admirer of the German people, Josef Vissarionovich Stalin, and you saw new cars all over the town, cars which, until this moment, had been only a joke in the West German newspapers to him.

He walked around for over two hours, looking at the place, comparing what he saw himself with what was always said about it in the West, yes, well, that's how it is on the other side of the border, not a state of affairs we can change in a hurry, but we can't by any manner of means approve of it. However, Heinrich thought he had nothing to fear if the country was really what it appeared to be at first and indeed at second glance, the people here didn't look hungry, for instance, they spoke his own language, and they were friendly and tired from work of a kind he did not know.

Perhaps it's only because I remember that girl, he thought, or perhaps I haven't seen anything to speak of yet, or perhaps I ought to read a paper (the newspapers here looked thin), walking around the streets like this you didn't learn much, for instance, about the parliamentary decision of the People's Chamber on 24 January passing the law to introduce military service, but he did like the women (just look at that tall, black-haired girl in the kiosk), and a young woman selling sausages actually hoped he'd have a nice day.

And what do you think of our country, Harms enquired, when once again Heinrich did not refuse the whisky and turned down only the third cigarette he was offered, but Heinrich couldn't talk about his impressions so soon, and then he had to think how it had been with his Dora, yes, he had to think about her. There you are, then, that's all there is to it, said Harms, summing up Heinrich's morning in his own way, and he turned all official again and started in on his famous questions, but no Dora surfaced in any of them.

Although more and more creditors had turned up in the days before he left, making ugly scenes without sparing a thought for any customers present, Heinrich entered the premises of the shop between Tändlergasse and Wahlengasse at eight on the dot; even on that last day he sat on one of the display beds, began reading the newspaper, and waited for customers. He had become almost used to the absence of his uncle and Lehmann and Fräulein Swoboda, chatting half the day away in the office behind the shop or in the stockroom, while he dealt with customers out in front, but there wasn't much going on that morning, even his creditors seemed to have better things to do, or alternatively they had long ago abandoned hope and were drafting long and complicated statements with their lawyers, sending final demands to Hampel Beds Ltd, and if no money still came in then the case would end up in the hands of the public prosecutor.

It proved useful, now, that Rosa had always kept her distance from his business affairs, staying at home like a good housewife instead, looking after the children and entertaining various business friends of his and their wives, or even more often all kinds of acquaintances from pubs and bars and certain shady clubs and private saunas, and they'd drink his good, expensive whisky and even better expensive cognac from his expensive glasses until late into the night, and only just before midnight would Rosa say it was time she went to bed and did so, saying: Sorry, it's because of the baby, the baby screams almost every night now.

The first customers came into the shop at nearly eleven, but although he went to some trouble with them, a young couple from a village near the border (we're getting married at the end of April), and patiently explained the pros and cons of the new French models, the young people couldn't make up their minds to any purchase, and bounced about on all kinds of different beds for almost an hour, making silly jokes and giggling, until finally Heinrich lost patience and suggested they go away and sleep on it, for after all he and his beds would still be here tomorrow and the day after that, so they finally went off and left him alone with his newspaper.

Well, I don't have to worry about you and your shop, his father had said over the phone, ringing up to wish him a Happy New Year, you know all there is to know about salesmanship and singing the praises of your beds, and now that folk aren't short of money these days they don't just buy refrigerators and television sets and the latest Beetle, they get new beds and pillows and mattresses and sheets and pillowcases, in their early twenties they start new families in those beds, or maybe they give themselves a bit of time before starting new families in their beds – his father would speak quite frankly to Heinrich these days. Why, your sales pitch could even sell me a new bed, his father had said, pleased with the expensive cigars on his name-day and the sixty roses on his sixtieth birthday, although Heinrich had probably been mistaken in believing that his father was pleased with the over-expensive presents and his second son's success in business in distant Regensburg – for after all, what was so great about a salesman of beds and bedding in sleepy Regensburg with two children and a seven-roomed third-floor flat? Still he was solvent, and generous when his mean-minded brothers were short of cash yet again, when they acted as if they were doing him a favour by spending his money on a new car or a new built-in wardrobe in the bedroom.

It was getting on for one o'clock when he thought once again about the money he had lent Paul and Theodor and felt angry with them, so he closed the shop and wrote two short, formal letters in the office, asking for repayment of their debts by the fifteenth of that month, but not yet mentioning his desperate situation.

When he had finished the letters he was hungry.

You could get knuckle of pork with sauerkraut and mash at his usual café over the road; he had them pack him up a take-away, took it back to his desk, and ate lunch there thinking of his brothers, and of Bella and whether she might look in again, he hoped she wouldn't.

He thought: okay, let my brothers think I'm asking for my money back at this very difficult point in time on some whim, and let Bella think I've gone for good.

Then he sat quietly there in his office, doing nothing at all; the end of the whisky he found in the desk was just enough for two glasses.

He had no plans to say goodbye.

He put the light out at four as if he would be coming back, lowered both the roller shutters, and crept out of the shop like a thief.

On his fourth night in the camp Heinrich woke from a dream in which he was back with Marga, and all of a sudden there stood his Rosa down at the front door, she climbed the stairs and saw Marga hastily throwing on a dressing-gown and stashing Heinrich's shaving brush and pyjamas and whisky away in the wardrobe, but Rosa had no eyes for any of that, or for the fact that Heinrich too was naked and drowsy, stammering out an awkward greeting and looking round in vain for a dressing-gown for himself. I only have half an hour, Rosa said in his dream, then I must go back to the camp, oh, it's horrible, I can tell you, dirty and miserable, but we all have great hopes, and the men leave stains on the sheets in their huts, one for every night. Can I have a drink? I know I oughtn't to have woken you but you're a handsome couple, all bare and naked with the sleep still in your eyes, and the traces of your last love-making left in the bed, yes, I envy you. Well, you've come at rather a bad moment, said Heinrich in his dream, but Rosa wasn't to be put off, so the three of them drank a bottle of wine in the living-room, and Heinrich said: I've joined the Communist Party now, don't you worry, a person can always make a new start.

He had soon become accustomed to life in camp. After breakfast he usually spent a couple of hours in the town which he had visited with Dora, or he talked to Tom about the new times and the old, and the subject of tonight's evening lecture (it was going to be given by the young woman chairman of the Society for the Dissemination of Scientific Knowledge), but by the end of the first week at the latest everything began to get repetitive: the evening lectures on the imperialist West and the peace-loving GDR, announcements from the camp loudspeakers, surprise raids on lockers in search of any smuggled books or radio sets, silent masturbation under the camp blankets, the noise of the children in the family huts, jokes about the useless appeals for more cleanliness and order, the morning crush in the wash-rooms, thoughts of families left behind, hopes for a new start.

What Heinrich liked best were the afternoons with Harms, whom he assumed to be busy almost round the clock with discussions or interrogations, yet the man always had time for Heinrich, asking his innocuously devious questions about Rosa and the past over a glass of whisky from Heinrich's bottle, which always seemed to have a little left in it.

I'm going to clam up once that bottle's empty, Heinrich had said on their fourth or fifth meeting, but Harms seemed to take no notice, very likely he had sufficient stocks of whisky for a case like this, and he always added enough to the bottle to keep it from ever running entirely dry. At some point or other Heinrich himself stopped bothering and just talked away unreservedly about his life, saying exactly what kind of work his father and Theodor had done before and after their flight, which people in the Jena glassworks Heinrich knew by name, which people he knew in Mainz, he thought there couldn't be any harm in letting them know that.

In the middle of the second week Heinrich tried to bring the subject round to his own future prospects again, but Harms explained that unfortunately, as a Stasi officer, he wasn't responsible for such matters, there'd be no question of Heinrich's going to Berlin or Dresden, but after all it was Jena he wanted to go to, right, you'll hardly know the city again, and you'll find a flat and a job without much difficulty.

So Heinrich thanked the Stasi man whose whisky never ran out and who conducted his interrogations in a conversational tone: See you tomorrow, then. Are those lads from Göttingen still here? No, the lads from Göttingen had left yesterday, Heinrich didn't know exactly where they'd gone, but it was somewhere in Mecklenburg, so now I'm the senior occupant of the hut.

Heinrich had attained that status after exactly seventeen days, and four days later Harms welcomed him with a handshake and said he had a surprise. We made contact with your wife a few days ago, he said, and just imagine, she got straight on a train with your two children, I had the news from our border troops an hour ago, so pack your things, you're moving into another hut, your wife and children will be arriving in the camp in an hour or so.

I don't believe it, said Heinrich, and Harms said he could hardly believe it himself, but he'd never given up hope for Heinrich, and she'd really sounded very cheerful.

Yes, well.

2

In autumn it still looked as if everything would turn out all right for Heinrich: business was going well, so was his marriage to Rosa, and then he had a trip away from home now and then, and Bella every other afternoon. These were his best months. We're on a winning streak, said Rosa, and Bella said, I'm happy with things the way they are, long may it last. She would have had no objection to continuing to welcome Heinrich to her little top-floor room, it was Heinrich who suddenly insisted on a change, and it was a long time before he would reveal anything about his plans. Only when he had signed the contract for a centrally heated flat with a view of the Danube, and spent a few thousand marks on furniture, china and expensive carpets, did he come out with it, handing her the key as if she need not be surprised to receive more such presents in future.

Oh, Heinrich, said Bella, overwhelmed, and from now on she felt indebted to him, but she forgot her indebtedness and enjoyed the three comfortable armchairs in different colours, and a bed as wide and elegant as if it were in a French feature film starring Lino Ventura or Jean Gabin. There were days when she sat in her rooms with their modern furnishings for a long time after work, marvelling at it all, unable to take in her good fortune in meeting Heinrich, who drove all round town in his van in the afternoons, delivering the beds people had ordered, and then he came to her place, where he was expected, he slipped inside her and stayed there, amazed by her readiness, grateful for her gratitude, sleeping half the afternoon away between her thighs. Oh, Bella, my clever, wise, insatiable, darling Bella, go on, put on that new dress, the blue one, or no, come back here, it's warm under the covers, and let me tell how I'd like to see you, a pair of new stockings on your pretty legs, lace over the round curves of your breasts, a silk dressing-gown against your skin; it was in such words that he clothed her at another woman's expense (his Rosa's).

There hadn't been anything much between him and Rosa at home with the children for quite a while, so it was mere high spirits which made him increasingly careless that October, or perhaps it was because he was bored by the monotony of the evenings when the shop had closed, the children were still awake when the TV news bulletin came on at eight, no visitor looked in to cut short the hours ahead of him with an exhausted Rosa, and there was nothing interesting on television. As for Rosa, she didn't seem to notice that he was coming home later and later, always giving the same kind of vague information about his movements between six and nine, and although she sometimes looked at him and tried to calculate the number of drinks he had put back she ignored the smell of other women on his hands, letting him think for a long time that she didn't know about his afternoons, and didn't mind when, at night, he tried something out on her which he had thought up with another woman in mind, repeating it for that other woman's pleasure.

Sometimes Bella told him off, saying: If she's going to keep quiet you must do it with her now and then. Don't think about me. Make love to her the way you used to, or the way you've learnt to do it with me, and next time you come here you can tell me what it was like. But Heinrich didn't care to talk about his nights with Rosa, and wrote only a line or so about them in his old notebook with his Russian girlfriend Lyusya's name in it, and all the nights, long and short, that he had spent with women since he became a man, and he let Bella look at it now and then and read out loud what he had last written: 29 September, afternoon B., evening Rosa. Remember the first time? Come on, the first time was good, and so were the times after that. But she's turned all serious, while Bella laughs the whole time and doesn't stop till it's over.

Well, that's true, Bella would say, or: I like it when you write those things about me, but I won't be really satisfied until I feature in your notes more often than all the rest of them put together.

Do you mind me laughing while we're doing it, she had asked him in the summer soon after Susanna's death, the first time he had slept with her, and she was very inquisitive and wanted him to talk about the women he'd had before her, and whether any of them was like Bella, but straight off he couldn't think of anyone who had been like Bella, only Lyusya just a little, but that was in Russia many years ago, and Lyusya was very young and inexperienced and had other reasons for her laughter.

It was in mid-October that they remembered what it had been like in the summer after Susanna's death, and what they had talked about after the first time, and now they had their own flat with a fitted kitchen and the latest Scandinavian furniture, and the entry in the land register was in Bella's name.

Heinrich didn't discuss business with Bella either, except once when he said: I'll have to keep a closer eye on my book-keeper, I've an idea he's fiddling the invoices now and then, and then I'll have to stand the loss, not knowing exactly what it is.

I don't know anything about book-keeping, said Bella. To which Heinrich replied: He helped you on with your coat twice on our outing.

Was that wrong?

I think he votes Social Democrat.

I suppose you'd know.

34

Heinrich had voted for the Christian Social Union as he did in the last elections. It was on the third Sunday in September, shortly before the polling stations closed, and they were just back from an outing up in the mountains: Heinrich, Bella, Lehmann and Heinrich's uncle, and Rosa didn't come but stayed at home because the baby had been sick in the night, and unfortunately had a slight temperature too. What a shame, Heinrich had said, and Rosa had agreed, yes, what a shame, but have a nice time, all of you, so he had simply asked Bella along, seating her in the back of the car next to the book-keeper, and they set off early on the Sunday morning. Let me introduce you: Bella Anton, a friend of mine; my book-keeper Lehmann, my uncle from Cologne.

Anyone know a nice place to go, Heinrich had asked, but nobody could think of a nice place to go straight off, so he simply started down the motorway in the direction of Passau, and they none of them said anything at first, thinking of Rosa left at home, while Bella kept looking out of the window and filled the entire car with her perfume. Do you absolutely have to drive so fast, asked Heinrich's uncle, because after all, someone had to say something, and then he went back to the subject of the hotel and what a good order it would be, a place with fifty beds, they were going to make their minds up early in the week. Do you think we'll get the order? Of course we'll get the order, said Heinrich, wait and see, they'll call us on Monday morning. In the rear-view mirror he could see the book-keeper casting Bella several sidelong glances, but keeping his mouth shut as he wondered exactly what kind of friend Bella was, and whether she'd have been in the party if Rosa had been one of the party too, yes, well, that was the question.

Everything all right back there, Frau Anton?

Yes, thanks, fine. Did I ever tell you I lived with my grandmother in Zwiesel for almost four years when I was a little girl? It's ages since I've been there, but Zwiesel's a pretty place, and the house where my late grandmother lived is worth seeing.

So it was decided that they would all go to Zwiesel that Sunday of the elections to the Fourth Federal German Bundestag, and that Heinrich and Bella would stop addressing each other by the formal *Sie* pronoun in front of the others, which no one seemed to mind. They drove on. Outside, the weather had turned hot again, with the warmth of late summer, and since Bella wanted something to eat when they reached Zwiesel they went into a café in the market place and ordered eggs and bacon and Sekt all round. Bella mentioned a couple of villages quite close, remembering walks there with her grandmother, and how they were once overtaken by a storm just before they reached the glassworks and had to shelter in a shed for over two hours before the rain stopped. They were talking away now. Lehmann paid Bella a compliment on her pretty freckles, and Heinrich and his uncle drank a glass of cognac, and then they finally decided to go and see the place where little Bella had spent part of her childhood, they'd make it to the glassworks easily in two or three hours. Just outside the town Heinrich's uncle said: Hey, my boy, that Bella of yours, I must say I understand you there. And Bella, who was walking a little way ahead of them with Lehmann and ignoring his *double entendres*, said: Isn't this lovely? To which Heinrich replied: Yes, beautiful. So simple, just wonderful, let's come back and take a room just for the two of us next weekend if you like, that would be even better.

For all of four weeks after that they kept talking about repeating this excursion back into Bella's past, but first Heinrich couldn't make it because of the hotel deal, and once Bella was finally installed in her lovely new flat she considered every hour spent outside her own four walls a waste of time. (But he persuaded her to change her mind.) Later, Heinrich remembered two rainy days in a hotel room with two old, worn-out beds, which they left only for meals down in the smoke-filled dining-room, and they spent the rest of the time as they liked to do, drinking wine and whisky straight from the bottle, forgetting about precautions and experimenting (Heinrich took some photos of the pair of them), and three weeks later Bella rang in a state of great agitation saying she thought she was pregnant.

It was on a Tuesday in early November that Bella surprised him with this bad news, and it was also in early November that Heinrich questioned his book-keeper on the where-abouts of various invoices, but Lehmann wouldn't let him get a word in edgeways, waxed indignant at being suspected by Heinrich of fraudulent practice, and said the question was who was defrauding whom, after all, as the firm's book-keeper he knew best how it was doing, and what would Heinrich's uncle say if he knew how Heinrich was squander-ing all that money, changing suppliers the way other people change their underwear, oh yes, thank you very much. If we carry on like this we won't even make it into our second year, said Lehmann, and soon after that Bella had phoned and they didn't discuss it again.

A few days later, Bella said: Oh, I was so scared when I didn't get the curse, and now I know it's all right I'm almost disappointed. We'll have to be a bit more careful in future. Promise me you'll be a bit more careful in future? He promised. (And didn't touch her for the next few days.)

All he knew about Rosa during those weeks was that she spent her evenings writing long letters to various women friends of some kind; or her friend Friedrich from the East, and took no notice of him when he warmed up his dinner in the kitchen at eight or eight-thirty, eating the leftovers from the meal she had cooked for herself and the children straight from the pan. Oh, Rosa, he would say, when Rosa didn't utter a word all evening, and he felt jealous of her friend Friedrich from the East and her women friends, to whom she wrote in her small, round handwriting, telling them all about her life, complaining and feeling sorry for herself.

Her letter to Friedrich, which he found in the television room a few days later, left Heinrich feeling oddly moved. At first he thought: So she's writing to me because I don't know what's on her mind, and I've never had a letter from her before, but he saw the other man's name, hesitated, and then read what she had written about him and kept secret from him: Dear Friedrich, I often think of those days in August when I told you everything, and it was all so new to you. Have you settled in here in the West yet? I'm sorry to say I'm feeling really low again today, I got around to thinking nobody would be sorry if I was dead. Heinrich went away to the mountains with her again last weekend, you can imagine what they were doing there and how that sort of thing hurts. I found lots of photos of the pair of them in Heinrich's wallet, there they were in the most impossible positions, I just don't understand it. I'd give anything to wake up and find it was all just a dream, I'd give my life for that: How are you getting on with your Robert now? Does he like you, at least? You deserve it. Love from Rosa.

Heinrich still clearly remembered Friedrich coming to their flat one day with nothing but his papers and the clothes he stood up in, and of course Rosa had said, we must help him, he doesn't have any family here in the West, after all, he doesn't know the simplest things, but he has lovely hands, and he looked so lost just now when I spoke to him in the café. For a moment Heinrich didn't know what Rosa meant when she said, we must help him, but it was only a few hundred marks, after all, so she went out into the garden with her Friedrich and made him tell her the full story of his Robert again, and how they had come to the West together a few days earlier, over the border, which was still open at the time. Friedrich had given two thousand Western marks to Robert, who was over forty, married with two children, and the poor fellow had to go and fall in love with a man like that.

So what does he say about life over there, asked Heinrich, when they were alone, and Rosa told him they had been terribly hard on Friedrich over in the East, because for one thing he was a sensitive musician and for another he unfortunately didn't fancy women. But had Heinrich seen his fine pianist's hands, asked Rosa, who may have been captivated by more than just his hands (she had said unfortunately), and a week later they were building a Wall in Berlin and Friedrich was one of the last to have got out in time.

The day he heard about the building going on in Berlin Heinrich was at the open-air swimming baths with Bella. She was wearing her new pink bathing costume specially for him, at first she didn't want to listen to the news on the little portable radio, but Heinrich wanted to hear all about it, forgot what his hands were doing and Bella, and thought of his father. It was only at his mother's insistence that his father had left the house in Jena back in October of fifty-one, and now one of the Party bosses was living in it permanently with his wife and kids, laughing his head off at that sick old man in the West who still thought it was all just a temporary arrangement, and the house on the Wilhelmshöhe in 1936 was still his property. Only a few years ago Heinrich's father had shown him a letter from the Public Welfare Housing Co-operative Society, saying the opposite (Your property has passed into the possession of the people. In the event of your return to the GDR, however, it will revert to you), and his father had also shown him the reply he wrote, to the effect that he would be back once the two zones were reunified, which in view of the constant efforts being made by both West and East must be in the not too distant future.

Presumably his father was thinking of all this when he heard the news in his room in the Taunus (for he had been a patient at the Hohe Mark sanatorium in Oberursel since the

39

beginning of the month), and he would probably be shaking his head over that man Ulbricht and his cronies, or alternatively, like Bella, he simply would not want to hear about the Wall being erected by heavily guarded troops of builders right through the city of Berlin by order of Ulbricht and his cronies, for the defence of the German Democratic Republic, for instead he wrote: Oberursel in the Taunus, 13 August 1961, well, children, my stay here ends tomorrow and I'll be coming home well again. As far as I remember it was Heinrich who couldn't keep anything down but porridge his first few weeks. Many thanks to you all and love from your father.

Do you really have to keep listening to such horrid things, Bella had asked, casting Heinrich one of her famous Bella looks, which meant no, you do not have to, why not think about your Bella instead, see how your lovely new bathing costume suits me, and if you're very good I'll tell you what ideas I just can't get out of my head in this heat.

Did you hear what happened in Berlin, Heinrich asked in the shop next morning. Yes, terrible, isn't it, everyone said, those criminals, but from the way they said it you could tell they weren't really indignant, for in order to be really indignant they'd have needed to be like Heinrich, with a father who had lost a house to those criminals, or a family which had stayed in the East and couldn't easily get out again now, that was the least they'd have needed. I just can't get my head around it, said Heinrich, and Lehmann said: Sorry, but we have to order more sheets, oh, and yesterday there was a mattress representative looked in; two reminders came in the post, and you have a delivery to make to Frau Sander at four. Wasn't that the brunette whose husband is always away? Yes, that was right, Frau Sander. There was something about her. She'd dropped hints even on his very first visit (the way she kept plumping down on the bed in front of him), but although he didn't think her unattractive he wasn't happy about going there today. He'd rather have talked to his father, or he would have liked to talk to Rosa, but her head had been full of nothing but Friedrich for days, she was glad to be able to comfort him over Robert, and he almost envied Friedrich for being comforted by Rosa over these last few days, because Rosa had always felt good when she was comforting people, and when she felt good she was very gentle and quiet and friendly.

At first Heinrich wasn't sure whether Rosa would have been angry to find he had read her letters in secret, or whether she really wanted him to find out how bad it all was for her, and how horrible she felt searching his clothes and papers for evidence of this Bella of his, and seeing the photos, and hating herself every time she looked at them.

Heinrich had not gone to any great trouble to leave her letter to Friedrich exactly where he found it, but either Rosa hadn't noticed or she had ignored it, and next evening the letter had disappeared, either posted or she was still wondering whether to post it, or perhaps she had hidden it or torn it up. Once he said (just because he felt sorry for her): Why don't we go away for a few days, it will do us good, but Rosa didn't want to go away for a few days because she didn't want him feeling sorry for her, which he could understand. Not much later she didn't welcome his love-making either, and then came the first difficulties with the shop, but for the time being everything stayed much the same, changing only when Heinrich fled to the East.

Now and then there had been some cash-flow problems with the business recently, and although he'd been able to meet his financial obligations it was beginning to be obvious that he was living beyond his means, providing himself and Bella and Rosa and the children with everything they wanted, without stopping to think what part of the sums at his disposal was turnover and what was clear profit. More than once over the past few months they'd had to change to new suppliers because the money wasn't there to pay incoming bills, so they were increasingly reliant on the patience of their suppliers, whether large or small, and were beginning to include the extent of that patience in their calculations. If a supplier began to turn ugly after the second or third reminder, Heinrich simply replied curtly, withdrawing any further orders, ordered goods from another firm, paid the first supplier's bills with the proceeds from the sale of the new supplier's goods, calculated the extent of his patience too, exhausted it, replaced him in turn with yet another supplier, and would go on playing this game to the bitter end, although he didn't believe in that bitter end for the time being, and perhaps it would never come (or the firm would make a miraculous recovery), all he needed was for no one to lose patience too soon, he and Lehmann (that trickster) mustn't overdo things, and if everything stayed as it was, or turned out as he hoped, it would be all right in the end, so he believed.

When they sent in the last invoices for the big hotel order at the beginning of December Heinrich said: There, you see, Lehmann, we can't be in such a bad way if we're pulling in orders like this and sending our customers big fat bills, and Lehman did in fact look quite surprised, or perhaps Heinrich only thought Lehmann looked quite surprised, but at least he didn't contradict what Heinrich had said.

And when Heinrich's uncle came to Regensburg in December for his usual three or four days a month, and sat around in the shop from morning to evening with no idea how to make himself useful, Heinrich painted a picture of the situation as rosy, indeed excellent given the circumstances, but in contrast to previous occasions his uncle made a rather sour face at Heinrich's optimism, Lehmann the book-keeper had dropped a few hints, he said, and what, might he ask, was the meaning of the reminders piling up in drawers, I see that if no one does anything about it they're going to cut off your electricity at the beginning of next week.

Ah yes, the electricity bill, said Heinrich, suggesting that his uncle was adopting a rather inappropriate tone all of a sudden, or did he think he could teach him, Heinrich, anything about the modern beds and bedding trade?

I've invested two hundred thousand in this business.

Yes, I know.

Without me as security the bank wouldn't have lent you a penny.

Yes, I know.

I've risked two houses on this venture, and I haven't said anything about that Bella of yours yet.

Please leave Bella out of this.

Is she such an expensive mistress, or why is it that you can't pay your bills?

I said please leave Bella out of this.

Then he took his uncle to the book-keeper's office behind the shop, saying his uncle was worried about the business, what did Lehmann think?.

Oh, one always has business worries.

As bad as that, is it? said his uncle.

To which Lehmann replied that he was only the book-keeper, but he'd not been lying awake at night worrying about the firm. They'd have to wait and see. Keep calm. Get the first year behind us, and then we'll get the second year behind us as well.

For some days after that, Heinrich thought about the money he been spending these last few years, but except for Bella's flat, a new car every other year, trips in summer to Holland, France and Italy, things for the children, for Rosa (whose wishes were modest), nothing in particular occurred to him. Well, all right, the wines they offered their guests were expensive, so was the twenty-year-old whisky he drank, and the Cuban cigars he smoked when he was pleased with himself and the world in general (and it was quite some time since he had not felt pleased with himself and the world in general), and as he thought about all this it struck even him as surprising to find himself beginning to do such sums, because as long as the money was there he hadn't given it a thought.

Nor could he remember at all clearly now just what it was like when he first started as a stockroom worker for old Franz, Beds and Bedding, bringing home a few hundred marks a month, eating Rosa's overcooked one-pot dinners in their little ground-floor flat near the Schleuse, while all the world and his wife strolled past their kitchen window looking in at them as they sat over a pot of tea dreaming about a new car, and some curtains for their damp kitchen, because they sat there for preference at the time. They'd stuck it out for a good two years there, two rooms with running water, WC on the landing, and after a while Heinrich became van-driver for Franz, Beds and Bedding, and next year he was promoted to salesman, and from then on they didn't have to think about money any more, and the curtains in the three rooms of their new flat in the Altstadt went right down to the floor and were made of the very best furnishing fabrics. Back then, in the summer of 1956, Rosa had said: I never imagined this, not in my wildest dreams, and Heinrich had said: Yes, it's not so bad here, but I haven't finished dreaming my own dreams yet, not by a long chalk.

Then Susanna came into their lives, and when Susanna had gone out of their lives again only four months later Rosa had made a museum of their flat, and but for Heinrich and that one secret afternoon he spent with Bella on the lemon-yellow sofa they would probably never have shaken off the thought of their dead child, who had no will to live, so that all their efforts had been useless from the first.

There hadn't really been any good reason to take Bella home on that occasion, but the opportunity was a good one, so he had sat on the lemon-yellow sofa with Bella telling her, over a couple of drinks, about his life as a husband (not much to it now), and soon after Rosa came home she found a perfumed scarf of Bella's tucked under the cushions and refused to stay between those familiar four walls any longer.

Let's make a brand new start, Heinrich had said, and within a few days he had found a new flat in Rote-Hahnen-Gasse, and Rosa had said, all right, one last time, but we're going to sell the sofa, and you give that Bella her marching orders by the end of the month, understand? Yes, he understood. He'd try, he said, and from now on we'll think of little Susanna as only a visitor.

The phone call sealing the deal on the Rote-Hahnen-Gasse flat came the evening before they left for Wiesbaden to celebrate Heinrich's father's sixtieth birthday, and since the estate agent suddenly seemed to be in a great hurry and Rosa hadn't seen the place yet, they made an appointment for ten in the morning, when they spent an hour looking round the empty white rooms marvelling at them and counting them, unable to stop either counting or marvelling. Heinrich, who had been there twice already, did not say much, and more or less left it to Rosa to say what she thought of each of the rooms: the kitchen with its built-in fridge and electric cooker, the little dining-room, the large square entrance hall, the living-room with a view of the cathedral, the children's room looking out on the back yard, the red-tiled bathroom, the green-tiled lavatory, the television room, the bedroom, the corridor. Yes, thought Heinrich, this is how it could have been between her and me, and as she made her plans, getting everything mixed up in the process and asking the estate agent thousands of unimportant questions, it seemed to him for a moment that he could give Bella up.

They had set off from Regensburg late, and they arrived late in Wiesbaden. Heinrich had insisted on stopping at a florist's on the way (sixty long-stemmed red roses for his father), so the rest of the party had already assembled at the Zum Heiligen Kreuz inn: Theodor with Ilse and their two children, Paul with his chubby Hilde, their beautiful sister Constanze (without Ferdinand), their stepmother, grumpy as ever in her grey suit, and Father at the head of the table in a new waistcoat, smoking a cigar; yes, he was in a good mood.

Ah, the Regensburg contingent, there you are at last, for heaven's sake, who are all those roses for, surely not Father? Yes, Father: Heinrich had bought his father sixty roses, one for every year. Father beamed. Crazy as it was, he simply beamed and sent the waitress off for three large tankards of fresh water. So how's business? asked Theodor, who had only recently borrowed five hundred marks from Heinrich for a new VW Beetle, but Heinrich much preferred to talk about the new flat, and asked if they had already ordered. No, they'd been waiting. I wish I had that kind of luck, said chubby Hilde, and Heinrich's father said it was obvious how happy Rosa and Heinrich were. Or were they perhaps expecting another little addition to the family?

On the way home Rosa said: I wouldn't have minded a bunch of roses for my own birthday, but it's a long time since you scattered any rose petals for me. Does she call you by your name when she comes? (The answer was yes and no.)

Between Christmas and New Year Heinrich and Lehmann drew up an inventory, and although he didn't understand by any means all the book-keeper's calculations Heinrich did realize that the outlook for the coming year of 1962 was not good, the stockrooms were half full, unpaid bills were piling up, and no rapid improvement might be hoped for in the months of January and February, which were not good for turnover, that was how Lehmann saw it too. The best thing would be to reduce costs and increase turnover. But what keeps costs high? Employing a saleswoman, for instance. And how do you increase turnover if you can't lower prices, if you don't have the staff to provide better service, and nor do you have the money for an advertising campaign? That was the question.

In the end Heinrich saw two possibilities: he must sack Fräulein Swoboda, and he must revert to the business methods he had used to raise turnover year after year when he was working for Franz, Beds and Bedding. Fräulein

Swoboda, to whom he broke the bad news personally at the end of December, proved very understanding, didn't even insist on the legal period of notice, and wished Heinrich the best of luck. His conversations with Bella and Rosa were more difficult. Rosa in particular wouldn't hear of any kind of dubious entanglements with lonely housewives or visits to customers outside office hours, nor was Bella very keen on the idea at first, coming up with all sorts of complicated thoughts about women in general and Heinrich's customers in particular, pointing out that there was a difference between feeling someone up a bit for business reasons (if absolutely necessary), and screwing them every week or so ('scuse her language) just to make some stupid sale.

Heinrich said: You've none of you any idea how serious the situation is. To which Rosa replied: I don't want to hear about your skirt-chasing. And Bella said: Oh, very well. I wouldn't like to take the responsibility for your ruin.

Then he waited.

Nothing at all happened in the first week of January. In the second week, he dallied more or less unsuccessfully with a young florist from Donauwörth, delivered a double bed on approval to Pettendorf and another to Wenzenbach, was offered a cup of tea twice and a cup of coffee five times on his visits to customers' homes, met a couple of jealous husbands and in addition various men who worked shifts, a failed artist, an unemployed family friend, an insurance agent off work sick, a resting actor, schoolchildren who dropped in and went out again, girlfriends and acquaintances who happened to be passing and then just sat there, and when it came to discussing the purchase of a new mattress all the customers wanted time to think it over.

Then, in the third week, Marga suddenly turned up. There she was in the shop at three-thirty in the afternoon, enquiring politely about a firm mattress (she was only passing through Regensburg, too), taking her time over trying out one of the new Belgian beds where you were practically sleeping on the ground, enquiring about silk and satin bedclothes, in fact she was full of questions. Heinrich must forgive her, she said, but she just loved that sort of thing, whenever she came to a new town she had to go straight into a store specializing in beds and bedding, if she had her way she'd buy a new bed and new sheets and other bedclothes every week or so. If he had time, perhaps he'd like to hear her tell a few stories about people and their beds, and how they die and eat and make love in them, but Heinrich had a delivery to make in Kumpfmühl and put her off until that evening.

She was back soon after the shop shut. She smelled of fresh lemon leaves, and from a distance of a fine brand of Italian red-wine vinegar, and when he kissed her for the first time she sighed. He judged that she was in her early thirties, and as it was getting quite dark by the time they peeled off their clothes among the beds and recliners, all he saw of her slim, almost boyish body was a few outlines.

Are you still there?

Yes, I'm still here. Look, carry on, don't wait for me, I'm very slow about these things, don't bother about that, and when you've had a good time and you're finished I'll ask you to do something for me.

That was Marga all over.

Before she left she told him how she'd found him (a woman friend had recommended him), and Heinrich said he'd be happy to give Marga the dark-green silk sheets and pillow-cases, and when she was gone he didn't even have an address for her.

These last few years he hadn't often happened to go to bed with a customer not knowing whether or how much she would buy in the end, here in the shop too, with its large display windows looking out on the Tändlergasse and at the back on the Wahlengasse, and anyone glancing at either of those display windows could see right through the salesrooms to the other side.

Even in his mid-twenties he had told old Franz, Beds and Bedding: Some bed salesmen are successful because they know a bit about beds, and some bed salesmen are successful because they know a bit about women, and the future belongs to the second sort. He could have written a book about his experiences, his wiles, his manoeuvres, and it would have been a hymn of praise to women: the little weaknesses they all had, the small beauties he discovered in them, their blemishes, their hidden longings, their greed, their gentleness, their feeling for colours and gestures, their love of tangible things, their tendency to squander money, on which he counted, he had immortalized them all in his notebook (the Russian one).

It didn't always work.

Out of those women who went shopping with their husbands or lovers some, in fact the vast majority, didn't really look at him as a man or even a salesman at all, and a few did notice something about him, and made a date behind their husbands' backs, or thought a date might be possible, and a day or so later there might be one of these standing undecidedly outside the shop windows, and then she would pull herself together and ask about the flowered sheets on display, or a double bed with one-piece mattress for her and her husband.

If women came in without male companions (and that was easily most of them), he had discovered that there were several possibilities. As a rule he preferred women who made their minds up quickly to the hesitant sort, women around fifty to women in their twenties, and women in their twenties to women between their early thirties and late forties, with all their little doubts and their backtracking. Sometimes all he had to do was comment on their clothes, or their make-up, or the way they did their hair, and they appeared very surprised and flattered, or sometimes very indifferent or stand-offish, but the mere fact that they realized he saw them as more than just customers made it easy for them to buy. And usually it went no further than these harmless comments and encouragements, and if he liked one of them, then given the right circumstances he might say something else, about her shoes and the pretty, slender feet inside those shoes, would hurry through his spiel about the advantages of expensive down from the far north of Canada, and by now they had sometimes reached the nub of the matter and were discussing sleep in general and sleep in particular, and what it's like slipping into a warm bed on a winter evening, just the two of you or even alone, but of course it was nicer with two of you.

After that, well, it all depended.

Having made such remarks many of them felt they had gone too far, and others again seemed to hesitate for a moment, and as they hesitated Heinrich would say he was sorry if *he* had gone too far, or he might say: We can let you have the bed and mattress on approval for a few days, or perhaps he might say: You know, I can't help myself, I really do envy your husband, or lover.

And after that, again, it all depended.

Most of them, of course, were indignant when he spoke to them so openly and with such obvious suggestiveness, or at least they pretended to be a little indignant with him, but a few replied: Oh, if you only knew! and it turned out that they were not keen on their present husbands or lovers, or they hadn't found the right man yet, but yes, in certain circumstances they could entertain the idea of that bed or this mattress.

Heinrich had thought up the idea of deliveries on approval when he was still working for old Franz, Beds and Bedding. When he began offering this new service as part of his own business it looked as if his calculations had worked out, even though, as he already knew, his successes and failures there in the shop could seldom be trusted, a rather shy woman could suddenly become incredibly sexy inside her own four walls, while those who had been particularly bold and forthcoming often showed their reserved, prudish side at home: you couldn't rely on anything in these matters.

In all cases, his maxim was: whatever you do keep calm. Keep working on the customer. Don't trust the earlier signals she was putting out, the encouragement she gave you, but don't believe what she seems to be saying now either. Don't commit yourself to anything until you have a gut feeling that the lady is not averse to buying, but she needs something else, something to make the decision easier for her.

Usually it just amounted to a bit of petting, or undoing a couple of buttons, and by then most of them had second thoughts. The brave who suddenly lost their nerve were mostly afraid of their husbands, fearing they might suddenly come in at the door and not recognize them in the arms of some jumped-up bed salesman, or else they didn't fancy Heinrich all of a sudden, or when he turned up they said this wasn't a good time, such were the obstacles he faced. Heinrich never lost his temper in these cases, he took all the blame on himself, and the more willing he was to take all the blame on himself (so experience had taught him) the readier his relieved customers were to sign even a very disadvantageous sales agreement.

Going all the way was the exception. And then many of Heinrich's lady customers felt ashamed, searching about for their clothing and underclothes in front of him, or they were overcome by an inexplicable melancholy behind which they hid their astonishment at both themselves and Heinrich, but it was really very pleasant when they were happy and full of laughter afterwards. His mistake early on (a beginner's mistake) had been to stay in touch in one or two cases. Making critical remarks about their bedroom furnishings, sometimes hailing them in the street. It was in these cases that he dreamed of them.

Nor had he told Bella by any means everything when he

51

began gaining his first experience of the new method in the spring of 1961, but Bella probably didn't want to know by any means everything either, or else she kept her thoughts to herself, and as long as that was all she did with them, that was fine.

In fact, Heinrich sold only a little more in January 1962 than he would normally have sold in any January, and although by now he paid close attention to almost every woman who came into the shop, scrutinizing her closely for her hidden wishes and desires, working out in detail what he must say at which moment to make her forget why she had come, and for that very reason end up buying a little more than she needed – in spite of all this, not much had come of it except for that woman Marga, and in business terms the Marga incident actually represented a loss. More than once he had found the book-keeper leaving his office door ajar and watching Heinrich's desperate attempts to increase turnover, noticing that by now he didn't even shrink from making eyes at women of well over fifty, never mind whether he could tell even from a distance that they were not available for his little games, or he might waste his time with widows who had been dithering anxiously over the sale of the conjugal bed for weeks, and wanted Heinrich to tell them whether, with a clear conscience, he could advise them to do it.

Although he remained patient even in such cases (he once even went home with one of the widows), the effect on him of his failures was clear from early February. He began making mistakes as a salesman, miscalculated his chances, did not use existing opportunities at the right time, often went too fast at the beginning of a deal and too slow at the end of it, (or vice versa), lost his over-all view and became confused. It was increasingly frequent these days for a customer to leave the shop hastily, in a state of indignation over Heinrich's manoeuvres, and he would sometimes run after her, either apologizing volubly or uttering imprecations. People began to talk. The first bills of exchange were made out, and although they gave him breathing space for the time being, he was already dreading the day when they bounced.

Friedrich's letter and Marga's picture postcard arrived on the same day. Marga had chosen a summertime urban view, and her message sounded as if she were writing to someone from the past whom she found it difficult to remember after all these years (it had been a couple of weeks). I'm walking down the streets of a city which is still strange to me, comparing them with the streets of the city where I met you. Marga.

Marga? asked Rosa

Oh, forget it.

Very well, I'll forget it.

So what's the news of your friend Friedrich?

He's going back East. Can't adapt to this country and its people. He's thought it all over this way and that for a long time, but he's familiar with everything over there.

What an idiot he must be, going back to the East of his own free will.

I took a look at the new Opel Kapitän when I was in town today.

Oh yes? Fallen in love with it, have you?

Hopelessly.

So he bought her the car. (He bought it for love, and because he owed her something.)

Of course Paul, who came to stay for a few days at the end of January, showed how impressed he was by the two cars, after Heinrich had set up in business for himself less than a year ago, so he didn't ask too many questions, everything seemed to be all right, and Heinrich was careful not to disillusion him. Paul had come mainly on account of his Hilde, who was in her sixth month of pregnancy and had been waiting almost three years for him to return from South Africa, where there'd been a Jewish girl from Johannesburg, and long lazy afternoons underneath the palms, or whatever sort of trees it was that grew tall and gave shade in that damn place South Africa, and Paul drank and laughed and screwed the Jewish girl day in, day out, didn't even have time to send the family a Christmas card. Hilde almost hadn't got him back to Germany at all, and now there was to be a wedding in the near future, and the person still hesitating about it was good old Paul. He kept on thinking of Rheina, he said. He thought of her every time he made love to Hilde, Hilde was so inhibited that way: in and out in silence. She had waited three years for him, even though it was really all over between them, said Paul, and at the age of twenty-eight he didn't even have a proper job, the idea of a wife and children was madness.

Couldn't he have thought of that before?

He had.

Look, let me give you a piece of advice, forget your South African girlfriend. Pull yourself together, man. Find a well-paid job and a mistress if you like, if your Hilde's such a drag, but for God's sake marry her and bring the child up. Has my marriage ever bothered me, do you think? Does it bother me that the bank won't lend me any more money? None of that bothers me at all. Not in the least. And we'll be coming to your wedding in two weeks' time.

Fundamentally, of course, it was crazy to go to Wiesbaden for a few days at the very height of the economic crisis and eat a lousy meal after the wedding in a cheap restaurant near the grounds of the health resort, but since it was Paul, and Paul had asked him several times to come, he made the long journey, danced more often than any of the other men with chubby Hilde who was now his sister-in-law, paid her a couple of compliments on her cocktail dress, which was much too tight, and cast her into confusion when he half-jokingly told her, whispering in her ear, what it did to him when her lovely soft breasts pressed close to him as they danced, and what other parts of her he suspected to be lovely

54

and soft, how sad that they were brother-in-law and sister-in-law.

It was an entertaining evening; the party didn't split up until just before three. Even Theodor had danced with his Ilse, and their father had danced first with their stepmother and then with all the other women present in turn. Just before one in the morning Paul took his brother aside and said: Well, what do you think of her? And Heinrich said: You've done well for yourself, you'll have plenty of fun with your Hilde, and if you don't it won't be her fault.

Back in Regensburg Lehmann was waiting for him with bad news: a bill of exchange had bounced, and furthermore the man from the bank had phoned twice on Friday and every two hours since this morning.

So now it's serious, said Heinrich.

Yes, it's serious now.

The lawyer whom Heinrich visited in his office on Tuesday morning had already advised him over his entry in the commercial register, and on the advantages of a limited partnership and the disadvantages of a limited liability company. He had wished Heinrich good luck, but now, when he heard about the bouncing bill of exchange and the sums Heinrich owed the bank he just shook his head and sent Heinrich away, telling him he'd better take a look at the criminal code, which he described as one of the most important books ever produced by mankind and a positive oracle in all imaginable cases of difficulty and crisis, Heinrich had better look up the relevant clauses there.

Back in the street Heinrich felt as if he ought to be grateful to the lawyer for the gloomy prophecies with which he was shielding him from the naked truth, and the truth was that Heinrich was in dire straits: anything was possible, from a hefty fine to a couple of years in jail. A sense of panic came over him as he sat in the library reading the clauses on the different ways of going broke, and as for the distinction drawn by the law between ordinary bankruptcy and a particularly grave case of bankruptcy, he didn't want to take in any of that at all.

Only after the third drink in his usual bar in Blaue-Lilien-Gasse did he feel more optimistic; he couldn't help thinking of Rosa's Friedrich and his idiotic return to the East. Would Rosa have had a fling with him if Robert or some other man hadn't been involved? Perhaps he ought to talk to her now, discuss some way out together, for instance he could sell the car at short notice, Rosa's Opel, or the jewellery she seldom wore, or he could ask Bella if she would help him out by giving up the new flat, so strictly speaking it wasn't too late after all.

As he crossed the Steinerne Brüicke to Bella's flat the situation appeared to him desperate but not hopeless. He was there too early, Bella was still at work, but when she came down the street he immediately felt enormously relieved. My God, she said, you look terrible. Didn't the lawyer hold out any hope? You'd better come in and sit down, I'll mix us a drink, and you can tell me what's up, or don't if you'd rather not.

Later she said: Come on, let's play our old game. Tell me what isn't nice about me but you like it. However, he didn't want to, and only long after midnight did he think of the things that he liked about her although they weren't nice, and by then she was asleep (he hoped Rosa was asleep too). The way she sometimes squinted when she was tired, or thinking hard of something. The little bits of dry skin between her toes. Her hair when it hadn't been washed for three days. In fact anything unwashed about her. The fact that she hadn't the faintest glimmering about politics. Her fits of rage for no good reason. The little rounded curves which came of whisky and the chocolate that was all she ever ate for breakfast. Her lack of restraint. The way she smacked her lips when she ate. The way she always spent for ever in the bathroom. She had never been jealous in all these years. A pity you were never jealous (he began composing his farewell), a pity you don't know this is the end.

It had been at the open-air swimming pool on the Schillerwiese that he first noticed her among a thousand beauties and never took his eyes off her, on the bank of the Danube back in the summer of 1957 when she was in her mid-twenties, swimming and diving like a man far out in the middle of the river, shaking the water from her hair (red hair) when she came back, lying on the grass with arms outstretched, taking no further notice of her surroundings, leafing through a book or magazine, now and then sending an excessively importunate admirer packing, thinking of nothing, warming herself up, then swimming and diving a second time, wrapping herself in an old green towel under which she changed into her clothes, never staying longer than an hour.

This went on for two or three weeks, and Heinrich couldn't think of anything to do but watch her from a distance as she lay there on the grass every afternoon in her raspberry-red bathing costume, unaware of Heinrich or all the other men surreptitiously watching as she climbed down to the river over the steps let into the slope of the bank, swam away, using every imaginable stroke, and came back the same woman as before. For the first three weeks he was thinking: I'll soon think up some way of approaching that girl in raspberry red who swims like a man, and when he still hadn't thought of one at the beginning of the fourth week he packed up his things one afternoon and followed her to her door, then waited for her at the same time next day, and for a week he followed her from Rote-Löwen-Gasse to the bathing place every afternoon, and back the same way an hour later.

And that was how it began. One day she said: Why do you keep following me like a dog, here, take my bag and buy us both an ice or a lemonade instead, and then we'll talk and tell each other why we're here, and see if there's any reason we might like each other. At the end of July 1957, lying beside her at the bathing place for the second time, Heinrich said: It's heaven-sent, that's what it is, finding you and lying here on the grass beside you, wondering what it would be like with you, and Bella simply said: Yes, this is the way it begins, so let's start, the two of us, I feel the same too, I'll take you home with me if you like and let you stay in honour of the day.

She was six months older than he was, and she herself didn't give them more than a summer together. At the end of that first summer she said: I like it this way, no ties, all swift and secret, and at the end of the second summer she said: I didn't particularly like you at first, but your mouth and your hands and your prick make me feel good, specially your prick. Sometimes now she no longer objected when Heinrich started on about his various plans for a shop of his own in the Altstadt and a flat with a view of the Altstadt for Bella. Discussing it all with you will bring me luck, Heinrich had said in the fourth summer, and Bella had replied: Let's hope so, and you must talk to your uncle, because if he comes up with the money you can get started in a few months' time.

It was in November, three months after Heinrich's twenty-ninth birthday, that he made the idea of the shop in the Altstadt acceptable to his uncle in two long nights of discussion, and then a few more months passed with the search for suitable premises and various financial transactions between the banks and Heinrich and his uncle, and in early February 1961 (her thirtieth birthday) he surprised Bella with a second-hand Karmann Ghia and an extract from the city of Regensburg's commercial register: an entry for the firm of Heinrich Hampel Beds and Bedding Ltd, dated 7 February 1961. Well, congratulations. Yes, congratulations, may it all turn out the way we hope, this is where life really begins, and Rosa too had said this was where life really began, with a healthy son not yet two weeks old and a firm in a very good position. Congratulations. Yes, congratulations, may it all turn out the way we hope.

When the shop opened its premises a week later Heinrich was drunk within less than an hour. He had chilled two crates of champagne, and ordered canapés on silver dishes, and everyone drank to his future and Rosa's and Bella's, and they felt relaxed and optimistic. Even old Franz, Beds and Bedding, had come, and Rosa with the sleeping Konrad, and Bella for a few minutes just before the shop closed, but by then Rosa and the baby had left. Fräulein Swoboda got so excited that she sold two sets of flowered sheets for the price of one, and Heinrich's uncle stood at the back with Lehmann beside the sprung mattresses from France and dreamed of hefty profits.

Heinrich was the only one who didn't dream. He would have liked to go round to Bella's, because then he could have relaxed with her for a while, and at some point Bella would have placed her hand on his painfully throbbing organ, whose importunate demands here and now, among all these customers and business acquaintances, struck him as a bad joke, and at the next opportunity he must put in a good word for it with his Bella, who suddenly had something very strange and distant and unattainable about her, and then there she was in the doorway, waving to him in a friendly and encouraging manner as if to say: There, you see, didn't I tell you? There's a lot you don't still know about me, and you'll be surprised yet by my kisses and my wantonness.

The first creditors came in early March. The creditors came as if they had ganged up together, some with reminders and threats and imprecations, others with concrete claims and a readiness to negotiate. Sometimes Heinrich paid them a small sum just to be rid of them for a while and prevent them from kicking up a great fuss on the stairs, giving Rosa and the children the impression that it was only a matter of days before he was arrested and taken away God knew where.

As for Rosa (his Rosa), he could only marvel at her. This could have been her hour, now that she saw it would be all over between him and Bella, and the humiliation which was linked to Bella, but instead she said little, and was very reserved and circumspect and quiet. Yes, I rather thought so, she said, or: I thought as much, but I never dreamed it could all happen so quickly.

What's to become of us, said Heinrich.

Yes, what's to become of us. You'd better think of something. Sell the new Opel if that's any use, or take my jewellery to the pawnbroker's, or perhaps your precious Bella will come up with a contribution, but do stop being sorry for yourself and me and your precious Bella, that's not going to get us anywhere. Because that was always your credo, wasn't it, life goes on and you can always begin again, remember? You can't let the world come to an end after the death of a child, we have to pull ourselves together, look to the future, make an effort: quoting Heinrich in 1957. Yes, I remember, said Heinrich, but if the doorbell rings again please will you answer it, I'll stay put. So soon Rosa was the only one barring the way to impatient tradesmen and suppliers early in the morning, or in the evening or at the weekend, getting rid of them as if they were children pestering her for sweeties, no, she was sorry to say they couldn't speak to her husband, no, he was away, yes, away on business, but when he gets back he'll be in touch, I assure you.

The days now passed him by in a kind of haze, and only when he was lying beside Bella, and Bella stimulated his weary member into life, did he temporarily forget his creditors waiting for him in Lehmann's office, slagging him off, wondering whether he'd cut and run or was drowning his sorrows in drink in the station bars and would carry on drinking and lamenting his fate until some waiter or waitress took pity on him and turned him out. It was a fact that Heinrich now regularly began drinking in the morning, but secretly and in small quantities, for instance a shot early in the morning on the way to the car, and another when he saw Lehmann opening up the shop at eight-thirty on the dot, acting as if it had nothing to do with a few sales more or less.

He was well known in the bars where he warmed himself up every few hours after his walks. Around noon he usually went to a café down by the river, ate the same dishes for days on end, chewed peppermints, wrote his father a picture postcard, passed the shop again, preferring to give it a wide berth, waited for Bella, made himself notes. Monday the fifth: the electricity company cut off the supply, no advance warning. Tuesday the sixth: got Bella mixed up with Rosa. Wednesday the seventh: Lehmann's made off with last week's takings. Thursday the eighth: the bank has said there won't be another pfennig, full stop. This is the end.

Heinrich still hadn't accustomed himself to the idea when old Franz, Beds and Bedding, suddenly phoned him at home on Friday the eighth and asked to speak to Heinrich, how would he like to go and work for him again, he hadn't forgotten his former salesman and what he'd done for the firm, and there was sure to be some solution to his present obligations or his debts.

It's easy for you to say that, said Heinrich.

I'm making you an offer, said old Franz, Beds and Bedding.

Well, no, I'm not sure, things look pretty bad.

You should know.

On Saturday morning Heinrich began saying his goodbyes. At first he didn't realize they were goodbyes, and that he was already walking the streets which had been familiar to him for years as if he were a stranger, or a traveller whose train will be leaving in an hour or so and is just garnering a few final details before he leaves the city, perhaps for ever. As on his arrival in Regensburg nearly ten years ago, Heinrich was surprised to find how short and easily surveyed its streets were, how close to him, how familiar it had all been. That

Saturday morning he tried, more or less, to sum it all up for himself.

All alone, Heinrich walked the streets down which he had walked hundreds and thousands of times. From the Altstadt over the Steinerne Brücke and on to the Schleuse, noting the difference between Bella places and Rosa places and places where he had been on his own, testing familiar and long-forgotten smells and sounds, looking with the eyes of the past at the little windows of their first flat near the big car repair workshop, once again standing with Bella in the dark, narrow passage leading to her favourite cinema in the back yard, sitting once more on the stone steps in the back yard of the Herrmann maltings, telling Rosa about his first sale of a double bed, remembering cafés and inns and bars and restaurants where he had been with Bella or Rosa or friends and business partners, calling to mind a customer whose name he saw in passing beside a doorbell or on a letter-box, finally growing tired after all his walking and remembering and forgetting again, and then he went home to Bella.

He hadn't felt like asking her about the flat.

He wanted her to retain a memory of the Heinrich he had once been, the Heinrich he might not so easily become again.

I didn't expect you so early, she said, adding that she was sorry but she wasn't feeling too good, she hoped Heinrich didn't mind but what she really wanted to do was fall into bed and stay there, the worst of it would be over by tomorrow morning, and he could count on her for the champagne breakfast on Sunday. Or had he changed his mind? No, it was only that so far Fräulein Swoboda didn't know anything about it, he was just going to look in on her and invite her, she might like to come or she might even have heard about it from that rascal Lehmann, who knew?

Why yes, she'd certainly like to come, Fräulein Swoboda had said, but what was there to celebrate, for heaven's sake, she did hope she hadn't forgotten anyone's important birthday, and Heinrich was able to reassure her there.

Must you really, Rosa had said, and Heinrich had said: Yes, I'm afraid so, Fräulein Swoboda is going to be fifty-five and has been looking forward to it for weeks, but with a spinster lady it shouldn't go on for more than two or three hours.

It turned into an odd kind of Sunday in a café in the east of the Altstadt. To start with, Fräulein Swoboda was surprised, wondering why they were celebrating the firm's first anniversary late and without Lehmann and Heinrich's uncle, but then the first glass of sparkling wine was served, and the breakfast, and Fräulein Swoboda enjoyed it, and so did Heinrich and Bella. Heinrich complimented Fräulein Swoboda on her new shoes, and Fräulein Swoboda complimented Bella on her elegantly plucked eyebrows, and later on a few people from Heinrich's regular table moved over and sounded off about the depravity of young people today, and the crowds of foreigners pouring into the country from all over the world and competing for work in the factories, and since it eventually became quite merry, with Sekt and cognac and a couple of liqueurs for Fräulein Swoboda, they all stayed there until late in the afternoon.

Later on, in the car on the way home, Bella said: I sometimes feel quite afraid of you, or else I'm thinking what you dare think yourself only in your most honest moments, and that was the last time he ever saw or heard her. When he thought of her later he always pictured her in her little flat with its view of the Danube and the Altstadt, and he knew she had a few photographs left, and half a dozen bottles of whisky in the living-room cupboard, she had taken a nip of whisky now and then when he was there at her door around four or four-thirty almost every afternoon, and he didn't tire of her quickly: he hoped she would remember that.

That same evening Heinrich wrote in his notebook: Bella Anton, 25 July 1957 to 11 March 1961. She had red hair, sang very prettily. Not too keen at first, but she got used to me in time.

Then he packed.

3

His first weeks in his new country were weeks of waiting, and those first weeks were difficult but full of promise, they were weeks in which he left almost everything to Rosa, who had a will of her own, might have been in her early twenties again, and ignored him. Even a full month after Rosa had turned up at the camp with the two children and didn't go away again, but stayed and suppressed her own sense of regret for the sake of the family, Heinrich caught himself thinking what it would have been like without the presence of Rosa and the children, and without the Birnstiel family who were giving them temporary accommodation, and who explained their new circumstances to them through the example of a pair of bathing trunks in a land formerly left in ruins. Heinrich envied the Birnstiels from the first moment on. He envied them their marriage, their house and garden, their conversations about anything and everything: the decisions taken at the last Party conference, the current seven-year plan, the future of heavy industry, international peace. Heinrich was not used to people in the West taking their own country's fate to heart in this way, with the most trivial things becoming important, whether you saw them through Party eyes like Friedhelm, or through the eyes of a working mother like Anneliese, who had to go all over town to buy a pair of children's shoes or red bathing trunks: well, that was the situation. We can't complain, Anneliese had said on the first evening, and Friedhelm had said: We're full of hope, the new border has given us a breathing space, and it's not the fault of the Party of the working class that Anneliese has to go all over town to buy a few oranges or a pair of red bathing trunks, that made the pleasure of getting them all the greater (said Anneliese), and after all the country was still in its early stages (said Friedhelm).

The two of them asked only the most general questions about Heinrich's and Rosa's life in the West; they seemed to know most things about it already, or perhaps they felt ashamed or feared comparisons, so Heinrich in turn spoke of it only in outline, told them how his father and brothers and sisters were, was quick to change the subject when Rosa started on again for the hundredth time about their big flat in Regensburg and their two cars, while he himself faced everything new with determined goodwill.

He often thought of Harms and what Harms had told him when they parted about this country where the apples and cabbage and meat and potatoes tasted of hard work: it was a quiet, modest and cheerful country, Harms had said, and it wasn't just the need to economize on energy that made it far less colourful and full of advertising slogans than the West with its brightly lit cities and advertisements and all its elegantly dressed women, yes, it's easy to dream of those women, but better to stick with a different sort, a simpler woman, the sort who doesn't have to know everything and have everything and be everything, and the sort who'll work hard and be reliable like the women here when the crunch comes. Heinrich would have to adjust to his new homeland, Harms had said, and you had to be patient with the country and its people (he spoke from experience), and I'll come to see you in three or six months' time and you can tell me all about it.

And so Heinrich got through his days, came to know the new smells coming from the sky or the greyish-brown floors of administrative offices, memorized the abbreviations and concepts of the new order, asked a great many questions and received answers, his mistakes marked him out as a man from the West, but his knowledge of the old days showed he was a local inhabitant: place of residence, the German Democratic Republic, university city of Jena (District of Gera), Number 6 Windbergstrasse, ground-floor flat on the right.

On the first evening the kind Birnstiels had said: We're very sorry, but we can only offer Heinrich a room in the house opposite, it was occupied by a professor of physics until he fled to the West last summer and the room's been empty ever since, it has a bed and a chair and a wash-basin by the door, we hope it'll do for the time being. When he stood at its window he could see the house where his father once lived to the extreme left, and the house in which the Birnstiels had given Rosa and the children a room opposite, but he didn't get to know very much about their life there. He and Rosa met only when he was invited over to supper, or by chance, or if there was an appointment with the housing department, when they became a couple again. Rosa probably sensed that he would have preferred to be on his own at first, or perhaps, conversely, she preferred to be alone herself coming to terms with the past, or resigning herself to the fact that things weren't very easy, but for the sake of the children one must pull oneself together, or one would be starting all over again like Heinrich, who was simply drinking their past together right out of his mind, collecting empty bottles like trophies.

And so the days passed by.

Prospects of work and accommodation were held out, but nothing had yet come of them, he did a good deal of walking, drowsed whole afternoons away in the room once occupied by the professor who had done a bunk to the West, and waking from time to time he would realize that he had been dreaming of Fräulein Swoboda again, she had rounded breasts like globes in his dream and spoke to him very earnestly, very reassuringly, like Harms: It took time to put everything behind you, yes, but no use getting into a state about it. Or is it? Well, not a state like this one, said the lovely Fräulein Swoboda with her rounded breasts like globes, Fräulein Swoboda who came from distant Silesia, meaning heaven knows what state, and if you kissed her (as Heinrich did in his dream), she murmured a little and clenched her little fists, or rather paws.

Rosa had lingered in his room only once, shortly after Easter, when she said: Come on, we have to talk, your brother has written, this is what he says, and you won't like it. Although she had instantly spotted the battery of bottles beside his bed, and remained standing in the doorway all the time, she had sounded quite cheerful in her white pullover with the black spots and the gentle curves under it at which he only guessed, just as her first letter to Theodor had sounded cheerful and carefree: Jena, 19 April 1962. Dear Theodor and Ilse, well, here I am sitting in the Ratskeller with Heinrich, and let me tell you, Jena is a fine city. We're staying with the Birnstiels at the moment, and the people here are all very nice. The Wilhelmshöhe is a really wonderful place. Your father's house has been very well maintained: yellow paint, green shutters; the man who lives there now is a university lecturer. Do please write – why don't you write? Heinrich sends best wishes too, you still owe him some money you had from him, please buy us a fridge and a TV set with it, and once all our things have been moved here I'm sure we'll manage.

Heinrich had added only a few meaningless greetings, saying that Rosa had passed on everything Theodor had said verbatim. Which was to the effect that Heinrich was no great loss, for heaven's sake, Rosa mustn't throw her life away on a trickster like that, in the last resort anything was better than a life behind the Wall, a life behind barbed wire: such had been his good brother's comments.

So what's he said in his reply?

It's about your father. And all the trouble the family in Wiesbaden has had because we left, and he says he and Ilse were always ready to help us, but now they're not so sure that was the right thing to do in every instance. He says that towards the end, about always being ready to help us, but this is the first part of the letter: We're just back from visiting Father, he's been very ill for the past two weeks, and for the last ten days he's been back in a psychiatric hospital. I suppose I don't have to tell you just why his nerves are in such a bad way.

Heinrich was inclined to feel rather cross with his father and his father's strange illness, and the way he always took everything so much to heart and sat in his big armchair at home for weeks on end without uttering a word, and then all of a sudden his mood would change and he didn't get a wink of sleep all night, he was euphoric and carefree, took a taxi to Aachen to see his brother Jakob, or ordered some wickedly expensive car for Paul or Theodor in a recently opened car showroom, when they always had to cancel the sale and had difficulty in explaining about him.

Theodor had said nothing more precise about the circumstances, but no doubt it was after yet another of his deranged purchases or long taxi rides that they had got him sectioned again, against his will, for it was in the insidious nature of his illness or loss of control that he was no trouble to anyone when in the depths of despair, but when he was happy and full of energy they shut him up in a hospital where he was strapped to the bed and had handfuls of tablets stuffed into his mouth, for only then did he calm down and became quiet and easy to deal with.

I'm sorry about Father, Heinrich had told Rosa, but I'm not sending any answer back to them in Wiesbaden about the rest of it, and Rosa had said: Yes, I understand, but they must still send us the things, for instance we could really do with a fridge for the summer.

Won't you stay a little longer? Heinrich had asked.

Yes, a little longer, but not for what you have in mind.

Oh. A pity.

Yes, it certainly is a pity.

The question is, where do we go from here?
That was indeed the question.

If it had been up to Heinrich he'd have liked to be a bed salesman in his new country too, but the woman in the employment office had held out little hope of that from the start, so he was not surprised when the authorities informed him in April that he could start work as a driver with the State Retail Organization, which supplied the shops and hotels and so forth, and would be delivering foodstuffs to various businesses in the western part of the city. Would he kindly present himself at the appropriate office first thing on the morning of 2 May, and Comrade Müller would tell him what the job involved, with Socialist greetings, yours truly.

He had liked the comrade from the Jena City Council at first sight, with her hair combed severely back and her tolerant smile when she heard what he would really like to do, replying that his experience in the beds and bedding trade was one thing, the demands of Socialist productivity quite another, how delightful that you chose in favour of our German Democratic Republic, and after all Heinrich need not remain a van driver for all eternity.

Rosa had said only: Well, at last, we badly need the money, I hardly know what to spread on the children's bread, and Friedhelm had added: Everyone has to start again here, and if you make something of the job and work hard then before the year's up they'll be asking you if you'd like to study, or register for management training, you wait and see. That would be nice, said Rosa, already imagining Heinrich bringing good money home, and at six in the morning on 2 May he began work. When Comrade Müller welcomed him in her office she gave him a cup of coffee, and explained what he had to remember as he drove around with the delivery van. The logbook in particular had to be meticulously kept at all times, Heinrich must always insist on signatures from all concerned, and if all that went well and everyone was satisfied after his probationary period, they'd be happy for him to stay on.

The older colleague or comrade who accompanied Heinrich on his first round did not at first seem particularly keen on initiating a Westerner into the Socialist art of delivering foodstuffs, or perhaps he had run out of words after all those years behind the wheel, or was waiting for Heinrich's first mistake, for instance in changing the cumbersome gears or filling in the paperwork.

Only some days later did Heinrich see that this was exactly where he had gone wrong: in not giving the man from Lusatia who had been driving milk and bread and rolls around every morning for over ten years, and meat and sausages and cheese every afternoon, the chance to spot a single mistake, however small. That would have been the only possible way for him to begin; a novice like Hampel was supposed to make a mistake sooner or later, so that he could be mildly reprimanded and set right, and told: Yes, the same thing happened to me once, come on now, tell us what it's like in the West, I knew a little sexpot over in the West years ago, the worst of Socialism on German soil is the way there aren't any nice little sexpots around these days, there's women like Comrade Müller, though, but it's best for the likes of us to keep our hands off them.

Heinrich would have loved to find out more about Comrade Müller, and why it was best to keep your hands off a woman like her, and he would also have liked to know whether she was married or divorced, but the Lusatian simply ignored his questions, nor did he seem really curious about this Western refugee, he thought him a nuisance, not worth trusting, perhaps not even worth suspecting.

But Heinrich learned a lot from him. He found out how to save time loading up at the depot, and how to save more time during deliveries, he picked up the subtle differences between the way to address management, sales staff and drivers, he noted names and faces, the packaging and weight of the goods, he liked being accepted by the men as one of themselves, and he liked the way the women would lend a hand and weren't afraid of a bit of dirt, and when they climbed out of the bathtub in the evening smelling of vanilla or lily of the valley their bones ached, but unlike Heinrich they had stopped noticing that long ago.

The Hampel household was content. Theodor and Ilse even sent a friendly present now and then, and Rosa would write one of her extra friendly thank-you letters: Dear Theodor and Ilse, what a lovely surprise when your parcel arrived today, the rice absolutely saved me at lunch-time! Heinrich doesn't get his first pay packet until the twenty-fourth of the month, but if we sell the camera we shall manage all right. We have so much news! We've got a flat in Jena East, and it will be ready for us to move in on 1 June. There's a large garden too, with seven fruit trees (the rent is 6.20 marks a month), and I can grow vegetables there. Heinrich has been very busy, working from morning till night. He's going to take the schools sixth-form exam in September and then begin studying. How is Father? I've written several letters, but I haven't had any replies.

I know why not, wrote Heinrich in a PS, Father's envious of me, that's why he doesn't reply. My big brother Theodor would never survive in this country, and if it hadn't been for Mother, Father would have stayed here.

Then we'd never have met, said Rosa.

But the house would still be ours.

On the second or third morning Heinrich had gone over the road to his father's house and introduced himself to the new tenants, that's to say what he really wanted was to see what had happened to all the little rooms and the garden with the old birch tree, and he briefly described the reasons why he was back in the city, but so unwelcome a sight was Heinrich to the new tenants, as if he represented some kind of threat to them, that he couldn't get more than a few sentences out. He just had time to say he had only wanted to see who was living in his father's house after all this time before they immediately interrupted, saying the house had been the property of the people of the GDR for years, and why should they care that he was the son of the former owner. Sorry, but that's how it is, the university lecturer had said, and his thin wife had made a face which, if Heinrich interpreted it correctly, expressed contempt for him and the whole pack of refugees in general, making who knew what fortunes in the West, and when things went wrong coming back and expecting to be welcomed with open arms.

At first she had reminded him of Marga, with her narrow mouth and suspicious little eyes, but then he wasn't sure whether it might not be doing Marga an injustice to compare her to a woman like this, but anyway what did it matter if he *was* doing Marga an injustice by comparing her to someone, after all, Marga was dead to him now, so to speak. Since his arrival he had thought of Bella merely as someone dead to him too, sometimes talking to her in his head and deciding that she was dull and boring, for instance he could hardly tell a dead woman like Bella about his first impressions, looking for the ways he used to walk and sometimes couldn't find again, or if he did he found them much changed. He could hear Bella, dead as she was, laughing at the Heinrich of spring 1962, and the way he walked the city of his childhood trying to take it all in, dutifully reading the big red banners, and dreaming, and applying their slogans to himself: All our abilities go to strengthen the Fatherland we love, using our forces to enrich it, that was how the students talked here, that was what he found inscribed over the entrance to the main hall in the Oberer Philosophenweg.

The ways he used to walk were from the Gänseberg along the Burgweg, down into town to the Camsdorfer Brücke, crossing the river Saale, going over the Marktplatz past the big Zeiss works in the direction of the railway station, the Westbahnhof, then going from the Westbahnhof down

Schottstrasse to Gate B of the works: this was Father's route. Between 1931 and 1946 his father had walked these streets twice a day with his thin briefcase, greasy from much carrying, but it was his mother who always dragged the heavy shopping bags containing food for at least seven people up to the Wilhelmshöhe. From the very first his mother had privately hated and cursed the way from the Camsdorfer Brücke along the Burgweg and up to the Gänseberg, just as her children were soon privately hating and cursing the way from the Camsdorfer Brücke along the Burgweg and up to the Gänseberg when their mother was lying in her darkened bedroom with one of her frequent migraines, giving them instructions in her pain: Heinrich, fetch a sack of coal, it's more than I can do, and Constanze, don't forget the potatoes, my husband your dear father won't carry coal and potatoes.

She would have been sixty-three this summer, and the way in the opposite direction up to the Fuchsturm had been her favourite, because up there under the Fuchsturm she felt rejuvenated, a new woman, and for a few hours she was once again the delicate, slender girl she had been in the late twenties: the photographs showed her full mouth, her smile slightly wry with excitement as she faced the photographer's uncompromising camera, her strong brown hair combed severely to one side in the fashion of the times, her eyes grave and dark and mocking, should mockery be appropriate. Small breasts hidden under dark, heavy garments, you wouldn't have credited her with five children, perhaps you wouldn't even have credited her with a husband. A beautiful woman. Mother had been strong and tender, gentle and cruel. His parents did not get on well together for long, took things too literally or on the other hand too lightly, were very different. He feared her sharp, stinging blows with the willow rod, her silences, her maledictions: You'll be the last nail in my coffin, Heinrich, let me tell you, and the day I go to my grave it will be all of you who did it.

On the second day the Lusatian accompanied him only as far as the Co-op behind the city church, and then took the tram back to the depot: Heinrich had grasped what he had to do quickly, he said, such a clever-clogs from the West would soon find out what little tricks the delivery van had besides those gears, for anything else he'd better apply to Comrade Müller.

Was she perhaps waiting to hear from him? Heinrich put his mind to this puzzling but fascinating question for a whole week, wondering whether it would be better to look in on her early in the morning or last thing in the evening, but every time he had decided on a certain time or opportunity he took fright at the last moment, loaded up the van at top speed as usual, saw her sitting in her office over balance sheets of some kind, and hesitated. Only once, early in the morning, had he seen her standing with a couple of the drivers at the very back of the State Retail Organization site, and for a moment Heinrich thought she had waved to him in a friendly way a couple of times, and though he wasn't quite sure if it was really a wave, or a demand of some kind, or a chance movement of her hand, he had made a gesture as if he were waving too, raised his hand in her direction and quickly drove off.

The first Saturday came, and his first Sunday off, and on Monday morning, just as he was loading the last loaf and the crates of warm rolls into the van there she suddenly was beside him, looking very young and appetizing as she stood there, just as if she might not be out of the question for him. Weren't you going to look in and tell me how you're getting on, she asked, and did he think she hadn't noticed him stealing out of the yard in the evening like a thief, casting sidelong glances at her window? Or was there something on his mind? No, well, yes, but it wasn't important. He must apologize to Comrade Müller, Heinrich said, realizing he didn't know how to address her, and although he didn't think he even really fancied her, for the moment he did fancy

75

almost everything about her: her rather mocking way of looking at him, her hand on the rusty roof of the vehicle, then her hand on his shoulder (for the fraction of a second), the way she smoothed her hair back from time to time, or put her hands reproachfully on her hips, she obviously used her hands a great deal.

She'd heard a lot of good things about Heinrich, she said, while Heinrich was still busy looking at those strong little hands, the Lusatian in particular had nothing but praise for him, and so did the managerial and sales staff, the packers, the drivers, they all sang his praises, but it was the Lusatian she really trusted. People can be mistaken, said Heinrich, to which she replied: Yes, and then you know the truth and you've been wrong again.

Saying this seemed to embarrass her, as if she had told him a secret or let herself be induced to make a politically dubious remark, but Heinrich thought it suited her to be telling him secrets and letting herself be induced to make politically dubious remarks, then looking embarrassed and fiddling with her fingers like a schoolgirl caught in the act of something, immediately noticing that she was fiddling with her fingers like a schoolgirl caught in the act of something and changing the subject, so now, unfortunately, they were well away on politics. Heinrich was suddenly reminded of Lyusya and how, the very first time, he had thought, so she likes this, she doesn't like that so much, all things considered there's no great mystery about it, but it might all be different with another girl, for at the time he didn't yet know a great deal about such things, did girls always retreat at first and go all quiet, and would Comrade Müller here have retreated at first and gone all quiet, such questions were occupying his mind.

I've remembered a Russian girl I knew, said Heinrich, but her mind was somewhere else entirely, and she said (breaking into his thoughts about Lyusya and other women comrades): My father was in Buchenwald from 1941 to 1945 for being a Communist, and again from 1945 to '46 for being a Social

Democrat, by then he'd had enough and didn't stand by his convictions any longer. He probably starved to death, or else they beat him up in that Buchenwald of theirs where the really obstinate either lost their false beliefs or died of them, we never did find out for certain. I was fifteen or sixteen when my father died of starvation or was beaten to death in Buchenwald, so I joined the Party at twenty and I do my best. I didn't want to do things the same way as my father who died for his beliefs, and I don't think he needed to.

That's why, you see, said Comrade Müller whose father had died in Buchenwald.

Ah, yes, Buchenwald, said Heinrich.

Yes, Buchenwald, she said.

I like your perfume.

It's Bulgarian. That's where my husband comes from.

And as for the other things I like about you, I'd better keep them to myself.

Buchenwald had also been the subject of conversation several times during Heinrich's weeks in the camp. Harms had advised Heinrich to go there when he had a chance and get a first-hand impression, and the day before they were allowed to leave there had been an evening lecture on *The Importance of Buchenwald in the German Democratic Republic's Struggle for Peace*, but there had been no mention of any camp at Buchenwald under Soviet occupation, or perhaps Heinrich hadn't been listening properly as usual, for on the whole he could well understand that the Russians had to put their defeated enemies somewhere or other.

As they said goodnight on that occasion Rosa had added: Well, this is your last chance, Heinrich, and it's going to be your last chance with me too, now help me pack, we're going to have a strenuous day tomorrow. Harms himself had gone to the gate with them, and Tom, rather hesitantly, had accompanied them halfway, and then the four of them had walked to the nearest bus stop, Rosa with Heinrich's rucksack, carrying the baby, Heinrich with Rosa's two suitcases, and in front five-year-old Eva, little Evi, that big little girl who had been overcome by amazement for days and weeks past and went very quiet in her amazement, for here they were at last in this foreign country where the people didn't look foreign at all, they even spoke the same language and called their country by three initials, rolling the third initial so nicely: Welcome to the GDRrrr, Evi.

Rosa too thought the new country was showing its attractive side in this spring-like weather, the buses drove slowly from one stop to the next like buses everywhere, it was just that everything looked a little less colourful than in the West, that was her first impression. An attractive German town, Eisenach, thought Rosa, noticing queues outside the shops here and there, but there were queues in the West too, the people looked content, just as people in the West looked content on the first spring days, it was still rather cool but sunny and bright, with the first courting couples out and about on the streets, so at least you still had a chance of getting kissed here under Socialist rule.

They reached Eisenach around lunch-time, and since there wasn't a train to Jena for the next hour and a half, and they had good reason to celebrate, they went to a State Retail Organization buffet on the station and ate bockwurst with coleslaw, and Heinrich had his first beer with it, and Eva and Rosa had a fizzy lemon-flavoured drink. Rosa thought the people gave them some rather funny looks, because they and their cases and the two children were taking up two tables, but Heinrich said: Oh, never mind, they're just envious because we're in a cheerful mood, celebrating being out at last, and they can't possibly tell that we're straight from the camp.

On arriving at the station in Jena, the Saalbahnhof, they were all surprised to find that the journey had lasted a whole hour and a half, but because it kept stopping and they were all very excited, wondering what Heinrich's Jena would look like and whether their postcard had reached the Birnstiels in time, the journey flew by. Heinrich was sure the postcard would have reached the Birnstiels in time, just as Rosa, for her part, was quite sure the Birnstiels had no idea they were coming at all, and sure enough there was no one to take their heavy luggage or help them in any way, but Heinrich didn't think that was too serious. When they had gone on foot from the Saalbahnhof across the Marktplatz to the Camsdorfer Brücke, he said: Now I'm home again, and Rosa thought, home, well, yes, but here and there it still looks much like Regensburg: the dirty river Saale is a bit like the Danube, what they call the Paradies district is as quiet and secluded as the Thurn und Taxis park, only everything was steeper and more hilly and fuller of nooks and crannies here, and when you finally reached the top of the hill you had wonderful views over the city and the country around.

When the kind Birnstiels had got over the initial first shock, Heinrich went to look at the outside of his father's house, and after that came the story of the red bathing trunks, and the first evening in the room left empty by the professor, but although he felt some longings, and stretched as he lay there and couldn't get Rosa's perfume out of his head, he was suddenly feeling careful, thrifty and optimistic, and didn't play with himself.

In the days after her confession Comrade Müller was formal, indeed cool. She was probably sorry she had told Heinrich about her father, or else she was annoyed by the non-arrival of a delivery, or else her husband was always bothering her at night, and when he bent over her secretly she always thought of Heinrich and didn't know why.

Heinrich didn't seem to be having any luck with other women in his new country either, or else he kept meeting the wrong sort and hadn't got his eye in for the right sort yet. He exchanged a few words with some of the salesgirls he met now and then, and of course they were always curious to know what it was like in the West, and whether it was as difficult to get hold of a good bathing costume for the coming bathing season there, and then they immediately took fright at their own remarks and questions, and treated him as if he were an informer.

At first Heinrich thought: it's because I'm only an ordinary van driver, an ordinary van driver isn't anyone worth knowing here either, but perhaps the people were afraid too. Afraid, said Friedhelm, what nonsense, no one in our country is afraid, and Anneliese said she thought it was probably something to do with Heinrich's clothes or the way he talked. People can see you're from the West just by looking at you, every gesture and glance and movement show it, they notice your expensive shirts and your white shoes and draw their own conclusions. There have been occasional disappointments with people from the West, explained Friedhelm, and Rosa thought he wouldn't get far in the long run with just one rucksack full of clothing anyway, so he was allowed to get a complete new wardrobe with her blessing in the last weeks of May, bought a couple of inconspicuous pairs of trousers, shirts, shoes, socks, and out of his own old things all he kept was the box of papers. He had even secretly thrown away his underwear one morning, just in case, so there wouldn't be any awkwardness, for instance he wouldn't have liked to hear Comrade Müller with her pretty, industrious hands saying he couldn't be serious about living in the new country, because a man who is serious about life in the Workers' and Peasants' State doesn't wear underclothes from the West.

Was she capable of that? Heinrich thought she was capable of all sorts of things, but whatever he thought her capable of he would probably be wrong. So he merely marvelled at her and the way she noticed everything, telling him one day that she missed his nice white shoes, and that was a pretty little girl of his, but she doesn't get that red hair and those freckles from you. Of course you know our drivers are strictly forbidden to take friends or relations or anyone else in the van with them, but I'll turn a blind eye on account of your daughter's red hair and freckles. Would he like to bring her along tomorrow or the next day? Yes, thanks very much, he would.

He had already told Eva about Comrade Müller and her office, which always smelt of Bulgarian perfume: they took to each other. Of course Eva had to start out by saying how a pot of sausage salad had fallen over one morning in her father's van, and the fresh rolls were always so nice and crusty, she babbled on, but she'd never taken more than one. Show me your perfumed office, said Eva, and Comrade Müller showed Eva the perfumed office, and then the big garage, and the even bigger depot, and could Heinrich spare her some time that evening, she had something to discuss with him, shall we say seven in my office? She knew a little bar on the western outskirts of the city, it wasn't very easy to find, a lot of Russian officers and Party members went there, but it was good fun.

You like my little girl that much?

Well, let's call it that.

The bar on the western outskirts of the city was called The Cosmonaut, and was only the size of a living-room, but there was plenty of French cognac and whisky and vodka, and after nine-thirty Comrade Müller danced, first with Heinrich a couple of times, then with a different officer after every glass. She was wearing a short, flowered summer dress, and didn't look at all like a Comrade any more, and the Comrades of the friendly Soviet Army thought she didn't look at all like a Comrade either, and took turns whirling her through the air. It was not until just before midnight that she danced up to his table for a minute or so and said: My first name's Gisela, and Heinrich said: Mine's Heinrich, and I hope you have a good head for vodka. Oh yes. Just don't get any silly ideas about me, she said, so many people have got silly ideas about me on evenings like this, but as my father's daughter I have my principles, and what's more I'm happily married. Shall I find you some company so you don't have to keep staring at me all evening while I amuse myself turning the heads of our Russian friends? I'll bring my dear friend Vladimir over, yes, why not, and she brought over Vladimir, who was from distant Siberia and, like Heinrich, stared all night at the Comrade in her flowered summer dress and the way she danced and whirled in the air, vanished among the dancing Russians, reappeared and then disappeared again. Vladimir talked about his Siberian home, and Heinrich talked about those past weeks in the camp, and then she suddenly left and went home without saying goodnight, what a shame. Yes, a shame, agreed Vladimir, ordering another bottle of vodka, we're not going home until they throw us out. Ah, Geinrich, what a woman, said Vladimir, and Heinrich, who had already found out that Russians always called him Geinrich, nodded a couple of times, thinking Geinrich and Gisela, the names went well together.

Next morning Rosa said: Sometimes I hardly recognize you, you're really hoarse, all grey and quiet and nothing to look at, and you were drinking yesterday too.

Yes, with Vladimir. Comrade Müller took me, but I've no idea what she was really after.

There's a letter from Eisenach, from that officer, Harms. But he only wants to know how we are.

And how are we?

So-so.

It had been a bad moment when Harms brought him the news that Rosa and the children were on their way, had set off first thing in the morning and would be here in the camp early that evening at the latest. At first Harms seemed surprised that Heinrich took it badly (as if they had died), but he asked no more questions, poured drinks for himself and Heinrich, and thought of a few cases in the past when, similarly, he had not asked the man he was talking to any questions but poured a shot of whisky to help the bad news down, and then such men lay beside their wives in silence for a few nights, began on their first embraces, whispering, were defiant and desperate, made love out of boredom or indifference or early in the afternoon after the last interrogations, when they were feeling very small and docile and patient, and they and their wives reassured themselves with one another, leaving the window open, and forgot the past, it wouldn't be so bad for a man like Heinrich.

You'll soon get used to it, Harms had said, I'll come to meet them with you if you like. It was just before six, Harms had kept Heinrich in his office, and after a while a brief phone call came saying Rosa and the children were at the entrance with their luggage, waiting to be told what to do. Rosa said immediately: You've been drinking, and Heinrich, unwilling as he was to believe all this, said he would never forgive Theodor. Then they fell silent, assessing their disappointment. Rosa stood there at the camp entrance with two large suitcases, the baby in her arms, and Heinrich stared at his daughter Eva and did not move from the spot. Harms was the only one to stay in command of the situation, he took the cases and said: Well now, you must be little Eva, and: Welcome to Eisenach, Frau Hampel, your husband has told me so much about you. This seemed to surprise Rosa. And where was she to go with all this luggage and the two children, they all had a terribly long journey behind them, and they were hungry and thirsty too. Of course, right away, said Harms, I'll show you your room at once, over there in the hut they'll give you something to eat, of course, a glass of juice for the children, a schnitzel, a local beer.

Later Rosa said: Just think of the kind of people they have here in the East, that man acts as if he were a friend of yours and went out drinking with you every other afternoon, whereas what he's really doing is sounding you out, and he'll use what he discovers against you the first chance he gets.

Something like that.

Rosa would have liked to say: You're not glad to see us, and Heinrich would have liked to say: You needn't think I'm glad to see you, but then they both said something else, and first they had to eat and then put the children to bed, except that little Eva wouldn't go to sleep before she knew what kind of a country it was where they had such funny houses and rooms and beds and bathrooms. Heinrich said: I only moved in here today myself, and the beds are called bunk beds. Look, the letters and numbers on the bedclothes show you you're in a foreign country, but in a few weeks you'll feel quite at home here.

It was a bad journey, said Rosa, and she didn't know when exactly she had realized that she couldn't go back, but if she could she would, like a shot. Theodor sent regards, of course, so did Ilse and Paul and Hilde, they had all seen her off. But her mother had suddenly regarded her as a Communist, and a woman like Rosa's mother wouldn't so much as spit at a Communist by way of goodbye.

Has that man Harms been giving you strong liquor, she asked, when the children were asleep at last.

That's another story, said Heinrich.

Yes, and I know it too.

You'll like him, honestly.

I doubt it.

She had not in fact got to know Harms at the time except from a distance, when Heinrich was leaving his office, or perhaps at the evening lecture, but she was sent to someone else for the usual interrogation.

From the first Rosa said little when she came back from the interrogation, which was in a hut set apart from the rest of the camp, she only said she was talking to a woman officer, and it was all pretty ridiculous, and no whisky or liqueurs would make her talk, apart from a few names and facts which, correctly enough, she judged harmless, they weren't going to get anything out of her. You can still go back, said

Heinrich, whom the new state had obviously regarded as one of its own from the first day, and Rosa had said she couldn't stand the stink of the camp and the children's eternal shouting for long, and whatever went wrong between you and me won't be any more easily set right in the West than here in the East, as Heinrich thought himself.

He soon heard from Harms that Rosa and the children had given a very good impression in general, he heard nothing but praise of Heinrich's Rosa, and what she said agreed with Heinrich's own statements except for a few minor details: so far, for instance, Heinrich had, so to speak, kept quiet about this Bella. Rosa had poured her heart out to Comrade P., he hoped Heinrich would forgive him, the German Democratic Republic regarded all this as his private affair, but did Heinrich know that in her youth Frau Bella Anton used to go out with an SS officer? We have his file here, I can show it to you: Peter Fehrenkötter, born 22 August 1922, joined the Waffen SS in February 1943, took part in various operations in Lithuania, White Russia and the Ukraine, resident since June 1950 in Aichach near Munich under the false name of Alfred Schuman, employed in the Upper Palatinate as a commercial traveller in chemicals. Wanted for assorted crimes against humanity, including several hostage-shootings and the mass executions of Jews, partisans and deserters. A quiet, amiable man in his late thirties when he met her at a swimming pool. A ladies' man. Disappeared in summer 1957, probably gone to South America. No, of course she'd never said a single word about the man. Just silly coincidence that she met him and didn't ask about his past, but she did better next time around. We suspect that Heinrich Hampel was a stroke of luck for Bella Anton. We may hope he'll be a stroke of luck for our new young state as well.

So these are your famous stories, said Heinrich.

What I tell you isn't necessarily true, although we do have it down in black and white in our files.

Not a word of it's true.

Every fifth word, perhaps?

Yes, bad enough.

A few days later, remembering this conversation, he told Rosa: Sometimes it starts quite harmlessly, and then they think up some story, and a lot of those stories are pure poison. You know they're invented, they've been thought up to confuse you or lull you into a sense of security, and you end up believing at least the conclusion or the beginning of the story, or some detail in it, because how else would anyone know that one particular detail, so you start believing it all.

This was at the beginning of his fifth week in the Eisenach camp, and Rosa, for whom it was only the beginning of the second week, said: I think I know what you mean, but I can't help you, we can only help ourselves.

Even little Eva had been interrogated once or twice (more as a joke than anything), and Eva, who didn't know she was being interrogated, was inquisitive and observant as usual, for instance she didn't want to tell that unknown woman in uniform about some of the secrets she shared with her girl friends. You don't do that sort of thing, said Eva, and you must remember not to, because if you tell secrets God will strike you with rheumatics, such was Eva's view of things, and she didn't think it so bad that the huts were crowded and noisy and dirty, not as long as she could go over and visit Tom a couple of times a day, she had taken a great fancy to Tom and he to her, it seemed; of the stories he told she always liked the true ones best.

At the end of the fifth week Tom told Heinrich: Your daughter's a clever little thing, and if you were half as clever as she is you wouldn't be spending your afternoons with Harms, I mean, he can't actually force you to take his cigarettes.

Rosa herself thought highly of Tom and his principles from the first, and the main thing she learned from him was that with these people it's best to ask the questions yourself, and just Yes and No when you're giving answers. Say you want to go home, launch into some subject of conversation, Tom had advised her, so at every interrogation, every session of questioning Rosa repeated that she wanted to go home (to Heinrich's home in Jena), and every day they spent sitting around here was a day lost to the Socialist Fatherland.

Perhaps we may be able to fix something up between us after all, said Heinrich in the middle of April in his penultimate conversation with Harms, and Harms replied: Ah, that's what I like to hear, why not start making your plans and you can be out of here in a day or so.

How does a person make plans? asked Eva.

Ah, that's a difficult question.

No, it isn't, it's easy.

Weeks later Heinrich still remembered how surprised he was to find that his little Eva had been forming her own ideas for quite some time, wondering how she could have been forming her own ideas while he, her father, had not the faintest notion of it. When she was five, in the summer of 1960, she had made him show her the moon and all the pretty stars up in the sky every evening for a couple of weeks on end, and they had collected a handful of pebbles at the bathing beach on the Schillerwiese every other Saturday, carrying them home in Eva's yellow plastic bucket. Then he forgot about her. He remembered the procession with Chinese lanterns at her sixth birthday party, in the evening, but after that nothing but the autumn and winter, his long negotiations with his uncle, the birth of his first son, the opening of the shop, his afternoons with Bella, his rift with Rosa.

He felt uncomfortable because he could think of nothing to say to Eva about his neglect of her, but she made it easy for him, taking things as they came, pleased when he took her for a ride in the delivery van, welcoming her new life in general as an interesting novelty, getting him to read her the words on the red banners in the city, envying the FDJ children in their pretty blue shirts, and after a few weeks she could identify the banners of all the fraternal Socialist countries, and we'll visit a different one every summer, she said, day-dreaming. She liked it when he came home in the evening and admired her latest landscapes in water-colour, listening when she told him about the girl with blonde pigtails who lived at the end of the street and called Eva a capitalist. Capitalist yourself, Eva had said, it was the end of May when she had said that, with no idea what she was talking about, and at the beginning of June they packed their things and moved into the new flat on the first floor of a long apartment building in Jena East, where the children talked the kind of language she understood, they hadn't even unpacked before she was being called by her new nickname of Carrot-top.

Heinrich had planned to do the move on foot, but one afternoon Comrade Müller said he could use the van, she owed him that after their crazy evening in the Cosmonaut bar, you don't feel a real human being until you have a place of your own.

There's even room for you and the children in the van, Heinrich had said, when he had loaded it up with his rucksack and Rosa's suitcases, and a couple of cartons full of crockery and pots and pans, and the bedclothes borrowed from the Birnstiel family, and Rosa had said: We have so little, here we are making a fresh start with so little to our name, remarks that she repeated later in the empty, dilapidated flat: We have so little, here we are making a fresh start with so little to our name.

We moved on Saturday, she wrote in a letter to the family in Wiesbaden on 3 June 1962, you can imagine what a lot of work there was. The place is in a terrible state, Heinrich is painting the window shutters at the moment. He's decided to work on renovating the place until nine every evening, and the living-room already looks reasonably good. I've organized a box bed with a mattress, and made a new cover for the old sofa which the previous tenant left behind, all we really need now is a new TV set, it's such a pity that you won't send us one. Well, the Birnstiels have lent me two duvets to be going on with, but I'm afraid we have no bed-linen, and bed-linen is very expensive here, particularly as Heinrich's earning only 520 marks. But you do still owe us 600 marks, so please buy me two duvet covers, and pillows and sheets, but not too expensive so that there's something left over, there's so much that you just can't get at all here, or if you can it costs a ridiculous amount. Eva has settled down well, she'll be going into Class Two in autumn, and the little boy isn't so little any more. I'm enclosing a list of clothes I urgently need for the children. It's not easy for us here (though I'm not supposed to say so) but we're not complaining either.

You look tired, said Comrade Müller when Heinrich was loading up the van at five in the morning these days, with a few splashes of peppermint-green bathroom paint in his hair, and later it was the dark ochre paint for the kitchen, what was he up to, she asked, and both praised and blamed him for his diligence in stripping old wallpaper for days on end, though he couldn't find the sort they wanted in the specialist downtown shops, but he kept looking, and in the end always found something from the small range available, just as if he'd been here for ever. She liked that about him, said Comrade Müller, plucking dried paint out of Heinrich's hair, and that was what he thought of when he lay on the new air mattress at night: the way she'd picked paint out of his hair, just as a lover might, while Rosa kept going on about the children and what they needed next, wondering when those things were going to arrive from Wiesbaden, but they kept on failing to arrive.

It takes time, said Comrade Müller when he mentioned it to her, and would he like to come and celebrate her birthday in the bar, her husband was off to Bulgaria for a few days tomorrow. The fact is I have a couple of pieces of jewellery

89

to sell, said Heinrich, and the Comrade said: Vladimir's your man. You can ask him. But it was clear that she was pleased.

In the last week of June, just before their eighth wedding anniversary, Heinrich thought they had earned a break, and not knowing exactly how to give Rosa a treat he invited her to dinner in the Zur Sonne restaurant, and paid the eldest Birnstiel daughter five Eastern marks to babysit.

Heinrich couldn't remember when he had last seen Rosa in a dress, and Rosa, wearing her new grey dress, couldn't remember when Heinrich had last taken her out for a meal, and since each was surprised in his or her own way by the other the evening was quite a success. Except that the two waiters were frantically busy and unfriendly, and seemed far from pleased to see people queuing up for braised beef, mashed potatoes and red cabbage on a perfectly ordinary Wednesday, waiting in line for a table, and once you did get in the place was half empty.

Now, tell me all about it, said Heinrich, when the waiter had shown them to a table near the door, and he ordered pork roulades in marjoram sauce for Rosa and knuckle of pork with broad beans for himself. So Rosa began to tell him what it had been like when Heinrich got into his car and drove to Fulda and didn't come back, and the longer she talked the odder Heinrich thought it that he hardly featured in her story at all for the two weeks before she left, and when he did it was as an idiot, a fraud, a two-timing bastard who had brought the world crashing down around the ears of Rosa and his uncle and everyone who trusted him, who didn't settle his bills, who made off for the East because that was where he came from. For some time she couldn't believe that her Heinrich had really gone to the East without a thought for her, so unsuspecting had she been, so little had she known him, and of course people claimed that he was spying for the Russians, and said they were surprised to find how unsurprising they found it.

On the evening of her return to Regensburg, the first doorbell she rang belonged to that Bella of his, but of course that Bella had been taking care of number one all this time, would have gone anywhere with her Heinrich but not to the East, oh no, not in any circumstances. I realized you'd gone, I cursed you for it. I cursed you most of all in the first few days when the creditors turned up, and the bailiff, and your brother Theodor came visiting, always telling me what to do and what not to do, and the only comfort he could offer was the prospect of a modest future as a home-worker for Bertelsmann in a flat on some new housing estate. They all told me: Stay here, we'll see you're all right, your Heinrich's affairs are none of your business, we'll help you, and a woman who's been so badly deceived all these years won't weep for the deceiver long. That's the kind of thing they said to me, they didn't seem to think it so bad that I couldn't pay the rent for the old flat, and the bailiff left his tags on even the least valuable things, and only little Eva had no idea what it was about and envied her father for being on holiday. I thought anything possible as I earned a few miserable marks cutting book covers out of transparent film in the kitchen, and your brother was regularly ringing up asking how I was, I'd have liked to make off into the wide blue yonder myself. I wrote to your father saying he wasn't to judge you harshly, you were a good, kind person at heart, and instead of answering me your father walked beside the river for hours on end, couldn't make out what the world was coming to.

Yes, Father, said Heinrich, well, he'll have to see how he can manage now, and so will you and I in our own way. And by the way, do you know what became of your Bella, asked Rosa, but Heinrich had no idea what had become of his Bella, honestly, not the faintest.

That evening in the restaurant Zur Sonne and during the following night, as Rosa told the story of her journey and Heinrich lay silent on the mattress beside her, listening, they made a kind of truce, concluding that the past was the past, and there was no point starting on the subject of Bella over and over again, and how everything at home in Regensburg had dissolved into thin air, and your uncle ended up losing his two houses.

What about the journey? asked Heinrich.

Yes, the journey. Eva had a window seat facing the way they were going, so as not to miss anything; Konrad, half asleep, was in the pushchair; and Rosa, both determined and wary, sat between them in her new Persian-lamb coat and her court shoes, with her hair pinned up. She didn't even have a free hand to wave goodbye to Theodor and the others, and like Heinrich she felt a momentary satisfaction at knowing how cross they all were with her, angrily accusing her of being a Communist before she had even set foot in their homes, saying she was heading for disaster, while she and she alone knew, or rather hoped, that none of that was true.

It had not escaped the notice of the other passengers in their compartment that the family were all standing round her until the last moment, talking urgently to her, assuring her that the children would be ruined, and now all those people were gaping openly, feeling sorry for the two children for having a mother like Rosa who was actually going East of her own free will to join her rascal of a husband. And the young border official who offered to help Rosa just after Bebra never seemed to have come across a case like hers before, and said that if ever she changed her mind he'd get her out, just let me know, here's my name and address on this piece of paper, I'll get you out.

That was because he fancied you, said Heinrich, and Rosa said: Who knows, adding that she had laughed at his offer, but he really did write a name and address and telephone number on the scrap of grey paper: Horst Lange or something like that, and somewhere between the two checkpoints she'd thrown the piece of paper out of the window, she had something to prove to herself.

Then they went a little further, and the train stopped, and went on, and the closer she came to her destination the more often she thought: For heaven's sake, there's someone with an automatic pistol every few metres, you're for it now. As soon as they arrived in Eisenach two Red Cross nurses took her to a room with no handle inside the door, only barred windows and *Das Neue Deutschland* on the table, and she thought: I must get out of here, Heinrich won't be angry with me, and while she was thinking that they began to check her luggage. They were looking for foreign currency and weapons, found a little small change and a gramophone record of Hitler's speeches, and Heinrich's new dinner jacket among a pile of shirts and blouses, so they immediately concluded that he must be a musician, they poked a pair of knitting needles into Rosa's pinned-up hair (finding nothing), they thought Rosa's make-up box suspicious (finding nothing), we have our orders.

So she entered the country, surprising herself and, as we have seen, Heinrich too, but he soon got used to it. She might not have minded if he'd made a pass that night when she finally got it all off her chest, talking until their eyelids closed, but Heinrich thought he owed it to her to act like the guilty party and listen to her stories, asking exactly what she was thinking as she was driven to the camp with the children, perhaps in the very same bus which had taken him there a couple of weeks earlier.

I wouldn't have been too happy in your place either, said Rosa, but by then Heinrich was almost asleep, and what he muttered neither he nor Rosa remembered, it was to be hoped it was nothing about Comrade Gisela whose Bulgarian husband was almost away travelling, and brought his Gisela back little round bottles of sweet, foreign perfumes, and then Heinrich would sniff her, enjoying it when she told him off, tilting her head so prettily as she told him off, making the

93

impossible seem possible, which of course he believed, calling her by her name while half asleep, feeling troubled.

Well, think of something, you two, Gisela had said on their second visit to the Cosmonaut bar, dragging Heinrich and Vladimir out on the little dance floor in turn, and then taking them off for another drink at the bar after every fifth tune, dancing and drinking the pair of them pretty well into the ground yet again, soon looking round for other men to dance and drink with, finding them, taking and enjoying what she needed, what she considered her right, and her two most faithful admirers, Heinrich and Vladimir, sat at their little table like schoolboys, dreaming of her kisses. What are the pair of you gaping at, don't you have something to discuss, she called to them from the little dance floor after a while, and then Heinrich knew she had already told Vladimir about the jewellery, the jewellery which Rosa had given him that afternoon wrapped up in thick brown paper: a couple of gold and silver rings, a brooch, two pearl necklaces, and the gemstones bought in the years 1954 to '61, emerald, ruby and rock crystal, hidden in the false bottom of a make-up box, yet surely the border people knew about boxes with false bottoms.

That evening in the Cosmonaut Heinrich and Vladimir became friends, or rather business partners, for they spoke the same language, and in the language they spoke the girls were called Lyusya and Sonya, and Bascha and Natalia, girls who dreamed of tall young officers winning victories for the glorious Soviet Union, girls who dreamed of making love in big beds, that was for sure. Come along, I'll show you where I live, Vladimir had said, taking Heinrich (against the rules) to the Zwätzen barracks, where they estimated the value of the jewellery and the precious stones over a glass of vodka in the officers' mess, and very soon they were discussing the lovely Gisela again, and how far they had got with her respectively, which was nothing to write home about. Vladimir thought that if he did Heinrich a good turn it would help him with Comrade Müller, and Heinrich thought, my friends' friends are my friends too, and if she turns all coy and doesn't want to, prefers to keep her kisses to herself, well, the goodwill of a Comrade might always come in useful.

Rosa was sometimes surprised by the respect with which Heinrich spoke of Comrade Gisela, and the way she could drink the men under the table by four in the morning, at a bar on the western outskirts of the city and then deliver long speeches next day about Marxism-Leninism and its importance in supplying the population with perishable goods for everyday use. Rosa thought it did him good, he was rather in love with this Gisela but he wasn't really getting anywhere with her, and although he gradually overtook Rosa in the art of adaptation, using language which she did not yet feel capable of employing, she was content with her old Heinrich now that he was a new Heinrich, for he was patient and industrious, drank only late at night as he wandered around their new rooms, enumerating for his own and Rosa's benefit the jobs he had already finished, was happy to talk about the children, and kept bringing up the subject of this Gisela, and Harms, yet how different everything was in the new country, for instance the women (so Rosa said) were often stuck-up and unfriendly, they were tired after working, they stood in queues, fetched their children from day nursery, there was always something they had to do. I'll never get like that, said Rosa, not knowing what she would in fact be like some day, nor did Heinrich, though in the case of any doubt, he said, just stay the way you are. She liked that. And she felt glad that she liked lying beside him at night again, and thought something might come of it, and laughed with him to think that here they lay spending their nights on a couple of dark-blue air mattresses, while only a few months ago they slept in wickedly expensive beds from France. Yes, it was good that she liked thinking about him again, and was waiting for him to make a pass at her and show what he could do, give her a son or a daughter, and in the end they did it out of defiance too. Are you thinking of her now? asked Rosa when Heinrich had given her a son (or perhaps the night after that) and Heinrich said, as if surprised at himself: No, but I'm thinking of Harms, remembering he was the one who wanted us to be reconciled.

After that they had a few good months, their things arrived from the West, and another postcard came from Harms. In the middle of one week, when Heinrich was driving bread and sausage and cheese round the city as usual, thinking of Gisela's pretty mouth or her new suit, two large wooden crates were suddenly deposited outside their door, one of them containing underclothes and bedding and the old washing machine, and the second their familiar clothing and the fridge, and a new transistor radio, a present from Theodor. Under the gaze of their neighbours Heinrich and Rosa and little Eva carried the things into their new flat like treasures which had gone missing for a long time, and then Heinrich went out for a bottle of Hungarian white wine to celebrate, and not two days later the second postcard came from Harms. How were they getting on, asked Harms, Comrade M. had told him this, that and the other, but he'd like to see for himself, he suggested meeting for a friendly chat at the Zur Sonne restaurant on Thursday. He'd like to know what Heinrich thought of the people and the country; and what people said about the country; and what Rosa said. A little chat between old friends, he'd expect him after seven, don't eat first.

If it was Tom he wouldn't go, said Rosa, who was now almost sure that Heinrich had given her a child on the air mattress, as she then told him, and Heinrich said: Yes, fine, but you can't blame me for feeling hungry.

4

The doctors had held out little hope from the first, calling the condition by its Latin name of *Spina bifida totalis*: split backbone. We're sorry, Herr Hampel, but we have bad news for you, the doctor had said, taking Heinrich into a small two-bed ward early in the morning of the twenty-sixth, and there lay Rosa, pale and looking shocked to death, amazed that he had come, and the little thing beside her was a few hours old and looked healthy enough.

This isn't a good start, Rosa had said over the phone the previous afternoon, come quick, I'm all wet, and half an hour later, on the way to hospital, she repeated: This isn't a good start, everything happening so fast, my waters breaking like this, gushing down between my legs like two brooks, why in such a hurry, my little darling, don't give me grief. It had seemed to Heinrich that he could smell the water which had come gushing out of Rosa like two brooks, and at the same time he could smell the traces of Gerda on his hands, because the woman he had just left was called Gerda, and smelled like sulphuretted wood.

It wasn't at all like this with our little Evi, our big girl now, Rosa had said in the taxi, and then she spent two hours in the delivery room and nothing happened, and she lay there for a third hour and then a fourth, and after eight hours she sent for Heinrich and didn't want him waiting around any more, walking his legs off, asking how much longer it was going to be and whether he ought to be worried about the time it was taking; no, he needn't worry. Look, go home, get some rest, keep thinking of me, have something to drink, it'll be over by tomorrow morning and I'll need you then, but I'll need you to be well rested, it's not unusual for the waters to break early in a woman's last month, and they just have to lie and wait and be brave, same as usual. You think so? Heinrich had asked (it was one in the morning by now), and Rosa said she was sure of it, there's some leftover cauliflower and roulade in the fridge, and if anything happens they'll phone you, or you'll hear the news in the morning.

He hadn't planned to deceive her again that night, to feel so impatient, to go back to Gerda out of boredom. Just because Rosa had let him go, or rather told him to go, Heinrich had wanted to stay, walking his legs off up and down the bleak, long hospital corridors, but then he felt tired and jittery, heard women screaming in the distance, hoped that it had just happened, quietly, and they'd bring him the news any moment. He went on pacing up and down for another hour, seeing the sisters, doctors and male nurses who hurried past now and again looking at him: tired, jittery, trying not to think of Rosa and not to think of Gerda who smelled of sulphuretted wood, something he had never known before.

Naturally Gerda was surprised when he turned up at her place so late, since she had already gone to bed and was asleep, but she welcomed him in, for she was often surprised at herself to think how wide awake she always was after his kisses, and what ideas she always had when he kissed her awake. She didn't know much about this man called Heinrich, she accepted him like a woman who knows that waiting around for a man like Heinrich is not a good idea, but when he visited her and made her warm and wakeful and yielding she didn't mind that, or the fact that she didn't know how he spent his days and nights. When he had left again she would go over all the details of everything he had done in her mind, stuff she didn't even tell her best friend Anna, remembering how he had called her *My little piggy* the very first time, and when he called her *My little piggy* he always did things to her which made her feel quite different, even days later, and remembering how the things he did to her made her do such indescribable things to him, her friend Anna wouldn't have believed a word of it.

He stayed two hours and then went back to his Rosa in the hospital, and what Rosa had in her arms neither she nor Heinrich yet guessed. My God, what have we done, Rosa had said, and she asked Heinrich no questions about where he came from and where he had been, she said: See how peacefully she's sleeping, you wouldn't know there was anything wrong with her, but if it wasn't for the dressing you could see right into her spinal cord. Heinrich didn't want to know what it would be like looking into Susanna's spinal cord, but then he saw the big dressing, and was horrified and frightened, and couldn't forgive himself. Don't be angry, she can't help it, he said, and Rosa said: Yes, I mean no, I'm not angry, only a little bit, and anyway we have little Evi.

He had begun seeing Gerda at the beginning of the year, he had been visiting a customer and she was still living at home with her parents at the time, sitting at the kitchen table with her mother and father, making eyes at him. Sometimes he was surprised to find how brazen and shameless Gerda could be when she was in the mood for it, living in a boarding-house near the Steinerne Brücke, cracking dirty jokes and laughing at them, perfectly innocent she was, and doing things to him in all innocence that he didn't know from Rosa, perhaps not even from his Lyusya back in that Russian winter of 1949 to 1950, when he was just eighteen.

It had been Anna who drew Heinrich's attention to Gerda, Anna was a student in her third semester, but unfortunately her attitude to love was rather complicated, that's to say she thought nothing of it, and wasn't bothered by thinking nothing of it when Heinrich did gymnastics between her white thighs every few weeks in her room in the student hostel, taking a great deal of trouble and trying experiments, and then she would suddenly get up in the middle of their love-making and say why didn't they go for a little spin in Heinrich's new 17 M, when we get tired of it we can lie down and just go on from where it was nicest. I think too much when I'm making love, that's why it so seldom works for me, anyway I don't understand all that, or why people are so mad about it, but if he kept on taking trouble surely she would one day, he was ambitious enough for that.

You ought to meet my friend Gerda, Anna had said after one of their failed attempts at love-making, perhaps I'll introduce you, the way your boss introduced you and me back then, you've probably been wishing for ages that he hadn't. No, I have not, Heinrich had assured her, remembering the Christmas party at the beginning of December 1956 when he discovered Anna, she was the daughter of someone he knew, the owner of a shop selling beds and bedding in Straubing, and she was studying English and French in Regensburg. They had argued about politics at the Christmas party, and Anna had said: I don't like the Communists but I'm afraid of nuclear war, and Heinrich had said: Oh, come on, nuclear war, in the worst-case scenario we have to show the Russians we mean business, I know all about that.

Even months later Anna might still ask him what it had been like back then in the faraway Soviet Union, so Heinrich had to tell her, taking care at the same time not to tell her too much, because if he did she would start thinking again, and when she thought too much it put paid to their love-making however hard he tried. Later, when Heinrich had begun seeing Gerda, he and Anna used to discuss Gerda, and what fun she had had when Heinrich was holding forth in her parents' kitchen on the advantages and disadvantages of Polish bed-springs, and bedsteads made of wood and iron and gold and silver, and how Gerda suddenly pressed her narrow little feet against Heinrich's under the kitchen table, or sort of snuggled them against his, they were really nice and warm.

Anna could have talked about Gerda for hours (not that it did any good), while the bold Gerda, on the other hand, never said a single word about Anna, perhaps she had her own misgivings, or she was ashamed, or didn't know how to talk about the things she was ashamed of afterwards, even to Anna.

That was the story of Anna and her friend Gerda. Sometimes he saw them only once or twice a month, and there were days when he would have liked to let them know they were both his mistresses, whose names he sometimes mixed up and whose faces, odours, movements, fluids mingled and were superimposed on each other, fluids which he sometimes drank, thinking of himself as the father of their daughters, their sons. Anna was always saying what a fool she was, letting a rascal like Heinrich in between her thighs, and then she would sometimes pick up her old camera and take a few photographs of her rascal, grinning out of the picture in his hat and coat, a Chesterfield in his mouth, as if he weren't the Heinrich she knew but some Chicago gangster, or looking casually past her into the distance, feeling good and thinking: so this is what it's like when everything's going fine, success all round, money coming in and women too, life can be so delightfully easy, Rosa was in her fifth month, and perhaps the only thing he didn't have yet was a son.

Heinrich couldn't really have said he was hoping for a son, but Rosa certainly was, and when they got to the point where she let him make love again, in fact encouraged him and worked out the most likely days in advance, he had always, for her sake, thought of a son. But this time, unlike Eva's conception two years earlier, it didn't work straight away, and Heinrich was quite glad it didn't work straight away, for unlike that first time this was all done carefully and with intent, and Heinrich thought it changed everything when it was done carefully and with intent, pouring his sperm into her and knowing it was just so that they would have a son, or a daughter if it had to be that way. He wasn't sure whether Rosa really understood him, but he felt very strong and virile and sexy during those weeks, and then it was like hard but enjoyable work when he took her, thrust into her and came, and waited for Rosa to come too, but she was thinking only of his juices.

He had a great many commissions that summer, not for the first time either, so to celebrate they bought two sets of the most expensive bed-linen, the idea being that they would enjoy it and not get tired, would be patient over starting their second child, neither Gerda nor Anna had yet come on the scene. He liked it, putting back the bedclothes with Rosa almost every evening for two or three months, making love, and when it finally worked there was a brother or sister for Eva on the way, Eva would be happy with whichever came along.

Although the doctors had held out little hope from the first, Heinrich in particular did not give up hope, wouldn't hear of the mortal danger of infection, wouldn't listen to the nightmares Rosa had in the early afternoon between his visits, when she gazed helplessly at the baby on her lap as if it were something broken, or the wrong Christmas present. In order to let Rosa know he was on the way and in a good mood, Heinrich had taken to tap-dancing again, he tap-danced whistling or humming down the hospital corridor, flung the door open like a clown, kissed her cheek or forehead and took the broken thing in his arms, the baby which must not, for heaven's sake, must not get infected or die in some other way, and whispered to her: I know it's hard, but you must keep going if only for Rosa's sake, she'll never get over it if you change your mind, so please, please. Even when he was driving the delivery van, or in the evening, when he wasn't with Anna or Gerda or at the Schillerwiese swimming pool, but making himself a solitary meal or putting a couple of frankfurters in a pan of hot water, he talked to his daughter, his second daughter, the one who had turned out all wrong, promising himself and her that it would be a good summer.

He had never said anything to Anna and Gerda about Rosa's pregnancy, but when he began feeling claustrophobic after a few days at home in the empty flat he did tell them, just to have someone he could talk to about his encouraging little speeches to Susanna, or perhaps because for the first time in his life he didn't know what to do, and every time he visited Rosa in her ugly two-bed room she expected that he would come up with some idea. Anna had said: How awful, come along, let's drive around for a bit, or why not come in between my legs, my turn to comfort you today, but Heinrich didn't feel like driving around with Anna or getting in between her legs, he didn't really take her seriously. Gerda had said: Oh, that's terrible, but I don't know what you can do either, you've upset me, maybe you've hurt my feelings, which really surprises me. Heinrich didn't see why Gerda's feelings should be hurt because he couldn't get his sick child out of his head, but probably she secretly believed that it was Heinrich's fault Rosa had brought a sick child into the world, and was imagining what it would be like letting a sick man make love to her every few weeks, a sick man who was pouring his sickness into her and thinking of something which was nothing to do with her.

I'm sorry, Gerda had said, I don't think I can do it, and Heinrich had said: All right, although he only half understood. He never visited her again, and during the month of June he visited Anna too only out of politeness, or if he knew he would have to leave straight away to deliver a bed to Lappersdorf or Harting, but Anna was not offended and didn't miss him.

It was a bad sign that even after a week Rosa lay there as if turned to stone, didn't want to breast-feed the little creature at first and banished her from the room at night, while the clever doctors were suddenly talking about possible infections, not a good prospect for the Hampels' daughter, they'd better take her home. They can't do any more, said Rosa, but I don't want to take her home, I'd rather stay here asking questions, and then if they come in one morning looking grave, finding it difficult to choose their words, I'll know it's over.

Heinrich took the precaution of simply not listening when the doctors said that unfortunately there was nothing to be done in such cases, obviously preferring to send people away with their damaged children, and probably it really was best if they all went home and didn't give up hope, the little girl might improve, after all, perhaps they could operate in a few weeks' time, or she might go on living with her big plaster.

By the end of the second week he had finally got Rosa to accept it, and on a Monday in the middle of June she wanted to go home too, just when he had discovered Bella, that is to say he had spotted her at the famous Schillerwiese swimming baths and thought she was interesting, well worth looking at, the mere sight of her put him in a good temper.

All they had said to Eva was: You have a little sister but she's not well, so she needs you to be very careful and nice and kind to her. Eva had not wanted to come and look at her new sister, she much preferred staying with Rosa's mother, because when she stayed with Rosa's mother in Lappersdorf she could watch Granny chop the head off a hen every few days, even if the hen had laid a nice brown egg that morning it was plucked a few hours later, chopped up and simmering in Granny's biggest saucepan with some celeriac and leeks and carrots. Tomorrow, Eva said on the telephone when Heinrich told her they were bringing her poor little sister home, and she had arrived next day greeting Susanna with the words: Hello, little sister, Granny killed a chicken, are you staying long?

Rosa at least seemed to have no regrets about coming home, and sat in the kitchen under the suspicious eyes of Eva, who was now almost three, pretending she need feel neither hope nor despair for little Susanna, who often cried in the night and refused the breast, or wanted it at the most inconvenient times, she knew about that from the first time round. Until the first week of July Heinrich was home around five every afternoon, looking through the kitchen window to make sure they were all there, passing the time together on those long afternoon hours at the kitchen table, or singing or cooking or playing games, but Rosa was usually too tired to do much with her two daughters, she did only the bare essentials. Six or seven weeks after giving birth Rosa looked as she had before her pregnancy, but she was thin and sad and bitter, and greeted him with constant anxious prophecies featuring the most minute details of their new daughter's present temperature and weight, the number and consistency of her bowel movements, the frequency of her feeds, the length of time she spent sleeping and waking, and depending on how Heinrich reacted she would recover hope or lose a little more of it. Heinrich sometimes thought Rosa was overdoing it with her hourly checkups, observing the tiniest changes for better or worse, but perhaps it was her way of reconciling herself to what might happen and arming herself against it, for the little creature had grown steadily feebler week by week, she caught coughs and colds, she regurgitated Rosa's milk and wouldn't take anything else. Heinrich was very patient with Rosa and the baby and the impatient Eva, who was more trouble than she was worth, and sometimes he was surprised to see how patient he was being, and he was still patient when he realized that this couldn't go on much longer, soon he was delaying his return on some evenings, drinking his first schnapps of the day in the storeroom at the back of the shop and another on the way home, going to the swimming baths to see Bella in the afternoons, taking flight, turning away, picking up the threads of his old life. He might still pick little Susanna up in his arms early in the evening, carrying her around from kitchen to living-room to bedroom, and whispering to her now, encouraging her, letting her go, giving her her freedom: No, you don't have to keep going, even for Rosa's sake, even if she never gets over it, we'll remember you with love.

At first Heinrich was alarmed to find himself talking to his daughter like this, leaving the decision to her as if she were grown up, no longer urging her to stay, no longer blaming her for not wanting to stay, not wanting to come to anything; he thought they had no right to do it. We can't force her, said Heinrich, and Rosa knew he was right, nodded, didn't listen, thought he was clever and wise and cruel; she still felt needy. It was the end of July, and Heinrich was seeing Bella at the open-air swimming baths every few days, but he hadn't approached her yet; he was giving himself time. He told Anna on the telephone: No, I'm not cross, it's just a misunderstanding, we can't force other people to do things, and for a moment Anna thought he was talking about himself and her and the future, but he was talking about his daughter, or perhaps about both.

But she's still alive, said Anna.

Yes, she's still alive; I'm beginning to think she likes it.

She gets that from you, said Anna. She could learn a few things from you, she added.

I'll be twenty-six in three weeks' time, and she'll probably be gone by then.

On his twenty-fifth birthday in August 1956 he and Rosa had spent the whole day in bed, and on his twenty-fourth birthday in August 1955 he had driven to the firm as usual first thing in the morning, and just as he was about to look through the list of deliveries to be made the boss had called him into the office behind the shop and made a little speech about Heinrich, a speech such as Heinrich had never heard before in his life. Well now, Hampel, I must say that your method with our lady customers, well, I don't even want to know how you do it, but since you joined the firm turnover has doubled. I've worked it out: mattresses up 72 per cent, bedsteads up 57, cotton bed-linen up 112, silk bed-linen up 143, quilts of all kind up 36 per cent, I suppose we could improve on that. He probably didn't have to tell Heinrich, said the boss, that old Franz, Beds and Bedding owed him something, and he pressed a brown envelope containing five hundred marks into Heinrich's hand, this was just to be going on with. Was there anything he wanted, the boss asked, and Heinrich, finding that words failed him, had said: Yes, I mean no, and thanks a lot, but it might just possibly be useful if in future he was out in the front of the shop now and then, because you had more chance there to meet lady customers right at the start, and deliveries can be made after six in the evening, after all, just a suggestion, in case it might succeed, and the boss was all for it. What good ideas you have, Hampel, the boss had said, and what's good for turnover is good for you and me and our families, my wife doesn't need to know how it's done, and nor I hope does yours.

Days later Heinrich was still pleased to think the boss had spoken of a *method*, for it would not have occurred to him personally that his success with the firm of Franz, Beds and Bedding was due to a method which, since the boss had never heard of such a thing before, he called the Hampel Method. Of course he couldn't tell Rosa that they owed the five hundred marks in the envelope mainly to the Hampel Method, but Rosa asked no questions, accepting the money as something that was hers by right, indeed almost like a personal present to her.

When Heinrich thought of this conversation over the next few weeks, it struck him that he had no memory at all of when, where and in what circumstances the first incident had happened, or when, where and in what circumstances he had begun cultivating such incidents, not disagreeable in themselves, in the course of business. He had never before been particular about the customers he visited as he drove the van, but now that he knew he had a method he took careful note

of the manoeuvres which proved successful, made complicated lists of names, words, gestures, and wrote it all up in his
notebook. Sometimes he thought: There are only ten or
twenty or a hundred different kinds of women, so there are
only ten or twenty or a hundred ways and means at most of
dealing with them – or on the other hand he might think:
Nothing is ever repeated, the hundredth time is as difficult as
the first. So there were weeks and months when something
happened every few days, and there were weeks and months
when almost nothing happened, and then he would let well
alone and stop to think, dwelling on a glance here and a hint
there, thought of the young widow from Hagen whom he
had persuaded to kiss him after working on her for weeks, of
husky-voiced Lotte who opened the door to him one
afternoon in a cocktail dress with a long slit up the side,
Corinna with her buttermilk kisses, Pauline who drank,
nervous Monika with her habit of bursting into laughter at
every opportunity, and then, if he moved inside her, she
went perfectly quiet, whimpering and grunting, you
wouldn't know her for the same woman. He often went for a
drink when he had delivered the last bed and the last mattress,
or he would wash himself secretly in the Gents of some pub
or restaurant, because a little of the smell of these women
always clung to him, it wasn't easy to say if the smell was
individual to them or was the same in all other women.

The baby died on a Thursday in the early morning, it was
Rosa who noticed, around three-thirty, Rosa, still half asleep,
who reached into the wooden cot, felt the cold skin in
surprise, and then she knew and was silent. Heinrich could
not say later why he had immediately woken up too, to see
from Rosa's face that something terrible had happened,
perhaps she had sighed or whispered and said it couldn't be
true, but if so she hoped in vain. The baby had gone quite
cold since dying and leaving them in the middle of the night,
and all Rosa could say was: Take her away, I don't want to

see her like that. And Heinrich said: Are you sure? Yes, I'm sure. Wait, I don't know, said Heinrich, putting his head down close to the dead baby girl, shaking her, blowing air into her mouth and nose a few times, but in vain, shaking her once more and putting her back in the cot; he still couldn't believe it. He dressed, wrapped the cold little creature in blankets, handed her once more to Rosa, for Rosa to say goodbye, and then spent two long hours driving all over town with the dead baby, completely at a loss.

Then he gradually got used to the idea; then they talked, and as he talked on and on he glanced from time to time at the bundle on the passenger seat beside him, the little bundle who hadn't wanted to live, but whenever he looked she had her eyes closed and was deep in whatever dreams came to her. It's all right, said Heinrich when he had finished and, in saying goodbye to dead Susanna, had told her something about himself, his travels to Russia and South Africa, his first years in Jena when he was a child himself, his first years with Rosa, and what was he to say to her big sister Eva when he came back without Eva's new little sister, the little sister who had only come to visit for a few days and had a big dressing on her back.

It took two whole hours for Heinrich to tell her about it all, and after two hours he took her back to the children's ward where she had been born. At six in the morning Heinrich was standing at the main entrance with dead Susanna, wrapped in blankets, ringing the bell and waiting, and letting the nurses' horrified glances pass over him, but then they felt sorry after all, and took him to see a doctor. Some time early in the morning, Heinrich had said, and watched the doctor shaking his head, then giving Heinrich his hand and listening to the child's chest, or perhaps it was as he listened to the child's chest that he shook his head, and then gave Heinrich his hand, saying: I'm very sorry, and now we must deal with the dead child's paperwork, he could leave her there, they'd see to everything.

Rosa was still sitting as she had been sitting when he left, and although the last few hours had, in a way, been a comfort to him, he could say nothing about that comfort in the face of a woman turned to stone, just put his hand on her shoulder and waited. Was Eva awake yet? Yes, she said, Eva was playing in her room, and what for heaven's sake had he done with the blankets, he must have forgotten them in his distress.

Then they waited. Wrote letters, picked up the phone, heard or read remarks about a mercy, or a release, but Rosa read and heard only the half of it, had odd ideas, dreamed of a terrible fever or journeys that could not be postponed, wanted to burn the dead child at a funeral without any guests, and afterwards she would happily go into a madhouse where he could visit her every few weeks.

Every day, Heinrich told her: Come along, we'll survive this, and at some point his twenty-sixth birthday came, and the day after his twenty-sixth birthday was the day of the funeral. About a hundred people had come, it was a hot day, and naturally they did survive it, by late afternoon in the Zum Roten Hahn restaurant he could laugh again. Come on, it's not wicked of us to laugh at a joke, Heinrich had said, but Rosa hadn't noticed that it was a joke cracked by his uncle from Cologne that had made Heinrich laugh, which was almost worse than her being angry with him. Heinrich said: Look, your mother's here, your brothers and sisters, your sisters-in-law, my brothers, they all want to stay and be useful and help the time to pass, but then one day they all went home and everything was as unbearable as before. Say something, do, said Heinrich at the end of the third week after Susanna died, but Rosa had only silence for him, and in that silence he always heard her saying the same thing: You're relieved that she's dead, but it's killing me, and I hate you for it, that was what she was really saying to him, and at the end of the third week she was still saying it, by which time he was, so to speak, well settled in with Bella. I thought as much, said Bella, and comforted him, didn't want to rush things, sent him home quite soon. But he said to Rosa one night (said it, or rather whispered it, only once): Come here and let me make love to you, we'll make another little girl, called Susanna or called Rosa like you. And he was glad he had only whispered it, the way he only ever did whisper near Rosa now, because it allowed her to ask: Did you say something? Or perhaps she thought: yes, I hear you, it's a kind idea but I can't bear you while I'm so sad, in a few weeks I hope I can bear it again, and then it'll be all right for you too.

Rosa mourned exactly three months and nine days for the baby with the big dressing on her back, who had died after exactly three months and nine days, and when her mourning was over she said, in Heinrich's own words: Come along, we'll make another little girl, I'm ready now, I'm your own old Rosa again. But Heinrich, who had given up expecting anything of her by now, removed her hands from him, and her mouth, and said: I'm sorry, I can't. Well, it's like this. Her name's Bella. I didn't really want to tell you. Can you take it so lightly, is it really so serious for you? Rosa had asked, and Heinrich had said: I don't know; could be.

Then Rosa had begged and implored him, just that one time: Heinrich, I was wrong, I won't nag you any more, everything was most unpleasant and it took Rosa until early in the morning to grasp it. She wouldn't have been squeamish, she said, if it had just been another of those sluts or his, well, let's call them his customers, but she could see from the expression on his face that it wasn't one of those sluts of his this time, because after them he always washed his hands before going home, or drank a fruit brandy or a gin at the railway station, but he didn't wash his hands after this Bella, just lay down beside Rosa as if nothing had happened.

She had said some angry things to him over the past few months, but when she tried to remember them she could recollect only her despair over the sick baby, and the reason for the sick baby was Heinrich's drinking and his affairs, which must have damaged his sperm and the embryo and the baby, and now he was actually relieved she had died, and he turned cold and ugly and shifty and had to get out of the house, she made sure of that. At first Heinrich had thought: I must give her time, she didn't talk to the dead baby, she can't forgive herself for that, she doesn't believe the horrible things she's saying. He had got hold of medical textbooks and read them to see if they said it could be anyone's fault, but from the medical viewpoint (he grasped that much) it wasn't even an accident, just a whim of nature, a statistical inevitability, the back of one new-born baby in a few thousand simply did not close up, but it was Bella, not Rosa, to whom he told this when they had known each other for two months.

He hadn't been absolutely sure he'd want to see her again after that first afternoon when she took him home with her from the swimming baths, washed his penis in her bathroom, walked naked and happy through the room and slipped under the white sheet, but Bella was willing and welcoming from the start, she liked the way he bent over her and took his time, thinking what she would like and what he would like himself, so he was happy to go back when she invited him again.

For about two months they were engrossed solely with themselves and their bodies in all kinds of variations, and after that came the first hours when there was time for questions, and what exactly Heinrich did to make women customers snatch the wares from his hands, did people always love men or women in the same way, or was it in a different way each time, this was a question which particularly interested Bella, who liked it when he didn't stop to say much but stripped her skirts, blouses, dresses and knickers off, who liked it even better when he talked about it first, describing exactly what he was about to do to her, no, close your eyes and don't listen to me, and then, when I say, look at me and tell me if it's all right for you, and what you'd like me to do next, and how long it takes to be good for you. It's all good for me, or almost all good for me, your prick's tired, let it sleep, I'll cover it up with my kisses, that's something I've learned from you, or maybe I learned it a hundred years ago, how should I know.

Sometimes he felt jealous when she talked like that, or when he realized she had a good deal of experience with men, or when she whispered in his ear: I've always liked that best, now think something up for me and tell me about it, talk dirty, the first time nearly drove me crazy, oh my little cunt-licker, my stallion, my mole, my lord and master, I don't wash for three days afterwards, and in the evening, when you're gone, I put my head down between my legs and dream of you.

It was early October when Bella began talking to him like that, so that he lived only for those afternoons, wearing himself out on his afternoons with Bella, somehow getting through his work as a bed salesman but failing to do his women customers justice, he simply didn't fancy them any more. Old Franz, Beds and Bedding, said: Your child died, just do the essentials, better times will come, Hampel, if necessary I can hire a temporary driver for a few weeks. But Heinrich didn't want a temporary driver taking over his rounds, and Rosa didn't want him to go to a lot of bother, so he forced and persuaded himself, had it off with a few customers out of habit, was unenthusiastic and automatic, they didn't always seem to mind. One of them said once: You're a nice lover, I must say, lazy and absent-minded, aren't you, you think I don't notice? And another said: Oh, this is no fun, have a good night's rest and come back in a few days' time, or don't if you'd rather not, we won't quarrel over a few sheets and pillow-cases.

Soon Bella herself was saying: You're running out of steam a bit, darling, and I'm glad to think I'm the reason, but it's not something I'd like in the long run.

I didn't know myself at all before I met you, said Heinrich.
I know.

Heinrich had quite often said that he didn't know himself
before this, that or the other happened, for instance in the late
autumn of fifty-five when his first daughter was born, and
when old Franz, Beds and Bedding promoted him to driver
he had thought the same, and a few years earlier too, on his
return from Africa when he was twenty-one.

Little Eva was just a few days old when Franz, Beds and
Bedding, opened his first branch, taking young Heinrich out
of the stockroom and telling him what he had decided, when
he pointed to a brand-new van and said, or rather decreed:
Your probationary period is over, Hampel, you can get
straight in that van, take it for a test drive, you'll be working
as a driver from tomorrow morning, I reckon you're wasted
on ordinary stockroom work.

Thanks a lot, Heinrich had said, and he got into the van
with the handsome gold lettering on a blue background,
drove once round the block and then round it again, and
neither he nor old Franz, Beds and Bedding, nor Rosa,
whom he told that evening, had any idea what was to come
of his driving round on deliveries, it wasn't until later that any
of them saw the catch in that, or rather the advantage of it.

Heinrich did get a glimmering of it during the first week,
but at the time he dismissed it from his mind, feeling
surprised, but he was gradually getting ideas of just what it
could mean to be driving all round town day after day in a
brand-new van, and out of town too, for a radius of fifty
kilometres around, delivering a bed or a new mattress to
some housewife or other. Sometimes the housewives forgot
that they were having a bed or a mattress delivered, and
didn't want their purchases after all, blushed red, apologized
volubly, offered him something to drink, were embarrassed
and pretty and vulnerable, were grateful to him for forgiving
them, and took silly ideas into their heads.

That was how it started. That is, it started with some Katya or Senta, the first whom he noticed getting silly ideas into her head, with a look on her face that made him entertain silly ideas too, so he couldn't help looking at her and making some comment on the red or yellow polka dots on her dress, she hadn't been expecting someone like Heinrich. Do you always do this, she had asked Heinrich when he was unbuttoning and stroking and caressing her a bit, just to see if she liked it when he unbuttoned and stroked and caressed her a bit, oh yes, she did. She was still quite a young woman standing there in front of him, glancing sideways at the new bed, blushing, and he liked the way she blushed and, cheeks still red, breathed out a few questions, while later she stood in her fitted kitchen looking embarrassed, asking when he would be coming this way again.

And so it became a regular business. Old Franz, Beds and Bedding, who was first to notice the increased turnover, occasionally asked why some of the women customers had recently taken to asking after an ordinary van driver, leaving brief written notes or phone numbers at the cash desk with some query about a lost wallet or a ring, and Heinrich knew at once that the boss had drawn his own conclusions and had no objections.

He was never happier, professionally, than in those first weeks when everything went so well for him, when it was all still entirely new, and each triumph, however small, came as a surprise. If Rosa asked how his day had been (but she soon stopped asking) he would say: Same as usual. Nothing special really. Driving around the neighbourhood quite a bit. Had it been possible, he could have told his Rosa a very different story, telling her how good his success made him feel, what a lot of money it brought in, and he thought more than once that she really ought to be proud of him, and how happy it would make him if she finally felt proud of him, but the first person he ever told in detail was Bella, of whom he thought no less highly for it, which was as well for her.

Bella had never minded the fact that Heinrich slept with other women in the way of business, working very hard on them (as she understood it), she just always wanted to know what it was like, in detail, and then she made Heinrich get undressed and lie down on her narrow bed, tell her what he had been up to and have a rest, and after a while she found various means of reviving Heinrich's powers after he had finished work, she put cold compresses and warm compresses on his weary prick, painted it with home-made salves and tinctures compounded of honey, cognac, sage, caraway and eucalyptus, often didn't actually touch him for days on end.

She didn't like it when the others left traces of themselves behind, but she was curious, tried to guess who they were and what it had been like by the smell of them, guessed at their age, measurements, the look of their breasts, their mouths, their thighs, how tight or how slack they were, whether they had borne children, what faces they made, what men they knew, what women; she asked about all this, meanwhile mixing ointments and essences, for as a pharmacist's assistant she knew a lot about such things.

Even after that first winter and the first spring it was still a surprise to Heinrich to find that however well he knew her he didn't tire of her, and sometimes they lay side by side on the stained sheet through a whole long rainy afternoon like brother and sister, waiting for time or their lack of desire to pass. Heinrich couldn't always stay so long, or they would let time run out on purpose and he would take her once or twice at the door of her flat like a stranger, just as he was going, calling her by the nickname he had for her in a whisper: Oh, Nitribitt, you lovely naughty clever whore, what a lovely firm bottom you've got, my darling Nitribitt, there's nobody like you, nobody so pretty and shameless.

In these early months Rosa had mentioned Bella only once, in the autumn just after the Rosemarie Nitribitt scandal, when it suddenly slipped out of her: I wish your Bella would die too, like that wicked woman; I'd buy the knife or rope or revolver myself. After that she never said anything about Heinrich's Bella again; she was waiting. I'm just waiting, said Rosa to herself and her women friends, hinting at it to the family in a letter to Heinrich's father, and to Heinrich himself one morning in March. I'm waiting, she said, and Heinrich didn't like to think of her waiting, thinking up some plan against him and his Bella, who laughed at the idea of being called Nitribitt by her rival, she didn't think her own life as rich and shameless and dangerous as all that.

Then Paul came to Regensburg for a couple of days, wanting advice about the project of his journey to Africa. And since Heinrich didn't want to give up his afternoons with Bella the three of them arranged a time to meet in a café in the Altstadt, where they did not have much to say to each other. Later, Bella couldn't help laughing at the way Paul had kept foolishly staring at her breasts from the first moment they met, his eyes moving from her breasts to her mouth and back to her breasts, he didn't like her any better for it but sat there over a second and third whisky, monosyllabic and disapproving, asking unwelcome questions. He had received evasive answers from Johannesburg, and he wanted to know just what had happened in the summer of fifty-three on the estate of their uncle and his young married niece Stella, it was to be hoped Heinrich hadn't ventured to touch, or had he? Nonsense, said Heinrich, and: Better not talk about it, he said, but go there, why don't you, our uncle's a rich man with his huge asparagus fields and his hundred and fifty black serfs, they said as much years ago in *Time* magazine, so he'll have a room to spare for a poor nephew from Germany, you don't have to mention me at all while you're there. I really envy you, Bella had said, and Paul had replied: My God, envy me, I'm twenty-five now and nothing in particular has happened in my life yet.

I mustn't keep biting my nails when we go out, just remind me of that, said Bella, when Heinrich drove her home, and now come here and let me think about your brother's nice eyes, ooh yes, do that, that's nice, your brother could learn a thing or two from us, wow, if he only knew what he could learn from us, there now, right this moment I'm the Bella I'd like to be, and now, right this moment, I've forgotten him already.

Over a year had passed since Susanna's death, but he still hadn't touched Rosa, nor did they talk to each other, but in the afternoons when little Eva was asleep or in the early evening he still thought she was prettily rounded, warm and appetizing. He realized she was still waiting for him, but since she saw no prospect of an end to the waiting she often locked herself in the bathroom and examined herself closely in front of the mirror, regularly awarding herself points for the firmness of her breasts and the circumference of her thighs, applying expensive face lotions and face masks, oils and powder, painting and perfuming herself, and was pleased if some man's eyes lingered on her lips or her new check skirt when she was out shopping, or when a little twerp patted her bottom at her friend Marie's New Year's Eve party, she could keep going for several weeks on that kind of thing.

At the beginning of the new year she had left a couple of letters lying about the apartment, and Heinrich didn't know if it was the little twerp from the New Year's Eve party or someone she had met out shopping, or heaven knows who, but something had happened, the letters sounded as if someone had staked a claim to her, her body and her thoughts, still, if that made her happy, it was fine by him. At Easter they went away together for a few days to see Heinrich's father, and all the family were there except his two sisters. Paul had an air ticket for Johannesburg at the beginning of May, Theodor was boasting about his latest salary rise and the flat, tastefully furnished by Ilse, but Heinrich just smiled, thinking secretly of his big brother as a dull bourgeois soul who probably hadn't had as many as three women in his life, who didn't know of a decent restaurant in the whole town, let alone a bar, of course, but who pontificated like a great politician on the Soviet ultimatums over Berlin, and the new law on premium bonds savings, or on the duck's-tail haircuts and American wailing of Messrs Presley and Haley, which he disliked, and of which he found it easier to express disapproval than the scandal of the dead prostitute, he said nothing about that, or very likely he was afraid he'd catch something from that girl, the tart who died, just by mentioning her name: Rosemarie.

Heinrich always tried to get away from such subjects as quickly as possible, discussions of the present situation and the world in general, the way everything kept getting worse and worse and at the same time better and better, and he would usually close ranks with his father, who also had few opinions on current international politics, and asked his father: Well, still polishing your shoes with cigar ash? Or he would say: Come on, let's go down to the river and look at the ships, but we'll preserve a polite silence about your marriage and mine, and the way my stepmother hides the expensive wines and the new potatoes under the bed when we come to visit.

His father had seemed cheerful and happy during those few days, but in the course of the summer his mood became darker, and suddenly the letters from Wiesbaden brought the news (from miserly Gertrud, his second wife): Your father's been under Dr Hahn again for his insomnia for quite a while now, and Dr Hahn has sent your father to hospital, he thinks a thorough course of therapy there will cure him (12 August 1960). He's not to have any visitors except for us, so that he can have a proper rest; we're told to expect them to keep him in hospital another two weeks (7 August 1960). Now he's certainly coming home on Friday, in fact he must, because Sibylle's wedding is just ten days away, and he'll be needed then (9 September 1960).

At first Rosa had refused to go to the wedding and act the part of happy, contented married woman for the benefit of

Heinrich's father and stepmother and the whole bunch of them, but in the end she allowed herself to be persuaded (Bella would happily have gone) and danced a pair of high-heeled white shoes into the ground by early in the morning, got a little drunk, was pleased because one of her admirers had followed her when she was going to the ladies' around midnight, and since he was so nice and had such lovely long eyelashes she let him kiss her twice down there in the basement outside the ladies' room.

It was at this wedding (while under the influence around two-thirty in the morning) that Heinrich first had the idea of setting up on his own account, and a few weeks later Bella had the idea too, and he still thought of it as a fantasy.

I haven't got that far yet, said Heinrich.

Oh yes, you have, said Bella. Do you think your Bella doesn't know when the right moment has come for you, and when you ought to wait a little longer? There you are, then.

Sometimes Heinrich was ashamed to think how seldom Rosa featured in his thoughts, and sometimes he wondered what would have become of him but for Bella (or but for Rosa), or but for the Russians and that man Hitler, because it had all begun with Hitler, and since it all began with him the Hampels had to go to the Soviet Union in October 1946 for war reparations work, and then, to make matters worse, found themselves in Ulbricht's East German state in January 1951. Or had it all begun in the West? Back when he crossed the border under cover of darkness, and boarded the next train without a ticket, and met the Bundestag deputy Dr Alois Sinnhuber in the train, and the Bundestag deputy Dr Alois Sinnhuber, a CSU member sitting in the first German Bundestag, took to young Heinrich at once, gave him a recommendation to old Franz, Beds and Bedding, in Regensburg, and then Bella came along, and he wasn't making plans for any other woman these days. Well, so what? she said, when Heinrich had started his but-for-this-that-and-

120

the-other game with her yet again, a game which she didn't like, she preferred to take life as it came.

It had been in the summer of 1951 that Bundestag deputy Dr Sinnhuber sent a written recommendation to Regensburg on Heinrich's behalf, but then came the South African business, and when that was all over he went to Regensburg because of the recommendation, and Rosa was pregnant and had to go with him. She had still been in Landshut when he got her pregnant in February 1954, after she hadn't heard from him for over a year. She had been thinking of him a lot, remembering what it was like when she got on his borrowed bike for the first time and rode over the bridge, but then she realized she would be in a bad way if she kept thinking about Heinrich day after day, and the wretched man didn't even send her a postcard in all those twelve months.

She had not the faintest idea that he was back in the country when he appeared at her door one Saturday, without any previous warning, but even in her initial surprise she realized she would forgive him on certain conditions, so he granted her girlish little conditions, gave a few vague explanations, his teeth chattering with cold, and warmed her up and impregnated her on a heap of birch-wood back in the shed where her mother stored apples and potatoes by the hundredweight, hoping they wouldn't freeze.

So now what about you, what about us, asked Rosa, and Heinrich, who had not been reckoning on Rosa at all, said: No idea, perhaps I'll go to Regensburg, or further west Aachen way, when you're untrained you can always find a job but one you like is hard to come by. I see, Rosa had said, and went on waiting for him, and when he finally turned up again he had a job as a stockroom worker in bloody Regensburg, that was the first she heard about it from him: I'm off to Regensburg, I've got a bed and a wash-basin behind the stockroom, and it's a thousand times better than here anyway. You hurt my feelings, talking like that, was all Rosa had said at the time, and Heinrich had replied: Yes, sorry, but I have to find a place to live, and one afternoon in April she was facing her parents and telling them she was seven days overdue, so they had to get married.

The register office wedding was on a Tuesday in May and took less than half an hour. Rosa's older brother Karl and her friend Marie were her witnesses, and after that they all went to eat asparagus in the Ratskeller, and that was it. Well, happy now? Heinrich asked, and Rosa said: Yes, but you can finally introduce me to your father as your lawful wife this weekend. May I introduce myself? Hampel – Rosa Hampel, Rosa had said to his father, observing a short pause, and in that short pause (this was very odd) Heinrich loved her with all his heart, and since his father saw that Heinrich really did love her with all his heart all he said was: Oh, very well, welcome into the family. We know each other by sight.

Do you think he's come round to the idea of me, asked Rosa later, when she was going to Regensburg every other weekend, learning about marriage in a hotel bedroom, and Heinrich said: Oh yes, do keep quiet, he's courting too, I persuaded him to, so why would he be angry with me? Courting, said Rosa, shivering slightly under the thin blankets of the Pension Erika, and Heinrich said: Yes, through a Catholic marriage bureau, but as far as I know nothing's come of it yet.

Rosa thought it was rather soon to be placing an ad only a year after your dear wife's death, looking for another already, but she said nothing, for fear of displeasing Heinrich, just as she said nothing when he got it into his head one evening that they must do it with each other now, in this cheap room in the Pension Erika, and start the baby she had already conceived all over again, after all, he said, his mind hadn't really been on the business then at the back of the shed, so they did it again, it felt a little strange, but it certainly got you nice and warm, so that was all right.

From the end of July onwards things began moving very fast. They found and furnished their first flat, Heinrich was busy working almost round the clock, and at the beginning of August they finally packed their few possessions and moved into their new home with them. She didn't have much experience of men, and it had always pleased him that she didn't have much experience of men, but she was a good cook, and it was because she liked cooking and was a little plump here and there that he had accepted the idea of her, which was something of a miracle, the fact that he'd accepted the idea of her, so it would work out somehow or other.

A year before opening the shop Heinrich would never seriously have thought anything could come of the idea, and since Bella saw that he was still hesitating they soon had their first quarrel. It had started on New Year's Eve, when Bella and Heinrich were watching the firework display from the Steinerne Brücke with a bottle of Söhnlein Brillant, wishing each other a happy new year. Bella had not the slightest doubt that this would be the year of Heinrich's great new departure, so in between a few quick kisses she spoke of the new firm as something to be taken for granted, speculating on the opening party, and Heinrich said: Yes, yes, we'll see, and when she still kept on about it: I think you're dreaming, I don't have any savings, so where would I get the money for the stock, the stockroom, the bank interest.

They had no experience of major quarrels, so for the present they both gave in and went back to Bella's; in this third year of their relationship they were going to her place at least every other night.

Afterwards it was Heinrich still talking about his own firm, but in a way that instantly showed he didn't believe in it. You just don't want to do it, said Bella one evening in February, and one evening in March she got really cross and turned Heinrich out of her flat, refused to read his letters or answer the door to him over the next few weeks, and when he called her at home at the usual time her line was always busy, or she didn't answer the phone, hoping to teach him a lesson that way. At first he thought: she's just joking, she can't seriously suppose that without money, and with a family to support, you can simply conjure up a business out of nothing, but then there were the letters she didn't read, and his vain attempts to reach her by phone or in the afternoon when she was back from the pharmacy, so in the end he took it personally, Rosa immediately welcomed him back with open arms, and after six weeks of radio silence from Bella he begot his first son. Then it was Rosa who had an idea about the money, she didn't think herself above that and was enjoying their days together to the full. Wasn't his uncle in Cologne rolling in riches, and didn't his uncle have a crippled wife in a wheelchair, and two houses in the name of his sick wife, who bored him? Why, yes, Heinrich's uncle. Why not?

Once again Heinrich didn't believe in it, but then bad news came from Wiesbaden in May, a letter from miserly Gertrud told them that Heinrich's uncle from Cologne was actually going to come and visit his insomniac brother in Mainz University Hospital, to persuade him to take his tablets every day and get better, and feel well and not be a burden on those around him. Getting no sleep for several nights can drive you crazy, wrote Heinrich's stepmother, luckily you two have no idea what it's like, you sleep like logs. So another few days passed by, and when they discussed the project for the first time in the last week of May, Heinrich's uncle was instantly enthusiastic.

They had both been alarmed by the state of Heinrich's father, who kept pacing the hospital corridor like a wound-up toy, in raptures over the virtues of his Gertrud, and going on about the new NSU he was going to order for her next week, but over a glass or so in a wine bar they soon got down to business, discussed past and future financial details, came to an agreement, asked for time to think it over. Heinrich, who was now coming to believe in it himself, painted the situation in the rosiest of colours to his uncle, acted modestly and with reserve, but showing evidence of ambition and self-confidence, he would quite understand if his uncle didn't want to offer financial backing, he would like his uncle to think it all over thoroughly and find out what the bank said, and what Heinrich's crippled aunt said too, and they left it there.

On the day of his return he went to see Bella with the latest news, and the fact that she didn't immediately slam the door in his face was something. Instead she listened to him for a time, nodding her head: Yes, not bad, I knew you'd find a way, but who'd have thought it would go so smoothly? He wasn't quite back on the old terms with Bella straight away, but then he hadn't been back on the old terms with Rosa straight away either, and then, when he was, along came Bella and resumed her old position. When she heard that Rosa was pregnant again she didn't believe it at first, but then she did believe it, and said it was a high price to pay. Heinrich was glad for Rosa's sake, because she had taken fright and was firmly counting on a boy, to be called Konrad, a name meaning 'bold council', which was what Rosa had given him.

Heinrich and his uncle met twice more in Wiesbaden that summer, to discuss the project of the firm and visit Heinrich's father in hospital, and when they had visited him in hospital together they went to the casino to discuss more details. The first time, in the middle of June, Heinrich's uncle said: The bank's happy with the idea, but I still have my doubts about the staff and the premises, and the second time, three weeks later: Agreed, then, but mind, it must turn out all right, I can't risk those two houses now I've re-mortgaged them. Oh, it'll turn out all right, said Heinrich, inviting his uncle to dinner both times so that he could see how seriously Heinrich was taking their firm, and he owed it all to his two women, whom he called in turn from the hotel in the evening to tell them the news. Great, said Rosa, who hoped this would at least put an end to his dealings with women customers, and Bella thought it was great too and hoped for goodness knows what, perhaps there was something she wanted to prove to herself with her Heinrich.

The search for suitable premises began at the end of September, and it was also the end of September when Heinrich went to tell his boss; he thought he owed him that. Yes, well, too bad, said old Franz, Beds and Bedding, counting up the weeks he would still have the services of Hampel as salesman. Three months, thought Heinrich, and he took no real pleasure in his work for Franz those last three months, but for that very reason he tackled the most difficult cases successfully. The wife of a cigarette dealer known all over town bought four sets of bed-linen in only two weeks, and he took a boutique owner who was really much too thin for him and nearly fifty to the cinema, where they saw a very exciting American film in which a girl was stabbed with a knife in the shower, and when the boutique owner didn't fancy spending the evening alone after that he went home with her, and found her bony and quiet manner quite interesting, all things considered. He met Anna one day in the street, in company with a man, but although he was perfectly friendly and waved, but from a distance, she was cool and remote, like a stranger, perhaps she did have some pleasant memories, or perhaps her lover was very jealous and couldn't adjust to her memories.

You talk in your sleep, Rosa told him quite often, but you don't mention women's names the way you used to, just the amount of loans and mortgage rates and numbers of square metres, what with all this calculating nothing can go wrong. Are you all right, asked Heinrich, and Rosa said: Yes, are you all right too? Yes, don't worry.

It was only Paul whom Heinrich worried about, for if he understood Paul's first letters correctly his brother had not found work in South Africa, nor had he made contact with his uncle, but instead was spending wickedly large sums of money living in a dilapidated apartment hotel where there were bottle parties almost every evening, with all kinds of irresponsible girls, and dear Paul, of course, was even more irresponsible than any of the girls, regularly drinking himself stupid, or going off to his room with a girl and having it off with her there.

Yes, I'm fine, wrote Paul in his third letter of October 1960, her name is Rheina, she works as foreign languages correspondent for a bank in Johannesburg and her father's a big noise in Cape Town, but because I'm German and she's Jewish unfortunately she can't marry me. I saw Aunt Felice only when I'd just arrived, I didn't see pretty Stella at all, everyone was very formal, including Uncle, it's not hard to guess why. I can guess what happened when you were here, old chap, but so what, I don't have to rely on the family anyway, my little Rheina is really very sweet, and she has almost every evening free.

He puts that nicely, about guessing what happened when you were there, said Bella, and your Bella can guess too, how would you like to tell me about it?

It wasn't what you think.

Well, who was it, then?

Aunt Felice, actually. She felt a bit neglected, but her library was piled to the ceiling with books, and she often read something aloud to me, she didn't bother about me. We wrote letters to each other, if you really want to know, but her husband had some kind of objection, so I left the country.

And that was Africa.

Yes, that was Africa, it's lovely there, perhaps I'll take you on a visit some day.

5

In the seventeenth year of the existence of the new state, the comrades on the Central Committee thought it was about time to write carefully phrased letters on the future of the divided country to the members and supporters of Social Democracy in West Germany, and Heinrich wrote letters now and then himself, but Comrade Gisela, who read them and smiled at them and tore them up at once had nothing but mockery for both him and the comrades on the Central Committee. The German working class won't be won over by fine words, she had said, and I won't be won over by your fine words either, supposing I don't want to go home some night or other I'll go to my Vladimir, he's the rough and ready sort but as affectionate and reliable as a brother, just for your information. And should you be in the area again, distributing our books among people without having read a single one of them yourself, kindly remember I have my principles, and I've got my principles mostly from reading books, but of course as a former bed salesman you wouldn't know about that.

It had been Harms's idea for Heinrich to increase turnover for the People's Bookshop in the Holzmarkt by selling books from the bookshop van out in town, hearing what people said in their businesses and on the street as they looked through his books, and listened to him urging them to increase the fighting power of the working class and fend off malicious attacks by the imperialist powers of West Germany, which didn't want international peace and most certainly didn't want a Socialist Germany. For the sake of Rosa and Harms and making a living for the family, he hadn't found it difficult to speak this new language, making the most recent Bodo Uhse or the latest Stalingrad novel from the Soviet Union palatable to the workers and comrades at the Zeiss or Schott works or some collective or other, or a co-operative working on commission, and when they were all satisfied and had gone off to work he still had time to drive to Lobeda and deliver a few apricot-coloured wash-basins, or he visited Vladimir and his friends over in the barracks at Zwätzen, they had time on their hands there.

Things could have turned out much worse in the new state, thought Heinrich, who was on the road a lot, just as he had been in the old days, and as usual Rosa, at home with the children, hadn't the faintest idea exactly what money they were living on and the kind of people he was mixing with in order to earn it. She had become used to the way Heinrich kept bringing these Russians home, negotiating with officers of all ranks in a strange, really horrible language over a couple of bottles of vodka, and she thought her own thoughts, watching in amazement but asking no questions when brand-new television sets straight from the factory were piled high in the living-room, and Vladimir and his friends took them away under cover of darkness, smelling of vodka and whores of some kind, and the man who wound them all round his little finger and had them doing as he wanted was Heinrich, and he by no means always decided on the cheapest of everything. (But no new Bella had come along.)

Rosa knew he had wasted a good deal of time over some woman called Gisela, and Heinrich knew that Gisela got into bed with Vladimir every other night and sipped vodka from his mouth, but he thought that if he kept on writing her letters she'd listen to him some day. Vladimir (his friend), with whom he would have shared her, always said: You'd better forget about Comrade Müller, my dear Geinrich, and Comrade Müller, when he visited her in her office scented with those famous Bulgarian perfumes, said: You drink too much, that's your trouble, and you entertain false hopes too.

In fact complaints had soon been made about the talented bookseller who could unload Bodo Uhse on the public, a man with a dubious past as a bed salesman, who now and then let himself be tempted into making suggestive remarks out of pure high spirits, and who whistled at the legs of FDJ girls much too young for him in the canteens, or who when under the influence of vodka compared the secretary in the Free German Trades Union office with a beauty from the West; that was the kind of thing. There had been two or three complaints in the year, and in the end they piled up; Heinrich was going too far. By now they knew him at the People's Bookshop only under the influence of vodka, so very likely some important comrade had complained, or alternatively Heinrich had delivered one of those important comrades a spare part for his Trabant in the People's Bookshop delivery van, something difficult to obtain, and next morning the comrade was suddenly stricken with a guilty conscience and repaid Heinrich's kind offices by blackening his name.

Even nervous Rita had looked at him oddly on that fateful morning in March, and then they told him in a few plain words that he was sacked and threw him out. We're sorry, we told you in a kindly way and we told you in a less kindly way, but unfortunately it did no good. So when do I leave? Heinrich had asked. At once. Oh well, Heinrich had said, and he walked out of the shop past Rita and all the others, crossed the road to the delivery van and brought back the keys; no one said anything. Only Rita said or rather whispered something: In half an hour's time outside the newspaper kiosk, she whispered, and was suddenly very brisk and brave and determined, because it was something of a piece of luck for her that they were turning him out then and there, she'd waited long enough.

So he went out with thin Rita for a while, collected her

from work and went to her place, a cold flat which didn't even have a bathroom. We must be quiet, my son's asleep next door, shall I fetch coal and light the stove? But Heinrich didn't want her to fetch coal and light the stove, for it was nice and warm under her bedclothes, and she didn't talk much, and since she didn't talk much she was just right for him.

Do you remember New Year's Eve? You didn't spare me a glance, said thin-as-a-rake Rita.

Yes, but it's all different now, come along and get under the covers, it's really cold, only not everywhere, luckily.

At first Heinrich had not wanted to go to the New Year's Eve party also attended by Rita, all his other colleagues at the People's Bookshop and heaven knows who else, but Harms had pressed him to go, saying a New Year's Eve party with colleagues from the book trade was an interesting opportunity, from the point of view of the authorities anyway, so Heinrich had let himself be persuaded and spent a whole evening in boring conversations about new titles and new prices, and whether the Bitterfeld Way was just a stage on the way to international proletarian literature or a direct short cut, all under the eyes of skinny Rita. In his reports Heinrich had always taken care over such details, noting whether it was Comrade Grab from Leipzig or that twerp Hanke with his unpublished poems who had called the Bitterfeld Way pure Stalinism, and as for whether that denoted approval or concealed criticism, his nosy acquaintance Harms could see what he made of it, but all things considered such expressions of opinion were few and far between.

Rita, whom he allowed to observe him, and whom he observed while she was observing him, as if she might be one of those questionable characters, talked half the night to a young woman from Leipzig whose husband had recently fallen off some scaffolding over in those parts of town where new building was in progress, she was still pale from the shock and at a distance reminded him of Anna, but since she was always with Rita all he got was a dark look now and then. In his New Year report to Harms, Heinrich actually mentioned the young woman from Leipzig whose husband had fallen to his death, and the fact that she didn't want to go home but had been out early in the morning on her husband's building site for days, standing there nodding and saying: Yes, yes, I know, we've lost one of our best men but our cities will be bright and friendly and forward-looking, constructing Socialism is hard work, his won't be our last death, we shall get over it, that's for sure.

Heinrich always wrote his reports on the same paper with fine blue lines which he used for his letters to Comrade Müller. It was poor quality and full of wood fibres, but that was just what Heinrich liked about it, as well as the way that he might have been writing something perfectly ordinary, for instance a letter to Theodor, as he sat in a café during the lunch break composing his fortnightly report to Harms and thinking up something which would please either the authorities or his Gisela, for he sometimes wrote to Harms and Gisela at the same time, telling her: Good morning, my sweet bold sister, blushing and devouring my letters with your grey eyes really suits you. If it were only evening I'd cover you up very carefully, or I'd kiss your lovely red mouth, but sad to say it's afternoon, so I'm being cautious and industrious. Or he might be writing: Report of 17 January (p.m.). A good deal of conversation at the People's Bookshop about the sacking of the Minister of Culture. Bookseller Garbe thinks there's some connection with the Biermann campaign in *Neues Deutschland*. Rita F. sings a couple of Biermann's songs. She says she can't get black stockings anywhere in the city in her size (34), she'd have to go to Italy or France for them. A girl in FDJ uniform says: My grandfather in the West has died, he exploited his workers shockingly, so none of us are going to his funeral. People are proud of their country, except they say that unfortunately

888,000 new homes won't be enough, and you can comb the whole city in vain for the latest Beatles record.

This was what Heinrich liked writing best: reports on the general mood, when he listened to people, neither restraining nor encouraging them, he named no names (or only in exceptional cases), but assumed everything and everyone was important, and merely hinted at what was really dangerous. He didn't write: A. or F. said this or that criticizing the state, or cracked a joke about the Party or the Soviet Union, because the fact was he didn't know anyone who would have made remarks criticizing the state in his presence, or told doubtful jokes, and it struck him that those who did (they were friends of Vladimir) had a perfect right to do so, and were not within the competence of Harms and his department.

Heinrich would not have called Harms his friend, even in the fourth year of their acquaintance, but Harms had always meant well by him, and since he still meant well he asked Heinrich to write everything down in his reports, explaining how important it was to the authorities responsible to have someone noting even the tiniest details, and if his reports led anywhere, well and good, and if not, they provided an insight into the secret wishes and longings of the working class, and then perhaps the Party could do something to fulfil those wishes, or perhaps, unfortunately, it could not.

Delicate, refined, anxious Rita featured only peripherally in his reports, since nothing he knew about delicate, refined, anxious Rita until that fateful afternoon in March seemed to him very significant, for instance it was a fact that she had hummed Biermann's songs only once. Three or four weeks before he was sacked he had asked her out for a meal, but she didn't hum any Biermann songs then either, for she was shy and cautious and nervous (which was typical of her), and scarcely uttered a word in two and a half hours. I sometimes worry about you, Herr Hampel, she said, I don't know why, and nor did Heinrich know why, but he sparkled in an effort to entertain her, he felt she was clothed in silence.

When the family back in Wiesbaden asked how they were during those first years, Heinrich said: We'll catch up with you yet. It took the German bourgeoisie over a hundred years to build up capitalism, we've had only two decades to start putting it right, and at least we don't suffer from arteriosclerosis, on account of the butter shortage, as Ulbricht said at the Sixth Party Conference of the Socialist Unity Party of Germany, 15 to 21 January 1963: I'm glad I don't eat much butter, because I look forward to surviving not only the Adenauer government but many other West German governments too, those were his very words. So there's no need for you to worry about us, I must tell you that no, we don't have everything, but we've worked hard for what we do have.

Rosa's letters always struck a different note: she had long, endless wish-lists, and to keep the lists from being too long and thus making the family in the West, providential as it was to them, stop sending parcels, she sometimes exaggerated the situation, calling it urgent when it was only difficult, thinking up things she and the children and Heinrich needed which couldn't be acquired very easily, even the other side of the border, and in general she complained. The least to come of this was one or two parcels every quarter containing real coffee, chocolate for the children, a toy for little Walter, two check winter coats for Eva and Konrad. However, Theodor and Paul and their parents declined to send a black and white TV set, we have to think of ourselves too, you know, we didn't leave the country overnight and we're not the ones boasting and complaining now, you must manage for yourselves, don't expect too much, though we can send a few pairs of low-denier tights now and then, and if Heinrich keeps working hard you'll have your TV set some day.

The deal involving the television sets stacked in the living-room, which would bring in a few hundred marks if everything went well and all concerned kept their mouths shut, had been Heinrich's biggest coup so far, it was in the fourth summer after he crossed the border and he felt rather uneasy about it, but that was the interesting part of such little sidelines, you felt rather uneasy about them but you ignored that and took a risk, just as if you were the businessman of the old days. If Gisela hadn't taken him to the bar on the western outskirts of the city, perhaps nothing would ever have come of these deals, or if Vladimir hadn't turned the jewellery into cash, for it was with this first deal on Vladimir's part that it all began, and with time of course he acquired contacts, and as it turned out they were almost always the right contacts, for ultimately, even here in the East, almost everyone had something to sell or wanted to buy something, and with luck Heinrich or Vladimir could provide it. Can you really? they would say in surprise over the tenth vodka, and Heinrich would say: Yes, really, it'll cost so and so and it won't be easy, but there'll still be stocks in Erfurt or Gera, right, let's meet again in ten days' time and we'll have got hold of it.

Usually it really wasn't anything much, a tool or household utensil in short supply, or a few thousand nails, screws, Rawlplugs and other items needed on building sites, that is, in time it wasn't anything much, because in time you knew the right people in almost every field, and you could persuade the right people in almost every field to sell this, that or the other. This was always Vladimir's great moment, for Vladimir had access to girls, and once Vladimir brought his girls into it no one could easily refuse, and you could sometimes get ten brand-new TV sets at cost price for a night involving a threesome, and there was no difficulty at all in selling the TV sets on and earning a tidy sum on the deal.

Heinrich didn't think Gisela could know exactly what deals they were doing with members of the Party elite in the Cosmonaut bar she patronized, but she must have had at least some idea, because once, when she and Vladimir were visiting Heinrich and she saw the vacuum cleaners in the children's room, she dropped a hint, asking whether he was now planning to set up as a vacuum cleaner rep in the GDR, well no, not exactly.

It was in the summer of 1965 that Gisela and Vladimir came to a Russian dinner consisting of several courses at 13 Hermann-Stapff-Strasse, and they didn't refuse the first and second bottles of vodka, or the third either. To German-Soviet friendship, said Heinrich, who didn't like to see Vladimir and Gisela acting like a young couple in love all evening, talking about their last night together over zakuski and bortsch, or petting in front of little Eva, not that little Eva seemed to notice, instead she chattered away about her afternoons with the FDJ, asking how old you had to be before you could spend your afternoons at the German-Soviet Friendship organization like Gisela. Would you like to come along on Saturday, asked Gisela, there's an outing planned and then we're all going for a swim in a big lake. Oh, yes please.

And so it was that they all went out into the country next weekend: Heinrich and Gisela and Rosa and the children (Vladimir was on duty), and Gisela and Heinrich immediately felt like stripping off, it was only Rosa who needed coaxing to join them all in the buff. Heinrich was slightly surprised that she needed coaxing, and he was disappointed in the conduct of the naked Gisela, for if she had wanted him at all in some secret corner of her heart (so he thought) then she would have been embarrassed too, like Rosa, who wanted him only every few weeks, and knew him as well as she knew herself. He tried not to look at Gisela walking into the shallow water ahead of him, but he saw her narrow shoulders and her pelvis, which was much too wide, and after that, unfortunately, he couldn't get them out of his head. I didn't want to see you like that, he wrote to her a few days later, in my head I keep wrapping you up in towels and coats and dresses, so we'll be back the way we were before, I hope you don't mind, because that's the way I first knew you and the only way I can bear to think of you.

In the first few days after losing his job Heinrich did nothing at all. His sacking hadn't really surprised him, and indeed he took the new state of affairs as a welcome change, visited Rita every other evening, felt cheerful and got used to doing nothing. Rosa, as usual, heard nothing about it, and he acted as if everything was still the same, got up, over breakfast he mentioned the routes he had to drive and the likelihood of delays, and off he went. On the first day Heinrich wandered through the city like a stranger, or someone revisiting it, hired a boat in the Paradies district, walked over the Paradiesbrücke, down Friedrich-Engels-Strasse, and then along the Holzweg to the Kernberge, and back through the Pennickental to Wöllnitz and Rita's little flat in An der Diebeskrippe.

That first week he fetched her from work a couple of times, and she was always pleased to see him outside the shop windows just before closing time, not ashamed to walk up and down as if he were a customer. Hello, good evening, she always said, and they usually did a little shopping somewhere or walked to her place, but he couldn't kiss her until they were a few streets away on account of her colleagues.

Heinrich had never known a woman of around thirty who kept wondering the whole time what her colleagues and friends and acquaintances were thinking of her, and whether it was really a good idea to take him home with her or just offered the community policeman a welcome opportunity to denounce her when she slipped past him into her flat, switched on the light, and before she had taken her coat off and while the door was still open Heinrich's friendly hands would take hold of her. She only liked to do it in the dark, and she liked to do it hidden under the bedclothes and in total silence. She liked it when he put his hand over her mouth at the last moment, and she couldn't help putting a hand over his mouth at the very last moment too, for with a son of not quite ten, and fear always there breathing down her neck, everything had to be done quietly, things that were delightful and important as well as those that were unpleasant and unimportant.

Heinrich had had no notion anyone could be so frightened, and although it surprised him at first he soon got used to it, and to the way she sometimes jumped out of bed for no obvious reason and ran to the door, looking and listening to see if there was anyone looking and listening outside, and then she always came back feeling contrite and relieved, and for a while after that everything usually went well. Don't be cross with me, I have my reasons, she often said, and Heinrich thought he had no reason himself to be cross with her, because if you weren't afraid of anything you could easily make mistakes, and he preferred not to think of what happened to people who made mistakes.

Thank you, said Rita, and Heinrich said: Aren't you exaggerating?

No, I'm not exaggerating.

And you trust me, of all people.

He would have liked to buy her an electric stove or a warm quilt to keep away the colds she caught, but he was afraid she would feel as if he were paying her, so instead he bought a schnitzel or a packet of mince for their evening meal now and then, to be eaten with fried potatoes and canned mixed vegetables Leipzig style.

Thanks, but I've eaten already, Heinrich would say when he got home after one of these evenings, to which Rosa replied: What a pity, I've got meat loaf and fried eggs, oh, and your friend Harms rang, he wants to see you on the twenty-ninth and said you'd know where, same arrangement as usual. Same arrangement as usual, thanks, said Heinrich, knowing that this time he wasn't going to that dump with the drawn curtains near the Westbahnhof, to discuss the cases in his report and their connection with the general situation, acting offhand, saying: Yes, fine, everything's okay, oh, and there's this, that and the other I ought to add, because it isn't in my written reports, but listen hard, my dear Harms, I want to feel I've earned your whisky.

In fact he really wouldn't have known what to tell Harms now he had lost his job, on the other hand the authorities must have known for some time that he had lost his job, and consequently they also knew about his Rita and the way she kept rushing to the door just when they were coming to the best bit, and when Heinrich really wanted her there would be an evening meeting of the German-Soviet Friendship Society or the Cultural Association, which she always dutifully attended.

Heinrich sometimes took a nap on her sofa then, or the boy might be there, and he would say: Hello, lad, I see your mother's not at home, and they listened to the children's radio programmes together, that was how he spent his days. You must look for another job, said Rita, and Heinrich said: Maybe Vladimir will think of something, you don't know Vladimir, but I'd have a hard time finding a better friend anywhere in the country.

Vladimir would probably have said: Come on, let's go for a drink, and don't let me down, Heinrich, there are deals to be done, or aren't you a real man, hiding away like that with Rita? Or Vladimir might have called Comrade Müller, getting Comrade Müller to advise him over the phone, as the former supervisor of their mutual friend Hampel who adored her and was looking for a new job. And then Heinrich would have had a new job before three days were up, but now three whole weeks had passed and Vladimir and Gisela still didn't know what had happened. He had hardly seen Gisela in the New Year (although he wrote her letters full of dirty language), and he had seen Vladimir only once, in passing, when he was shopping in the Army Store for the friendly Soviet soldiers in the Zwätzen barracks.

Heinrich had been unable to believe his eyes when, some years ago, Vladimir first took him round the famous Army Store, and how proud Vladimir had been of being able to show Heinrich all this, while Heinrich, as he still remembered, could hardly get over his amazement. Choose something, old friend, Vladimir had said, showing Heinrich the shoes, the coats, the trousers, and in another room shelves stacked high with cans and bags and bottles. It's just for us officers, said Vladimir, showing him the vodka, the black and red caviar in small flat tins, along with open tubs of pickled cucumbers and cabbage, Crimean champagne and tea and blancmange powder from the Ukraine, not to mention rarities like dried seaweed, mussels preserved in oil and vinegar with garlic, bottled peaches and apricots from Hungary, jars filled to the brim with sweets, dried fish from Riga, fresh fruit, vegetables from the Thuringian forest.

Vladimir had begun making him presents both large and small on this very first visit, although it was like a present in itself for him to let Heinrich wander round among these delicacies from all over the world, and the salesgirls let him have a taste of trout mayonnaise and tongue in aspic, you could neither buy nor even see such things in ordinary shops. Heinrich had always liked it when Vladimir gave him canned fruit from Hungary, for the sweet peaches and apricots tasted of travelling in far-away lands, and wonderful drinks could be mixed with the cloudy juice, or the children drank the juice and Rosa topped a cake with the fruit. It was not usual for a civilian like Heinrich to go in and out of this Army Store, but because Vladimir had given permission, and so did the other friendly officers, there was never any trouble, and he didn't turn down the freshly made piroschki or koulibiaka, nor did he turn down the occasional offer of one of Vladimir's girls either.

The matter of the girls came up one day like this: Heinrich would never have thought of it by himself, but Vladimir had a guilty conscience over Gisela. I can't help it, he said, the fact is she's crazy about me, but look, why not take this girl out, she's just started studying in Ilmenau and is feeling lonely, so be nice to her and she'll be nice to you in return, and best wishes from Gisela, she still enjoys your letters, she loves people talking dirty.

So once or twice a month Vladimir tried providing him with comfort in the shape of one of these women students or tourists from Poland or Czechoslovakia, and Heinrich liked some more than others, but he still couldn't help thinking of Gisela and his friend Vladimir who could have her whenever he wanted, and when he didn't want they talked about Heinrich and his girls, or about politics. So what's it like with her, Heinrich had asked, when the affair between his friend Vladimir and Comrade Gisela was in its early stages, and he would hear something along the lines of: Very well, old friend, I'll tell you what it's like, only don't go complaining to me later: this is what it's like with her, and he enumerated it all, first, second, and third.

However, they still went on doing deals, Vladimir and Heinrich the loser with his letters and his longings, for that was one thing and the deals were quite another. They liked each other, as it had seemed they would from the start, although Heinrich did not have much experience of male friendships. Rosa, however, had difficulty from the first in taking to Vladimir, she saw only the colourful orders on his chest and the fact that he was an officer in the victorious Red Army, for a Red Army soldier on his victorious way to the West had killed her father just outside Breslau in January 1945, and his comrades, who saw him die, had not been sparing with the gruesome details on their return.

Well, that's life, said Heinrich, and Rosa said: I'm afraid it is, but that doesn't mean I have to like my father's murderers.

Heinrich could clearly remember the day when Gisela and Vladimir became lovers and no longer hid the fact that they were lovers from Heinrich, her red cheeks told their own tale, even hours later when they met in the Cosmonaut bar as usual. It was on the day of Otto Grotewohl's death that they told him, yes, even though it was the day of Otto Grotewohl's death they had told him the good or bad news, up there in the Cosmonaut bar, unfortunately they couldn't tell anyone else but Heinrich was their friend, they could tell him, he was to be the witness of their new-found happiness. We just can't believe it, said the happy Comrade Gisela who had once been his supervisor and who had a birthmark between her shoulder-blades and who knows where else, we're over the moon. Have you heard about Grotewohl's death, Heinrich had asked, so as not to have to comment on their happiness, but they didn't want to know. Oh, come on, don't be a spoilsport, it could have been you but as it happens it's your friend Vladimir, long live German-Soviet friendship: so said Gisela.

Weeks later Heinrich was still complaining in his letters that she had said: *It could have been you*, but she never said why it wasn't. I'd have given anything to be in his place, he wrote, I'd have lavished every attention on you, or I'd have been rough and inconsiderate like Vladimir, I'd have taken you even against your will if that was what you wanted. I'd have read all the books for you, and learnt Ulbricht's speeches by heart, or Lenin's *The Next Tasks Confronting Soviet Power* as printed in my Civics Handbook, the one old Harms once gave me to educate me. Do you talk about things like that when you've been doing it? And which language do you speak? Do you know dirty Russian words because Vladimir whispers them in your ear to get you excited when he's being rough and inconsiderate, and does Vladimir know dirty German words? I'd have loved you in two languages and with two mouths and two pricks and a thousand hands, and now you're missing out on all that, you faithless woman, you friend of the Russians and the Party, oh yes, you have your principles, I've no objection to that, but after all the kisses of a

Marxist-Leninist won't taste so very different from anyone else's.

Rosa immediately realized that he had not spent a pleasant evening up in that horrible bar, the Cosmonaut, and she was glad, because if he had spent an unpleasant evening up there it could only be on account of that woman Gisela, the woman he thought about when they were making love, because they still did make love now and then, except that with her nobody had to learn speeches by heart or lavish every attention on her, that was all nonsense. She had once found one of these passionate missives addressed to Gisela in the waste-paper basket and read what it said, and she kept smelling him in the evening but found nothing, and was reassured that there was no new Bella, only some cheap little tart from time to time, she could live with that. She wasn't going to ask what had happened that night, but she sensed that he took it as a defeat, and since he always needed comfort after any defeat, either major or minor, she was kind and attentive, took him by surprise and won him round. She wanted him to say the other woman's name, and she wanted him to do it to her as if were doing it to that other woman, and naturally he demurred at first, and then he was surprised at her for pretending to be another woman, telling him how good he was and saying: Close your eyes, it's me, and my only name is hers.

Later he was ashamed of himself for letting her persuade him into this game, but Rosa said: Well, it was nice, wasn't it, or didn't you have your money's worth, oh, good heavens, Heinrich, said Rosa, and Heinrich said: Yes, it was all right, any news? Yes, Tom phoned again, said thanks for the other evening and hopes you haven't taken offence.

It had been the weekend before Heinrich's defeat that Tom from the camp suddenly appeared at their door, bringing with him a few memories of their time in the camp and a few surprising items of news. He had changed a good deal, wore a suit and tie and the little Party symbol on his

143

lapel, so you knew where he stood at once. May I come in? Yes, come along in, Heinrich had said, although it was only early afternoon and he wanted to go out again, these were stirring times. Whisky? asked Heinrich, meaning it as an allusion, and Tom immediately understood the allusion and didn't beat about the bush, he'd tried one thing and another, he said, and now he was living with his wife and child a couple of cities away from here in beautiful Götha, he'd been with the firm for three years.

The firm? asked Heinrich.

Yes, that man Harms, remember him? He gave me the idea. Hasn't he ever asked you to join the firm?

Not that I know of.

The first difficulties came two months later. Rosa still didn't know he'd been sacked, but Rita was now going on at him almost daily, she was gentle but persistent, wondering what was to become of her and her somewhat silent son, so one evening Heinrich put back the bedclothes, got dressed and went out to meet some old acquaintances, as he now did almost every evening, meeting acquaintances old and new up in the Cosmonaut bar and asking if there was anything they wanted to buy or sell. He had lost some of his enthusiasm in the last few weeks, found that what had once been a welcome change was now a burden, was sometimes success-ful, sometimes less successful, ran up debts with suppliers and customers, invented difficulties, learned how to manoeuvre in the new state too.

Early in May it looked as if all might yet go well. He had driven to Leipzig in a van provided by Vladimir to collect some spare parts for cars, and a few days later he went almost as far as the Czech border for a consignment of mattresses, in fact this was the first time he had been on the road in connection with beds and bedding, it was like the old days, and he was as cheerful as if he were back in his former life.

It wasn't easy to be a successful dealer in the new state,

which did not approve of people supplying goods to make up for such shortages as might occur, and Heinrich was a little lazy, so customers were soon asking him about unkept promises, enquiring after a boiler for the bathroom and the fur coat belonging to a dead neighbour of his on which they had put down a deposit, and Heinrich always had to think hard about his answers, and out of habit or idleness they believed him and kept quiet for a while. (The same old game.) Since it was now some time since enough money had been coming in, he broke into his last savings, secretly sold Rosa's remaining jewellery, and although he sometimes thought, this is like what happened back then, it can't go on much longer, just as it didn't back then, things went all right all through May and all through June, and at some point in July, when Rosa guessed the truth, he almost felt relieved.

Rosa didn't say much when it finally came out, but she was prepared when Harms suddenly turned up at the door a few days later, asking after her husband, they'd had a date on the twenty-ninth, but Heinrich didn't turn up at the appointed time, he said, and where was he now; oh yes, on the road, was he? Rosa would rather not have let him in, but Harms had made it quite clear that he wanted to come and have a word with her, had to say how anxious he felt, in reply to which she thought, or said she thought, there was no cause for anxiety, Heinrich had been ill for a while, and if he didn't mind her saying so her husband was in general extremely reliable.

May I come in, asked Harms, and immediately started talking. She didn't need to stand up for her Heinrich, he knew all about it. Well, I'm afraid I don't, said Rosa, and Harms repeated: Yes, it's a pity he won't look facts in the face, and he hasn't drawn a winning ticket with that Rita either.

Rita? asked Rosa.

Yes, these last three months, said Harms, and here he fell silent for a while out of consideration for her, and when it had had time to sink in he comforted her and promised to have a serious word with Heinrich about looking for a new job, and ask if that woman Rita was really worth it when he had a wife like Rosa and three children, Eva, Konrad and Walter, who had turned out well.

After this visit they waited, Rosa full of hope and Heinrich full of anxiety, but although they were respectively hopeful and anxious Harms did not seem to be taking the matter any further, so they soon stopped expecting to hear from him and forgot him, and life went on. Heinrich missed his friends, because Gisela was away for three weeks' holiday in Bulgària, and Vladimir had gone on a training course in Moscow, so he visited Rita as often as possible, ate with her and slept with her, was grateful and affectionate and went to the bar no more often than necessary. There were evenings when he hadn't been there half an hour before he had to leave to avoid impatient customers, and there were evenings when he was in luck and watched the Russian officers and the girls from Poland or Weimar dancing half the night away, but there wasn't a woman like Gisela among them, and there wasn't a man like Vladimir among them either, only good old Harms who turned up a day before the World Cup final between England and Germany, of all times.

Heinrich's heart almost stopped when he suddenly saw Harms sitting at one of the neighbouring tables, drinking and chatting, and Harms waved in a jovial manner like an old friend, pointed to the girl at his table and then, as if in explanation, to his watch, talked a little longer, and was smiling as he came over to Heinrich's table, still sounding perfectly friendly, had Rosa mentioned his visit, how was he getting on without a job, he was behind with his reports, wasn't he? Ah yes, the reports, said Heinrich, and Harms said: I think I could help you, I can even find you something in the beds and bedding line if you like, because you do seem most at home in the beds and bedding line, you aren't so happy delivering bread or books. Would that be a good idea?

Yes, it would, said Heinrich, unable to believe he was getting off so lightly, I'm very grateful, that would be ideal.

So who's going to win at Wembley tomorrow? Two – one after extra time, that's my bet.

Yes, and then I'll start on the reports.

Only later did Heinrich remember what Harms had said about gratitude on one of their earlier meetings, it would have been in the spring of 1964, Harms had chatted for a bit, and said that grateful workers were always the most reliable, or, as he said, quoting one of the secret service instructions from memory: A sense of gratitude engenders a desire to do fruitful unofficial work, that was how those in charge had put it.

Heinrich had never felt at ease from the first in the shabby flat near the station, and he hated the way he had to steal upstairs to the second floor, not meeting other people's eyes or responding to their greetings. He always felt like airing the place, drawing back the curtains, but Harms was very cautious in such matters, warned Heinrich of creaking boards, offered him a chair and then got down to business. Like criminals hiding away because they have a murder on their conscience or they're planning one, Heinrich had said on one of their first meetings here, but Harms had merely replied briefly: Well, that's how the class enemy would see it, but whether a citizen of the German Democratic Republic might legitimately look at things that way was another question.

What news of the lovely Comrade Müller and her good Lusatian, Harms had asked in the spring of 1964, and when was he switching to the bookshop job, no problems, he hoped; such was his preamble. Heinrich had said: No, everything was fine, except that recently there'd been a bread delivery which wasn't complete, and some of the bread was mouldy, so of course everyone blamed the bakers and the packers, complaining of people who go to work without sleeping off their hangovers and nobody gives them a rocket. No indication of hostile or negative activities and incidents?

No, no indication of hostile or negative activities and incidents; this had always been their little game, and even Comrade Müller with her lovely legs featured in the little game, although Heinrich would actually have lied for Comrade Müller and her lovely legs.

Comrade Müller had not been too pleased when Heinrich said he was changing his job and going to work for the People's Bookshop, and Harms had given him the idea, but since it had been Harms who gave him the idea she did not show her displeasure, but said she hoped she'd soon find a replacement. Best of luck, she said on the morning he loaded up the delivery van for the last time, and when he came back early in the evening she had left without waiting for him. Best of luck, said his new colleagues in the bookshop next morning, so this is the famous Hampel, well, a man who knows how to drive bread around town will know how to sell books too, both are good fare for workers and peasants; it was a comparison he liked.

Gisela had found a replacement for him quite quickly; she sat in her office as usual late into the night, and he would visit her from time to time and watch her struggling through accounts and lists of supplies and deliveries, groaning and despairing, and his company always did her good. Sometimes Heinrich thought: she's sorry I've left, or else she needs someone, and in fact she sometimes did make remarks with a double meaning, and wondered why he never asked her out for a meal or a boating expedition on the Saale, she saw she meant very little to him. Far from it, said Heinrich, and asked her to go on a boating expedition at the end of April, on one of the first fine weekends of the year, and sure enough she did not think it over for long, but laughed and beamed as he made his way along the river among a throng of other rowing boats, feeling hopeful and fearful, and making the best boat trip of her life and his own out of it, and that evening, when they came into the moorings in the Paradies district much too late, she kissed him on the mouth as she was getting out of the boat.

That was when he really fell in love with her, and that was when he began writing letters of adoration to her, but he never managed to repeat the daring felicity of the first letter, for when he visited her after that one she was embarrassed and happy. You shouldn't write to me like that, she said, so he knew that he should, and she'd be waiting for his letters, waiting like a lover for every one, but she never would grant him a night with her or another boat trip. Tell me what you're wearing, send me a photograph, reply to me, yield to me, said his letters, and depending on her whim and her mood she replied thanking or reproaching or encouraging him, for when you write to me, she said, I'm a different woman, I begin to glow. Believe me, I read each letter only once, she wrote, and then I tear it into countless pieces, but I luxuriate in what you write.

The day Yuri Gagarin came to town, early in October 1963, Rosa had said: I can't wait to see what your famous Gisela looks like, and then Gisela was wearing a dark-blue suit with a white blouse and a gold belt, and looked boring and narrow-lipped and severe, like a spinster getting on in years. Even the Lusatian had taken an hour off to help give the renowned Soviet cosmonaut a suitable welcome, and wave and gawp at him in his much-decorated uniform, as he shook hands and called something out in Russian to the people from among all the black Volgas, and Heinrich and Rosa and the children had come, but as they were late and couldn't make their way through the crowd with the pram they had to watch from the back rows. Heinrich's mind was instantly occupied with Comrade Müller's new perfume, Rosa had her work cut out with Walter, who was bawling, and little Eva read the wording on the red banner hanging from the front of the old Zeiss building out loud to Vladimir, hesitating briefly only over the word republic: The republic needs us all, we all need the republic.

What does a cosmonaut do in his holidays, asked Eva, and Gisela knew the answer, because cosmonauts went travelling on their holidays, and were proud to think that even little girls like Eva knew who they were and asked questions about them, and dreamed of flying through space as cosmonauts themselves some day, or so she supposed. Not me, I'd rather be a teacher, said Eva, and Gisela thought being a teacher was a good career too, and after a while the famous cosmonaut had driven out of town in the middle of a column of foreign black cars, and then they sat together over a cup of coffee for a little longer. The Americans will never forgive us for Gagarin, said Gisela, and Vladimir, understanding only the word American, shook his head and said manned space flight had always been one of humanity's dreams, what do you think, you good, you fabulous woman, my dear Rosa: you've given Heinrich two sons and a delightful, clever daughter, and you grow lovelier all the time. Oh, thank you, thank you very much, you make me feel all embarrassed, Rosa had said, thinking that Vladimir's manners could almost be called good, for a Russian, unless Heinrich had not interpreted accurately. She's like a Russian woman, like a Russian woman, your good, your fabulous Rosa, she must have Russian ancestors, was literally what Heinrich had been given to translate, but it always sounds a bit over the top in Russian.

All Rosa said about Gisela afterwards was: I can't think what you see in that Gisela, her perfume's terrible, and how stern and cold she looks in the blue and gold get-up, and then there were her legs too, had Heinrich noticed her knock-knees, at least that Gisela certainly wasn't his type.

Well, what do you know, replied Heinrich, kissing Rosa on the mouth, for at this time he was still kissing her on the mouth when he did not entirely share her opinion, and that evening in the bathroom, when she was naked, he looked at her as he would look at a woman who gave him pleasure.

Don't you get bored with me, she asked, adding: I've got a little plump, look, oh, dear me, I'm really plump there, and there. Almost like a Russian woman, said Rosa. Do you like me all the same? Yes, always, all over.

In October Rosa had taken him by surprise a couple of times in swift succession, so they were always much occupied with each other, couldn't wait until the children went to bed, didn't answer the door when the bell rang, waited and listened and lay where they were for a few minutes, yes, no, wait, come on, it doesn't last long, but every second is delightful and terrible and lovely.

Nor would Heinrich have answered the door on the Sunday of the election at the end of October, but Rosa had suddenly remembered: Oh, my word, the election, everyone in the building has to go, everyone's supposed to vote by noon at the latest. Harms was obviously a happy man when they met a few days later in the new café on the Holzmarkt, 99.95 per cent of the vote to the Socialist Unity Party, and were they all happy after their first year here, little Eva was already making a name for herself in the Young Pioneers. This went on for half an hour, and after half an hour Harms ordered something to eat, and when they had almost finished he started on about politics again: what did Heinrich really think of the new state, what was there that could be improved, things that he and Party people must think hard about some time, for unfortunately there was a lot they didn't know, or they knew it only too late, information was needed.

You're trying to recruit me into your firm, Heinrich had said, very well, I'll tell you something, for instance I'll tell you something about Comrade Müller, her father was in Buchenwald, but she's straightforward and honest as the Lusatian himself. My wife says she can't get the right sort of bread for dumplings in town, and she does miss a bit of well-trimmed pork, but she could live without a car and a fridge.

You're laughing at me.

Not at all, said Heinrich.

Maybe you're not working in the right line, said Harms, and came up with the idea of books, Heinrich could try the book trade, that was a good line of work, he'd get to know the country and its people better and have something to report on too.

All right, said Heinrich.

All right, said Heinrich in October 1966, when he was up to his neck in trouble and Rita was going on at him: Do you have any work yet? Promise me you'll soon have work and remember my boy and me? Yes, all right, said Heinrich, and saw things repeating themselves, for by now he had debts enough for three. He would have liked to ask Harms for his advice, but there had been no word from Harms for weeks, and he had no telephone number or address where he could reach him. Probably getting him the new job was more difficult than Harms had expected, or else Harms was holding out on him, or had difficulties and anxieties of a different nature, not that he really believed a man like Harms would have difficulties and anxieties.

A week before his arrest Heinrich had entirely lost his grip of the overall situation, and while there were days when he still felt completely carefree, there were other days when he was realistic and did calculations, coming up with terrifying sums. Exactly a week before his arrest for flagrant debt Heinrich took on his last commission: a delivery of red roof tiles and seven sacks of mortar. He had promised the friend of a friend to deliver these items within three days, payment in advance, but then found he could get them only at far too steep a price, and they were not available at all locally, so he had to go to Gera and Erfurt and Plauen, had no luck in Gera and Erfurt and Plauen either, and came back to Rita like a dog with its tail between its legs. Nothing again, then, said Rita by way of welcome, and said as if to herself: Nothing is going to come of us, and then at last, one evening: That Harms came to see me, he said you don't mean badly but the

152

trouble is nobody can rely on you. It's not what I want, but his advice was for us to separate, he said I should send you packing this very evening, because you won't go of your own accord. Well, so I say to this Harms, I should hope not, as far as I'm concerned he can stay, as far as I'm concerned he can stay till the Day of Judgement, so now get out of my flat, I tell him, I never invited you here, and then he went.

It was as if he felt he had to warn me against you, and warn your Rosa too.

That's what his sort are like.

After that everything moved very fast. One Monday in November Harms told him that unfortunately he had made no progress in the matter they had been discussing; next Wednesday Rita went to see Rosa, and around seven on the Thursday morning officers from the criminal investigation department were at the door asking for Heinrich Hampel, born 25 August 1931 in Jena, resident in that city with his wife and three children, address for deliveries of letters and parcels of all kinds 13 Hermann-Stapff-Strasse, I'm afraid we must take you with us, you've been reported to the police.

Rosa? said Heinrich, and waited until she came, and then they took him straight away with them, refusing to tell the deeply shocked Rosa where. Heinrich, what is it, she cried, and Eva said: Those men were in our garden looking up at our window, will you be coming back soon? In retrospect, all Heinrich saw was Rosa in deep shock, and himself waving to her and Eva as if he were going to stay the weekend with friends, and then they put the handcuffs on him, led him off before the children's eyes to a waiting car and took him away.

At first he couldn't grasp the fact that they were really taking him away, driving him in this car to Gera and the remand prison as if he were a criminal. Sixteen thousand in less than a year, said the public prosecutor, that'll be three years without probation, and even now Heinrich couldn't grasp it, or what those numbers meant, sixteen thousand in less than a year: his debts.

People were still friendly to him, his cell was reasonably all right and so was his first meal. I want to speak to Herr Harms of State Security in Gera, said Hampel, but even he didn't believe anything would come of that, they probably wouldn't make so much as a phone call for someone like him, or they'd act as if they didn't know any Herr Harms in Gera, or they'd say he was away or sick. He thought of the children, and what it would be like for them, not seeing him for a couple of years, and he thought of Rosa's curves, and as for Rita, he thought only of their first days. He spent a whole evening trying to remember exactly what she had last said to him, but he simply could not recollect it. You're late, hurry up, tomorrow is another day, was what she had probably said, because recently, when he said goodbye, he had taken to whispering a few indecent remarks in her ear, but if he'd known this was really goodbye he'd have said something nice instead, she had earned it.

After a year in the East everyone told him: The first year is the worst, your first year was difficult, things can only get better, we try hard, we're old hands at trying hard, not that it's done us much good so far. Things can only get better, Heinrich had said, and Rosa had said: Yes, they must, but all the same it's bad enough, everyone has trouble getting coal and butter and meat, and not everyone has a full stomach, and it gets me down in the long run, standing in line waiting and having to be content with the bare necessities. People had been queuing outside the shops for every little thing for months, there was nothing to be had but carrots and onions and potatoes, and every variety of cabbage, there were articles in all the newspapers telling you how to make delicious salad out of cabbage, or a vegetable dish with bacon and onions, and how long it was best to steam the cabbage, with the lid on or off the pan, you found the same smell on the stairs and in the corridors almost everywhere.

Harms had regularly asked after them, sending small

presents for the children and a bunch of carnations for Rosa's thirtieth birthday at the beginning of January, unfortunately, he said, he didn't have much time to spare, his new task and the situation as a whole called for all his energies, but he would certainly come and visit in February or March when the baby had arrived, and when he did finally call and suggest a date it was the end of March, and Rosa had a few days to go.

Harms had grown a moustache since last time, the first time in the Zur Sonne restaurant, and was talking with great enthusiasm of the Party conference in January. Yes, we've made mistakes, he said, but none the less mankind's old longing for a life of freedom, dignity and social security is becoming reality, step by step. I quote from Walter Ulbricht in *The Programme of Socialism*, he had said, where you can also read this exhortation: Socialism, the ancient yearning of the people, is Germany's national good fortune. But no one can satisfy that yearning as a gift to our people. Its fulfilment must be worked for, and fought for, and then worked for all over again, worked for and secured again and again.

Heinrich would not have been surprised if Harms had asked him the second time what he asked him the third and fourth times (We need a man of good will), but instead he spent the whole time talking about meat and butter, and how the people in the West have cars, but they eat less meat and butter than we do. Do you remember our first evening in the Zur Sonne restaurant? he asked, and Heinrich did remember just how they had been cautiously sounding each other out half the evening, he was suspicious and hungry, and the lukewarm red cabbage with roast meat tasted of smoke and fire, but it was good. I'm not for the West, Heinrich had said, thinking of Theodor, but I can be for the East only if my children are properly fed and my wife doesn't have to wear herself out running round town looking for a kilo of potatoes, or 100 grams of sweet almonds and 25 grams of bitter almonds for her Christmas baking.

Yes, I can understand that, said Harms, and he sent Rosa chocolates when she had the baby, and a blue tractor and trailer loaded with coloured building blocks from the People's Republic of China for little Walter (a name meaning a man who is strong). I hope you didn't pay for it, was all Rosa said, still very weak on the second day but happy and relieved because the birth had been so quick, at five in the afternoon as she lay on her side in the delivery ward of the University Hospital and pushed the little thing out into the world with just a few contractions.

Sometimes I curse you for all this, said Rosa, when her milk was coming in on the third day, and the baby clamped himself to her breast and sucked, unaware that this was his beginning, but from the way she said it he knew that this was indeed a beginning for Rosa, and the events of the past year had just been skirmishing. He looks like you, she said. And it's typical of you that he looks like you, just don't let him go to the bad, take care, bring in the money, find ways for us to live, but be careful not to burn your fingers, a person could burn his fingers very quickly in this bloody state, you wouldn't get away with it as easily as you did back in the West.

We're not living in a prison here.

But sometimes last summer all we had was bread and that horrible margarine.

In the first six months Heinrich had talked quite differently, for everything was new and strange and tolerable then, so they talked a lot about the meat and milk and butter that were unavailable, and the empty markets and shops that opened only in the morning and sometimes for an hour in the afternoon. Those early days were both difficult and carefree, and Rosa counted the weeks and accepted the strict rationing and the shortages, and all the work entailed by the shortages, like a storm which would pass over. Just think, today I couldn't get any peas at all, either yellow or green, her account of it would begin in the evening, and then she would enumerate everything else she couldn't get: oatflakes for Konrad, rice, pearl barley, potato starch, Ericona-brand Hungarian goulash soup, cinnamon, ginger and marjoram, sweet biscuits and savoury biscuits, chewing gum for Heinrich's long drives with the delivery van. Once she managed to get hold of some Russian bread, a packet of the chocolate wafers called Pischinger Ecken, some peppermint brittle for the children and a few Cuban cigars for Heinrich, available in three differently priced grades, and jam and mustard was sold out of big tubs because of the shortage of glass jars. Well, it won't kill us to go without coffee, Rosa had said in the first few weeks, but only half a pound of meat a week, we can't live on that, and then you have to listen to the butcher saying oh no, I'm sorry, Frau Hampel, you've had your ration, look, it says so here, and of course you mustn't get cross, you must look as friendly and patient as possible, as if you were grateful to him for letting you come back and sit on a stool waiting hours for a piece of pork belly almost entirely consisting of fat.

And that's what they've gone and built the Wall for.

Not for that, Rosa. And: It was your decision to come, Rosa.

Yes, I'm afraid it was.

At first he said once or twice: You didn't have to come, you could have spared yourself all this if you hadn't come, but then we wouldn't have had the weekends down in the Paradies district and the boat trips, or you and me on our narrow, blissful air mattress, there wouldn't have been any of that. I'm just not giving Theodor the satisfaction, he said, and you can't deny that they're going to endless trouble here in this country.

So they adapted and accustomed themselves to it. Without the parcels from Wiesbaden, almost always containing two pounds of coffee, and a few cans of vegetables, and once a pair of nylons size 42 for Rosa, they wouldn't have known how to manage, and sometimes the kind Birnstels looked in and brought cabbage from their garden or a packet of cake mix, Annemarie had found it right at the back of the kitchen cupboard when she was turning the cupboard out, and they drank a cup of coffee together and chatted about the good old days, although if the good old days were really to come back with all the fuss and bother and the dreadful war and the anxiety and the worry about the children – no, a horrible thought.

Cuba, said Friedhelm, all I'll say is, Cuba, and Heinrich, who was not really especially concerned about Cuba, said: The West will be careful not to start a war with Cuba, I'm sure the Americans won't want the Cubans teaching them another lesson.

He was still practising, yes. But he asked that man Harms all kinds of unwelcome questions in the Roter Hahn. We do indeed have difficulties over supplies of meat and sausage, Harms explained, but he did not agree that there wasn't enough to eat and drink in general. No one in this country starves, but things will turn out badly if this goes on, if no one puts an end to slackness and the mistakes made out of ignorance and lack of ambition. Dates aren't met, extra work has to be done, the quality's not good enough: that's the bitter truth of our export industry. The newspapers say: Meat's in short supply in the shops because good production workers are in short supply, and that's a fact, so let me invite you out this evening, what luck I'm in Gera now, that way I can keep in touch with you, this has been a promising start, so let's drink to my hope that it will go on the same way.

For the first three weeks Heinrich thought it would be only a few days before he was taken to court, but then nothing happened, and Rosa didn't visit, and nor for a long time did Harms, whom he had been expecting, but then suddenly there he was one day in Heinrich's cell, talking and preaching sermons as if he were a friend or father. Good heavens,

Hampel, said Harms, you've been up to things I don't like at all, but we offer the hand of friendship to those who see the error of their ways and make an effort. You ought to have listened to me, he said, you ought to have been more careful, and more suspicious of your so-called friends. As I said to you at the start: We have to be patient in this country, a man who wants to go onwards and upwards needs stamina, so try to make the best use of the time you serve, that's my advice. Two or three years are quite a long time.

Two or three years: the words echoed in Heinrich's ears (it was the second time he'd heard them), and he was horrified at the thought of those thousand days; it couldn't be true, a thousand days for debts of sixteen thousand marks, but Harms didn't seem to have any other ideas, or else he thought the punishment just, or perhaps he himself had helped to work it out, had approved it. Then they both fell silent, and when they had both finished with their silence Heinrich said thanks and goodbye, and Harms also said thanks and goodbye, Heinrich wouldn't be forgotten, our authorities have a good memory. Was there any favour he could do for Heinrich, he asked, and Heinrich said: Yes, Rosa, and sure enough she was allowed to visit him a few days later. Rosa looked tired and thin, but also determined and unsympathetic. She did most of the talking, admonishing him and carrying on at him, and he nodded and looked at her, noticing things about her, laying in provisions for the future.

Eva sends her love, and Vladimir and Gisela, they came to see me the other day, your Gisela just couldn't believe it.

I'm starting work with Zeiss on Monday, said Rosa, Friedhelm asked if they had anything for me, it's in the wages office, oh, dear me, but we have to live on something.

We must see it through, he said.

My God, see it through, said Rosa.

What can I say, said Heinrich, thinking she was making it easy for herself by making it difficult for him, for after all she had the children and could go in and out of her own four walls just as she pleased.

You're cross, he said, and Rosa said: I'm just thinking what it could have been like, because you'd have got off more lightly in the West. It wouldn't have been easy, but we'd have kept our friends and our flat and our nice life.

And now it's turned out differently.

Things always do turn out differently.

But it was good on our air mattresses, wasn't it? Say it was good on our air mattresses.

Well, yes, I'll say that.

She did not touch him in that half hour before the long trial of their patience began, Rosa was all he had, and Rosa was all Rosa had herself. He stayed more or less the same in prison, but when she came to collect him after almost a thousand days he didn't recognize her again.

6

Of course it could all have turned out quite differently, for instance everything could have turned out quite differently in Africa in 1953, but he was indolent and impatient then, he had no great aptitude for market gardening and construction work, and he had a rather strange aunt who climbed into other people's beds when the moon was full, an aunt who walked in her sleep. He had great plans for himself in Africa, a place where a lapsed monk and a pregnant servant girl could make their fortunes, so surely a young man like Heinrich could do the same, although it was a pity the voyage was so long and uncomfortable, taking almost three weeks from the day when they sailed from Southampton.

The ship was just moving away from shore when he saw Jeff the sailor far below on the quayside, waving and shouting something, but unfortunately he couldn't hear any sound from down there by now, only the thudding of the heavy engines, and the cold west wind blowing, and the passengers on deck talking and shouting. I hope you find something, Heinrich had said as they spent that last hour in a smoke-filled pub down by the harbour, killing time, and Jeff, who had been looking for a really good berth for months without finding one, had said: Yeah, you bet I will, but you be careful with the married women, now, I really envy you your Stella in that photo.

Heinrich couldn't make out why a man like Jeff would hang around Southampton for months, moving from one cheap pub to another, running up debts, and wasting time in ever cheaper pubs because of those debts. Sure, fine, next week, I promise, had said Jeff, a man who'd been living entirely on shipboard for nearly twenty years now, so that the only girls he knew were the tarts in rundown brothels, and he had wished Heinrich a good journey, good luck and come back soon, though by the time you do I hope to be on the way to Madagascar or lying beside a beauty from Jamaica or Bristol, those were his parting words.

Even when the ship was a few hundred metres out from the shore he could still see Jeff standing by the quayside waving, until at last they gained speed, and Jeff and the colourful crowd on the quay grew smaller and smaller, and then they turned and put out to sea. For almost an hour Heinrich stood by the rail in the gathering dusk, thinking of Jeff, that odd character, and why he hadn't had a girlfriend for years or even a fixed address, because if he had Heinrich might have written to tell him what distant South Africa was like, and exactly what Stella was like, and his uncle and his aunt, who had retained her youth, yes, he might have written to Jeff about all that.

For a while, in the distance, he could still see the lights of the city of Southampton, of which he knew nothing but a cheap pub in the harbour, and after one last look he finally went below, and found his cabin among the people crowding the corridors in second and third class, but there was no one else there yet, only a large suitcase on one of the two plank beds, plastered with colourful stickers, which unfortunately told him nothing about its owner's background.

At dinner, just before eight, Heinrich sat with two Indians and an elderly lady from London, and they gestured with hands and feet as they told each other where they came from and where they were going, pausing for breath and letting their eyes wander, that was the kind of thing one did in the first few hours, and Heinrich soon spotted a pretty woman here and there, looked into a pair of dark or light eyes, kept his thoughts well away from his father and his dead mother, and relaxed.

Perhaps he might be able to think soberly and objectively about past events after all, he reflected, drinking a last beer at a bar between decks before returning, at around nine-thirty, to his cabin, where he found the owner of the large suitcase, a Belgian from near Liège who was South African rep for a firm manufacturing industrial sewing machines, spoke a rather curious German, and was not very forthcoming at first. Not too bad, said Heinrich to himself, although he thought it odd that the Belgian suddenly undressed in front of him and did some press-ups, stark naked, went to have a wash, still naked, came back, covered himself up and turned away from Heinrich, as if he sensed that at the age of twenty-one Heinrich couldn't yet bring himself to strip in front of a stranger, a man of around forty, of whom he knew nothing except that he lived near Liège and had the hard body of a soldier.

Only hours later, as he lay there still awake, did Heinrich feel happy, glad his voyage had begun at last, glad he was beginning to live his own life, as for what lay behind him, it was ridiculous, not worth mentioning. He would have liked to dream of Stella that first night, but the girl of whom he dreamed was called Rosa, he dreamed of Rosa sitting one cabin away, weeping over seven suitcases and wanting to go home.

The bad news had reached them early in the evening when they were all just back from their daily visit, when they had moistened the mortally sick woman's lips once again, waiting for one of those now rare moments when she was conscious and recognized her children and her husband, since she had something to say to each of them, words of farewell, or comfort, or simply something baffling. Up to the last it was for Heinrich alone that she had no words of farewell, or comfort, or even anything baffling to say. Then she whispered: Oh, Heinrich, or perhaps it just seemed to Heinrich that she was whispering, oh, my son Heinrich, what a shame, to which he replied: Yes, I know, Mother, it's a shame, but the thing consuming you and taking you to your grave comes out of yourself.

It was on the Tuesday or Wednesday that he spoke to her for the last time, and now it was Friday and the neighbour with the only telephone for a long way around had brought them the news. Oh, Father, oh heavens, said Constanze, leaving the neighbour who had brought the message standing in the doorway, and then their father knew too, went to the door and thanked the neighbour, bowing and nodding to him. Heinrich said: Well, she's got it over with at last, and the others turned on him saying that as usual he was thinking of no one but himself, never sparing a thought for anyone else, the living or the dead. Now, now, children, said their father, adding that they must go one last time to say goodbye, although when he saw her like that, and touched her and she didn't move, he knew he would feel shattered.

Then he sent a telegram to Theodor, and next he called a taxi, and after that he drove off with Paul and Heinrich to say goodbye to the dead woman. Heinrich kept a few metres away from the body, but his father kissed her hand a couple of times, looking at her like a lover, while Paul just kept studying the tag tied to her left toe: Elisabeth Hampel, born 15 August 1899, died 2 February 1953, she was already different now. Come on, let's go, said Heinrich, but his father didn't hear, so he and Paul went out into the corridor for a cigarette and stood there, not knowing what to talk about.

Theodor arrived next morning, recognized the situation at a glance, and since he saw that their father was incapable in his grief of doing the simplest things Theodor took charge himself, said a few words of comfort to their sisters, sent Paul out to buy food and Heinrich to visit an undertaker two streets away, a man who always knew the right thing to say, who immediately recommended a plain coffin from the first part of his brochure, had drapes and shrouds which their mother would have liked, the dear departed, your wife and mother, the ways of the Lord are unfathomable and wise, but those who live in the faith have patience and courage, and know that the dead have only gone ahead. We must discuss the gravestone too, Herr Hampel, said the undertaker as he left, or perhaps you could send one of your sons over at the beginning of the week, and the lot fell on Heinrich. Even Theodor gave him a free hand to choose a stone that would do her justice and last a long time, hard, unhewn, unpolished, that was how he thought of her, but bright, with a touch of red, a woman like granite.

Then they had to get through the first weekend, silence and tears behind closed doors, or at the dinner table when Heinrich served up canned soup with Viennese sausages, and no one felt hungry. Theodor spend almost two days sending death announcements here, there and everywhere, while their father sat on the sofa with a mug of camomile tea, motionless and perfectly silent, they didn't know what to make of him or exactly how bad he was feeling, nor did they know whether it was now that his sickness first struck root in his brain, or if it was on the day of the funeral, when the temperature was minus twenty degrees, or over the following weeks and months.

It had been so cold on the day of the funeral that all the bunches and flower arrangements instantly froze: their father's red roses, the cyclamen wreath from Schott, the brightly coloured arrangements from Heinrich's brothers and sisters, the floral tributes from Aachen, they all froze immediately. When Rosa visited Heinrich a few days later and saw how miserable his father was, she just said: He still can't find the words to express it, but I can see you're already feeling it like a release. You have nothing on your mind but your journey, she said, and how you can get out of here and leave everything behind, including me. Nonsense, Heinrich had said, I'm just thankful it's over, if you like I'll send for you in a few months' time, and then we'll see, but Rosa didn't really believe he would, because not much had yet passed between them, she knew he had other girlfriends as well as Rosa, and not two hours before his train left he was saying nice things about her soft places as if for the last time.

When Heinrich woke up in the morning the Belgian was lying on his bed already dressed, reading an American magazine, and said something about Heinrich missing breakfast, and by the way, he talked in his sleep now and then, had a girl ever told him so? Not that I know of, said Heinrich, soon discovering that the Belgian felt well disposed to him, knew a place between decks where you could get a late breakfast up to mid-day, and barely moved from his side for the next few days; he always rose early, woke Heinrich or let him sleep late when they had been drinking at the bar until well after midnight, or Heinrich had been dancing the night away in his white shoes, spending a week casting his spell on a pale English girl, throwing money away on her as if he were rolling in it. In the end he didn't really have much success with the English girl, who was just nineteen and travelling with her nearly blind grandmother, had pointed little breasts, and was so bored by the end of the second week in first class that she wanted to be kissed, for the days and nights were long, amusements were few and far between, you lived as best you could from one meal to the next, growing fat and lazy and fretful, so Heinrich cheered himself at night or in the late afternoon with various thoughts of this girl Julia, or far away Rosa, or Stella, that prize won by his cousin Alfred, Stella whose skin was brown as cocoa.

He had only a fuzzy black and white photograph of Stella, standing half concealed behind a peach tree in blossom, wearing a straw hat with frayed edges and a pale, flowered summer dress, her feet bare. He was still sorry it was not she who had written to him but his aunt, in her pretty, rounded, girlish script: My dear Heinrich, my poor boy, she wrote, we've never met, but after all these dreadful weeks I want you to know how much we're looking forward to seeing you.

Heinrich could not say exactly what he thought of his aunt's writing such things to him in her pretty, rounded, girlish script, not seeming to notice the difference in their age, or mentioning his dead mother. He might not have been surprised if Stella had written to him in such terms, saying she kept thinking of him and looked forward to seeing him, perhaps it was because down in South Africa they always looked forward to visitors from distant Europe, or perhaps it was just his aunt's way, or perhaps Heinrich reminded her of an earlier love, after the event, of course everyone was wiser.

He didn't talk much to his Belgian companion even after the first week, but that was what he liked about the man, the fact that they could lie side by side in their cabin for hours on end, or think about their families after their third or fourth drink at the bar, and the days and weeks separating them, for they were both more or less in flight. Well, it went all right for a few years, said the Belgian, and then it went badly for a few years, and one day she was off and away with another man, and I hope she's regretting it. That's life, Heinrich would comment, or else he would say nothing at all but gaze out of the big wide windows at the sea, or look behind him to where the pale English girl sat in a corner with her nearly blind grandmother, who didn't notice when he sat down at her table and made approaches to her Julia, which was how he spent his days. Have you written home, asked the Belgian when they put into Madeira on the fourth day, and Heinrich could only stare at him: what could he have to write about after a week, except that he was still alive and wasn't thinking of them much, only thinking of Rosa's famous soft places, and what it was like when she sighed under the touch of his hands, or showed them something, and when they had come off the right track or she wanted them to find it she guided them back again.

But his mother had not liked Rosa from the first: what kind of a housewife was it who didn't scoop the very last of the egg white out of the eggshell when she was making cakes, just threw it away instead, what a wicked waste. Oh well, Heinrich had said, you know what Mother's like, for back then in the late summer of fifty-two it had just begun between him and Rosa, and he couldn't help thinking of that at the end of the first week at sea, when he stood by the rail for a long time after lunch, looking out over the water, looking south, where a new life was waiting for him, and so were Stella and his uncle and aunt, and thinking of all this he took out the photograph of his mother and tore it up, throwing it unhesitatingly straight into the sea.

At the beginning of the second week Heinrich invited his English girl to the tea dance, and when he took her back to their cabin early in the evening, and neither of them was sure what was going to happen next, there stood the Belgian in the doorway all of a sudden, looking at them as if they were two schoolchildren caught in the act. She's only a child, said the Belgian, adding that he'd do better to think of his Rosa, and had Heinrich ever thought of a man in the way he thought of his Rosa, that was what he particularly wanted to know, that was what he was leading up to. Heinrich couldn't believe that the Belgian was suddenly asking him to confess such things, so he simply shook his head in a vague way, waited a moment and said: Well, no, and then thought he should have said it more firmly, in a chillier tone, but instead he just sat there, thinking the questions not so bad in themselves, or the silence, in fact feeling flattered.

Later he was ashamed of having allowed a man to say such things to him, but at the time, on his bed, he was not ashamed or frightened, he just listened in surprise and said thanks, but no thanks. A pity, said the Belgian, when he had finished paying Heinrich compliments in his peculiar Belgian-accented German, and said he hoped they would still be good friends for the rest of the voyage, he felt sure they would, and he wouldn't say another word on the subject, except that when he was falling asleep, or late in the afternoon up in the bar when the hours passed so slowly, he would like to think of Heinrich. (Well, yes, no objection to his doing that.)

You're very kind to me, said Heinrich, and the Belgian said: It's because of you yourself if I am, I can't help it, now listen to me, I've made a useful contact for you, he's expecting you up in the dining-room: a rich farmer from near Cape Town who emigrated to South Africa in the thirties and now he's on his way home after four weeks in Europe, you'll like him. Well, we'll see, said Heinrich, and for the Belgian's sake he approached his former countryman, a man of around fifty who had been born in Wuppertal and kept interrupting his much younger wife, boasting of his success and his wealth at such volume that you could enjoy the joke several tables away.

He took to Heinrich immediately, and his little wife also took to Heinrich immediately, but she kept quiet almost all the time, asking few but pertinent questions, didn't pity him for what had happened and thought his wishes, dreams and plans were justified. Heinrich had really just meant to exchange the time of day and wish them a good voyage, but stout Felix from Wuppertal made him sit down with them, there and then, and they had scarcely reached the second bottle of Cabernet Sauvignon before it turned out that they had a long-standing connection already: it was seven or eight years ago, said Felix, that he once met Heinrich's uncle at a political gathering in Johannesburg, everyone knew that Heinrich's uncle was far too soft on the blacks in general and his workers in particular, is it a crime to hit a naughty child or a black who doesn't work properly, that was what they'd been arguing about at the time. What was it that Heinrich's uncle grew up there in the north? Oh yes, asparagus. An eccentric, Heinrich's uncle, a man who didn't beat his workers, he was known practically all over the country, well, I mean known among us Germans, my kind regards to him, please, and kind regards from my little mousie here too, not that she knows him, I didn't have you yet back then in Johannesburg, did I?

A moment followed in which it seemed she might say something, but he was talking on again, taking no notice of anything she might say, or perhaps she had long ago accustomed herself to saying nothing on her own account in front of him, keeping it for later instead. Over the next few days Heinrich met her once by chance in the ship's library, and then again early in the morning down near the lavatories, and on each occasion Heinrich spoke to her first and stood beside her, giving her time to sort out her clever little remarks and her friendly questions. She was not exactly pretty with her grey-blue eyes and in her close-fitting costume, but she liked to listen, and didn't conceal her envy of his youth and the way he still had everything ahead of him at the age of twenty-one: as if she felt that the best of her own life was already behind her.

I don't know why it is, but I have faith in you, she would say, or she would get him to tell her how he was going to send his Rosa a ticket in a few months' time, but before that he'd be driving his uncle's fresh asparagus round the country, selling it at wickedly high prices to the big hotels on the coast, and after a while his uncle would be congratulating himself on buying his nephew's ticket and would make him a partner or something.

There was nothing more to it, except that once, just for a moment towards the end of the voyage, when stout Felix was in reflective mood over dinner, scrutinizing his little mousie and Heinrich, he said: I hope you two aren't keeping any secrets from me, and she actually blushed like a young girl, and seemed happy and proud to be blushing, that was all.

A few hours before they reached Cape Town she visited his

cabin once more to say goodbye, and the pale English girl said goodbye too in her own way, writing him a note in English on scented paper, too late now for anything else, she said, unfortunately. Well, fancy that, your English girl, said the Belgian, who translated it all for him before the two men exchanged addresses, just in case you ever happen to come to Liège and need a place to stay; and with that the Belgian went ashore.

This time it was Heinrich waving and searching the crowd with his eyes, calling out a last-word message to the man he was looking for, but in vain, for it went unheard, and later on they reached the harbours of Port Elizabeth and East London, and at six-thirty on the morning of 21 April they arrived in Durban.

Hours later, during the long drive in his uncle's black Chevrolet, his aunt was still amused to think that their nephew from Germany had been waving at a young black girl in a straw hat for almost half an hour, erroneously taking her for Stella, but the lovely Stella hadn't come at all, just his uncle in a check waistcoat with his jacket slung over his arm, not looking at all as if he had driven 700 kilometres across country. He and Heinrich's aunt had been standing on the quayside since eight in the morning, and it was his aunt who first spotted their nephew from Germany, but as he kept looking over their heads and waving to the black girl they didn't meet until two hours later, when he had completed all the formalities. You look tired, my dear, was the first thing his aunt in her summer dress said, and his uncle said: Welcome to our state, the land of the Boers and the British, and a fine land too, as you'll see, everything here is always ready six months earlier or later than with you, but it's never really cold and unpleasant.

So they drove away, going on and on, north past Johannesburg, through parched land with stubble fields, and an occasional village of round huts thatched with straw, a broad river flowed sluggishly along in the distance, there was

Heinrich's first sight of a giraffe under tall trees, and zebras, herds of cattle crossing their path, four donkeys trotting along the dusty track pulling a cart, and the light and the constant dust, the tall sky above the endless countryside: those were his first impressions.

Later he must have dropped off to sleep for a while, for when his aunt woke him, touching his shoulder and asking if he was coming in with them for a bite to eat, it was the middle of the afternoon and the sun over the self-service restaurant was mild and warm. Had a good sleep? asked his uncle, and wouldn't be relieved at the wheel of the car for the last hundred kilometres, sang German songs to keep himself awake and prevent Heinrich's aunt from starting to ask questions, we want to get home first, have Abraham bring us a nice cool drink, and then you can both ask questions so far as I'm concerned.

The house with the long, sloping roof over its veranda seemed surprisingly small to Heinrich. There were only three tiny rooms and a kitchen, a bathroom with the lavatory in it, we don't need much, you see, when you're farming you're almost always out in the fields or the glasshouse, as you'll find out. Come along, I'll show you your room, said Heinrich's aunt, taking him into a bedroom with a bed, a chair, a cupboard, and a window looking out into the yard, where he was to stay until he had a place of his own and the money he'd need for it, which would take a while yet.

His room was between the bathroom and the main bedroom, and until a night ago had been used by the faithful Abraham for taking a little nap after lunch and resting from his labours; they'd employed him for nearly eight years now and were satisfied with him, he was reliable and quiet and had no other choice, at almost fifty-seven, but to stay with them. Are you hungry? asked Heinrich's aunt, gazing at him as if she really had been looking forward to seeing him, and Heinrich said yes, he'd like something to eat, expecting something African, but it was a German dish, to celebrate his arrival. His aunt and Abraham had been leafing through old German cookery books, thinking, coming to a decision, so in honour of the day they would have braised beef with potato dumplings, her nephew would like that, and indeed he did.

Not until dessert did she ask about his father and the rest of the family, and since his uncle wasn't really listening he said only what was most necessary, mentioned Theodor's professional success, avoided the subject of his fiancée Rosa, and soon went to bed. He listened for a while longer to various unfamiliar sounds in the garden, heard through the open window, or sounds from further away, from his uncle's fields and meadows, which you could hardly see in the dark, those were probably cicadas chirping, or crickets, he knew crickets from the Paradies district in Jena, and later he heard doors opening and shutting, his uncle's deep voice, his aunt's mild reply as she said (unless he was dreaming it): Be kind to him, he's little more than a child, poor boy, I've been looking forward to his visit, so leave him to me, do you think he's serious about this Rosa?

It was on the Sunday after his twenty-first birthday that Heinrich first promised to marry Rosa. Come along, I've got a surprise for you, said Rosa, and Heinrich hadn't the faintest idea what she meant, but behind the bushes at the swimming baths she looked at him suddenly, looked at his hands, took one of them and showed him the right place, and what a man could do to make a girl of nineteen enjoy herself and close her eyes, the rest would come all in good time, like everything else. Yes, there, said Rosa, and now stay there, and be nice to me and think what I'd like, because this is my birthday present now you're a real man, and Heinrich thought it was exactly the right birthday present for him and said he wanted to marry her on the spot. What on earth are you talking about, asked Rosa, taking this as one of his exaggerations, closed her eyes, noticed when he was unsuccessful with some small detail now and then, but gave herself up to him, for what he said was one thing and what his hands were doing was something else again. Are you disappointed, she had asked as they went home long after dark, picking the grass out of their hair and clothes, but Heinrich had said no, taking his slight disappointment as a promise or an invitation, for next time *he* would prove himself to *her* there behind the bushes, and he had both guessed and failed to imagine what it was like beneath her hands: such bliss.

When he found his mother in the kitchen he thought: She'll know I've been behind the bushes with Rosa just by looking at me, or she'll be able to tell from the smell on my fingers, but the only person who did notice anything, and as usual had no idea what it was all about, was good old Paul, who wondered why Heinrich kept sniffing his fingers and didn't know they smelled of Rosa, which to Heinrich that evening was the most delightful smell in the world.

That was the summer when his mother fell sick, or when the disease finally showed itself, leaving the first traces behind. Even over coffee and cakes at the silver wedding in June his mother had suddenly stood up and excused herself, leaving the room in the middle of her last good day, and in July she had a couple of breathless turns down in the hot laundry room, that was how it began, the cancer in her liver and pancreas was giving her trouble by then. In August, when Heinrich came home smelling as he had smelled only once before, back in Russia, even a suitable reprimand had been beyond her, and in September they had a visit from Heinrich's uncle in South Africa, who thought his mother needed a change, what was Heinrich doing with himself all day long, and that was how the idea of Africa came up.

But what would he do there with no training, asked his mother, and his uncle said: Yes, well, my blacks have no training either but there's no shortage of work, work enough for a lifetime. Well, why not, said Heinrich, and wanted to go straight off and tell Rosa all about it, but suddenly his mother was herself again and said Rosa was of no significance at all, he'd do better to sit down and listen to what his uncle was telling him. So his uncle started right in, telling Heinrich how he had believed in the future of asparagus-growing back in the year 1926, when he was a monk of the Order of the Holy Ghost in the Orange Free State, and planted the first little crowns in the soil of the mission station garden in Harrismith, praying away over them, only I'm afraid that one day women came along and interfered, and since I'm afraid it was in the form of your Aunt Felice that women interfered they write long articles in America about me and my blacks and the asparagus which doesn't make me rich, but not poor either, we can afford a passage from Southampton to Durban: that was his offer.

Think it over, Heinrich's uncle had said before flying back to Africa, and keep an eye on your mother, all of you, you still need her, and they all agreed and did think it over, and soon they had other anxieties, for the pain in their mother's bowels was getting worse and worse, and when even a pilgrimage to the shrine of St Corbinian in Freising did no good they took their mother to hospital to die in the middle of November.

Heinrich was the only one of them who would have nothing to do with the pilgrimage and stayed at home, where he dreamed of his Rosa and how he would show her everything in the evening, show her what to do to make a man of twenty-one close his eyes with bliss, and the rest would come all in good time, like everything else. Yes, there, said Heinrich, when she was there at last, and he did not think of any mother or father, he paid attention to her hands, her clever, busy hands, and Rosa was very serious and immediately recognized every hesitation, every sensitive place, perhaps she was keeping something from him, or alternatively it was love which made her so tender and wise.

They just had time to throw the bedspread over the bed when Heinrich's father came into the room, pale with anxiety, asking him to put together a few things for the hospital, and his mother, bent double with pain, said nothing at all, just looked at the girl Rosa and at Heinrich, the clothes they had straightened in a great hurry and the heat in their faces, and she was not angry, and it was because she was not angry and didn't mind their doing something of which, in her heart of hearts, she deeply disapproved, that Heinrich knew she had reached the end.

Up to the last he took her fruit juice and fruit from distant lands, but towards the end she was quiet and grey and had no appetite, and didn't want to listen to anyone, what did the living know of the hard work she had dying, and yes, she liked to have them close, but when matters are really serious you would rather be alone, brace yourself and get it over with, and whatever happens next may not be like paradise, but at least it must be better than this hell.

Next morning his uncle gave him a brief introductory lecture on the reasons for his success as a market gardener, the plants and flowers he raised in his hothouses and the fields stretching behind them as far as the eye could see, fields where asparagus grew in the African spring, those were the two sources of his wealth, he called the people whom he paid to work for him his black children, and when they all greeted him and the guest with him too, he always knew them by name. Basically, we use the hothouses to grow anything that flowers and gives people pleasure, depending on the time of year, said Heinrich's uncle, and I'd say we don't live badly on it. I've invested my hopes in asparagus for a long time now, and it depends on three things: first, light soil with a good humus content; second, regular irrigation; third, patience and yet more patience. About fifteen thousand crowns, that's the best number, you put them in at a depth of some twenty centimetres, and then you have to wait till the end of October or the beginning of November to begin harvesting. You'll see what a laborious business it is for my people, walking slowly along the mounds looking out for the little tips, then cutting them and bringing the fresh asparagus to the light of day as lovingly as if it were a little black baby, it's so delicate and easily injured, and the whole thing has to be done twice a day until Hallowe'en. We don't have a very long time to get rich in, said Heinrich's uncle, adding, about the blacks: you'll get used to them in time, they're human beings too, and had Heinrich ever seen a black person before, well, yes, he had. There had been a few around in the Paradies district of Jena in the summer of forty-five, when the victorious Americans were still in control of all central Germany, and although there were some black men among them everyone thought a golden age was dawning. Yes, a mistake, that, said Heinrich's uncle, and Heinrich nodded, realizing that there were at least two kinds of blacks, some who cut asparagus in the African spring in the fields belonging to a lapsed German monk, and others who liberated the country from Adolf Hitler and his gang.

What do you want me to do here, asked Heinrich, and his uncle instantly came up with things for him to do, for instance the almond and peach trees needed pruning, and then there were all kinds of odd jobs to be going on with, things it was difficult to get around to: weeding, watering, applying fertilizer, replacing a broken pane in a hothouse or mending a hose, not to mention various repairs in the house or on the car, shopping for your aunt, these, more or less, were his uncle's suggestions. Yes, fine, said Heinrich, feeling that it was fine for a start, but he didn't plan to grow old doing all these piffling little jobs.

He wrote home to say he'd arrived safely and the food was good, but he hadn't seen Stella yet, she was away on a trip, he wrote, but when she's back again we'll be driving over to visit, it's only fifty kilometres, that's nothing. So he worked, and was surprised to find he wasn't worn out in the evening after spending the whole day hanging around the hothouses, keeping his eyes open for this, that and the other, seeing the dirt accumulate under his fingernails until washing his hands wouldn't get rid of it.

About ten days passed like this, and on the afternoon of the tenth day his uncle's sister came over with her Alfred and his brown Stella, who was five months pregnant and didn't spare the visitor from Germany so much as a glance. She doesn't like me, thought Heinrich, surprised to see that she had taken against him from the first, and held Alfred's hand while they had coffee and cakes, or stroked her stomach and went into raptures about the trip they had just taken to the Kruger Park: he might not have been there at all. Yes, it was a good time, said his uncle's sister Maria, who had left Germany quarter of a century earlier because of her illegitimate son Alfred, who now had a wife as slender as a gazelle, with breasts as round and lovely as the hills of her home in Tongaland. We'll see, thought Heinrich, waiting for her to notice him and say hello or ask him a question, but in the end it was Alfred who asked one, what had he found that he didn't expect here in lovely South Africa, so Heinrich said his aunt's braised beef, which made pregnant Stella smile. It was a start.

From early May onwards he sometimes went along when his uncle visited outlying farms owned by various friends and acquaintances, to whom Heinrich's uncle enthusiastically recommended asparagus-growing, why not have a go themselves, he could supply asparagus crowns and the benefit of his experience, and chemical methods of controlling the principal enemies of all asparagus growers, the asparagus fly *Platyparea poeciloptera* and the asparagus beetles *Crioceris duodecimpunctata* and *Crioceris asparagi*.

Heinrich liked to hear his uncle praising the advantages of the South African asparagus varieties over their European counterparts, pointing out that asparagus had always been a vegetable for kings and emperors, while it also made a good decorative plant and was useful as foliage in bouquets of cut flowers, you could easily make a large profit from a comparatively small area of land. Heinrich's uncle knew and talked persuasively to his potential customers among the farms of the provinces of Transvaal and the Orange Free State up to a day's drive from his own, so they spent the night in a motel now and then, visiting Stella and Alfred and Aunt Maria for a coffee on the way home.

He still wasn't really getting anywhere with Stella. Her replies to his questions were civil but brief, for instance when he asked about her family background, why her father had emigrated to South Africa in 1933, how he met Stella's mother and had the good fortune to hang on to her, such were his questions. Stella never let him see whether she was picking up the message, whether she even felt pleased that he was taking a great deal of trouble over her, just as Alfred once did, some time ago now. Heinrich liked the fact that he didn't know what pleased Stella, and he liked the way she remained very aloof, particularly in front of Alfred, who never took his eyes off her for a second, a blind man could see that. He and Stella were alone on only one occasion, when she was standing in her mother-in-law's kitchen – her mother-in-law who had fled from Germany years ago – slicing fresh peaches, apricots, apples, pears and grapes into a bowl, and said: Here, you can squeeze me some lemon juice if you like, if you have the time, and Heinrich was glad that she had thawed out, but then she ignored him as if it had been a bad idea.

His uncle said: Yes, Stella, we had to get used to her too, and now here she is carrying our dear Alfred's baby, they got married in 1949 just in time, before the new laws came into force. She's very nice, said Heinrich, acting as if he had merely registered her name and adding that he had something else to ask about asparagus, to which his uncle said: Go ahead, ask away, but mind you don't drive off the road those last few kilometres, you're a very fast driver.

Over the following days and weeks Heinrich was to return to his ideas about asparagus repeatedly, but at this time, driving off after their second or third visit to Stella, he was still cautious and disguised them as questions: Did his uncle have any connections with the big hotels on the coast, why not send Heinrich to sound them out some time, there was promising business waiting there, after all, or the asparagus could be exported to Europe or overseas, why not? Good God, what an idea, said his uncle, refusing to listen, Heinrich had better keep his feet on the ground, his dear nephew hadn't even earned his ticket to South Africa yet, what did he think he was doing, giving his uncle advice, or do we look as if we're on the breadline? I know other people on the breadline, or has your father, my brother, won the lottery? There you are, then. And for God's sake don't tell your aunt any of your wild fancies or she'll take ideas into her head. Ideas? said Heinrich, unable to imagine what kind of ideas they might be, since his aunt had given him the impression of being a woman with her feet on the ground. The long days without his uncle and without distant Europe probably depressed her sometimes, but she had her nephew now, her impatient nephew who wanted to prove something to himself and her and everyone who knew him, perhaps she had some good advice. Well, for one thing, he'd better keep his hands off Stella, said his aunt, do you think I haven't noticed you watching her, challenging her to do heaven knows what in front of us all?

I'm doing no such thing, said Heinrich, I'm not thinking about her at all, maybe I'm not even thinking about any other girl.

What a pity, said his aunt.

Oh, I don't know.

Well, I do. You think of nothing but making a pile of money, and you think of your Rosa, but I know what's good for you.

This was the first piece of advice his aunt gave him: not to make trouble for himself over a girl like Stella. The second piece of advice was not to try making helpful suggestions to his uncle, if he had an idea why not just follow it up himself, hire a car in town, drive to the coast to see how the land lay some time when his uncle wasn't at home. All right, that's what I'll do, said Heinrich, and waited until his uncle was going to Cape Town for a few days at the end of June, and expressed no surprise that his nephew from Germany wasn't coming, since he didn't seem particularly interested in flowers and the big trade fairs where his uncle annually showed the latest varieties he had bred.

Off you go, then, said his aunt when his uncle set out one morning, Heinrich will keep me company, or he might like to go to the sea for a few days, he's still young and ought to see something of the world, good luck and have a safe journey. Yes, have a safe journey, said Heinrich, and stayed behind another night himself, seeing his aunt go sleep-walking through the house at three in the morning, but when he called out to her by name, with a question, he stopped short, for she neither saw nor heard him, but was in a different world.

Heinrich did not achieve much on his first and last drive through the huge, wide land of South Africa, but he saw the sea and the harbour town of Durban, where there were several large hotels and a few chefs or hotel managers who said they'd think it over, considered the royal vegetable expensive but delicious, talked about their favourite recipes and their reminiscences of the European cities where they had trained or lived, those were the days.

When he got back all his aunt wanted to know was whether he'd gone sea-bathing, had he been thinking of Stella; he had, but he had not driven north up the coast from Durban to Tongaland, where she came from. Good boy, said his aunt, and said (or claimed) that Stella had already complained of Heinrich and the way he looked at her and his manner, but she had complained only as a joke, and his father had written mentioning that girl Rosa who seemed to be in love with him, why didn't he talk about her, or wasn't he sure of himself? Yes, no, I mean I don't really know, said Heinrich, and let her stroke the hair back from his face while she asked questions just like the Belgian, but in contrast to the Belgian's questions Heinrich didn't mind hers as she probed his mind, trying to find out what he was like as her nephew, as a young man, and he found he could tell her all about it: he could tell her exactly what had happened with his Rosa when his parents went on the pilgrimage, or at least hint at it, but in such a way that she understood and nodded, put her hands on his cheeks and laid his head in her lap, where he fell asleep.

Early evening came, Heinrich's uncle still wasn't back, and when Heinrich woke up she took him into her little den where she did the ironing and read books, and showed him an old English atlas of 1911, in which she went for lengthy, complicated journeys in her mind now and then, longing for European rain. Heinrich felt rather embarrassed to have her showing him all this, and then she opened a drawer and took out some old photographs and letters from before she was twenty, when she had gone out with a soldier for a few months, a soldier who was so stupid that he shot himself in the stomach one day by accident. My Jim, said Heinrich's aunt, he was so stupid, so much in love, he shot himself one day while he was cleaning his gun, and I'd so much rather he had gone on writing me his loving, clever, daring letters, because he was brilliant at writing loving, clever, daring letters. You remind me of him, said Heinrich's aunt, but mind, I haven't told you any of this, I don't want to upset your uncle, it was all long before his time.

I'd have fancied you then, Heinrich thought or even felt bold enough to say, meaning her fine hair in two plaits, her eyes as brown as hazelnuts or earth dark with the rain. He ought to have thought about you less, your Jim, he said, and his aunt said they'd have gone to France together, she and Jim, but of course nothing came of that with the stupid bullet in his stomach.

Oh dear, Europe, she said. Do you think I'll ever get back there?

America would be nice.

Oh yes, America.

You could afford it, you and my uncle.

Ah well, your uncle, I think he forgot about me long ago.

A year ago, in Ulmenstrasse on the long evenings of February 1952, Heinrich had been talking of going to America, because one day he'd have the money, jump into a plane, leave them all behind and come back with his fortune made. I only have to ring Colonel Reynolds and say I want a ticket, Heinrich had claimed, but then he couldn't find the telephone number or reach Colonel Reynolds, and moreover there was Rosa all of a sudden, with her soft places and her promises, just the kind of thing he liked, never mind if they cost him something.

Out of the few hundred marks he earned as an unskilled labourer with Schott he could treat her to the cinema now and then, or the new ice-cream parlour in the market-place, and what was left over, after subtracting what he paid for bed and board at home, was just enough for a few cigarettes.

Even before the six of them moved into their new flat in Ulmenstrasse, Mother had taken a piece of paper one evening and noted down on the left-hand side of it, in front of them all, the money coming in: Father's salary, what his sons Heinrich and Theodor were earning, the loan from the works, over five thousand marks, the small amount of money they still had from the East, and on the right-hand side she listed household expenses for the flat, food and clothes, plus a new cupboard and a table and the beds they needed, because you can't, unfortunately, take a cupboard and a table and three beds with you when you get away over the green border, and then there was their father's daily cigar, and the radio they all wanted, with luck they could find a second-hand set.

So that's the situation, Heinrich's mother had said, and they all knew it was not a comfortable one, and the family had to take money from Heinrich and Theodor, we need every pfennig. Theodor had better look for a place of his own, said Mother, and then there'll be a room for us and the girls, a room for Paul and Heinrich, a bathroom and the living-room cum kitchen, that'll have to do for us. Yes, that will do, their father had said, and that evening Heinrich said: I'll be off soon anyway, when I'm twenty-one this summer at the latest.

They had moved into Ulmenstrasse at the beginning of February, and Father had debts of some ten thousand and had left his house behind in the Eastern zone, but when he fell into yet another gloomy mood Mother was cheerful and determined as ever, calling him an old skinflint, or do you really want to go back to the East where yes, we had almost everything we wanted, but at what a price! It wasn't as bad as you make out, said Father, and Mother said: It was so bad I just can't describe it, and although I have little or nothing here (I mean, this place amounts to nothing), I can sleep and breathe freely, as I could in the mountains, or in the first years on the Wilhelmshöhe before the war, but time never turns back.

We have to make up our minds, she said.

You made up your mind long ago, said Heinrich's father, so now we're here, and here we must stay and make the best of it.

In those first weeks Father had invited all manner of people from Schott to the living-room cum kitchen on Sunday afternoons, where they talked about the good old days over coffee and cakes, with a cigar later, telling each other how one man had come over to the West very early and another quite late in the day, but so far no one had regretted it. This sleepy little town on the river Isar wasn't such a bad place, except that the business of the new factory wasn't decided yet, since the city fathers see us from Schott as proletarians, more or less, and they don't want their town to be proletarian.

I probably won't be here after this summer, Heinrich told Rosa, at the point where he knew her name, and they both thought each other quite nice, but when they secretly imagined this, that or the other they got no further than a walk along the river-bank. She was a good two years younger than Heinrich, and addressed him by the formal *Sie* pronoun when he first pushed his bike over to her, and he liked the way they called each other *Sie* and acted as if love was as serious and as dangerous as in the cinema. I don't expect you'll be in this town much longer, she said, having been born there herself and knowing every corner of it, so he told her his story, pleased with every question, pleased that, as he noticed, she had questions enough to last seven days and seven nights, which was the good part of every beginning, the way the questions never ran out, and the waiting, the venturing, the doubting every word spoken or left unspoken.

They began in this very slow and equivocal way, always with the formal *Sie*, and Heinrich liked the way it all went so slowly and equivocally and politely, because once they began addressing each other as *du* the rest was only a matter of time. I dreamed of you, said Rosa the first time she called him *du*, and Heinrich said: Yes, I know about that, I even dream about you in the day-time with my eyes open, that's the point we've got to. Oh no, we haven't, said Rosa, to which Heinrich said: I dream bad things, lovely things, and suddenly she turned shy. I'm only nineteen, said Rosa, who was indeed only nineteen but perhaps didn't mean to be taken entirely seriously, and she let him kiss her and promised him something, but said she was afraid he would have to wait another few weeks.

In her first and only letter to him, written in the middle of July, Rosa said: I haven't heard from you at all, do write some time, we're all waiting for a letter, me too. Or have you forgotten me? Marie says he'll be very busy, he just doesn't get round to it, but I know better: I'm afraid you're no letter-writer. Do you at least think of me, the way I think of you when I'm standing in the shop from Monday to Saturday running myself into the ground as I help customers try on shoes, I have plenty of time then. I remember your hands, that first kiss which missed, the way my stomach contracted when I thought this minute, or in a few moments, he'll think something up, and it will begin, or end, here and here, and then I close my eyes and let myself be deceived as usual, love from Rosa.

Her letter had seemed to Heinrich like something from the past and very far away when he read it one morning, or rather skimmed it, among flowering hydrangeas in one of the hothouses furthest from the house, and then he put it in his trouser pocket with his earth-stained fingers, kept it for later, didn't feel like answering it. Heinrich got his hands dirty in the hothouses all August and September, planting and hoeing, and he sometimes made long speeches to his uncle, trying to convince him of the merit of his own plans, which featured large seaside hotels and steamed asparagus as part of every other dish on the hand-written menus of the elegant restaurants. Still dreaming asparagus dreams, are you, said his uncle now and then, and his aunt said: Come along, I've got a freshly baked cake and I've laid the table for coffee in the garden, work can wait but your aunt can't. Don't be cross, said his aunt, comforting him with these afternoons in the garden, and she gave him comforting glances too, and once or twice spoke to his uncle (in vain), and finally had the idea of sending an express letter to Sinnhuber the Bundestag deputy, who never replied or never read the letter, while whoever did read it must have thought importing South African asparagus a crazy notion.

At the beginning of October, when the fruit trees came into blossom in Heinrich's first and last African spring, when their fragrance wafted in through the open window until long after midnight, his uncle went to Johannesburg for a few days as he did annually, to recruit a busload of seasonal workers from the townships for the forthcoming harvest, staying away three nights after he had left this time, and on the third night Heinrich's aunt got into bed with him, mistaking him for someone else. It alarmed Heinrich to find his aunt sharing his bed in her sleep, confusing him with someone else and putting her hand on his member as if he were indeed someone else, someone from the past, her lover from the days before she met his uncle, about a thousand years ago.

What's the matter with you, Heinrich asked the sleeping woman, who might not be asleep at all or might just be dreaming she was asleep, and who kept her hand on his member as if she must watch over it or take care of it, as if she knew nothing of the longings she aroused in him, tormenting him by keeping him in suspense. Heinrich half feared and half hoped that she too was just waiting and listening, the way he himself was listening in the dark, holding his breath, his eyes open, wondering, weighing it up, coming to a decision and placing her hand on the sheet beside him, and in the morning his aunt had gone back to her own room, and knew nothing at all about it.

Around noon next day Heinrich's uncle came back with a bus full of black women workers, singing and glad to have been picked, delighted with the huts, ten or twenty of them sharing each, and with the certainty of a job until the end of December, a job they either knew already or could picture to themselves, for some of them had no idea how to cut asparagus. They'll learn, said his uncle, who valued experience but liked a pretty face too, so he used to go round the huts the evening before harvest began, indulging himself. I don't mind, said Heinrich's aunt, who was acting as if nothing had happened, and Heinrich himself acted as if nothing had happened, feeling sorry he had not been bolder and looking for some sign that she forgave him, or else was

187

encouraging him, in which case he wouldn't be sure what to make of it.

One morning he did say he'd been dreaming of Stella's baby, and he had dreamed of his aunt and uncle too, but it was all confused. Yes, said his aunt, blushing because he kept looking at her hands as if she were not a sleep-walker but some kind of teacher, for that was what he dreamed of now: that she would visit him again in her sleep and teach him what no waking woman could, putting her hands on his member, and then he would wake her up and beg her for it, or give her what she wanted, depending which way round it was.

The day after the black women arrived they began harvesting, and Heinrich was to do a proper job of work at last as well, so his uncle took him out into the fields early in the morning and taught him the difficult art of cutting asparagus. You haven't got the hang of it yet, he said, and wondered aloud why he was spending so much time with his aunt: as if you weren't a grown man. Asparagus is like glass, said his uncle, adding that you had to see it and feel it and guess where it was, because once it was really showing above ground you were left with lower-quality spears with the tips turning purple. Your aunt was a good asparagus cutter soon after your war in Europe, when we were just beginning here and the work was endless, we often went out together and made a game of it, but your aunt always won, she noticed every spear I'd missed, carefully uncovered the tip and put her hand deep in the earth, freed the spear from all the soil around it and cut it with the knife at its deepest point, brought it carefully to the light of day. It takes a few days or weeks to learn how, said his uncle, my women will be happy to help you, or ask your aunt, she can still do it better than anyone. Heinrich would very much have liked to ask her if she would come out in the fields again for his sake, but he was too proud or too shy, didn't ask his uncle's women either, but just watched most of the time. After four hours he hadn't even cut five kilos, and they stopped for a rest, the women with their brightly coloured head-scarves or sun-hats fetched water from the hothouses or ate the fruit they had brought with them, melons, peaches and apricots, as if they were all living in paradise.

You poor, good, tired boy, said his aunt, when he brought her his asparagus that first evening, like a present for her alone, and she took it and peeled the ends of the stems and cooked a kilo or two to be eaten with ham and new potatoes, trickling hot butter over the asparagus and biting the tip off each spear first (a habit of hers). The first asparagus is always the best, said his uncle, and his aunt said you just had to be patient and keep your eyes open, and then everything would come your way of its own accord. Really? asked Heinrich, intending a double meaning, and his aunt said: Yes, really, and perhaps she intended a double meaning as well, or was putting him to the test (naming her conditions), and all the time his uncle was eating Heinrich's asparagus, wondered what was up, or perhaps not wondering, for his mind was still on the past day and the first big delivery for the Krugersdorp market: they weren't doing badly for a start.

Heinrich felt with increasing frequency that he and his aunt were conducting secret conversations at every opportunity about sleep-walking and about the possibilities of the nights, either that or he was just imagining it all, brooding for a whole morning in vain over a look or a silence, and when he touched her in the kitchen as if accidentally, and kept close to her instead of moving away, she took no notice, or only as an aunt would notice, for after all he was still a child to her.

At the end of the first month of the harvest season Stella came over with her Alfred, and as soon as she arrived she began laughing at Heinrich, saying he'd never earn a living cutting asparagus, the spears he took out of the soil were so damaged, their tips spoilt by the light. His aunt stood up for him, saying he wasn't used to working in the fields, his hands were trained for lathes and in glassworking skills, he had a man's hands, why did they think almost all the workers his uncle employed in the fields were women, it was in the nature of women but seldom in the nature of men to be gentle but firm.

Heinrich would have liked to laugh too, at his cousin Alfred, for instance, and the way he couldn't keep his hands off the pregnant Stella, as if she were his personal possession. If you only knew, all of you, thought Heinrich, thinking no one was as beautiful as his aunt that afternoon, for she had had a life before his uncle, and with luck would have one after him, so from now on he left the fields on the sly in the early afternoon and went to join her.

At the end of November she said: It's not right for you to be leaving the fields behind your uncle's back, to say nothing of your reasons for it. Look, my hands are old, the first dark age-spots on them came when you arrived, you're still young, you don't realize that your uncle is losing faith in you, and in my own way so am I. I don't see you staying here long, said his aunt, but your uncle will get over it, and you certainly will, young Heinrich.

Oh, but I am staying, said Heinrich.

Yes, well, you can stay a little longer.

Days later, on the journey home, Heinrich still couldn't have said exactly where he made his mistake, whether he had been too hesitant or too forceful, but you'll learn with time and your first girl, she had said, and the day when you do know it you'll be a man. It had been the middle of December when his aunt told him this, and in the middle of December it still seemed as if she would have Heinrich there for ever, watching the blacks working in the fields, mingling with the brightly clad women for a few hours if he felt like it or his aunt couldn't do with him just then, digging and cutting and pulling the spears out of the ground until he had twenty kilos or so, on occasion even thirty or forty.

You'll learn yet, said his aunt, who was not so sure about his staying, and not a week later came the business of those two afternoons when he crept into his uncle's and aunt's bedroom and looked at her as if she were his captive prey, for there she lay with her eyes open, her body spread out like a lover's, and when it had gone on long enough she dismissed him. Later, he thought: I can't think what got into me just to leave her lying there, I can't think what got into me to send me back, failing to hear my uncle, because there he suddenly was standing in the doorway and found Heinrich's aunt with her body spread out like a lover's, except that it wasn't Heinrich's uncle she was waiting for and perhaps not Heinrich either. Get out of here this minute, whispered his uncle, and then she could be heard talking for a long time, and after supper, over coffee and cognac, his aunt told Heinrich he must pack before Christmas and leave the house for Durban, where they would book him a third-class passage to Southampton tomorrow, unfortunately they just didn't suit each other. A severe disappointment, said his uncle, adding not a word after that, and his aunt said, as if to soothe all of them: You have to be born to it, you see, and if you aren't, well, there are other things you can do, no reason for him to feel ashamed.

After this incident Heinrich spent all of four days in his bedroom, and then confirmation of his booking came and they parted on the morning of the twenty-second, when his aunt was already waiting in the black Chevrolet with the engine running, to make sure the goodbyes were quick and painless, and no one had to search for many words. Well then, said Heinrich's uncle, and Heinrich said: Well then, all the best, to which his uncle replied: Make something of yourself, short cuts aren't always a good idea, but nor is the longest way round either.

So he went all the way back to Durban with his aunt, and when they arrived there were still three hours to go, they were both hungry but didn't eat anything, and repeated almost the same parting words. Well then, said Heinrich's aunt, and Heinrich said: Well then, and all the best, to which his aunt replied: Make something of yourself, write and tell me when you have, or just send a postcard with your name, I'll be expecting it. Heinrich would have liked to tell her how he disliked her making herself out an old woman to him, but then he decided you couldn't say that kind of thing to an aunt, and it was as her nephew (not as someone who had been watching her lying in her bedroom) that he waved down to her for a while from the rail, and saw her turn away and walk back into her old life.

He spent the first part of the voyage almost entirely on his plank bed, as if he had been doing hard labour for the past few months, reading about the events of 17 June in East Berlin in an American magazine or trying in vain to write a letter to his aunt, regretting the absence of any travelling companion, leaving the cabin only for meals. Christmas passed, and so did New Year, and except for a few tables with seasonal decorations in the restaurant they were the same as any other day. He sent his father a telegram from Cape Town, saying he would be back at the beginning of January, unfortunately he'd had some health problems, Merry Christmas and Happy New Year, love, Heinrich.

From her photographs, Heinrich would have put his aunt in her early forties, but then she told him one day that her fortieth birthday would be on the second Sunday of 1954, a birthday she was now celebrating without him, waiting, hoping that he would write. Dear Aunt, wrote Heinrich, stumbling over the word Aunt every time, tried using her first name, tried dear and beloved and bloody and horrible as terms for her, in turn, by then he was in Southampton and back in the smoke-filled pub where he had once sat with Jeff, and he wrote: Dear sleep-walker, I hope you will burn this. I'm in Southampton, in the England you love and miss. Best wishes on your fortieth birthday! Send me good wishes on my own some day! Be brave, regards to my uncle, tell him not to be angry, I fancy trying my luck as a salesman, and I fancy a slice of your cake too sometimes, I mention it just in passing.

He had exactly twenty marks in his pocket when he exchanged the last of his money in Brussels and caught a train going south, working out an explanation he could give, something wrong with his circulation, he'd say, and he was still young with the world before him, oh, and I'm to give you all warm regards from Aunt Felice.

7

So Heinrich served his years of apprenticeship in prison in Gera and Leipzig, when he became and remained a different man. To Rosa, who visited him once every six weeks, he just said: Prison's prison, the same everywhere, but you get used to it. Only you don't get used to the eternal thin cabbage soup and the rotten vegetables, slopping out and the creaking of the mattresses when everyone's jerking off so they can get to sleep, it takes a long time to get used to that. There are a lot of false friends in prison, so you always have to be on your guard against false friends among the screws or the inmates, people who'll punch you in the face when they're in a bad mood and laugh at you, you have to make sure you keep your mouth shut about it and think of some excuse that lets them off taking the blame. It was in Gera they beat me up, I was still stupid and talking big in Gera, as if I were a paying guest and the food wasn't up to scratch, or the bedclothes weren't as clean as in that hotel in Salzburg, do you remember, we'd just fallen in love and all we saw of Salzburg was from three in the afternoon onwards, because we didn't get up until then.

Rosa was allowed to stay a whole half an hour when she visited, and they sat with all the others in a badly overcrowded room telling each other what their lives were like, or whatever each thought it was safe to tell the other about a life which was such a mess, speaking in general terms, saying the children were being very good, and the things in the food parcels tasted delicious, praising each other for being so patient, saying nothing about the sudden incursion into their lives of a tenacious Karl or a Friedrich to populate their days and nights, someone there under the covers when it was cold, why bother about all that? They learned to spare each other in the weeks and months of the first and second years of his absence, when the children were growing up and remembered him as a kind of uncle.

Halfway through, at the beginning of April 1968, Heinrich was sick and feverish for a few days, but then he pulled himself together and celebrated the fifteen months now behind him with Karl and Gappy and the Bavarian, he had a good portion of dripping with crackling for everyone, and the pickled gherkins Rosa had bottled, and in the afternoon a mug of Western coffee from a packet sent by kind Paul or Constanze. Even the Floozie stayed for a while to celebrate, sitting on his bed filing his nails, but he was soon off again in the usual way, hanging around outside the storeroom next to the kitchen until evening, and anyone who stopped and gave him a little present knew the Floozie would do whatever he wanted and be patient and shameless about it, making no trouble afterwards.

Here's to Hampel who'll soon be out of here, and here's to the Floozie and his customers, said Gappy, who had lost his front teeth getting into a punch-up in the port of Rostock, and they all drank to that, each of them counting the days he had left to serve, but no one else could count them as quickly as Hampel. Young Karl, who had already been seen with the Floozie, had mugged an old lady years ago because he needed money for a ticket to Dresden to see his girlfriend, and Gappy was banged up for brawling in several pubs, while women were to blame for everything, as usual, in the Bavarian's case, it was because of a woman he'd gone to Halle in fifty-nine, and then he was bringing gold and silver rings and necklaces and brooches home for her, and not knowing how to pay for it all he dipped his fingers in the till of the People's Metalworks in Gotha a couple of times.

Gappy and the Bavarian seemed untroubled by the thought of their crimes, but slender young Karl often thought of writing to the old lady some day or paying her a visit, wondering whether he was still the same man as the Karl who knocked her down in the dark for a few marks, the thought would not let him rest. Go on, then, write to her, said Heinrich, and he thought people did remain more or less the same, but at those bad moments they're different, they don't know themselves and even later they never get to know themselves. Or forget it, he said, realizing that the idea of the Floozie kept preying on his mind, and the way young Karl had got in under the covers with him one night, when the Floozie was awake at once, asking in a whisper what he fancied. So what was it like? Heinrich had asked, and Karl had said: Good, almost like with a girl, a tight one or a virgin, at least, that's what you have to keep telling yourself, and how would we know what it's like for a girl?

It was a couple of days ago that Karl had told him about his night with the Floozie, and taking the girl's part himself, and ever since then he kept thinking of it, watching the Floozie whenever he cast glances at Karl, because he was casting glances at Karl himself. He would have laughed if anyone had said to him: Yes, you and Karl, who else? Even the evening before he let Karl in under the covers with him he would have laughed out loud at the idea, but then it all turned out perfectly simple, and it was a little like being with Rosa and a little like in Karl's story, only with the roles reversed. Heinrich was very quiet and silent and watchful, he hesitated the way he had once hesitated with Rosa, he sighed and he thought of Comrade Müller.

He had written to Comrade Müller a couple of times during the first year, but although he still struck the old, intimate note, teasing her and telling her in his own way how he adored her, he had never received a reply, and no doubt she was right not to reply asking about his life in jail, because it was monotonous and boring, or anyway couldn't be explained in the few lines allowed. He thought of her only very seldom, and then in the same way as he also thought of Rosa, or one of his other girls from the past whose little song he still knew, the smell of her armpits, her underclothes, what she said to him in the morning. Then he longed for those things, and became quite foolish with longing, and what it came down to in the end was either this business with Karl, or you deadened your mind, or you hanged yourself like fat Ludwig before Christmas, an incident which cast them all into gloom, and they had no appetite for a long time afterwards.

Do you think about me, asked Rosa on her twelfth visit, in the middle of March 1968, so for her sake he nodded and invented a couple of dreams featuring her, which pleased her. They had long ago worked out firm rules for their afternoons together, beginning as usual with Heinrich, they agreed that he mustn't give up hope, they wouldn't let things drift. I'll send in another ten petitions for early release if I have to, said Rosa, and she told him she was wondering whether to go and see his friend Gisela, someone like that was bound to have connections. Forget it, said Heinrich, and Rosa said: But she liked our little Eva, not to mention our silly big Heinrich. Eva, she added, had been very unhappy recently over trouble with a teacher who didn't want diligent little Eva to be treasurer of the Young Pioneers on account of her father, but the class did want her and elected her, and got their way.

And all because of me, said Heinrich, and Rosa said: Yes, and when anyone asked Eva what her father did for a living she had been told to say: He's a lorry driver, my father's a lorry driver and unskilled labourer, and just at the moment he's away on a job in the People's Republic of Yemen, or else she must say he's seriously ill, we all hope he'll soon be better. Think of her lying for you, said Rosa, not adding that she was still telling lies herself, inventing the most improbable of journeys for the benefit of nosy neighbours, by now she knew the names of all the states in Asia, Africa and Latin America which were friendly to East Germany, that clever-clogs Harms had been quite surprised.

Heinrich sometimes missed Harms, who of course wouldn't want any more to do with a man like Heinrich, but his colleague Opitz the liaison officer did, he came to ask this and that sometimes, when Heinrich and this Opitz would sit in the library discussing a headline in *Neues Deutschland*, or Opitz would look over his shoulder, checking the entries on the grey index cards. Heinrich took to regularly reading the newspapers laid out in the library, out of sheer boredom, or because he was thinking of Gisela, or because he wanted to please this man Opitz, so he knew the exact words in which Walter Ulbricht had rejected Chancellor Kiesinger's sugges-tion for a rapprochement on practical matters in a divided Germany, he thought of Theodor and what his brother Theodor would think of the rapprochement on practical matters in a divided Germany which Ulbricht had rejected, and of why it wasn't right for his brother to think of life in the other Germany with nothing but contempt, that was how his train of thought began. And he would laugh at Theodor and think of them over there when he read about the upheavals caused by the so-called student movement in West Germany, whereas we in our German Democratic Republic have the first Socialist constitution on German soil, and we have treaties of friendship, co-operation and mutual support with half Europe, we have books from all periods stacked to the ceiling in our prisons, more than you could read in a lifetime, you just remember that.

Even Gisela would have been surprised to see all the books he read in the library these days, for instance spending an afternoon leafing through *The Eighteenth of Brumaire* or *British Rule in India*, dipping into *On the Idea of a United States of Europe*, and *One Step Forward, Two Steps Back*, because he liked the title. He liked to remember that Gisela and Vladimir had quoted Marx and Lenin too, and so had his Lyusya years ago, and just think how surprised they would all have been by the new Heinrich with his Marx and his Lenin and those guides and philosophers of the German working class Grotewohl and Pieck and Ulbricht.

Rosa kept telling him: You must study when you come out, for instance you could train to be a good civil engineer, then you could build roads and bridges for the country, you could build your round little Rosa a house. This was because she still hadn't given up hope, and had taken to sending long wish-lists to the West again, ordering expensive things from the catalogues of the big mail-order firms for herself and the children, though heaven knew where the money came from.

She must have someone else, said Karl, adding that he was sorry, but he could sometimes wish she did have someone else.

What things you say, said Heinrich, who hadn't really been paying attention to him so far, fancy saying a thing like that.

I'm not saying the worst of it, said Karl.

As bad as that?

Oh yes, Heinrich, as bad as that.

Rosa had drawn up three wish-lists for the family back in the West. The first, sent in early January, was still quite modest: 1 nylon anorak for Heinrich, 1 kg red knitting wool, 1 pair black shoes with straps, 3 pairs socks, green, red and pale blue (size 37), 1 pair brown walking shoes (size 39), seven and a half metres curtain material, 1 bag plastic clothes pegs, 1 plastic washing line, 1 shopping basket, 1 turquoise cushion, 1 kg feathers to stuff a pillow, 1 wicker chair, that was what she wanted, what she needed, without it she'd have to put the children into a Home, and everyone knew what became of children in Homes, for instance Heinrich's friend Karl had spent most of his life in Homes like that.

I know it's not easy for you, wrote Rosa at the end of February 1968, but we really do need them, and as she was by now experienced in sending wishes and making out orders she divided her squared paper into two columns, one containing numbers of items and details of metres or grams, the other listing things not available in East Germany: 1 pair white Romika gum-boots (size 38), 1 Knirps umbrella with nylon cover (multi-coloured), 1 silk headscarf (bright green), 5 metres kitchen curtaining (blue check or red), 1 Rowenta automatic toaster, 1 bread slicer, 2 pairs latex knee-length socks with decorative border, 1 bottle Seborin anti-dandruff hair lotion, 1 bottle 4711, 1 jar shoe-cream (white), 250 g coffee, any brand. We can afford it, was all Rosa would say, and Heinrich replied: Yes, but how, wondering if they'd come into money over in the West, a legacy from some uncle in America believed to have disappeared or something like that. You'll be surprised, said Rosa, just wait till you're home again, and then Heinrich thought what that would be like, and refrained from asking about the bottle of anti-dandruff hair lotion and whether there was some man in the flat who needed it, or was it for Rosa herself or the children, after all, what business was it of his?

Is anything the matter with Father, asked Heinrich, noticing that recently she hesitated when he asked about his father, and he wondered whether his father was back in hospital, or puffing away at cigars at home in his mean wife Gertrud's company, or marching up and down the stairs on bad days until he was exhausted, but it would be the small hours of the morning before exhaustion really set in. I hope nothing's the matter with Father, said Heinrich, and Rosa said (but very hesitantly): No, why should there be, he's bright as a button, spends half the day down by the river ship-spotting as usual, and when the sun shines he looks at his reflection in the shoes he polishes with cigar ash.

I'll be so glad when you're back again, she said, and she had made a third list which she knew off by heart, like all the others, and which she recited to him as if it were a long poem, or a song you might sing in the morning while doing the laundry or on your way to the shops: 2 jars Nivea Cream,

1 bottle eau-de-cologne, 1 nylon dressing-gown size 42–44 (pink or pale blue with white lace trim), 2 sleeveless nylon overalls (blue and green), 1 pair each summer sandals sizes 37 and 39 (white), 2 pairs knee-length socks (plain with border), 1 Nyltest shirt (white), 2 bow ties, 2 lengths Nyltest fabric each 3 metres (pale blue and pink), 1.5 metres trouser fabric (pale grey), 2 metres jacket fabric (blue), 1 fashion magazine with dressmaking patterns, 2.20 metres women's suiting (honey-coloured) with buttons and lining material, and 3 Orion pullovers size 44 in lemon yellow, bottle green and cornflower blue.

When she had left Heinrich thought: I don't really believe in the man with the hair lotion and the two bow ties to wear with the blue jacket, or perhaps they're for me when I'm expected home, but I'm not ready yet, for that was what always crossed his mind when she talked about the future and his new life outside: he thought he hadn't yet come to terms with himself and his past, and Karl with his glowing eyes and his body like that of a hundred-metre sprinter or a high-jumper after his last attempt.

Karl had arrived shortly after the New Year, and since Heinrich was still new, and didn't trust Gappy and the Bavarian and the others, they had got together and talked, telling each other what their trials had been like (short), why they had been sentenced and for how long. Gappy in particular had not liked it when they got together, occupying the two middle bunks and discussing their girlfriends, speaking from one bunk to another, while the others just heard the names and when they'd done it: as if Paradise was only a few days off or a few buildings away. Shut up, Hampel, do we have any secrets from each other, Gappy would say, sticking out a leg to trip Heinrich when food was being given out, or another time an elbow, but after a while you pulled yourself together and shared things, not just the parcels but stories of the old days too, and the women you'd had in the past, and which of them you had unfortunately had only briefly or not at all. Come on, Hampel, tell us about your red-headed Bella when she sang, let's hear about prudish Anna and Gerda, and Heinrich would tell them what it had been like with his red-headed Bella and with Anna and with Gerda, and when they still hadn't heard enough he invented a few more for their benefit, and with luck that gave them all enough to think about overnight, keeping their thoughts to themselves as they dropped off to the sound of the creaking mattresses, when would this wretched life ever be over?

Heinrich's trial had been at the end of November, by which time he had been in custody on remand for over a year and the sentence came as something settled and familiar: two and a half years without parole for *speculative hoarding of goods*, together with *fraud prejudicial to personal or private property*, in fact he was getting off quite lightly. Heinrich scarcely had time to say goodbye to anyone before they brought him into court, and no sooner was he sitting at the front of that tall, stately and pitiless courtroom than they were sending him down for the famous thousand days, saying he had better use the time to think and improve himself, the state and its elected judges were kindly but stern, it sounded almost like what good old Harms had said at the start.

The trial lasted an hour or slightly longer, and then they took him back to a cell for the night, and next morning, around seven, they put him in a police van without any breakfast and drove him to Leipzig. The van had four windowless cabins or cages, with a smooth plastic wall to the left and a door with a spy-hole on the right, and the occupants sitting there probably being watched included, besides Heinrich, two men convicted of robbery with breaking and entering, and a woman from near Karl-Marx-Stadt who had murdered a child. Heinrich looked only briefly at the white container on the lorry, which was painted to look like a laundry van to disguise it and deceive the public, it even had an address and telephone number painted on it, but the prisoners who spent the next few hours in it had no addresses or telephone numbers, with luck mankind would be spared their presence for good, or perhaps, like Heinrich, they still had the *old bourgeois consciousness*, weren't a part of Socialism, were strange to it or not yet at home with it, they were *rudiments of the old society* who would disappear in time or change with time, for instance, it wasn't too late for this man Hampel yet.

The drive from Gera to Leipzig lasted some six hours, although it should have taken an hour and a half at the most, but presumably they didn't want the prisoners in the cages working out the route, or else the cells in Leipzig wouldn't be vacated until nearly evening, or the driver was always choosing the narrowest streets and the minor roads for fear of the population's watchful eyes, stopping for a break every half hour, making a wide detour around Karl-Marx-Stadt or even Dresden, someone in Heinrich's situation had plenty of time on his hands anyway.

On arrival they all went through the double gates and along various long corridors, and they passed through the hands of the unfriendly warders, hoping for a good cell, and to be alone a good deal or in the company of people like Gappy and Karl and shy Anselm, he didn't even know them by name yet. New here, are you, right, lie down there and keep quiet, we want some sleep. That was how it began, and the very first night someone stole his little tin for cigarettes and the satchel Rosa had embroidered, it was only after that night that he got wise to what went on and was watchful and cautious, most of all he didn't trust the fat Saxon, for the fat Saxon was still alive then and thought nothing of a newcomer like Heinrich, he had the rope under his pillow already.

So what's our new friend's name? asked Gappy and the Bavarian. Hampel, he said, his name was Heinrich Hampel and he had a wife and three children, his dear wife's name was Rosa, she was going to the public prosecutor's office every few weeks and he'd be out of here in six months at the latest. Of course they laughed, and Heinrich didn't know if it was at the idea of his Rosa going to the public prosecutor's office, or at the name of Hampel, or because he hoped to be out of here soon, once he was out of here he'd begin all over again, but avoiding the old mistakes, and he would no longer be ignorant of Lenin (Gisela's Lenin).

He wanted to make himself useful straightaway and work in the library, or volunteer for building work, or for sports and Russian lessons in the evening, he knew about all this from Gera, in fact he had made quite a name for himself that way in Gera before he got his thousand days and knew it would be over in a thousand days at the latest, and if he tried hard and got into the good books of someone like Opitz he might save himself a few months. Yes, all right, Hampel, the library, Opitz had said, when Heinrich had asked about it in his first few days, ignoring the warnings of the others, because it was not well thought of for an inmate to go to such people and let them soft-soap you, but Heinrich had experience, didn't he, no harm in asking, and if he asks about you lot I'll tell him you like the food and the work and the cell, so what's the matter? Good management, Heinrich, I must say, the Stasi man had commented, and then he started on about the humanity of man, and work in general and work in a Socialist society in particular, so that Heinrich felt much flattered and was already subtracting the first few weeks.

Barely six months after Opitz had hailed Heinrich as a new man he heard from the prison governor's office, in mid-May, that he would be able to pack and walk out into freedom at the end of July at the latest, because they knew a little bit about him now, in future they wouldn't be taking their eyes off him in a hurry, so they didn't plan to drag things out any longer, they had great hopes of him, we see everyone, after all, and glad to, so let's forget the past.

It was a day before Rosa's thirteenth visit that Heinrich heard of his forthcoming release, and went to tell Karl the good news, but Karl couldn't welcome it straight off. What a shame, he said, so now it was all over, why had Heinrich never gone back to him, why was he avoiding him, yes, all over now. I'm afraid so, said Heinrich, thinking in his own way about Karl and their one night together, and why he didn't want anything of that kind to start and develop and get more than they could manage, although he himself wasn't sure why he felt like that. His thoughts always made a wide detour around that one night, but it was like making a wide detour around something very valuable, irretrievable, and one day he said: Come on, help me peel the last kilo of potatoes and then we'll go next door and I'll cheer you up. You don't mean it, said Karl, and Heinrich said: Yes, I do mean it, it's a mystery to me why I should feel afraid of you.

Next afternoon, when he was sitting in front of Rosa, he thought she must see just by looking at him that he had been with Karl, spending almost half an hour in the storeroom exploring the way to go about this new kind of love, but Rosa was drawing up another of her lists and saw no sign of their embraces on him. Unfortunately, she had also brought bad news: Heinrich was not, absolutely was not to be alarmed, but they'd found an ulcer the size of a tennis ball in her, sitting there in her uterus, and it mustn't be allowed to go on growing much longer. It's because you haven't slept with me for so long, said Rosa, and Heinrich said: But someone else visits you now and then, which she denied. Nobody visits, except sometimes Friedrich with his fine pianist's hands, she said, and sometimes he puts the children to bed and hasn't brought his own pyjamas, but when he stays and gets undressed, it's as if he were my brother.

I never could understand that: a man who fancies other men.

It's perfectly simple, you just have to imagine you're the woman, and everything about a man is strange and special for a woman, and well, you know the rest of it.

I've almost forgotten.

But you'll learn again, with me, I hope.

Not for the first time he told her how much she had changed, and when she said: Yes, but for the better, I have the grief and anxiety to thank for that, he couldn't think of anything to say, hoping it would be like the old days, he'd be bringing money in again and this new Rosa would stay at home with the children, just as they remembered from the past.

I don't suppose we'll miss any of this, he said, when the last few minutes had come, those last few minutes in which, as everyone knows, the most important things are said: that he would change for her sake, that he didn't need to change for her sake but he must for his own, as he was always promising her, and he felt like promising again now, she should just hear how they all believed in him, and praised him at work.

Good, said Rosa, and that was all, and for a moment it seemed to him that she had managed nicely without him for quite a while, and he sometimes felt she didn't need him any more, he might as well stay where he was, it was a kind of life, after all. Nonsense, said Rosa, and after a pause: It's just that I've made a life for myself too while you were away, that's what it is.

Are you looking forward to me coming back?

Of course, we're all looking forward to it. Evi is always asking: Am I going to have a new papa now, or is it still the old one? And I usually tell her: We won't know until he's home again, but if you're lucky it'll be a new one and the old one too.

You don't believe that.

I haven't given up hope.

Here in the prison they say I work hard enough for two, they won't want to let me go.

Yes, empty words, she said. I don't mean words, I mean action. And is a prison any place for action?

Yes and no.

Rosa said: They've shot a student over in West Germany.

To which Heinrich replied: And we still gang up with revanchists like that to send a joint team of athletes to the Olympics.

That's the way you're talking these days?

I'm talking that way because I've learnt my lesson.

I can't wait.

Six months earlier in Gera, Heinrich had been talking quite differently, for then he was still waiting for his trial. He had been waiting over a year already, and there still wasn't even the vague prospect of a date when one day they sent along a lawyer with glasses and a briefcase, the trial would be held before Christmas, did he know what he might expect, it was possible that a few of the thousand days he'd been told about might be subtracted.

Everyone had warned him against lawyers who promised you the earth, and what they'll do for the likes of us if all goes well, but they're really all in cahoots with the judges and the public prosecutors. It was all fixed ages ago, just how long they'll keep you shut up here or over in Leipzig, don't let them fuck you up, they all lie like crazy, same as we'll all lie like crazy if it does us any good, what do you expect?

Heinrich had nurtured few hopes of the forthcoming trial, and what difference did it make whether he got a few weeks more or less? Only Rosa had nurtured hopes, because when it was all over she would finally know if she had to count every mark, sharing the potatoes out carefully on the children's plates, and the little bit of meat every other weekend, that, she said, was what she hoped for. We mustn't hope too much, Heinrich had said, and Rosa had laughed: I don't hope at all, I just need to know where I am at last, so that I can manage my energies properly, because they won't hold out for ever.

This was another frequent subject of conversation in the cells: girlfriends and wives and how long they would hold out, the eternal waiting for the sentence, brief visits, answering the questions of friends and relations, the longing, the lies when they came and left again, pretending it was all a children's game, and if it was all a children's game to them they'd be faithful and brave and – it was to be hoped – wouldn't look at any other man. Wishful thinking, said Georg, who didn't trust himself, far less his Marianne, who was twenty and had been doing practically everything there was to do since her sixteenth birthday, so why would she stop now. Jeremias knew about girls only from looking at them and defended every one of them, Oskar had a lover himself until he was arrested for anti-social behaviour, and the Swiss (from Saxon Switzerland) didn't trust his dear Regine in the least. What about you? they asked Heinrich, but he never knew, or else he would say: Why should I bother about any lovers Rosa has while I'm away, we all have to live our own lives, and in a year or less I'll be wiser and so will she.

The redheaded man in particular could never get enough of such stories, and although he knew little about women he told dirty jokes about them at every chance he got, and he knew how to do them when they didn't want it too. No sooner had a newcomer joined them in the cell than he would launch into his stories, inquisitive and talkative, telling everyone why he only ever went for the tight ones who had firm little arses, it was no fun except with the tight sort and you could tell them by their firm little arses. A girl had once told him how women know if what a man has in his trousers is any good or not, they can tell from our noses or our thumbs, apparently, or anyway this girl would look at a man's thumbs and draw her famous conclusions from them, and in three out of four cases she was pretty near the mark. A man's thumbs mustn't be too long, but strong and regular, she said, she even ended up wanting to have a baby with me, she came on strong every chance she got, oh yes, she was trying to trap me, lucky thing I noticed in time.

Then they moved on to the subject of the children they had, or they missed, or like the redhead didn't want to have, but most of them liked talking about their sons, daughters, nephews, nieces, and all they could do, all it was to be hoped they were learning, every last one was a miracle in his or her own way, and if they ultimately turned out badly it certainly couldn't be blamed on the new state, or the way mothers in the nationalized factories and production co-operatives had no time for their children, or were exhausted after working the early shift or on Sundays and holidays, when they did overtime to exceed the norms set in the latest plan.

What Heinrich liked best was talking about Eva and her love for the stars, clouds, flowers and stones, and how she had recently taken to writing letters to all sorts of people, although he wrote to her himself only once in all those months. Dear Eva, he wrote at the end of November 1967, for her thirteenth birthday, I don't have to work today so I'm finally going to write to you. I'll give you my present later, because I'm afraid I can't send presents from where I am just now, but the people here are nice and they all wish you many happy returns. I hope you're still working hard in school, I'm sorry to say your father never learnt anything properly in his life, but that's all going to change, I want you to be proud of your father, please think of him, because he can do with your thoughts.

Heinrich had written to Rosa a couple of times too, but generally he didn't know what to say and saved his stories for her next visit, or he stumbled over the opening sentences, wanted but couldn't manage to say what he was thinking, what he dreamed about, for he thought and dreamed of nothing, decided his days and nights were not worth describing, or would simply make painful reading for anyone on the outside where there were seasons, and festivals, and the ups and downs and routine of a hard-working life.

He did write her a letter in the second week of October 1967, because in the second week of October 1967 he had dreamt twice running of his father, who had suddenly taken to doing the most peculiar things and was not the father he knew. In the dream his father was cheerful, carefree and slightly intoxicated, because they were standing together drinking in the kitchen in Wiesbaden, and as they shared a bottle of Forster Schnepfenflug his father told him about the joint of meat he had put in the oven an hour before, spiked with caraway seeds and garlic, with carrots and onions braising underneath it, and though he'd never cooked a meal in his life before now he suddenly knew how you spike a joint of meat to flavour it, and you mustn't open the oven door for two hours: I'm telling you just to make sure there's no trouble, I don't want anybody complaining of me afterwards. In the second dream his father had been suffering from a bad cough, and even though it was the worst cough he'd ever had he sat on the sofa chain-smoking and talking, a couple of sentences between two coughing fits, so sorry about this nasty cough, with luck it'll finish me off.

Heinrich could make nothing of his dreams for a long time, and since he could make nothing of them for so long he took them as an omen and wrote his father in Wiesbaden a letter, asking if everything was all right, surely his father hadn't taken to cookery in his old age, or are you by any chance dead? It's a funny thing, Heinrich wrote to Rosa, I'm worried, and Rosa wrote back: Yes, a funny thing, but there's no need for you to worry, only recently I had a long letter from your stepmother and she didn't mention any illness, quite the opposite, it seems those weeks in hospital in Saffig did him good, that's the last news I have.

That autumn of 1967, closely guarded, they had been re-surfacing the road to Eisenberg on the outskirts of the city, with Oskar and Jeremias in the party, and they all three enjoyed the last sunny days, and when a girl appeared a few hundred metres away, waved and stopped for a moment, it was like living their old lives again. Sometimes Heinrich was surprised by the thought of last summer's Heinrich, when he was thirty-six and felt the past building up behind him, his girlfriends and the rooms, the flats, the houses where he'd had them, and then he had doubts and tried working out whether he was still living in the first half of his life or whether he'd reached the second half, and if so when exactly had the middle of his life been, for the past and future are balanced in equilibrium in the middle of your life.

Such were Heinrich's thoughts, and he was surprised at himself for having them and being unable to shake them off, he even pestered quiet Jeremias with them, but it was all a waste of time as far as quiet Jeremias was concerned, what did it matter whether you were old or young or somewhere in between, better not start thinking such thoughts at all here in jail, because everyone here in jail is old as the hills, which is the basic principle, or perhaps one should say the lesson we're to learn: the idea is for us all to feel old as the hills and brood over the past, and when we're finally done with it they'll let us out and say: Okay, ladies and gents, that's it, that's all we wanted, now see how you can manage, we mean well by you, only we might not feel the same next time.

All right, all right, said Heinrich, thinking of his little Eva, his clever, thoughtful Eva, and he guessed that in Jeremias's place she wouldn't say anything at all, or else she'd say: What questions you ask, Papa, as if he were the child.

Everyone can keep walking forward in the usual old way, she would say.

Yes, so they can.

I like walking backwards.

You can easily stumble, walking backwards.

Practice makes perfect.

The bad times had begun in mid-July when Rosa failed to turn up one day, because his Rosa had two sick children, a job which kept her at work from eight to five, and she didn't feel like visiting distant Gera, or else she simply forgot him, went swimming with a woman friend, and was lying in the sun half drowsing, half keeping an eye on the children, when it suddenly struck her that she actually had forgotten him, but by then it was too late to go.

Only two days later did Heinrich receive the letter in which she explained everything but still left him in the dark, it was only a few hastily scribbled lines, yet she wrote as if she didn't even have time for a few scribbled lines: Dear Heinrich, she wrote, I'm sorry about Sunday, I didn't mean to keep you waiting but it was no good, the children and the job are getting too much for me, six weeks isn't such a very long time, I'm sure I can manage to get there again next time, love, Rosa.

She wrote this as if she were a distant acquaintance, and of course he was quick to get ideas into his head, couldn't shake them off, wondered about everything, and in his position when you're wondering about everything you get bad-tempered and careless and invite violence, as he did a few days later over the food, although complaining of the food to one of the screws was known to be the most stupid thing you could do, your best course was to keep your mouth shut, take whatever came and eat it.

The very afternoon of the day he had complained Heinrich learned the meaning of fear, he was on the way to the library when there they were, barring his way, warning him, shouting at him, the first blow in the face hit him in mid-question: Had Hampel had enough, Hampel was a right pile of shit, we know how to deal with your sort, we don't hang about, we have our methods, you bastard, take this and this and this and this to remember us by, and learn your lesson, for every word was a kick in the kidneys or a punch in the face, next time we're going to murder you.

They let Heinrich lie there for a while after they were through with him and he had learnt his lesson, and then they took hold of him and dragged him, or rather carried him back to Oskar and Jeremias in their cell, unfortunately, they said, Citizen Hampel had fallen on the stairs, and they all knew at once what kind of fall that was, and laughed at Heinrich and kept their mouths shut. We did warn you, said the professor who was now spending the last days of his sentence with them, and Jeremias said: Come on, lie down, I'll make you a cold compress, you'll have forgotten all about it in a day or so, of course you could go to the doctor and get a sick note, only it was to be hoped he wouldn't be so foolish.

He lay awake a great deal in the following nights, brooding about his Rosa and whether she thought of him when she was sleeping with another man, and whether the children asked about him or about that other man who perhaps lived only a street away and had time, plenty of time, a man who was there, could be touched, sent out to buy a few last-minute things for the evening, who was cheerful and lively and knew nothing about the world of prisons except from books. I don't talk about you much, Rosa had said once; for months she had been living in two worlds, as it were, two worlds which knew little about each other, every six weeks she came through the two sets of doors and then went back to her dreary life, almost always bringing a little of the outside world in with her, and then taking a little of the prison world out again, but she forgot about the rest of it, left it or dropped it on her way, put it down as she walked to the bus stop early on Sunday morning, and as she went home late in the afternoon. She herself said this forgetting was hard work, but it was necessary for the good of all concerned, how could she possibly talk about the life of the convict Hampel and the reasons why he hadn't been home for months?

But there were the children, thought Heinrich on those nights when he mulled everything over, lingering for the thousandth time on the presents he would take Eva and Konrad and Walter when he came home, they'd be so surprised and ask questions, and seize on the presents he had brought back from his travels in distant foreign lands, there now, off you go and enjoy yourselves, play nicely and leave Mama and Papa alone for half an hour, they have a lot to talk about after all this long time, and wasn't it worth the wait?

He hoped so. He would even act like an uncle to them for a while, and go carefully with Rosa, making no advances until eventually she came to him of her own accord, remembering the old days and saying: Well, shall we do it then, my dear, can you still do it? I think so.

During the month of June, when he had only a few weeks left to serve, there were moments when he thought: I shall miss all this, I shall miss Karl and the way my days are regulated from morning to night, work in the kitchen or on the building site, the smell of shit in the cell morning and evening, Karl giving me the signal that he's coming in with me or asking me if he can come, sure, every night as far as I'm concerned. Sometimes he thought: how simple it all is with a man, or perhaps it's only so simple with Karl, or because we're still learning, trying experiments, changing roles, and we're almost always in agreement, which was the best thing, almost always being in agreement, and still wanting each other, because the moments when it was possible and the others weren't watching them were secret and precious, though they were all fast asleep after midnight at the latest.

They never stayed together long, but got up quickly, rearranged their clothing, didn't wash, and got back under the covers alone, exhausted and satisfied. Their love-making was always quick and precise, no fancy touches, that was something they both wanted and had not found with their women. They only had to be careful of the suspicious eyes and ears of the others, and when one of them sometimes said: Shut up, you bastards, it was to be hoped he had merely been talking in his sleep, but they would stop and wait, holding their breath, whatever point they had reached, and in a way those were the best moments, when they were waiting, sighing and trembling at every movement, however slight, as if this were the first, the last, the very best time, for by then everything was far advanced, they were ready, on the point of coming, and didn't want to wait any longer.

From mid-June onwards Karl and Heinrich were meeting almost every night, sniffing round each other, leaving stains on each other, and they often spent time together in the day-time as well, since Karl had volunteered for kitchen work, so they put the watery soup for lunch on early in the morning, cutting up the rotten potatoes and carrots and celery, with the meat of old boiling fowls once a week, chopping it very fine and thoroughly so that they had plenty of time to talk, and time to feel each other up behind the big pans and whet their appetites for later on.

At first Heinrich wasn't too comfortable about having Karl hanging round him almost all round the clock, not to be shaken off, but soon he was taking it as the last opportunity to learn something about himself and Karl and men in general, on the whole the two of them knew and liked and preferred the same kind of thing. Once Karl said: Maybe I'll leave women alone in future and look for someone like you, or maybe I'll come and see you some day, arrive on your doorstep begging for one last time. But Heinrich got quite angry and made a long speech in defence of women, with whom, after all, everything was much nicer and more delicate and smelled better, women were smooth and supple and could be tractable, not to mention the songs they sang or their sighs. Or are you just joking? Well, yes, to some extent Karl was just joking, but even that evening, hours later, he seemed offended.

So they forgot the incident and counted the days still left to them, each in his own way. Later on, he never mentioned his friend Karl and their whispered confessions, but when Rosa saw someone resembling Karl she would drop hints, wondering what it was like, and had Heinrich really and truly had something going with that boy, she'd often talked to his mother, I just can't believe it, was that it, then?

Yes, that was it, but different too, I can't talk about it, said

Heinrich, I forget everything, I've forgotten all that long ago, let it be, he asked her.

I must wash myself for you first, Karl had said.

No, stay the way you are, don't keep me waiting.

Like last time?

Yes, like last time, last time was good.

But you're still ashamed.

I'm not at all ashamed. Now, keep quiet and get on with it, it's perfectly simple, I know, this is the kind of life we lead, pitiful really but very nice.

During his early days in Gera Heinrich would have denied that his life there was any kind of life at all, for at this point they were moving him to a new cell every few days, waking him in the middle of the night to interrogate him, always asking the same questions, whom exactly had he been doing business with in those illegal deals prejudicial to the good of the beleaguered Republic where, fortunately, there were always watchful citizens and authorities bent on taking action, so let's have the names, come on, one two three, if you want to help yourself, if not we can do it differently. (He was familiar with this tune.)

Rosa advised him for heaven's sake to confess everything, and if the authorities were dead set on having names to invent a few if necessary, but as usual Rosa was talking off the top of her head, and was extremely angry with him at the time too, going on at him because of the children every time she visited, saying that but for the family in the West she'd be at her wits' end, but for the family in the West and me having to beg for a parcel every few weeks we'd have starved to death by now because of your debts.

I'm earning just a little, Heinrich would say, and Rosa herself was earning a little more than just a little, he added, better times will come, we simply have to believe in that, but when he said such things they made her lose her self-control, or shout at him and then fall silent, and walk to the station buffet in Gera, where she might write to Heinrich's sister Constanze, thanking her for the last parcel: I've just been to see Heinrich, I'm sitting in the station buffet in Gera with an hour to wait until my bus leaves. I want to thank you very much for your letter, Heinrich's just read it and it really moved him to know that you're not prejudiced against him. I can visit him once every six weeks, though only for thirty minutes, such a short time when there's so much to talk about. I'm still hoping he'll get early release, he works hard enough for three or four men, I'm sure everything will be all right. I think it was a firm hand and more love he needed as a child. He talks about your mother and father so much, if you ask me a man like that can't be all bad. He's tanned very brown, he works in the open air on a building site all day, and I'm glad he's settled down a bit after the first difficult weeks, because after all he's my husband, despite everything, and the father of my children, and we need him. Love from Rosa. It was along these lines that she described the situation when she wrote to the family in the West, saying Heinrich was very talented, but sad to say he always made friends with the wrong people, and carelessness and high spirits mingled in his character, he was blind to facts at the crucial moment, as she supposed she didn't have to tell them, only unfortunately I'm the one who has to pay for it, as usual.

She had four different jobs in the first few months, she spent a few weeks home-working – sewing girls' check dresses for a firm in Apolda – she sold toys in a shop in the Altstadt, she helped to look after the children at a nursery school, and didn't like any of those jobs because either the pay wasn't right or the people were stupid, so she went to work as a wages clerk for Zeiss, deciding at least to give it a try. She told Anneliese, in those first few months: I can't do it, or I can't do it very much longer, things just have to get better, she said, because if they didn't get better soon she'd be going on the streets here in the East. There were said to be women at the Leipzig Trade Fairs who offered themselves for sale, helping those fine gentlemen from the West to pass the time, you sometimes went to a room with them and asked what they liked, took the money and went along with it all, hated it or didn't hate it too much, washed your hands and mouth and everything, well, it's probably just a job like any other.

In those first months after Heinrich's arrest Rosa had been reduced to seriously contemplating going to the Leipzig Trade Fairs some time and putting out feelers, finding out just how to let men know what you are so that they'll take you to a room for a fair price; yes, she had been reduced to that. She wouldn't tell Heinrich if it did come to that some day, for he couldn't have borne to think of her selling herself for his sake, or giving the children up, he'd sooner have killed himself or Rosa or both of them. Oh no, he had said when she once put the idea of the Children's Home to him, saying it was the best solution for all of them for a time, so she knew she mustn't talk to Heinrich about it, nor must she mention Leipzig to him, and in the end she kept the idea to herself, practising, becoming accustomed to her life, perhaps something else would come up, or she might do it at home in the flat; anything was possible.

At this time they were both beginning to accustom themselves to everything, but Rosa didn't realize at once that she was accustoming herself and coming to be in control, for last winter the money wouldn't even run to a little butter, she needed a couple of hundred East German marks every month for Heinrich's creditors alone. In those first months all she had to spread on the children's bread was the cheapest kind of margarine, with salt or sugar or a spoonful of last summer's blackcurrant jam, and sometimes a tiny scrap of liver sausage at the weekend. I'm afraid we're not rich, said Rosa, talking to the children a lot about Heinrich's travels, but Eva soon stopped believing in those travels and the presents her father would bring them when he came back; it was all lies.

At first Rosa told him everything, and it was obvious that

she enjoyed telling him everything in detail, letting him know how she sometimes begged Anneliese and Friedhelm for a jar of pickled cabbage, or of sliced apples in cinnamon, these were their rare luxuries. At the beginning of March 1967, on her third visit, she said: I ought not to tell you what I think when I'm running short of money at the end of the month, because then I think you're a bastard, and I didn't deserve any of this, and I say to myself: this is the last time I tell him how miserable we are and let him comfort me, or maybe wait in vain for a word of comfort, I mean, the man who got us into this mess us is safe and snug in jail here and couldn't care less for any of it.

If only you knew, Heinrich had said, because at this time they were still waking him almost every night to interrogate him, but although they were still waking him almost every night to interrogate him he was saving every pfennig he earned for the children, he avoided the little kiosk in the prison courtyard where inmates could buy things, and he never smoked more than three cigarettes a day, that way at least they'd have money for a few plants and seeds for the garden, or something for Rosa to put towards a pair of new shoes or a summer dress or a costume, the grey costume she had bought in 1962 was already looking rather threadbare.

The interrogations by day and by night went like this: if they came for him at night they offered him a cup of coffee to wake him up, or if they were in a bad mood they didn't offer coffee but started straight in on the questions, which were always the same: Hampel had been in touch with members of the Soviet army, and he had been in touch with various Party officials, so let's have names, please, or we shan't be very happy, and wasn't he ashamed of himself for plunging his family into misfortune and leaving a mountain of debt to everyone's disadvantage. Furthermore, Hampel had been known to the authorities for a long time, except that what the records said about Citizen Heinrich Hampel didn't really seem to add up: born in Jena 1931, flees to the Federal

Republic 1951, returns to our Socialist fatherland of his own free will 1962, and not five years later here he suddenly is in our jails, or have we left something out? No, not that I know of, said Heinrich, and it was a fact that he ought not to have gone over back then, because then he'd have got much further in life, he wouldn't be here, but he wondered if they were trying to make a rope to hang him with out of his crossing the green border at the age of just twenty in the year fifty-one, he hadn't even come of age in the West.

The People's Chamber passed a resolution saying we don't prosecute people for that any more, they said, and Heinrich said yes, it must have been three or four years ago, because three or four years ago the comrades of the Central Committee had divided history into separate chunks, calling the time before 13 August 1961 *The Construction of the Foundations of Socialism*, and the time after it *On the Way to a Fully Developed Socialist Society*. Just as well for you, said the officers, because they liked repeating themselves, and different officers kept visiting him, and the new ones never knew what part of the Hampel case had already been cleared up, and what he hadn't told yet.

Over the first few weeks Heinrich had stuck obstinately to giving information only about himself, but then they had turned to their tried and tested methods, refined over the years, pushing and poking the tired Hampel during the interrogation, or shouting at him and leaving him to spend a few hours in a cellar where he had to stand and couldn't sit down, just so that friend Hampel would finally come to his senses, good heavens, it was only a couple of names they wanted. They pushed and nudged him very gently and cautiously, in an almost friendly way, and they hit him only with the flat of the hand, they owed him that, and had he, they asked, finally thought of something down there in our nice cellars, and lo and behold in the third or fourth week he did think of something, why not; Heinrich gave them two or three names, but the names of Vladimir and Gisela did not feature in his confessions.

You're always so tired, don't they let you get any sleep, said Rosa when she was visiting for the second or third time, and Heinrich said: I can make up for it later, once I'm out of here I'll sleep for a solid week on end.

But you can't make up for all this.

I can make up for everything else.

I'm not so sure about that.

At first they had left Heinrich in peace, that is to say, at first they hadn't pestered him with nocturnal interrogations that often lasted hours, but they would send for him by day, when he wasn't expecting it, and every few nights he was moved to another cell with other faces, other life histories, other ugly incidents. People would rather not talk about what happened on those nights, when a few names were mentioned now and then, for instance if someone complained about the food and another about a state where it was possible for them to give you food like that, well, you could never know whether the man was just talking or had been planted in order to listen and talk, all their stories sounded much the same. Some cases were grave and others less serious, there were habitual lawbreakers and opportunistic lawbreakers, but most were in for embezzlement and theft prejudicial to public property, and now and then a case got into the newspaper and was written up as a warning to all who didn't care about what was mine and what was yours and what was ours, kindly take note.

They sometimes talked about all this among themselves, that is to say when they felt quite sure of each other they sometimes talked, for generally it was dangerous anyway, someone might call one of the screws a bastard, which he was, but if another man couldn't keep his lip buttoned then the others knew in advance what the punishment would be, they knew how many days' detention for a couple of men bawling a song or so in unison out of the window in the evening, and why you had better keep it to yourself if you didn't want to go on any longer. There was evidence for that in the case, some months or years ago, of a man who didn't want to go on any longer, and had already collected the razor blades for Day Zero, and next morning they came for him early and beat him back to life in their cellars.

It was just before Christmas of sixty-six that the tale of the unfortunate man with the razor blades was being told in the cells and in the corridors, because it was well known that Christmas was the time when someone almost always hanged himself in his cell, or cut his wrists at the first light of dawn, hoping not to be found, for if he was found it was a pretty nasty business. Heinrich never really listened to these stories, but he often thought of the old days, and he thought of the children and Rosa, and Vladimir and his Gisela always feeling each other up so eagerly in public, and when they closed the door behind them late in the evening they would fall on each other at once.

Around Christmas in particular, and again after the New Year, he expected a letter from his friend Gisela almost daily, and when no letter from her came he made odd bargains with her, gave up meals or a cigarette now and then for her sake, took it as a bad omen when a tap dripped, and as a good one when the screw failed to switch the light off in the evening, he pinned his hopes on such things. Then he sometimes got angry with her, or told himself it was a just retribution that she had forgotten him so entirely, and returned to brooding on the mistakes he had made in the old days, the good times and the bad times, and God knew what they had depended on.

There were days when he was surprised to find how soon you were repeating that phrase to yourself, in the old days, words that could not be recalled: in the old days, and it was in the old days that he made his first few mistakes, but unfortunately these so-called mistakes were fun too. Bella had

222

been a mistake, it all began with that, he thought, and he thought of their first afternoons together, and he thought of Rosa too, since but for his mistakes, or perhaps he should say his acquaintances (and Rosa herself had once been just an acquaintance) he would hardly have existed at all.

He had to work through all this in the first few weeks, finding out which memories he could live with and which he absolutely could not, for instance he couldn't live with his successes but he laughed at his failures, and the way his book-keeper had cheated him, or some comrade or other had grassed on him, that made him laugh. He thought it unlikely that anything of that kind would happen to him again, but he did hope that a Bella or a Rosa or a Rita would happen again, except that he'd better not think of that kind of thing for the time being, he could think of it only for a split second, or just before falling asleep when he was tired out, which meant not often now.

The night before his release he got into bed with Karl one last time, and that one time they both stayed lying there, not bothering much about the others, so when they woke up next morning the goodbyes had been said. Heinrich was released at around two in the afternoon on 25 July 1968, but before they released him the prison governor gave him some good advice: the remainder of his sentence had been commuted to probation, so Heinrich must make sure he was diligent while on probation, carrying on from where he had left off here in the prison, since only those who will work shall eat, to quote Lenin freely. Heinrich was to report to the appropriate authorities in the next few days, there was work waiting for him, the collective of a construction co-operative in Jena had said it was ready to put the prodigal back on the right path, so take good advantage of that and don't refuse the helping hand of our Socialist state.

The liaison officer Opitz gave Heinrich advice too, describing the Hampel case as an instance of the superiority of

Socialist law over the monopolistic legal and governmental system of West Germany, of which he knew from sad experience years ago, and now you've had some experience of our state for yourself, no one can fail to see the difference. He was allowed back to the cell once more to say goodbye, and then, in the clothing store, they gave him back the watch and suit and underclothes he had been wearing on the day of his arrest, and a grey envelope containing his wages for the month of July, which had just begun, and then he was a free man.

Never again, he thought, as he walked through the two sets of doors like Rosa on her visits every six weeks, and the big outer gate opened to reveal a bright July day. It was so bright he had to blink a couple of times, and suddenly he saw someone waving and the person waving was Rosa in a summer dress he hadn't seen before. Heinrich blinked three or four times, and then he saw a man standing beside Rosa, a man who from a distance looked like Harms, and he thought: For heaven's sake, surely she hasn't brought Harms with her, but on looking more closely he saw that it was indeed none other than Harms, his famous coat slung over his arm, waving just like Rosa, as if they were all the best of friends.

Goodness, you're brown, said Rosa, kissing him on the mouth in her old way, and Harms said: Anyone would recognize him, though, quite the old Hampel or rather, as I hear, quite the new Hampel, welcome back. Well, good to see you, said Heinrich, laughing, and they all went to a café to celebrate, ordered fizzy mineral drinks and got used to talking to each other. You've lost weight, said Rosa, and asked if he'd heard about Prague, the situation in Prague was getting more critical every day. Yes, well, Prague, said Harms, this Prague business will soon be over, the counter-revolution will not triumph, we'll soon have things under control. Let's hope so, said Heinrich, unable to remember anything about Prague in the newspapers, and wondered what were the children up to on a fine Saturday like this, first

224

of all he'd like to go straight to see the children. Yes, of course, I quite understand, said Harms, but once you've settled in take a little time off for me, and then they paid the bill (Rosa paid it) and drove to Gera railway station in the official car allotted to First Lieutenant Harms of the State Security Service. Then he and Rosa didn't know what to say next. As a matter of fact, I have some bad news, said Rosa, after a silence, and Heinrich said: Yes, my father, I've thought so for some time.

One afternoon he turned the gas tap on and put his head in the oven, so it would all be over quickly.

Oh, so that was it, said Heinrich.

Yes, how odd, isn't it, you guessed as much.

Your lists gave you away.

I see, the lists.

I have to get used to it all first.

Of course, we all have to get used to it.

Later, in the train to Jena, he tried to imagine how the children would react to him, and for the first, for the thousandth time in almost two years he tried to imagine doing it with his Rosa: Do you hear your heart beating, do you hear mine? I'm still just tasting you. Dipping in here and there. Can I undress you? Would you like some music on? How dark it is now; how delicious you are, your delicate, clever, exploring hands, your finger tips are like a thousand little sparkling kisses. Can I ask you what you were thinking last time? You can ask me anything. Can I come on top of you? Yes, you can come on top of me. I want to be naked for you. Yes, me too.

8

The first problems came up in February, when they had been back from Russia for a month to find circumstances so different that they sometimes hardly knew the country, or the customs of the new masters who had been imposed on it by the Soviet Union, or the people of the old days. A month after their return from Russia Heinrich was still wearing the clothes he had on when they arrived at Schönefeld airport, and was going about like a Russian in felt boots and galoshes, with a heavy dark overcoat and a brown fur cap. Theodor and Mother were no longer at all sure whether the new Republic, founded to the sound of the poet's hymn, was the right place for them, but Heinrich and Father thought you couldn't tell yet if it was the right place or not, you'd have to wait a while and get accustomed to it, learning the language as if you were abroad, that's what we did in Russia, and it's to be hoped we shall feel more at home here than in Russia.

Out of the frying pan into the fire, said Heinrich's mother, and his father said: Well, time to get to work and look around, and he went off with his sons Theodor and Heinrich to get to work and look around, they all knew the long way down to the Camsdorfer Brücke, across the market-place to the station, and so to the works, they knew it by heart. Only occasionally did they see something new or restored, like the roof of the city church which had been bombed in the spring of 1945, or a building somewhere along their way, while the bridges, streets and squares had new names, and there were red banners with the slogans of the present rulers, who didn't trust the population of workers and peasants already living there, but were optimistic about men of good will, like Heinrich and his father, who still hadn't paid off the mortgage on his house up on the Wilhelmshöhe, and hoped to adapt to the new ways.

The words VEB Schott & Gen. stood above the factory, showing that it was now state-owned, a *Volkseigener Betrieb*, and on the second or third day they stopped noticing, and early in the fifth week the Party Secretary summoned the Hampels, father and sons, to report to him, beginning with the unskilled labourer Heinrich Hampel. They sent for Heinrich in the middle of the morning break on a day early in February, and he spent a good hour sitting in the local Party Secretary's office listening to his sermon and his admonitions. A number of remarks had come to his ears, he said, remarks which unfortunately we can't overlook, this kind of thing has to be rooted out, the imperialist class enemy takes advantage of such remarks, but of course Heinrich wasn't to know that in such cases, after five years in the Soviet Union, we ask people to come and have a little talk first, leaving any other necessary measures until later.

Well, so what was it like in that friendly country the Soviet Union?

Very nice.

But you talk like a class enemy in the lunch break.

I never say anything unless someone asks me a question, and I don't add anything or leave anything out: that's what I call telling the truth.

A nice sort of truth, I must say, whipping up feeling against the Soviet Union among the people here, said the Party Secretary, and he picked up a piece of paper and read what he had been told was publicly stated by the Hampel brothers: the Russians were in a bad way, poor bastards; people were starving in Stalin's Russia; people were pursuing a false ideology; what kind of Communism was it anyway when

227

some people lived the good life, while others hadn't had enough to eat for over thirty years and lived like slaves.

It's true about people starving, said Heinrich, and was quite surprised to see the other man nod, ah, he replied, but it was the Fascist Wehrmacht and the barbarity of Hitler's regime that brought famine to Russia, or did Heinrich think famine just falls from the sky like some divine punishment, or because Communists don't know how to harvest the crops? All this was the usual imperialist lies propagated by America and its friends and accomplices in London, Paris and Bonn, but the Party of the working class expected a man who worked at Schott to form a correct picture of the situation, so please bear this little talk in mind, we won't be giving you a second warning, kind regards to your lady mother and your good father whom we know from the old days, he lives for nothing but his work, and there's work in plenty to be done here.

With that Heinrich was dismissed and sent to talk to his brother Theodor, who as usual had formed instant opinions about everything and did not conceal them, getting into argument with various convinced Socialists in the canteen and shooting his mouth off, risking his own neck and his brother's too. Just be careful, will you, said Heinrich, who had not yet formed any opinion of German Socialism, and in all cases of doubt thought like a Russian, for he had learnt how to eat and drink and starve and make love from the Russians, but here in the Germany of the Socialist Unity Party everything was cold and grey and prudish.

Heinrich's first German girlfriend initially struck him as prudish too, and boring, her name was Dora and he met her when the Hampel family were re-clothing themselves from head to foot at the beginning of January, buying beds and chairs, cupboards, tables and chests of drawers in a furnishing store as if their house up on the Wilhelmshöhe had just been bombed, they still didn't feel at home there, and were regretting the furniture and clothes they had sold for far too low a price back in Russia, they could have done with them now. Heinrich's father had gone to the factory very early on the morning of 3 January to get a chit stating that they really did need everything on his mother's long list, and then all seven of them drove off in a car belonging to the now state-owned Schott works, went to the best stores where only the Comrades usually did their shopping, and started in on their spree with three sets of seven towels and several face flannels, Mother leading the way, list in hand, Father beside her, assessing their purchases and nodding, the children gradually building up what they had bought into a huge pile of suits and dresses and curtaining fabric and tablecloths and bed-spreads, together with all kinds of crockery and cutlery, and domestic utensils for cooking and cleaning and laundry work for the use of Heinrich's mother, who had not a glance to spare for her surroundings even hours later, nor did she notice that this was a shop for high-up functionaries with permits allowing them to travel who would shortly be going to China, Cuba or the Soviet Union as members of a delegation, and they were not a little surprised to see people like the Hampels there.

This continued for half an hour, with people gaping at the Hampels and their purchases, and finally one of the staff in the store felt it had gone on long enough and informed the Volkspolizei that there was a family of seven here buying up half the shop, and they don't look like Party members either. Right, we'll sort this out, said the Volkspolizei officers, shouting at the Hampels, demanding to see their papers and asking why they were buying mountains of textiles without a permit, this was a fine thing, they must say, whereupon all hell broke loose. This is the end, said Theodor, and Father said: Keep calm, do, to which Theodor replied: Look, these are the facts of the matter, and just why are the police coming down on us like this, who, might he ask, has been throwing his weight about claiming we're some kind of smugglers or black marketeers, but of course no one would own to that. Right, said Theodor, so now we see what kind of country this is, to which the two police officers said: It's not that bad, Herr Hampel, just a misunderstanding, calm down, we have our reasons, but they're nothing to do with your family.

Mother had spent two and a half hours crossing item after item off her long list before they visited another furnishing store a couple of streets away, and it was in this other furnishing store that Heinrich fell for his first German girlfriend, who was one of the salesgirls in the beds and bedding department and loved Josef Vissarionovich Stalin, that wise leader and saviour of the Soviet people, more than anyone else in the world. She had even dedicated her diary to Stalin, and after work every day she began her entries with the place and the date, noting what the weather was like in the beautiful city of Jena, and under the date of 3 January 1951 she wrote: Dear Josef, we had some weird people in the store today, they bought six beds all at once, for the whole family, they've just come back after five years in Moscow, there's the father, mother, two daughters and three sons. One of the sons looked Russian, with nice blue eyes and a voice like I'm not sure what, and I'd love to ask him what those five years in Moscow were like, and if he's been to the Bolshoi or to see Lenin in Red Square. I don't think about him all that much, but I have so many questions to ask, enough for two afternoons on end, we could speak Russian together, such was her record of their first meeting.

Heinrich probably wouldn't even have noticed her, but someone called her by her name, which he liked, and then he liked the girl whose name it was, and her smile when Father said: We want to buy six beds, please, one double and five single. Six at once? she asked – she had a sharp nose as well as her deep voice – and Father trotted out the usual explanation: We're just back from Russia, and asked her advice. Heinrich immediately thought: She's nice, and she has a nice job too, selling beds would be a really good job, you get to talk to people at the same time and it can't be very hard work, so he listened carefully to hear how she did it: they had the latest models in now, frames with elasticized webbing, very comfortable to sleep on, and for the young people she'd suggest wooden beds with plastic bases, they were welcome to lie down on the beds to try them out.

So you can't even get proper beds like before the war, Theodor grumbled, and he thought she didn't hear him, but she suddenly turned round and set him right: Even Comrade Stalin sleeps in a bed like this, so it ought to be good enough for a young gentleman like you, but she spoke in friendly tones and as one in possession of the truth, and Heinrich thought he'd like to see her again another day, or indeed, if he could summon up the courage or chance favoured him, why not tomorrow?

Next day, during the lunch break, Heinrich had left the works and walked past the Westbahnhof to the Altstadt, to visit Dora in the beds and bedding department of her store, where he asked after her, but unfortunately she wasn't in today, and when he went back a few days later he was told that Fräulein Dora had reported sick, and they weren't handing anyone's address out to strangers.

The whole of January passed by, and half of February, and then came the first of the interrogations and the problems, which meant that he didn't remember her in detail any more, or only one detail at a time: her sharp nose, her pale hair tied back, her laugh, much too deep for a girl of her age, or should he say a woman? He often lay in the bedroom he shared with Paul in the evening and couldn't help remembering that it was in the bed *she* had sold that he lay down to sleep, and before he went to sleep he sent his thoughts in her direction, hoping that she would notice and send hers back to him, that she was hoping just a little that he would come and pick her up in the evening long after dark, when the shops closed, and she went home to her beloved Stalin in his books, or in the diary entries she addressed to him.

At this time even Mother was pleased by the way things had worked out, bringing them all home safe and sound from Russia (including Heinrich), to find the house still standing, and the tenants finally out of the first floor: everything back to the way it used to be. She merely complained of the steep hill, and of never getting any help from her husband and not much from the children, who either went off to work like Theodor and Heinrich and weren't back until evening, or had their own problems at school like Constanze and Paul, who found it hard to adjust to the curriculum laid down by the new authorities. There was always something the matter every week: either they couldn't cope with the English lesson, or like their brothers they were spreading incorrect opinions of the great Soviet Union from which they came, where they knew about the queues for flour and sugar twice a year and wrote about them in their compositions, this is how workers live in the Soviet Union, they told their teachers, and we have no way of knowing how workers live in the United States, but they can hardly be worse off than people living in the workers' and peasants' paradise.

Oh, children, said Father, refusing as usual to listen to them in the evening, not wanting to know just why their neighbours' two children were in jail, and wouldn't get out in a hurry, on account of letting off a few stink-bombs in protest against the ceremonious conversion of the Schott and Zeiss works into state-owned firms, and did that make any impression at all on the country's new masters? Those bastards with their bloody Stalin and their three-times-bloody Ulbricht, Theodor would say, and since it was Theodor saying so, and Dora would not have liked to hear it, Heinrich called him a defeatist and asked why he didn't go straight over to the West, they'd welcome the likes of you there with open arms. Oh dear me, said Father, and Mother said: You're not going alone, anyway, and it was in March 1951 that she first began talking about the West, and the only members of the family who didn't take her seriously were Heinrich (because of Dora) and his father (because of his house).

Yet Heinrich wasn't even sure if he would recognize Dora again, but he saw her one Tuesday coming out of the door of the new furniture store after it closed, and he waved and hesitated, then smiled, hello, she said, what did he want? Was something the matter with the beds? And why didn't he look like a Russian any more, that was how she remembered him, as a Russian, he hoped it was a pleasant memory. Could he ask her out? Yes, he could ask her out for a coffee. But he must tell her all about everything in detail, anyone who'd come from Stalin's country must have a lot to tell her about it, she'd like to visit Russia herself in two or three years' time, she said that was her dream.

And so he began at the beginning, and took his time over it, and when he was finally through with his tale she had more questions, asking Heinrich about the Russian girls, and had he ever been to one of the big May Day celebrations, or an anniversary parade in honour the Great Socialist October Revolution? He would rather have talked about her life as a salesgirl in the beds and bedding department, or as the daughter of Regional Secretary Helmbrecht, she'd been born on 22 October 1931, the same year as Heinrich, and eighteen years later, on the day of the founding of the German Democratic Republic, she came of age and celebrated on the streets of her beloved Jena, singing a song in honour of the day of triumph: *A song such as never was sung, with music to gladden the ear. We are marching, the old and the young, no longer to feel dread and fear. A light on our glad hearts is shining, so bright that it dazzles the eye. And banners wave high, the streets lining, flowering red as the marchers go by.*

Johannes R. Becher, I know it by heart, said Dora, to which Heinrich replied that he didn't know the poem, but could he see her again? Well, yes, if you like, you're welcome.

For a long time he had no plans for Dora, but Dora had plans for him from the start, and sent him a poem or a speech by this man Becher once or twice a week, and when they met again he had to tell her what he thought of them, for instance the *Hymn to the USSR* and the *Song of the Blue Banner*, which she liked best, since she knew from experience what it was like when the Freie Deutsche Jugend marched under blue German skies in the merry month of May, as the song said: *Bright shines the sun in skies of spring, shedding light on German land. 'Left!' and 'Left!' the columns sing, Free Young Germans hand in hand. Let us build the state anew! Firm together we will stand! Blue the sky, and banners blue waft o'er our new fatherland.*

Could anyone put it better? asked Dora, quite hoarse with excitement, and Heinrich agreed that no one could put it better, yet so far nothing had passed between him and this small person in her blue tunic, not even a kiss. I can see it all, said Heinrich, because he did like her (and it was only because he liked her that he said so), I can see it all, my Dora out in front with the big blue banner and the first freckles on her face, that's what I see as clear as if I were there myself. It would be really nice if you came along next time, she whispered, referring to the many evenings when she attended FDJ meetings, helping to prepare for the forthcoming referendum against remilitarization, but when she came home tired her thoughts always went straight to Heinrich, and his attractive eyes, and his mouth, which looked as if it would be nice to kiss, so that she felt quite ashamed of herself. Sometimes she even neglected her diary these days, writing a hasty note in it to say how busy she was, but when this is over I'll think of you again, dear Josef, I'll tell you all the details the same as usual.

One Sunday at the beginning of April Heinrich introduced her to his mother, who had little to say about Dora except that she disapproved of the girl's sleeveless dress and the way she kept carrying on about Stalin, it was positively embarrassing, as if Stalin were her God. That morning his mother had

234

baked a cake with apples and cinnamon and sugar, and they all sat down around three o'clock, goggling at Heinrich's girlfriend in surprise as if she had dropped from another planet. What business of ours is your girlfriend, said Theodor, and Constanze said: It's not right, bringing her here, even Father's against it, only Father is so polite and weak-willed you don't notice. A nice girl, Heinrich's father had said, taking Dora out to show her the garden, and later, under the fruit trees, she let Heinrich kiss her for the first time, in fact it was the first time he had ever kissed a German girl, and immediately it was almost like being back with Lyusya.

You must have learnt that in Russia, said Dora when she stopped to take breath, and was dwelling on the thought of that first long kiss of her life, also keeping an eye on the kitchen window over Heinrich's shoulder, and he said: Yes, never mind, that was a good start, so come along, let's go for a walk, I know a good place up by the Fuchsturm, but now he was going too fast for her. Take it easy, my dear Heinrich, my Russian Heinrich, I'll have to think about it overnight, or maybe by the first of May in ten days' time, I hope we'll see each other then, and she told him to keep looking at the blue banners, because she hoped that then he'd have to look hard at her and see how pretty she was. Will you come and see me at home some time too, she asked as he went part of the way back with her, escorting her to the new buildings in Maxim-Gorki-Strasse, and he promised he would, and was very well conducted and proud and hopeful, no need to tell her the nasty things Mother had said.

Well, that's a fine girlfriend you've found yourself, said Mother, referring to that big shot in the Party, Dora's father, it's such folk who go locking other people's children up in their prisons for years on the pretext that it's for the good of Socialism, I can do without that sort of Socialism, thank you.

She's only a girl, said Father.

But she carries on about the Party over coffee and cakes as if she were on the staff of *Neues Deutschland*.

That's the way times are.

Times aren't that way everywhere.

But it's only here that we have a house of our own with a garden.

I couldn't care less about the house either.

Is it that bad between us?

Even worse.

So the first of May came, and the whole city was out and about on the first of May, with red and blue flags and banners everywhere, and Dora in the middle of them with her kissable mouth and the first of her summer freckles, looking very serious and happy. She didn't look at him long as he stood there waving and watching her, in fact she just glanced his way once and nodded, and then seemed to spot something else, and at home that evening, when she was going over everything again, she didn't say a word about him.

Even days later she had to keep telling Heinrich what a lovely feeling it was when they were all singing together, and marching as they sang, like in the poem, and why she was carried away and right out of herself at such moments, but it was only at such moments that she was *really* herself, and he'd have to take her that way, take her as he found her.

In the first week of May they went to Eisenach, for the weather was very sunny, and they were out and about a great deal and went for long walks on the surrounding hills and meadows and pastures, because they didn't know where else to go, and they had by no means finished with each other, that first kiss in the garden, it was to be hoped, was just the start.

Heinrich always came to collect her when they were going for a walk, and once they went to the *Lutherkanzel*, and another time up the Jenzig, and with every walk, as they lingered and looked and marvelled, they made new discoveries. Down in the Paradeis district they had both been hesitant, not sure how to start, but at the *Lutherkanzel* they didn't hesitate, they savoured it, then getting in some practice, living from one embrace to the next. She's quite different from Lyusya, thought Heinrich, counting her thirty-one freckles as he ventured on his first little explorations of her, and she liked it when he ventured on his first little explorations of her up in the Zwätzen vineyards, but when things began to get serious she removed his hands from her body and laughed, because she liked feeling his hands on her silly, thin body, but before he forgot himself, she said, she must tell him she had her own stipulations.

What are they, then, asked Heinrich, and had to listen to her telling him there'd been a lot of talk about the two of them in the FDJ, and what exactly was young Hampel's political attitude, there were certainly a few things he needed to learn. It'll be a kind of game for me too, teaching you, said Dora, and came up with her first idea at once: Molotov, Vyacheslav Mikhailovich, born 9 March 1890 in Kukarka, active in the Revolution from the first, editor of *Pravda*, People's Commissar of Foreign Affairs and Foreign Minister, and a cocktail of petrol and phosphorus for close combat with tanks in the Great Patriotic War of 1941 to 1945 was called after him, you know the rest.

I'll learn about Molotov, said Heinrich, and I'm learning about the sensitive little places behind your ear too, and where you like to be touched; he wanted to learn everything. Right, when do we start, he asked, to which Dora replied: Now, this minute, so it was decided that he would learn something new from her daily, and years later he was still connecting each and every part of Dora with the name of one of the early or later revolutionaries, and remembered how he would kiss her feet and toes thinking of Bebel and Rosa Luxembourg, and all the fine works and deeds mankind had to thank them for.

After the first few times she rather neglected her political tests, or would begin on them only after he had begun on something else with her, but she started by being very strict, punishing every mistake with yet another testing question, so they sometimes lingered quite late up there in the hills and fields above the city of Jena, practising the art of love step by step and leaving no stages out, she made sure of that. He had even explored her with his mouth now, up at the Dornburg Castles he had explored her with his mouth on a park bench, making free between her thighs as if he had been at home there or a welcome guest for years. They had been discussing Trotsky just before he claimed his rights as a guest, and until they reached Trotsky and Dora's first experience of ecstasy in the grounds of the Dornburg Castles high above the valley of the Saale she herself hadn't done much to Heinrich. She had touched him *down there* with her hands only once, very briefly, and then immediately took fright and was grateful he didn't insist on any more, but was content to wait for another time, which was now, in the Dornburg Castles park high above the Saale valley, where he was looking at her hopefully. I can't, she said, quoting a line from a poem, *When you and I unite, becoming one*, she said, and was startled to find herself suddenly quoting such lines, for once they had been said you couldn't recall them. Not yet, said Heinrich, and took her hand and showed her how to do something, and then it was all right and didn't last long: not too bad at all. He looks like a child when we do that, she thought, and the poet's words came back into her head: *And while my shoulder rises, falls, bearing up life, we feel ourselves hovering with a happy smile – ah, a mere rest after our heavy labours, for nothing ever can be given free.*

Thank you, said the Russian Heinrich, the Heinrich she liked, thank you, thank you. No need to thank me, I have things still to learn, said Dora, to whom all this was happening for the first time, and now she was almost looking forward to his taking her one day, making a woman of her, which had to happen some time anyway, yes, she looked forward to it, and really did use that phrase. Will you make a woman of me? I'd love to.

After that it was all quite simple, or it seemed to both of them that it was all quite simple. Trotsky? asked Heinrich, meaning what they did on the park bench up in the grounds of the Dornburg Castles, and Dora said without hesitating: Oh Heinrich, yes, Trotsky, I'd like that, even if Trotsky's own story came to a bad end when he was in exile in Mexico, well, I hope ours won't come to a bad end. It was late May by now, and in late May, on the occasion of his sixtieth birthday, the poet Becher was given the freedom of the city of Jena, so they had something to celebrate, with a red rose from Heinrich for Dora, and a piece of chocolate out of Dora's mouth as a surprise for Heinrich. I'm looking forward to doing it with you, they often told each other, and were just waiting for the day when they would have an opportunity and a room to themselves for a few hours, because they wanted everything to be very good and really special the first time, they'd need a blanket and a sheet, and an old towel for the blood, they both had one in reserve at home for when the moment came.

They finally had their opportunity early in June. At the beginning of June Heinrich's mother said she was going away on a visit, they'd all have to cook their own meals or make themselves a sandwich, because next weekend she was going to Aachen with Sibylle for a few days to see her mother, who had been sick in a nursing home near the border for months, and I want to see what it's like in the West now too, you hear this, that and the other about it.

So the day came when he took Dora up to his room, lay on top of her listening, and couldn't hear anyone. But his father was in the garden as usual, hoeing weeds, so they had to be very quick and very quiet, to start with anyway when she was standing there in his room, rather shivery and shy and feeling scared. I'm only looking, said Heinrich, putting back the quilt for her, and it was lovely just looking at each other for a while, enjoying the sight of what they had only guessed at before (though their hands had seen it), for instance her breasts, which were only of modest size.

What's your father doing, whispered Dora, sending Heinrich to the window yet again, but he was still there among the beds in the garden, pulling out weeds and humming, and then at last Heinrich lay down with her and did the things he had done with Lyusya, and with Lyusya it had always been easy, a walk-over, but with his Dora it was a disaster. I don't think you're going to fit into me, said Dora, and Heinrich said: That's only because it's the first time, but it will all be fine the second time. I'm sorry, said Heinrich, when he didn't fit into her the second time either, and wanting to make it easy for both of them he said, this just isn't our day, and his apology made Dora weep, and it all got terribly complicated.

She would have liked it to be the way it was before, although she couldn't possibly tell him she preferred it the way it was before, but then her dear kind Heinrich read her wish from her lips, made it all right for her, and she did the same for him. Your father's calling, whispered Dora, having heard something that sounded like a call, but Heinrich said his father could call all he liked, and if he catches us and he's surprised, well then, he catches us and he's surprised, he can guess what we've been doing, and very nice too with one tiny reservation, but after all, this is only the start.

His mother came back four days later, and what she told the family was brief but gave him cause for concern, for after just four days in the West, Mother seemed ready for anything. At first she said: Yes, it was very nice, but I can't say yet what that might mean for us. Only a few remarks later, however, after a few questions and answers, she knew perfectly well what it might mean for them: people aren't rich in the West either, but they can breathe freely, and walk with their heads held high, and have nothing to be scared of except their own past and the Russians, just like us. My mother sends all of you all her love, she said, of course she doesn't take much in any more, poor Mother, but she does know we have to think it all over carefully, what with the house and the children, in the past year alone some two hundred thousand people have crossed to the West to try their luck, so why not us.

I'm staying, said Heinrich, and brought up Dora's name, saying he planned a change of direction in his job too, he liked the idea of going into the beds and bedding line like Dora, as a salesman.

Sounds just the thing for you, said Theodor, and this comment made their mother very angry: Nothing here is just the thing for any of you unless I say so, she said, and Heinrich had better put that girl out of his head. (As indeed she thought.)

Even in July Heinrich would have liked to stay, and go on trying to fit into Dora one of these days after all, but then the Theodor business suddenly came up, because his clever big brother Theodor couldn't keep his trap shut and got across the new authorities. They were threatening his brother with the Aua uranium mines, it was three days before his twenty-third birthday that they threatened him with the Aua uranium mines, so three days later he asked Schott to pay him his wages, bought himself a train ticket to the border, and was up, off and away to the West.

Nice sort of brother you have, said the Party man when they questioned Heinrich about it a few days later, asking Heinrich what his own view was, so he cautiously said that Theodor's decisions and opinions weren't his, he was still learning, to which they replied: Yes, very well, but that no-good brother of yours takes his money and runs, we're shedding no tears over him, they're in deep trouble there in the West with all their unemployed, and the former soldiers, and people arriving from the East, let it suffocate them.

Heinrich's mother wept for two days and two nights when her eldest son left without a word, and she discussed the future with his father until late into the night, but Heinrich was still thinking of his Dora and what he could try next, so as to fit into her and give her a good time, nothing else interested him. Dora made no comment on his brother's flight, saying only that her father had said at once Theodor should be in jail, where they taught people what really mattered in East Germany in the seventh year of the Cold Peace, and if they wouldn't listen then you just shut them up for ever and saved yourself a lot of trouble.

Heinrich had not wanted to tell her about Theodor at first, but it turned out that she knew already and was horrified, though she was relieved that it wasn't Heinrich, loved him very much and let him try again, up in the woods by the Fuchsturm this time, and it was a crying shame. She explained it mainly by her youth, or perhaps Heinrich was simply a size too big for her, or perhaps he only fitted into people in Russia or the West, what am I doing wrong? What am I doing wrong, said Heinrich, and Dora at least thought he was doing everything right with her, that's to say he was doing everything right with her except for just that one thing, oh, what a nightmare, what do you think it's telling us?

I don't think it's telling us anything.

Yes, it is.

They talked of little else, and one day she suddenly brought her cousin into the conversation, saying she and Heinrich needed a rest from each other, so the idea of a visit to the beautiful city of Berlin was very timely, her cousin, who also worked in beds and bedding, had recently invited her.

You certainly fancy bed salesmen, said Heinrich, meaning it as a joke, but Dora was perfectly serious and said: You're not a bed salesman, and you can forget about those plans for a shop of your own, the time's not right, nothing will come of it, and nothing will come of you and your Dora either.

It was in Dora's room at home with her parents in Maxim-Gorki-Strasse that she said this to him, and Heinrich said (joking yet again): But I still have so much to learn from you, and who was going to teach him about the Revolution now, and test him and question him, because he always liked being tested and questioned by her, and she liked it too. So what's the matter, asked Heinrich, and Dora said they just weren't right for each other, it was a matter of social class, her father had recently explained it all, explained the difference between a real proletarian and one of the Lumpenproletariat, who deep down inside has no notion of correct conduct and no manners, you'll never get along with one of them in the long run.

It's a shame, I liked you, said Dora, and only now did he realize what was up, that is to say only now and then did he begin to realize, so he was prepared for it, in a sober mood, and made his first decisions. She had written him a letter, he was to read it when he'd gone home and was in his bed, their bed, then he could read what she had written to him. Don't take it hard, my little Lumpenproletarian, she had written in farewell, my father doesn't mean it like that, but you'll never be happy with someone like me in this country, you'll probably never be happy at all in this country, so be sensible. I expect you'll be gone by the time I'm back from Berlin, I'll give you an address just in case, he's an old school friend of mine, you can trust him, we're still almost all of us fellow countrymen. Love and kisses, she had written, and then, as if in another hand: Dora H., who likes Trotsky among other things, you know what I mean.

For a long time, therefore, Heinrich thought of Dora when he thought of Berlin, the distant, great, ruined city of Berlin, which unfortunately he knew from only a single night and a morning when they had arrived overnight in January 1951. It was pitch dark on their landing at Berlin-Schönefeld airport late in the evening, and there stood the seven Hampels in the profound darkness, alone and abandoned on the huge airfield, each with a bundle of clothing, disappointed that there was no one to meet them. Father would have liked to celebrate the occasion by going to a hotel in the city centre, but they wouldn't even let the family into the big airport building without money and papers, so for a start there were a great many questions and answers and protestations of legitimacy to the officials, and then they were finally allowed in and taken to a lavishly decorated reception lounge with thick red carpets and armchairs as big as beds. Seeing it's you and you have a long journey behind you, said the porter, and they had good reason to marvel, in view of the fact that usually only VIP foreign guests were allowed in here. Only please would the Hampel family take their shoes off, to spare the carpets, so then they all walked about very carefully for a while on the thick red carpets belonging to the leaders of the Party and State, studying framed photographs of the faces of international guests whom only Dora could have identified, along with the friendly countries from which they came, pleased to visit their great little brother state, the first in Germany, a state that loved peace more than any other, a home from home for all Germans.

They spent an uncomfortable night in the armchairs reserved for the guests of the leaders of the Party and State, and their first breakfast was modest too, but people were very friendly to the seven Hampels who had spent five years in the Soviet Union, and gave what help they could. A Soviet officer even got them bus tickets to Friedrichstrasse, since he thought from their accent that they came from Moscow, yes indeed, that was where they'd been living until recently. Dora would have been pleased to think that her Heinrich passed so easily as a Russian to a Soviet officer, and indeed it sometimes seemed to him later that she might even have been there at the time, since she had this cousin in the beds and bedding business who had lived in the Russian sector of the ruined city of Berlin for years, it was practically her second home.

They spent over an hour in the bus driving all round south Berlin to Friedrichstrasse station, and of course it was immediately obvious that the work of restoring peacetime conditions was far from finished, what with all the rubble from the buildings destroyed in the war, with the human souls and administrative offices in them, and not by any means all of it could be recycled for these new and better days. The city looked dead, early in the morning, there were just a few labourers out in the streets on their way to work the early shift, and at Friedrichstrasse station a few men and women in big dark overcoats beneath which they were hiding some American Chesterfields, or an old family heirloom made of gold, or some stockings and suspender belts, all for sale.

It didn't take Heinrich half an hour to sell their two tins of caviar and a handful of Kasbek-brand Russian papyrossi cigarettes at Friedrichstrasse station, and give Father the money, for only then could Father phone and ask the factory to send a car, yes, we arrived yesterday, the accommodation's been terrible, we're glad to be back. Sure enough, the works management immediately sent a new Opel Blitz convertible for the home-coming Hampels, loading up the seven Hampels and their dirty bundles to be driven home, it all went quite smoothly. They did have some more problems over their passes on the city boundaries of Berlin, for the new Volkspolizei officers had never seen a whole family on the move without papers before, but the Russians, who had, simply waved them through. No more of that, said little Sibylle, meaning the Russian language and the years she would now forget for ever, and when he reached this point in his memories he dismissed Dora from his mind too, since he feared that his Dora was up to something in the pretty Pankow district, or in beautiful Buch, where her distant cousin was a bed salesman, and after closing time they'd go home to his place and enjoy the way everything fitted together so nicely. It doesn't always fit like that, Dora would say, laughing and thinking briefly of her Heinrich, but thinking of her Heinrich only very briefly, and then she had to think of her cousin from Pankow or Buch again, because things don't always fit together so nicely, but it's lovely when they do.

So it was Dora who brought him to the point of going across the green border ten days after Theodor. It had taken Heinrich a long time to think it all out, and the way he saw it now, Dora was the one who sent him out of the country and into the West, probably for ever.

The address she had given him just in case was in Jena East near the Schillerkirche, and no sooner had he mentioned Dora, daughter of the Second Regional Secretary, than the man knew what it was all about and nodded, named a price, waited until Heinrich had got accustomed to the price, and crossed the street to an Opel Blitz, a car with which Heinrich was familiar, offering to take him to the border in it. Call me Dieter, he said, adding that he'd known Dora since they were playing in the sandbox together, but it was a long time since he'd seen her, Dora didn't send people like Heinrich every day. They'd be off on Friday, said Dieter, who had known Dora since they were playing in the sandbox together, and Heinrich said: Right, Friday around five at the Zwätzen barracks. They would meet there, and make a delivery round to be on the safe side, being a plumber Dieter always had a few lengths of piping or something like that with him.

Up to the last day Heinrich had wondered whether to say anything to his father or Paul or his big sister, but then he decided he had better just disappear and get in touch afterwards, and then if there were any difficult questions at this end his parents could say they had had no idea and were very upset, fancy our sons giving us all this grief and trouble, whatever are we to do?

Mother was boiling the laundry when he said goodbye, as if he were just going round to Dora's again, although his Dora was still in the pretty Pankow district talking about beds and their role in the intensifying class struggle, or perhaps she would have wished him goodbye differently, perhaps she was congratulating herself, thinking of her two men friends driving towards the border on one of the last weekends in July, talking almost entirely about her. Dora's a bit peculiar, said Dieter, I mean she's a Stalinist, but just because she *is* a Stalinist, and unlike her father, she thinks people must be allowed to leave if they don't feel good here, or give offence, or don't say the right sort of thing, because that way, says Dora, only the good people will be left and we can build the new state with them. I've always been able to rely one hundred per cent on Dora and the people she sends, and he wondered whether Heinrich had had a fling with her, well yes, just a bit of a fling, Dieter couldn't really imagine it. Difficult, that one, said Dieter, adding something else about the people she sent him: They're classy people, the refugees she sends, but there are classy people in the Party too, and the weird thing is they all keep saying it's for the best.

I've no idea where we are, said Heinrich when they had driven south-west for a good two hours, but Dora's childhood friend knew the road by heart, he said he always stopped in Unterlind, the next village is called Judenbach, meaning Jewish Brook, and where there are Jews you can be sure the capitalist West isn't far away, that was the joke he made as they went the last few kilometres.

So they drove to Unterlind, and in Unterlind he got Heinrich to hand over the money, gave him a wry smile, and then led him across fields and woods to the border. Over there, see that pair of guards walking along, when they and their dogs are out of sight jump the brook and run for your life. *Now*, said Dora's childhood friend, giving Heinrich a push in the back, good luck and all the best over there, and Heinrich was running, then he hesitated, then he ran again, called out little Dora's name, Dora with her thirty-one freckles, hoped she'd think of him when she was back home, but now stupid lovelorn Hampel had to run and run as if his life were at stake, so he jumped the brook and he ran and there he was in the West.

For almost half an hour he did nothing but gasp for breath and wait, listening, and when he had finished gasping for breath and listening and sending his farewell thoughts in Dora's direction in vain, he pulled himself together and walked through the woods and the meadows towards Ebersdorf, where they had experience of people like him. He was wearing a pair of Western shoes, a shirt and tie, and a suit made of cellulose-enriched fabric, he had a shabby briefcase with some underclothes and shaving things, that was the way those poor bastards from the East had been arriving over the last few months imagining it would all be perfectly easy, people would be delighted to see them, so overjoyed that they'd set the table for dinner at once and give them a bed for the night, well, they were dead wrong about that. Even at the parsonage Heinrich was sent packing, nobody wanted to mix with refugees who didn't know if they were coming or going, but if he had any money, took it to the bank and exchanged it, the rate being one to five, he could ask a farmer to let him sleep in the barn, or ask one of the farmhands, they can do with a few pfennigs and one of them might give you his straw mattress for the night.

Heinrich was still expecting it all to be perfectly simple in the train from Neustadt to Coburg next morning, since he had eaten a good breakfast at the farmer's and his pockets were full of money, he'd only had to open his mouth and say he wanted to get to the nearest railway station, and the farmer offered his old tractor as a taxi and drove him the few kilometres to Neustadt. Oh, Dora, thought Heinrich, thinking she ought to see all this some day and compare it to the East, even the landscape here immediately looked to

Heinrich brighter, more emphatic, livelier, they'd have so much to talk about. For instance, the people here didn't look rich either, but they greeted each other cheerily and laughed, cracked a few jokes about exiles or refugees like Heinrich, enjoyed seeing an inspector appear in the train because it always turned the refugees so deathly pale, or sent them sprinting for the lavatory, though they might be the slow sort like Heinrich, who was dreaming and kept looking out into this new, strange West Germany, dreaming of his girl, like a soldier, or dreaming of all the money he would make, or a good hearty meal, except that he didn't really look at all starved.

Two of the border police officers had boarded the train with their German shepherd dogs, and they only had to look at him to spot the peculiar suit he was wearing, let's see your papers, please. I only have Eastern papers, said Heinrich, so they led him straight off and said not a word until Coburg. Once in Coburg they led Heinrich off again, put him in a police car and drove him to the nearby school, which was serving as a temporary assembly camp for refugees who had been picked up like Heinrich and where the people in charge talked to them for a bit, and when they'd picked up enough refugees for the day one of the officials made a short speech, informing them that they were being transferred to the Soviet zone, we expect the lorries to be here around four.

At first Heinrich couldn't believe his ears, but then he rose to his feet and explained: You can't do that, not to me you can't, I've spent five years in Russia, so if you send me back I'll really be for it. This tune struck them as an interesting one, and they lent an ear to it, and began phoning round and fetched someone over from the American secret service. Russia, was it? said the man from the American secret service, and Heinrich said: Yes, I spent five years in Russia, and all of a sudden he was in the back of a Mercedes 170 with no handles on the inside of the rear doors and a sliding glass screen, rather like something out of a film. They drove

Heinrich all round Coburg to confuse him, not that Heinrich knew Coburg in the slightest, nor did he know the villa where they took him, he was told they kept a room specially for such cases, Heinrich might like to rest for a while or take a shower, they guessed showers were pretty well unknown in Russia.

My name's Reynolds, said the officer to whom he was taken an hour later, and he started straight in with questions about where Heinrich came from and where he was going, then suddenly switched languages and asked Heinrich, in Russian, about his five years in the country and what exactly it was like there, what it was like in the towns of Klin and Lytkarino near Moscow, and Heinrich had to tell him. Well, in Klin, he said, they'd played a lot of volleyball in the first couple of years, and there was an airfield nearby which always had a few new MIG 17 aircraft standing on it, at which the officer called Reynolds pricked up his ears, and asked exactly where he had always seen the MIG 17 aircraft standing in that first couple of years, and when he looked on his map (for the American secret service even had a detailed map of Klin), sure enough the orientation was right.

This went on for a good hour and a half, and after an hour and a half they said they'd want to check up on what Heinrich had told them, talked a little more, and by now it was almost evening. At the end of his long day Heinrich was actually invited to eat with the officer called Reynolds, who was clad in a brightly coloured bush shirt and old grey slacks, so for the first time in his life Heinrich ate steak and chips, followed by canned pineapple and strawberries, all he wanted, and he was much taken with the idea that things were like this in the West, or with this officer called Reynolds anyway, he'd soon be finding out more.

I could easily get used to this, said Heinrich, and the officer called Reynolds asked: Have a whisky? So they finally got to talking about girls, and since talking about girls over a glass of whisky is pleasant, Heinrich mentioned his girlfriends Lyusya and Dora, and the differences he'd noticed between them and what they had in common, and the officer called Reynolds kept pouring more whisky. Once he said: I don't believe it, can Russian girls really be like that, and he said Heinrich was a lucky bastard meeting Lyusya, he wouldn't find that kind of thing so easy here in the West, which is why we have whisky here in the West, and as for what else we have — well, we'll see.

He sprayed Heinrich's food a few times with saliva as he talked, this American who had given him the first whisky he had drunk in his life, and he talked a lot about the Korean crisis, and in the next breath returned to his sweet Cindy back home in Kansas City, saying everything was equally important, quite simple or sometimes quite difficult, like the Russian presence in Korea, but the Americans were going out there to settle it all, well, what do you Germans think happened to your Hitler and his gang?

This was the way Heinrich began his life in the West, and it hadn't begun badly at all, thought Heinrich, they even brought you a glass of fresh milk in bed in the morning, they gave you plenty of time to wake up and shower and think things over before they said: Well, everything you told us checks out, and asked where he was planning to go now with his stories, and what about Giessen, since they were afraid there was no avoiding the Giessen transit camp.

Giessen, no, he was afraid not, said Heinrich, and the officer called Reynolds said: It's not so bad, we'll call and tell them about you and then everything will go smoothly in Giessen, and we've packed you a bite to eat so you don't starve to death on the journey, and here's two hundred new German marks for you and a second-class ticket, you change trains once, in Frankfurt am Main.

They even took him to the station, these nice Americans who thought of everything and had everything and made everything easy, see you in Kansas City, said Reynolds, at the last moment handing him two large American paper bags containing cigarettes and chewing gum and sandwiches, and then he was off, going further and further westward from this part of the West, smoking and chewing gum and looking at what called itself the West, few people wore uniforms, for instance, and they were reading thick newspapers as if there might really be some news in them.

Just after Fulda Heinrich went to the buffet car and spent some time watching a young couple with two heavy rucksacks, and when he was still staring at them after quarter of an hour they suddenly rose to their feet and lost their tempers, so this is what Germany's coming to, you get total strangers undressing your wife with their eyes, not surprising with all the filth and trash that gets screened in the cinemas these days, they went on and on about it, calling him a dirty swine and saying people like Heinrich would once have been silenced, they'd have been taught a lesson, there was no hanging about back then in the camps; it was the husband who said all this, dragging his wife into it with him, and Heinrich had only a very vague idea what the matter was.

I see you're surprised, said a fat man at the next table, and asked if he could join Heinrich for a moment, immediately introducing himself: Sinnhuber, Bundestag deputy, on my way to Bonn, I'm a Christian Socialist Union member of parliament. My name's Hampel, said Heinrich, I've just been with the Americans in Coburg, I was in the Soviet Union before that, and then I left Jena and came over the green border at Unterlind, my brother Theodor's here in the West already.

Very interesting, said Sinnhuber the Bundestag deputy, and explained things to Heinrich: first the Soviets, second the Americans, third the Germans. They recently showed a film with a naked woman in the cinemas, hence all the uproar, and of course the Americans are responsible for naked women appearing here on screen all of a sudden, and the Russians are the Russians, same as usual, and as people who've been conquered and overrun and occupied we knuckle under like the good folk we are, we don't protest when they take away our land in the East, so there you are with Ulbricht and his friends in the middle, and incredible amounts of envy and resentment in the West: it was bad. Could he offer Heinrich a beer? Yes, he could, he could even offer Heinrich a second and a third beer, although Heinrich had his pockets full of money, everything was still new and baffling, for instance, he said, back in the East he'd never heard about the film with the naked woman in it. It's a sin and a shame, said Sinnhuber the Bundestag deputy, adding that just about everything was a sin and a shame wherever you went, and one of these days he might join the League of Exiles and the Dispossessed where at least they talked politics, and it's on behalf of the right people they talk politics, I mean people like you, Herr Hampel.

Oh, politics, said Heinrich, and was about to say something about American whisky as compared to Russian vodka, but Sinnhuber the Bundestag deputy, unlike the Texan officer Reynolds, seemed to think little of such subjects. However, the Bundestag deputy did prick up his ears when they got around to the subject of Schott and the train which took forty-one of its glassmakers away, and he asked what kind of work Heinrich expected to find here in the West, it wasn't so easy at the moment.

I'd rather like to work in beds and bedding, said Heinrich, and could hardly believe his ears when Sinnhuber immediately came up with an idea: as a Bundestag deputy he travelled a good deal, he got to meet all kinds of people, very likely including people in the beds and bedding line, he'd be happy to ask around for Heinrich, and now, before they drank their fourth beers, perhaps he'd take down the address and phone number of Sinnhuber the CSU Bundestag deputy from Bonn, call me some day soon and I'll have news for you, this was ridiculous.

He got another two hundred marks as well, it was just

before reaching Frankfurt that the Bundestag deputy came up with two hundred marks for this interesting refugee from Jena, so now he was on his way to Bonn, while Heinrich was going on to Giessen, see you some day soon.

Heinrich stayed two nights at the Giessen camp, and after that he got his papers and went back to the pretty town of Landshut to join Theodor, who was not exactly delighted. That's all I need, having you here, said Theodor, but he found Heinrich work at Schott and a room with his landlady, who had four rooms to rent in Unter den Kolonnaden in the Altstadt, and asked the extortionate sum of thirty Deutschmarks per bed per month, no girls in the rooms, no cooking. Do you have a girlfriend? Heinrich asked, looking at Theodor as if he surely must, well, at least there was Ilse, whom he had known before they left for Russia and who was the first person he'd asked after on his return, it so happened that someone could in fact provide information and gave an address in Kaiserslauten, which was where she had ended up and was now living, waiting for Theodor to come back or not, as the case might be. I have other things on my mind, said Theodor, and he didn't even ask about Heinrich's flight, only about Mother, and when the rest of the family would be coming, never mind about the house, well, now I have to go to work.

Even on Sundays, Heinrich often saw his brother sitting up until late into the night drafting plans of some sort, with a job in Mainz in mind, for if nothing came of Schott and its proletarian workforce in sleepy Landshut then he'd just have to see if he could make his way in Mainz, and meanwhile Theodor was already designing his first furnaces and tanks and melting baths, and making himself a name which, thanks to the great Soviet Union, would not be easily surpassed in the glassmaking craft in either East or West.

At first they had nothing suitable for Heinrich at the works, and asked what he had learnt in Jena apart form burning his fingers every few days on the glass while it was still hot, putting the glass on shelves to cool and looking for small flaws, that was about it, but since he was a Hampel and the firm owed his brother and his father a good deal they'd make an exception for him, he could start on Monday, but there wasn't a lot to do at the moment. As for Heinrich, he liked not having a lot to do at the moment, or having to think too much about Mainz or Landshut, or having to account for himself to anyone, and he thought about Dora and the beds and Sinnhuber the Bundestag deputy, who he hoped would help him find a job in beds and bedding, or if need be in some other line of work. It was still too soon to ring Sinnhuber the Bundestag deputy in Bonn, but it wasn't too soon for a new girlfriend, something could be done about that, with his four hundred marks for instance.

It was around now that Heinrich began frequenting various swimming pools almost daily in the summer, studying the girls, getting his eye in, rehearsing for Bella or plump Rosa, whom he didn't notice at all, or didn't think worth a second glance at this time. But he was still young, only starting out, and although he studied the girls a good deal, and enjoyed getting into conversation with them beside the water or over at the ice-cream kiosk, he was hesitant that summer, and dithered, and the odd thing was that the girls liked it when he hesitated and dithered, excusing himself on the grounds of his parents or his work. Some other time, then, they said, and they were not as bold as they seemed, for instance he wouldn't have got as far with them as he did with Dora up in the grounds of the Dornburg Castles. It was only on his twentieth birthday that he stayed quite a while with a girl, she was very quiet and friendly, with pale blue eyes, he'd never known such a delightfully silent girl in his life. This girl Clara spent the whole afternoon with him in silence, sitting beside him drying her hair and saying nothing, letting Heinrich bring her a bottle of lemonade and saying nothing, and like Heinrich she had no questions to ask, said thank you when they parted in the evening and went off, but she didn't come back next day, perhaps she had thought of something else not to talk about, or perhaps she was already engaged and had a fiancé and wasn't happy about him because he was away travelling so often, and when they kissed he tasted of blood sausage and liver sausage.

Later, Heinrich thought: I'd have liked to take Clara to the movies that evening, since they were showing the film with the naked woman who committed suicide at the local cinema in the evenings, and the two of them could have sat there in silence eating a bag of Texan peanuts and wondering why people got so worked up about that naked woman, you only saw her for a couple of seconds anyway. This was what Heinrich liked about the West, the fact that they showed movies where a naked woman was visible for a couple of seconds, while what he missed most about the East was his naked Dora, who could be touched and held, and lasted half a summer, except that unfortunately he never did fit into her properly.

One Sunday early in October his mother and the rest of the family arrived at the door, and the first person to say anything was Paul, who had a letter for Heinrich, he had hidden it in his underpants for Heinrich for two days and two nights, if they'd caught us with it I hate to think what would have happened. I think it's from Dora, said Constanze, and Paul said: She turned up in our garden one day, asking after you, what were we supposed to say?

Ah, here you are at last, said Theodor, who did not like this particular subject, did everything go smoothly? Yes, it's all in order, said Mother, adding that Father had gone to see the people at the Schott works and would arrive later, you look as if you've made quite a comfortable start here. Do sit down, said Heinrich, immediately opening the letter, so she had written to him once more after all. Dear Heinrich, wrote Dora, this is my really and truly last letter, I'm writing to you just this once more to say goodbye, not a word after this, we'll go our separate ways. Berlin was nice, you remember I had to go to Berlin so you'd finally understand and leave me alone, but bed salesmen are very boring, not a trace of Trotsky there. The big Stalin-Allee was lovely, though, and there I was all on my own in Stalin-Allee in the great city of Berlin, and I missed you, you see I really am very stupid.

Yes, it's from Dora, said Heinrich, because they were all looking expectantly at him, but then they wanted to tell the tale of their long journey, and their anxieties, and their arrival in the proud capital of the Republic. It had cost them three thousand Eastern marks to find someone local to help them get away, everyone thought they were going to a wedding in the country near Potsdam, this was on a Saturday, they climbed into an old car with a wooden carburettor and all went well until they were past Dessau. Then came the first check-points, and the awkward questions, and they made the acquaintance of fear. Where was their wedding present for the happy couple? Oh, here, in this bag. Open it, please. And was the gentleman at the wheel also a wedding guest? Yes, he was the witness to the marriage.

So they were allowed to go, and the two girls in the back felt their knees knocking until they were past Treuenbrietzen. It was three in the morning when they reached the capital of the German Democratic Republic, and by way of celebration ate their first or rather only breakfast there at the railway station, the Ostbahnhof, and then they took the suburban train west by way of Friedrichstrasse station, oh heavens. The first thing Mother had said was: I need a schnapps to get over the shock of this, and it was nearly thirty years since she'd had a schnapps, but she now drank two in succession in a bar at the Zoo Station.

Then came all the waiting about, the various hostels where they stayed, the fear of being dragged off in broad daylight and taken back to the East, that was the worst of it. The constant suspicion was bad, and it was a pity Paul and

Constanze were staying some way off in Dahlem with a lecturer who had fled from Erfurt, while Mother and Father and little Sibylle were in a Kurfürstenstrasse boarding-house which would accept Eastern money.

But Berlin was lovely, said Constanze, now that it was all over and they had been recognized as political refugees, there was even coloured knitting wool in the shop windows, and white Lux soap and as much chewing gum as you wanted. She and Paul had eaten the first banana of their lives in West Berlin, and they'd seen a colour film with Peter Alexander showing at the famous Zoo-Palast, he sang that song about the legs of Dolores which kept the señores from falling asleep, it was terrific. Berlin was very cold and very expensive, you were out and about almost all day marvelling at the things on sale in the shops, and the things flown over in planes from America or the new Federal Republic which had room on the return journey for people like the Hampels, people with the famous C classification who must not fall into Soviet hands.

We flew on a TWA Super-Constellation, said Paul, it was after an endlessly long ten days that the Allies flew them out of the frontline city of Berlin into free Nuremberg, and one Mr Brown of the British secret service asked them a few last questions in the waiting-room, both Heinrich and Theodor knew about that sort of thing and how it worked in their favour.

So how's Father taking it, asked Theodor, knowing that his father would be taking it badly because of the house, but in time he got accustomed to it and worked for Schott in Landshut and later in Mainz, jobs already fixed up by Theodor for his father, and the poor man didn't necessarily have to know that he wasn't really needed in either Landshut or Mainz.

Yes, well, your father, said Mother, he was carrying on as usual, but when Father arrived he seemed perfectly cheerful, and late in the afternoon they all five went out to Ergolding and a country inn there, recommended by the Schott works, where they could stay for the time being.

No East ever again, said Theodor, and Heinrich said: Yes, let's drink to that, for his bottle of whisky (the first Heinrich had bought) was still a good half full.

9

So Heinrich trained and had another seven years, his last fat years, and they were fat years too for the Republic where he lived, which was celebrating treaties and agreements and friendships for all it was worth. People celebrated over Crimean sparkling wine and champagne and vodka, dreaming until early in the morning of the fully developed Socialist society at home and in the fraternal states to the east, and perhaps tomorrow in half of Asia, Africa and Latin America, such were the bold ideas of the time, and they dreamed of love and respect for the land and its people, and wanted even the likes of Heinrich to be involved, wasn't it quite something that they had given him a chance on the big construction sites of the Gera administrative district, even overlooking the death of a man and the occasional carelessness of his reports.

Heinrich had wrested seven fat years from the masters, servants and women of the German Democratic Republic, along with seven mistresses and seven times seven bouts of drinking himself senseless, and then the seven fat years came to an end, and one morning in October 1975 Rosa woke him with words he knew well: Get up, Hampel, we have a date in court, it's eight-thirty and this time I'm not going home until I'm divorced. Oh, leave me alone, said Heinrich, feeling the effect of all the previous night's glasses and bottles and doubts, but Rosa, gentle and insistent, didn't stop talking until he got up, steeled himself to face the day, and washed and dressed as if they were going to a wedding or the Socialist initiation ceremony for their youngest child Walter, who would only call his father Ede, and crossed to the other side of the street when he saw that man Ede, his father, coming, or spat scornfully in front of his feet.

The date in court lasted less than fifteen minutes, and then the Hampels were divorced after twenty-one years of marriage, and didn't know quite what to say. This is the third time I've petitioned, Rosa had said, I can't take any more of it, and she totted everything up: the seven mistresses and the seven times seven bouts of drinking himself senseless, the lies, the pleas, his sordid way of life; the way he hid brandy and vodka all over the flat, the afternoons when his sons found him drunk and hauled him on to the sofa, heavy as a corpse, her feelings of disgust, how she felt sorry for him and stopped feeling sorry when he took to turning the gas tap on now and then, like his father but intending to be found (Eva found him), how she kept discovering bottles in the box of sheets under the bed, in the lavatory cistern, among his underclothes or the potatoes in the cellar, not to mention his promises to drink less and think of his children as a father should, except that his sons could scarcely remember him as a father. I can't take it any more, said Rosa, and the judges understood and asked her daughter Eva which parent she would decide for, good heavens, decide, anyway she said she was afraid she had to get to a lecture on dialectical and historical materialism, she was in her second semester studying economics, her fiancé was waiting outside in his car, he'll drive me there.

Well, see you later, said Rosa, when the documents were all signed and the Hampels shared only the flat and their surname, but not a bed and not their meals, which was nothing new. I'll be back in an hour or so, said Heinrich, shaking hands with her as he left as if she had won a sporting contest, and then he had a few drinks and waited for Harms in the new flat which was their meeting-place, good old Harms, who seemed rather surprised and could utter only commonplaces: To think it can all be over so quickly, said Harms, adding that twenty-one years was a small eternity, it was a small eternity ago that they had founded the new state which wasn't quite completed yet, back then on Dora's eighteenth birthday, he still had not the slightest doubts of it.

However, he said, Heinrich's reports had given him cause for concern recently, there had been mistakes in them, false accusations or things played down, he seemed to be mixing incidents up now and then, or else all the vodka was confusing him, what was the matter? Well, he needed money, and a new flat well away from Rosa and the children, because they didn't get on with him, so it would be better if he avoided them for a while, put some distance between himself and the family, Rosa thought so too, she was relieved, and in her relief she looked very pretty.

Come on, one more time, said Heinrich when he saw how relieved and how pretty she looked, it was a very strange thing for him to ask, and she looked at him and smiled and said yes, maybe. But only this one time, she said, hesitating, and undressed quickly, like one of those girls from Leipzig, only she had never told him that years ago she nearly became one of those girls from Leipzig, so he didn't notice, and thought her as loving and attentive and egotistic in her love-making as usual, as if they still needed each other.

But never again, said Rosa when it was all over and done with, and she let him sniff her again, and noticed the way he sniffed her for the last time, noticed everything, and then she had to get straight into the bathtub and sing, because when she was singing in the bathtub she felt her world was still in order.

It had been a very hot summer with temperatures well above thirty degrees at the beginning of August when the new bridge from Lobeda to Burgau was opened to traffic, and Heinrich Hampel, civil engineer, answered questions put by a woman reporter about the general principles of Socialist building, and how many tons of steel and concrete it took to build such a bridge, she wanted to know everything, every detail of the plan, how the norm was to be fulfilled, how many extra shifts were needed to exceed it. A norm of one hundred and four point two seven per cent on the project, Herr Hampel, you should be proud of yourself and your men, said the reporter from the *Thüringische Landeszeitung*, looking into the distance for a while, her eyes straying to Lobeda West and the new high-rise buildings on which she had once written a piece, and where she might have liked to live herself some day, although this was merely a suspicion on Heinrich's part, and he waited for the next approving remark or the next question, but it didn't come: just silence. She even took her dark glasses off, silent and feeling at ease with the silence, and it was at such moments that he came wide awake and knew just what to say. There's a lovely view, particularly in the evening, said Heinrich, not meaning it as a proposition, but the reporter from the *Thüringische Landeszeitung* took it as a proposition, just for a little while, Herr Hampel, please, I need a story.

She had changed before meeting him on the new bridge from Lobeda to Burgau to enjoy the view, although she didn't even make notes on it; it was so beautiful, the heat of the day still lay heavily on the landscape, and then suddenly she said: There's something else I was going to say, Herr Hampel, the fact is this heat gives me ideas, you can kiss me if you like, here and now and for as long as you like, that's what I wanted for my story, a kiss and a man and his bridge, that would be just the thing.

She took her glasses off before kissing him, and she went on and on kissing, and said: Cola with cognac, I don't know which brand, and placed his hands underneath her check jacket, all this on the bridge in the middle of all the people driving by and gaping and envying them, who knows. You must say something about my bridge, said Heinrich, when she put her glasses on again and assumed the expression of a reporter specializing in civil engineering, so she said something else nice about Heinrich's bridge, and something very nice about Heinrich's kisses on the bridge, it was a pity she didn't have a car so that she could drive over it, she went everywhere on foot or by bus or in cars belonging to various men on the construction sites, but she guessed nowhere near all of them were as nice as Heinrich with his mouth that tasted of cognac and cola, he must have been celebrating a little.

Then there were seven hot days, and every evening of those seven hot days he asked if Rosa wouldn't like to come and enjoy the view on the bridge from Lobeda to Burgau, but Rosa always said: Not today, I'm afraid I can't come today, surely those photos in the paper gave her a good enough idea, that young reporter seemed to be dotty about him, or why would she write so much.

You don't build bridges every day, said Heinrich, hoping she would change her mind, because then he could have shown her where he had got them to cement the bottle of brandy in, a farewell gesture to the booze from hard-drinking Heinrich Hampel, since at this time he was still making good resolutions, but she knew best why nothing ever came of his good resolutions.

She had treated him like a dog since that night in the summer of 1972 when he stood outside her door until early in the morning, begging and whimpering and in his thoughts already licking her hands, her firm little hands, those clever hands which knew all about him and despised all they knew about him, the hands of his enemy Rosa who had forgotten him and no longer spared a thought for his successes, or the chasms of failure into which he poured cognac and cola, and sometimes on Sundays a bottle of vodka from his Russian homeland, the Union of Socialist Soviet Republics, capital city Moscow.

He was already doing his first undercover deals with goods ordered for the building sites at this point, and once again he was going in and out of the Zwätzen barracks, where they still tolerated him as a former friend of Vladimir. You and your Russians, Rosa often said when he brought officers home, just as he did in the old days, and got drunk in his room with them, drinking the memories out of his mind as he had drunk them away last spring after their second date in court, or the year before when he lost his best labourer in an accident and drank for three days on end, but the drinking didn't drive the images away, and after another three days Rosa said: I wish *you* had died on that building site, you give me the creeps.

It was in the kitchen, around noon on New Year's Day, that she first told him he gave her the creeps, when Constanze and Ferdinand had gone into town with the two children to stretch their legs and see the sights and wonder about the state of the Hampels' marriage, and their sons Konrad and Walter, there must be something wrong there, what with the way they had instantly fallen on the visitors' suitcases asking for their presents, taking them without a word of thanks and talking about filthy capitalists, well, what do you think, the best people are all here with us.

Heinrich's sister and her family had come to stay for nearly a week, and they chatted comfortably away and drank to the increasing rapprochement of the two states, after all, we were once all the same country. On the first evening Heinrich's sister said: So this is the way you live here, we had no idea, interesting, not bad at all, and the Goethe House in Weimar isn't bad, and it must all have been meadowland once up by the Fuchsturm, wasn't it? If you only knew, said Rosa on the second evening, and on the third evening Heinrich said: It's lousy here, Constanze, absolutely lousy, but at midnight, on the third bottle, he was suddenly talking like a Party functionary.

They had not let their relations from the West see that they could scarcely get hold of the bare essentials to eat, or notice how their debts old and new were weighing on them, but then the happy families act put on in the East by the Hampels was finally over, and Rosa went to the public prosecutor responsible for such matters and asked for an immediate divorce. You don't mean it, said Heinrich, and the public prosecutor said: You don't mean it, Frau Hampel, not with three children aged eleven to nineteen, we do trust you can pull yourself together and cope, and you had better stop drinking, Herr Hampel, drink has been the downfall of better men than you, and worse men than you have won the battle against it.

Come on then, let's pull ourselves together, said Heinrich, and she remembered the promise he had given then, in the shape of a string of a couple of dozen pearls which he got from the West for his Rosa, because he was still owed some money by the family in the West, and it was an investment in Rosa, to make her stay with him a little longer and not find it too difficult, but Rosa thought it a high enough price for a few months of patience.

Soon afterwards she had the idea of drying-out treatment to cure Heinrich Hampel of his addiction to alcohol and make him better, and he did indeed go for treatment, approaching it like a holiday or an adventure, but after ten days he had had enough and wanted to go home to his Rosa and his bottles, rang the doorbell grinning from ear to ear, rang the bell again, how dared he, how on earth did he dare, good heavens, Hampel.

You don't seriously mean to come back, said Rosa, and Heinrich said: I've fallen in love with a Polish girl, and I thought I was going to burst.

I'm so ashamed of you, said Rosa, feeling all her old fury against Bella, and knowing how ridiculous it was to feel her old fury against Bella, for she had long ago buried the thought of Bella and Heinrich, and everything that had happened to her Heinrich since Bella: all over and done with.

On their second date in court, in the spring of 1975, he

had been the old Heinrich again, kissed Rosa's hand in greeting, moved her chair in for her, told the woman judge tearfully how much he loved her, and the woman judge was impressed by a man who would declare his love for his wife on the day of their divorce and shoulder all the blame himself, all was not yet lost for the Hampels, she said, and she suggested another six months to think it over, honestly, none of them had the faintest idea.

As before, he tried to bribe Rosa, asking how she would like a piece of gold and silver jewellery, there were all sorts of things in the catalogues of the Western mail order firms with a number beside each item, from car tyres to the platinum brooch costing one thousand nine hundred and ninety marks plus postage and packing, what was it to be? From you, nothing, said Rosa, and if you ever touch me again, or open my door when I'm asleep and stare at me, I'm going to call the police and tell them about your deals with that man Gerber, the man who died, I'm just warning you.

You wouldn't dare, said Heinrich.

I'd dare to do anything.

But there's no need for this.

You've been leaving stains on the sheets recently, she said, and asked him to use a towel, which he promised to do.

The afternoon when they found the dead man Heinrich was enjoying one of his visits to Vera, who lived in one of the new panel-constructed buildings nearby, and every few days had half the afternoon off from her job as a sixth-form college teacher, when she would play her little game with Heinrich, or they might ask plump Jana, Vera's neighbour at the end of the corridor, to join in and play little games with them too. These were not the last women in his life, but there were afternoons when he was depressed by going to a great deal of trouble to do gymnastics in these stolen moments between four and five, before she could climax he always had to knock at her body somewhere as if it were a door, so that she could say: Hello, who's there, I'm the door, you go in and out of me – she had such odd ideas in her head, calling herself his little golden thimble, or his garage, come along in, there's plenty of room.

She was a little difficult compared to Rosa, thought Heinrich, but it was a long time since he had last slept with Rosa, and difficult Dora with her Stalin was far away in the past too, so one had to look around, try things out, be patient with this sports and mathematics teacher with the two ex-husbands who had found her rather difficult, or didn't know the ways and means, because in the end you could always get into her somehow, or she would help you a little with her comments, or a hand between her thighs might do the trick, and then you pulled her on over you, like a stocking or a pullover, and there you were.

The dead Gerber was lying on his back with his eyes open when Heinrich arrived on the scene, and he thought: He's just asleep, Gerber's lying down in the middle of the site having a nap, but there's a lot of blood running out of his head, particularly from his mouth, as if he'd had a bad fall. They had found him around noon, and it was still not clear whether he had been careless, or felt unwell up on the wall before falling several metres to the ground and landing unluckily, right on his stupid round head, and he was married with two children, and alone at the site on Heinrich's advice.

The Volkspolizei had already told his wife, and there were a great many questions to be asked for a start, and when they were through with their questions Heinrich got into his car and drove to Winzerla to see the widow. She didn't want to let him in, she was so angry with Heinrich and his talk of all the money you could earn on the building sites of the Gera district, or the money you could get by doing shady deals, and now I'm left with my children, and yes, I've got a washing machine and a television set and a telephone, but who's it all for, what's it all for, tell me that.

He stayed less than a quarter of an hour, then he drove to the bank and back again, and put two thousand marks down on her table, this was just to be going on with, so that she would have the money for a proper gravestone and for the children and something nice for herself to wear and flowers and wreaths for the grave. This went on for a good three weeks, with Heinrich bringing her something almost daily, spending every free moment with her, going in and out of the place like a member of her family or a lover, yet she wouldn't even speak to him, though he was always buying her things, giving presents, re-papering her rooms, hoping she would finally accept what had happened, renewing the bathroom fittings, making a cupboard for her children, unable to get a good word out of their mother even after two months, until he had finally had enough of it and gave up.

You have nothing to reproach yourself with, said Harms, when the investigations were called off, and everyone was congratulating him as if he had won the lottery, or an official charter allowing him to leave her to her unhappiness. Eva, yes, the widow's name was Eva, and she was the only person about whom he wrote nothing in his reports during those weeks and months, along with his daughter, about whom he wrote nothing in his reports either, because she was still nice to him after all these years, or so he hoped.

Instead he wrote: My wife Rosa wants to go back to the West, she was born in Landshut in the Federal Republic of Germany on 3 January 1933, has been a citizen of the GDR by her own choice since 1962, he wrote, suggesting a few ways of preventing her from leaving and putting the wrong ideas into anyone's head, yours faithfully, the undersigned. Or he wrote: Vera N. is reading a book about Bolshevist mathematics, but she doesn't believe what it says. Jana S., lover of Citizen Hampel, the man with the vodka, is jealous and gives our afternoons together numbers like Party conferences. He was getting certain things mixed up in his reports these days, days which were blurred, one just like another, they passed and were forgotten, but he couldn't get out of his head those pictures of dead Gerber and firm-fleshed Rosa, the Rosa of the old days, that was the worst of it.

You should have stayed in the West after the funeral, said Rosa, no one here would have missed you, certainly not me.

They had given him three days and two nights in the autumn of 1973 to go and bury Gertrud, second wife of his father who died with his head in the gas oven; and at the age of forty-two he had a choice again, although it was probably only a joke that first Harms and then Rosa (each hoping for a different outcome) said he had a choice, acted as if they were saying a long goodbye, fearing, hoping he wouldn't make any mistakes in his brother Theodor's country, as if he'd be welcome there after eleven and a half years.

My brother wouldn't thank me, remarked Heinrich, getting into the train early in the morning, and on arriving that evening he saw that they had gone to some trouble for him as a citizen of that other, that hated Germany, they'd prepared a three-course meal, followed by whisky and cigars, not bad at all. Heinrich arrived in the West not twenty-four hours before the funeral, and had been considerably surprised by the freshly painted houses, the vineyards, the river in the last October sunlight, the women in their startlingly short miniskirts, which he tried to ignore, but when he gave his brother the present he had brought, some Bürgel china, he said very confidently: We're proud of products like this, we're proud that only skill and knowledge counts with us, no one who's just pretending, putting on an act, will get a look-in.

At this Theodor smiled, not wishing to argue, although Heinrich did want to argue, and had a derogatory remark to make about his brother's garden, and another about the new living-room fireplace, did they have to take this sort of thing from an ex-convict from the East, that lousy state.

Our state, said Heinrich.

Your state is run by dilettantes, said Theodor, everything's mediocre, and the leaders are a bunch of criminals by conviction who make sure it stays that way.

I'm not taking that, said Heinrich, and a nice sort of capitalism they had in the West, he added, where a working man can't make anything of himself, let alone an ex-con, but there in our state they make a man like me into a civil engineer: I've been learning all about the theory of bridge-building, the physics and economics of construction sites, dialectical and historical materialism, practical gravel extraction, blasting and digging foundations.

Congratulations, said Theodor, and poured him another whisky, but by now Heinrich was taking offence at everything he said, at the way he kept wrinkling his brow as he made any remark, or didn't really listen, said nothing, was sarcastic and then fell silent again, as if he were wondering whether to think of Heinrich as a nut-case or a lost sheep, Heinrich was a product of the system, maybe even worse, an informer, or why was he talking all this stupid stuff, no one can hear us, we live in a free country, you just don't notice, and that's the worst of you folk from the East: You make your gulags and your Bautzens for yourselves, and every word you say, with due respect, is pure kow-towing and catch-phrases.

Say that again, said Heinrich menacingly, and Theodor said it again, and his brother from the East stood up and said this was a warning to him, if all this ever falls into our hands you'll be right at the top of the list and they'll take you away and teach you and your sort the meaning of fear.

And that's how you speak to me as my brother.

That's how I speak to you as a citizen of my state, we'll see who's in the right of it.

Right, said Theodor.

Right or might, said Heinrich, and that was the end of their conversation. Next day the funeral took place in wind and rain, followed by a bowl of lumpy soup in a café not far from the cemetery where their father who had put his head in the gas oven was buried too, so they all got around to talking about their father again and the two women in his life, some saying they had been as like as two peas in a pod, others claiming that they were total opposites. So this is how we meet again, said Heinrich, unable to get used to the idea that even Sibylle was over thirty now, and he couldn't get used to Constanze's short hair, it had still been long last summer. You could stay, said Sibylle, not noticing how the others all froze and waited for Heinrich's answer as if it were their death sentence, but he just laughed and went on laughing for quite a time, ask Theodor, he said, like hell he was going to stay, he was off back to the East by the first train tomorrow, that's where his home was now.

You don't have to pretend with me, said Sibylle when she went to the station with him, and they still had a few minutes left, and Heinrich said something about what his visit to them had been like, whereupon Sibylle repeated: You could stay, think it over, you only have to get off the train and phone me. All right, said Heinrich, and thought about it, but during the quarter of an hour's wait in Bebra before the train set off again he got out only to buy something for the children and the blouse Rosa had been wanting for so long. There was even time left for a quick phone call to Marga, but a little girl of about three answered, saying in her childish voice: Mama, there's a man on the phone but he isn't saying anything, and Marga said, in the distance: He must have dialled the wrong number, just say Hello, wrong number and then hang up.

Rosa did seem just a tiny bit pleased when he came back on the evening of the third day, handing out his presents at supper time, and it was a long time since he had been welcome to her as the bringer of presents or news of any kind, but this time it was all from the West, where she herself had come from and where she didn't stay: the great mistake of her life. Sometimes she could say, to the exact day, when she had made her next mistake, and how each mistake had always led to more, while those mistakes had a long story going far back to the days before Heinrich, who forgot about her and got her pregnant and forgot about her again, her mistakes were so dazzling, so smooth, and cost such a lot that in the end you could string them together like pearls, and go through life adorned with your mistakes. How pretty you are, said Heinrich, for which she always hated him and kept out of his way in the flat in the evenings, reproaching herself for the children's sake, and for her own too, because she sometimes missed having a man with her in the night, but when it came to the point she never did anything about it.

That man Gerber, for instance, had once made up to her for a whole evening over supper, the spring before last, that was, when Gerber and Heinrich were fixing their first undercover deals, and by way of thanks Heinrich took him home to meet Rosa on account of her stuffed beef roulades, or because she was feeling rather lonely as the wife of the nearly qualified civil engineer Hampel, and she really only needed to say the word, it was all arranged, all set up and Gerber was ready, but she wasn't letting him have her for the simple reason that Heinrich was letting him have her, served up on a plate as if she were starved of such things, quick and delightful and slow as they could be, thank you very much but no.

He liked you, said Heinrich, and thought of Jana whom Gerber had recommended to him weeks ago, or rather had handed him as a possibility or a gift on approval. So he and Jana had met a couple of times and talked about Gerber, he was too wild for her in the long run, she said, she liked things cosier and said exactly how she fancied it, but in hints rather than straight out, for instance she liked water, in fact anything liquid, the thin clear soups she made in the evenings after her shift, and they could be drunk out of her or sipped from her, but very slowly, slowly, for at least as long as it took you to read *Neues Deutschland* (how long that took you all depended), and these were the titbits he included in his reports for Harms and his weird ministerial department, he'd been writing reports for it for years, he wrote enough about Jana alone to fill a whole lined exercise book in those first weeks.

Harms said he didn't really need to know all this: these personal habits of Jana's, and whether or when she made her fluidity available to Heinrich, but it was interesting to know that she expressed negative opinions about the new figures in the plan, because only at the beginning of the year she had been singled out as best woman worker in the firm, and you wouldn't really expect the best woman worker in a firm to say such things.

It's all innocuous, said Heinrich.

That's what you always say: it's all innocuous.

I've been saying so for ten years, said Heinrich, referring to the certificate and the money in an envelope which Harms had given him in spring for ten years of faithful service, adding a few questions about Hampel and state security, I think that to some extent we can speak to each other as friends.

Friends, yes, said Heinrich.

He had written a great deal in ten years, but no arrests had ever come of it, only warnings, a few measures were taken, a few people put on probation. On the one hand, they were not dissatisfied with their Hampel, but on the other there's more to life than having it off with women.

But women like to talk.

For instance, the decisions of the Eighth Party Conference don't feature in your reports. People must surely be thinking of what the Party said about the country and its future in the decisions of the Eighth Party Conference.

Oh, that, said Heinrich, feeling that his reports had been misunderstood, and in fact if anything it was reassuring that people didn't talk about the decisions of the Eighth Party

Conference, it meant they were happy and contented and took life as it was.

But you'll have to watch your drinking, Harms had said on that occasion, not that it had really begun at the time, and perhaps it wasn't all over yet with Rosa and his two sons, who at this point were still calling him Father and not Ede: rather a long time ago, all that, golden days, you might say.

On the morning after the divorce he heard Rosa singing in the kitchen, she was so glad it was all over and done with, either that or he was in luck again and owed it to his prick that she was so cheerful, oh, really, Hampel. She was in fact quite friendly when he came in, looking surprised, she was only a little cool, not uncivil, all right, she said, sit down and listen to her, she had something to tell him but he wouldn't like it, she'd been down in the cellar in the morning and found his bottles, two hundred and eighty of them hidden among the potatoes and jam-jars and pickled cabbage and bottled tomatoes in store for the winter, good heavens, a sea of bottles, and think of all the money they cost, think of the wasted days and hours, half your life, half our lives. She didn't say: I'm worth as little as that to you, then, you have as little self-control as that. She said: I've got everything ready, camp bed and bedclothes, the lamp, an old towel in case you need it, you can have all that. But my 600 marks won't run to food, and you must wrap up well at night, so off you go now and see how you can manage, said Rosa.

I have bad news of your brother, she wrote to Constanze that evening, it's very sad but I divorced him yesterday. From now on he's sleeping down in the cellar, we've already turned the heating on here, so I hope he'll be nice and warm. I found two hundred and eighty empty bottles in the cellar this morning, the story of his life, always the same old tune. He's been in poor health for weeks, gave up his job a month ago, and the debts are piling up because he's out of work, except there's always enough for another bottle, it all goes round and round in circles. I just hope he won't go the way his father went, he's very sick somewhere inside him, and he doesn't get any state benefits because we don't have unemployment here. I hope you can supply him with some provisions, please, he can do with them. Do you have any cast-offs for Konrad and Walter? It looks like being a hard winter, and no one wants to be spending day and night in bed like Heinrich, or perhaps he's warming himself up with that devil's brew which makes you warm at first and freezing cold in the long run, I don't really care much now.

In those first few days Heinrich thought: Well, she's got what she wants, here I am perishing miserably, dying in this cellar where it's so dark that I don't know what day or hour it is, for he was full of self-pity and extremely sorry for himself, Hampel without his wife and children, without his work on the construction sites and in the new housing facilities where he had it off with a couple of women every few days. You wouldn't have known Hampel, so lethargically and point-lessly and indolently did he pass the precious days. Sometimes he made grand speeches for his own sole benefit, knowing the reason for everything, or he read his old notes in the evening or the morning or at mid-day (time was all blurred), those sacred notes, for they were his legacy, that was all that would be left of him in the end: the fact that he had slept with these women and noticed everything about them, sometimes immortalizing them in a single sentence, the way they lay in bed, the arts they had mastered, the arts it was to be hoped they might yet learn, he read it all and found the passages, little poems, dramas, novels in two sentences, working his way steadily back through them.

Rosa 1975: Places where she's still young. The earlobes don't age, or the hollows behind the knees, or the mouth. Vera 1974: I could eat you up, skin and bones and all, but then I wouldn't have you any more. Jana 1973: Like certain flowers, or wounds which are always healing over. Marga 1969: You probably fuck differently here in this country.

Rita 1967: Sometimes she wept with happiness. Gisela 1965: If I could have you then I could forget you. Marga 1962: The way she gets up and buttons her blouse all wrong in the dark. Senta 1961: Always pulls back the covers and airs the bed, takes the stained sheets away to soak, brushes marks off with her hand. Anna 1957: She used to bleed every two weeks, another reason why she found love-making difficult. Bella 1956: Can I cut your toenails? Rosa 1954: I'd quite forgotten her. Dora 1951: Say Josef to me. Lyusya 1949: She loved me out of pure hunger, put her mouth round my prick, couldn't get enough of it.

Our friend Hampel always felt much moved by himself when he read all this, or he would come in his shirt or on Rosa's old towel, walked through his past as he used to walk through his days and nights, the thirty thousand that a life contains if it lasts, and that was quite a number he thought, counting up his days, counting up the times he'd made love, the times he'd thought about it, the nights of nothing now accumulating. I don't miss you at all, he said, I really don't much miss you at all, not so very much.

The beginning of the end had been the day when she made him move out of the bedroom, his fortieth birthday too, that was her birthday present so that he'd finally get the idea and see what it was all about, and from then on there were locked doors and only as many words as were absolutely necessary, for instance when a bill came in the post, or the building site phoned him, or a woman, when she would say: Here, it's some woman for you, and here's this bill, I need money for Konrad's new shoes and for Eva, she wants to go to the movies with her boyfriend.

At first he thought she meant it just as a warning or a game, or to teach him a lesson, so he accepted it and took pains to please her, gave her a bunch of carnations, found a book of knitting patterns she had wanted for a long time in a shop in Lobeda, asked how her day had been, and about her

277

worries at work with Zeiss or over the children, suggested weekend outings, came up against her first rejections, swallowed the snub, went shopping without being asked, didn't even get a thank-you, was angry with Rosa for not opening her door, despaired of that locked door, couldn't get used to it. Eva once saw him in the middle of the night, begging to be let in, or he would lock himself in the bathroom and rummage about among Rosa's dirty under-clothes, then he had to tell her what it was like rummaging about among her dirty underclothes and remembering what it used to be like, for heaven's sake, this couldn't go on, do see sense, Rosa, or do you want me to turn the gas tap on like my father, because sometimes I really don't know what else to do.

On his fortieth birthday his two sons had given him a bottle of brandy with a red bow tied round it and a note: For our father Ede who can't leave the stuff alone, and at first he didn't know what to do, and thought, I'll throw it away, they don't mean it kindly, only Eva means well by me, she had shaken hands with him, a long, firm handshake as strong as a man's: Well, Father, what shall I wish you on your birthday?

This was when he was still going to evening classes two or three times a week and dreaming of a life as an engineer, at least, in Rosa's letters to Paul and Constanze she spoke of these dreams and how difficult it all was, but they were giving him a good chance here in the East, and if he didn't pass an exam straight off or missed taking it they would turn a blind eye, knowing he had three children and a wife and a lot of responsibility on the big building sites of the Gera administra-tive district and in the city of Jena with its new high-rise building, all twenty-six storeys of it, our country is modern and self-confident, what does a failed marriage matter, or a personal file in which not everything is to our liking, because no one in quarter of a century is going to ask whether everything is to our liking in every personal file, but it's to be hoped that the cities and the human souls in them will stand firm and last till the end of the story, the coming of the Communist paradise.

At this time he was drinking only just enough to keep himself lively and cheerful and elated, taking his first shot in the morning and his second around noon, and only when they all went to a bar after the last evening class did he drink more, and then he would sometimes get it all off his chest, telling his companions how she wouldn't let him into her bed any more: her door was closed, her cunt and her heart and her mouth, all closed. What a life I lead, said Heinrich, but the others already knew about Heinrich's life or some variation on the theme, or else they acted as if they did and laughed at him, talking about conjugal rights and how to sue those who have undertaken to supply them for restitution of your conjugal rights, or alternatively go to the girls in Leipzig or take a mistress, those were their stupid and hastily proffered suggestions.

Even weeks later he still saw it as an unjust punishment, or a thunderbolt which had struck him out of a clear sky and the meaning of which he didn't understand, and he tried to remember what had happened, and what mistake he had made with his Rosa, for instance something must have happened in the spring, just before Marga visited him, but it all seemed the same as usual, perfectly normal. Rosa had been tired, that was all, but he was used to her being tired and not feeling like it, and sometimes she would do it just for his sake, half asleep, drowsing off and pleased if he had a good time, giving it as a present, she was in her mid-thirties and couldn't help it, and now all of a sudden she was fed up with him and everything that reminded her of him.

Marga had visited Heinrich in the East twice, on the second occasion in May 1971 when the Party of the working class was just holding its Eighth Party Conference and acclaiming its new head of state, they hoped for better times to come. Heinrich was still on the building site in Lobeda East when they elected that well-educated roofer from the Saar to be First Secretary of the Central Committee, it was early afternoon in distant Berlin, his friend Marga the West German Communist had been there, and a day later he suddenly found her with Rosa in the kitchen in Hermann-Stapff-Strasse, talking about her life as a Western Communist, and the songs sung by German Communists in the West, he hardly knew what to say. You, here, said Heinrich, and Marga said: Yes, I can see you're surprised, I arrived by train at three, and now here I am chatting about Ulbricht and Honecker and the children and life in general over coffee and cakes, I hope you don't mind.

She had taken a room at the International for a night, and Heinrich simply couldn't grasp that she was here and walking beside him through the new city of Jena, for that was what she had wanted: to go for a walk through the new city of Jena, looking and marvelling and stopping outside the multi-storey research institute, a hundred and thirty-eight metres high, they had blown up half the Altstadt to build it in the summer of two years ago, it had been in early July, just before he gave her a baby in the International Hotel, you could hear the detonations as she was washing herself in the bathroom.

She was still fond of him, the bed salesman of the old days among all the mattresses and the dark satin sheets, and liked the way he was still pleased to see her, and knew exactly which buildings they had blown up for the sake of the new Socialist city of Jena on the Saale, which was on the way to becoming a big city, the fourteenth such city in the country, and the man who was helping to build it had aged at least ten years and was the father of her daughter Nora, who didn't know him.

Eating in the Café Orchidee in the Platz der Kosmonauten, she said: You don't look happy, if I may say so, and so they talked about this and that, Heinrich's marriage and the passing years, the mistakes he had made and was still making, but now he was finally training and beginning to get a grip on things, he had great hopes for himself and the country, he said, well, we'll see.

We have great hopes too, said Marga, your GDR is among them, for instance, and the German Communist Party won one point three per cent of the vote in the Rhine and Ruhr elections.

But there's the border, said Heinrich.

The border is because of the West, and it will be there either till the end of time or until we've won the battle between systems, which could take quite a time.

I ought not really to be here, she said.

But there's desire, he said, not entirely serious in speaking of desire, probably it was just a case of sentimentality, or because she knew no one else in the Workers' and Peasants' State, while as a Communist she must be interested in life there and its difficulties.

Mustn't you?

But I do know someone here, someone who's the father of my daughter.

You could be wrong, he said.

And the sky could fall on our heads, she said, anyway, why should you care?

He would have liked to buy her a cocktail in the hotel bar, but Marga wanted to go straight to bed and rest before her long journey back, since she had to set out at eight-thirty in the morning, so they stood about for a while undecidedly, waiting and not knowing what they were waiting for.

We'd better not, not today, she said.

The comrades who forget their pyjamas, yes, I know.

Something like that.

So what else? Heinrich asked.

What else? She says my name already, and she doesn't look at all like you, or she looks like you only when she's asleep or if I narrow my eyes, yes, then she does a bit, we're doing all right.

Good, replied Heinrich, and said he would like a

photograph if she had one to spare, and she was pleased that he wanted a photograph, because he would certainly have liked little Nora, daughter of a West German Communist and a bed salesman who had crossed to the GDR and would never know her, or aren't you happy? Yes, of course he was happy, said Heinrich, well, have a good journey tomorrow, we can always write and think of each other, can't we?

Once again she had written only a postcard, but this time she wrote from the great city of Frankfurt am Main, where the comrades were busy with the *Land* elections at the beginning of November, and Marga had a little daughter in Frankfurt, Nora Luise is her name, life isn't what it was but it's all right the way it is, I'm not angry with you.

Marga? asked Rosa, remembering the day she had said it for the first time, and why on earth should Marga be angry with him after all these years, the card came from Frankfurt, didn't it, or was there something else which she hadn't heard about, a journey or a visit, for instance, these days even Herr Brandt and Herr Stoph had taken to travelling between the two Germanies, meeting in Erfurt or Kassel to take soundings, but only as one politician to another over a long and heavily laden table, she couldn't really see Heinrich and his little tarts doing that.

So our Herr Hampel had given her a child, had he, that was all he needed, and just now he was so taken aback he could hardly utter a word and said: Oh, it's just a financial matter, forget it, so Rosa forgot it and didn't mention it any more, for very early next morning they were all five going away in a Wartburg borrowed from a woman colleague, their first holiday for years, they were going to Lake Mirow and had rented a little cottage where they could stay, with running water and a toilet in the garden close to the banks of the lake, and a rowing boat which they could use, it had been an inexhaustible subject of conversation between the two boys and Heinrich for days.

They had almost unbroken fine weather by Lake Mirow, which was very nice, so all of them were always out until late in the evening, fishing in the lake on their boat trips, catching something now and then, and then Heinrich would light a fire late in the afternoon and grill the minnows they had caught or sometimes a roach for his sons, and if they hadn't caught anything then he grilled shashlik or some sausages out of a jar. Rosa was the only one who was not happy, because there were just two hotplates to cook on, but there was a proper bedroom for the parents with dusty old pillows and bedspreads, and the room beyond it had space for three blue air-mattresses on which the children slept like exhausted puppies, never going to bed before ten in the evening.

Heinrich and Rosa took it easy, and Heinrich thought a lot about little Nora and Rosa thought about who knew what, and around midnight, when the couple in the big house opposite fell avidly on each other, as they did almost every night, they lay awake in silence under the dusty covers listening. Putting on a good show, Heinrich would say, or Rosa might say: He's tired tonight, or maybe someone's complained, but they discussed it as something very distant and of no concern to them, and kept their spirits up, after all, they could go back to it again any time, for instance in winter or when a dream or a memory put them in the mood, that was how they saw it.

Sometimes he would have liked to tell Rosa that he knew just what little Nora from Frankfurt looked like: not as slender and delicate as her mother the Communist, but strong and energetic, her hair rather darker, with a short nose and plump little arms and legs, a smile which she threw around like confetti, as if she had enough smiles for two and was generous with them. Sometimes he thought: Rosa would accept it and take in the child as if she were her own, or another Susanna, but then there was Marga to think of, Marga who was looking after the little girl and didn't need a

283

man like Heinrich, and they lived in two different states and their wishes for each other didn't really suit.

For a long time now he and Rosa had not had wishes for each other which really suited either, but none the less she still hoped he would improve, she thought that a human being changes when he learns something, for it was never too late for that, never too late to learn something in life, and meet the right people while you were learning, for instance, she hoped there might be some of the right people at those evening classes. I hope you don't have anything going with anyone there, said Rosa, you'd have plenty of time, and how do I know who you go drinking with afterwards, and something could suddenly happen and then there you are on the sofa in some woman's home, it's been known, then she has to go and do something in the kitchen, put water on for the coffee, that's been known too, and while you're waiting she quickly changes her underclothes, dabs on a few drops of her new Bulgarian perfume, rubbing it just behind the earlobes, on her pulses, then she's ready and willing and you only have to take her.

You seem to know a lot about it, said Heinrich, who had only had something very small going with someone, something really minute and tiny it had been, and unfortunately she had run out of coffee, he sat there waiting and waiting and when she finally came back it was two-thirty in the morning and he soon had to go.

They spent a pleasant holiday by their lake. When he woke up in the night he had a drink.

His sons were completely unknown to him. But when the new, unknown little girl smiled she had two dimples in her cheeks, just like his.

Marga had arrived unannounced on the first occasion too, in the third week of July 1969 when they were beginning to blow up the first buildings in the city centre, and the long anticipated delivery from Wiesbaden had just come, a second-hand washing machine paid for out of his share of his father's estate. You can't imagine how wonderful it is to have a proper washing machine again after seven years, wrote Rosa in one of her famous thank-you letters, and Heinrich does the washing now, I only need to leave everything ready for him and he can do it, and our Evi is going to a party with Chinese lanterns on Saturday, because as usual she has a very good report, my four dear ones always have good reports, Heinrich included, your Rosa is very proud and almost happy.

Later it turned out that Marga had gone looking for him on the big demolition site, for she had come on behalf of the German Communist Party so that she could tell them something about the new city of Jena and the five thousand workers for whom new housing was being built in Lobeda West and Lobeda East, and after a good deal of questioning someone had told her that Herr Hampel was preparing the fuses at this very moment, and he lived at such and such an address and would be at home at such and such a time.

She had put a note in his letterbox as she stood outside his flat, not wanting to meet Rosa: Hotel International, Room 105, only if you want to, she wrote, best wishes, Marga. And of course he did want to, and sat with her in Room 105 of the Hotel International and admired her as he had before. Well, just think of you being here, said Marga, meaning the explosions, and the way the old town had to be demolished to make room for the new and one of those involved was Heinrich Hampel, former bed salesman and now a rising civil engineer, I'm so pleased to see you. And I'm pleased to see you, said Heinrich, and it was obvious what was going happen next after all this time, what with the good start they had already made years ago, or so it seemed. Heinrich was lucky, this was a good moment in time, said Marga, for it was quite a joke: a West German Communist and a former bed salesman now in the East making a baby in the Hotel International, maybe better not.

She said: I felt I wanted you because you're so masterful and old-fashioned and straightforward in your own way, and you're a good lover, but I've given up going into shops selling beds the way I used to, those times are over, I mean, there aren't any beds at all in my flat, just old mattresses with stained sheets, this was something she had to explain. It sounds odd, she said, but she hadn't been living on her own for quite some time, there were seven or eight of them in her huge flat in Frankfurt, and they had one room in common for everything: the big living-room cum kitchen where we eat and talk, the room full of mattresses where we all sleep and do, well, you know what, they got together to write a new pamphlet condemning the Vietnam war every few days, and when they'd done it they went into the room next door and swapped partners, cunts, pricks, mouths, did not feel that their partners or the comrades' cunts and pricks were anyone's personal property: this was roughly the way she described her new free-as-air life to him.

She was still very slender and very guarded, at the age of thirty or more, but she spoke this new, unfamiliar language, and was not to be compared with the Marga of 1962. I was thinking of that all the way in the train, said the Marga of 1969, who also spoke freely of cunts and pricks and fucking, he'd just have to get used to it and to her calling him a petit bourgeois, but the way he could scarcely bring himself to utter these new words was what she liked about him, it was really very funny.

She said: I always liked screwing with you, that was what she called it, and she wanted them to wash each other before they fucked here in this hotel in the GDR, she washed him and teased him, gave him and his prick a few butterfly kisses, and then they were in full swing. I'm imagining what you were like as a girl, said Heinrich while they were in full swing, and tried out one of the new words, and she liked it when he called her a girl, so she was his girl for this one time, and that charming scoundrel got her pregnant, and they could hear the explosions from the Eichplatz through the open window.

She was his girl three or four times that weekend in July 1969, when the Americans flew to the moon to go for a walk on it, and in the end Marga went back to her comrades in Frankfurt and the Vietnamese leaflets and the mattresses and stained sheets, and Eva went to her Chinese lantern party and had a lovely time.

You could have come and helped at the party, said Rosa, when he came home and washed his last hours with Marga off his skin, as a precaution for Rosa's sake and so that there would be something when he wrote his report, just a couple of sentences, saying that Marga called herself a Communist and praised everything here, but from the way she bore herself and the way she spoke and talked in another language in general, you could see she was one of them from the West, over here for a few days, praising us and going away again and knowing it was a blessing that she could go away again, even though she was a Communist.

I know nothing but good of her, wrote Heinrich, I never know anything but good of anyone, that's the kind of country I live in.

In the first summer after his release, when the Prague business was drawing to a close, the people from the construction combine first put him to work driving sand and gravel and stone about, or unloading freight cars carrying slaked lime or heavy sacks of cement at the Saalbahnhof, and then driving all over town in his lorry from morning to night to the big building sites in Lobeda and back again. Bread first, then stones, said the new Rosa to whom he could not get used, for it suddenly seemed she could do sums, she held the purse strings, and wouldn't let him have more than a couple of bottles a month. We're going to do things differently this time around, she said, and she was generous but thrifty, had ideas of her own in bed too, she often said no but sometimes yes, or perhaps, she made rules and stipulations which either applied or did not, depending on how she felt. If Heinrich said: Why don't you make those beef roulades again, she might reply: Yes, all right, I'll make them on Saturday, but you go and buy the meat and a kilo of potatoes to go with them, or then again she might say: I don't feel like making beef roulades, they're a lot of work and I'm tired when I come home from work myself, you make them.

That's life, said his sons, who were five and seven and almost always called him by his first name, as if he were a mere acquaintance or a guest on whom they were reluctant to rely. There've been a lot of changes, he told Constanze in a letter, but I'm very glad you were so good about helping Rosa, I want to thank you for that. Father's sad end has upset me terribly, though, I heard about it only three weeks ago, Rosa was very brave, the children have grown much bigger but they're like strangers, I hope we'll get used to each other yet.

At first he had thought he could simply pick up his old life where he had left off, and saw himself sitting up all night in the Cosmonaut bar once again with Gisela and Vladimir, just as they did in the old days, or little Rita welcoming him back, Rita who was afraid of anything and everything except Heinrich, but it soon turned out that timorous Rita had left town long ago, and Gisela was very formal, was expecting a second child by her Bulgarian husband, and didn't want to remember the old days up in the Cosmonaut bar and how they used to dance there, and as for their good friend Vladimir, he'd gone back to the Soviet Union just under a year ago.

So here you are back again, how are you, she said, sounding like the Gisela he had known once more, well, much the same as usual, he hadn't meant to bother her and now he was, because unfortunately the paperwork for the deliveries wouldn't wait, and she had to pick the toddler up from day nursery, he wished her good luck with the second.

He found the city and its people so changed in under three years that he was glad when Harms rang up with a question about some detail he didn't understand in Heinrich's first reports, so they stayed in touch and tried the new café in the Altstadt for coffee and cakes: it was almost like the old days.

Just before Prague Harms had said: Well, what shall I say, so far as we're concerned everything can stay as it is, same as usual, and then some troops from the Warsaw Pact countries had to get into Czechoslovakia fast to put a tottering world back to rights, and when the tottering world was back to rights Harms said the situation was serious but under control, all the authorities responsible were on high alert, and the authorities needed both new people and the tried and trusted sort like Heinrich Hampel, lorry driver and inquiry agent.

It was at the end of August that Harms described the lorry driver Heinrich Hampel as an inquiry agent, and early in September the papers were reporting the latest decision of the Council of Ministers on the rebuilding of the inner city of Jena, where a man like Heinrich would be indispensable, and suddenly there were ambitious plans in the city of Jena on the river Saale and in the Hampel household, where they were drawing up wish-lists from catalogues to the amount of nearly two thousand marks, the sum due to them after all these years.

Heinrich and his Rosa made out two wonderful long lists, which they kept reading out to each other, all those things you could get from the Schwab mail order firm in the rich West, so what do we need: Well, we need a new washing machine, and an electric boiler, a grill, a cassette recorder, a camera, fifty marks' worth of film, that was Heinrich's list; your turn now. But mine's so long, said Rosa, wanting a red pinafore dress and a black blouse size 34 for Eva, and a pair of shoes, a ring and a necklace, because at thirteen Eva was suddenly beginning to have her own wishes. I'd like two pretty nighties for you, said Heinrich, wanting her to think of herself too, and they both finally decided that the pink nightie was very pretty, and they also ordered her a dressing-gown and a green costume and a red Trevira dress size 42, which came by mail at the end of October.

And now, how are we doing? asked Rosa when the pink nightie had arrived, and Heinrich called her his little girl, and his new little girl Rosa felt all soft and velvety in her nightie, he didn't have to tell her. We're doing fine, just fine, he said, and Rosa said: In honour of the day? Oh yes, in honour of the day.

One day in November he disappeared, that's to say he disappeared from the ken of Rosa and the children, because he was feeling cold under his blankets in the cellar from which the central heating ran, maybe he was in another town, or he'd died, or gone over to the West, who knew. Rosa had actually bumped into him once or twice before he finally disappeared, and he was always friendly and optimistic, talking about some idea he had, and how surprised she'd be when he really got to work on it, he even asked after Eva and, out of politeness, after his sons.

It turned out later that he had been to see Gisela again before disappearing for a couple of years, and Gisela had said: Come in, what's the matter, you look terrible, you look as if someone in the family had died or you were on the run, come in, sit down and have a drink and tell me about it. He had asked her straight out for money, and although she knew it was not a good idea to give a drunk money she did give him a few banknotes of various denominations, and even the small change she had on her, it wouldn't bankrupt her, and she hoped to get rid of him faster that way.

Don't do anything silly, Heinrich, she said, it's not worth it, nothing is worth it, and Heinrich said: What do you mean, anything silly, good heavens, my whole life consists of silly things and you were one of them, so he looked at her again, the lovely Gisela with her Party badge and her Bulgarian perfumes, and she was really very boring after all with her

Socialist Unity Party and her husband and two children in their three-roomed flat, which was bursting at the seams, and when he asked her if she'd come out for a farewell drink with him she was afraid she had to cook dinner, her husband did like home cooking, sorry, it's just our habit, and thanks anyway, be seeing you.

So then he went for a drink on his own, and after that he went to the Cosmonaut bar a couple of times on his own too, it had got a bit shabby in all these years but everything else was the same as before, he even did a few last deals there, and now he had the money for a room at the International Hotel just like back then when they were blowing up the old city centre, although sad to say 105 was already occupied by a businessman from Kassel.

They had been suspicious at the hotel because he had no luggage, so to soothe their fears he bought a suitcase in town and two white shirts, shoplifted a tie from a place in the Altstadt and a pair of socks from another place in Lobeda, because this was the idea that had come to him one morning down in the cellar from which the central heating ran, or rather it was a part of the idea, it was the preliminaries, the prerequisite for the idea, he was in no hurry.

After the event, they thought in the hotel that they ought to have noticed something in view of the way he walked to the lift with a heavy suitcase three evenings running, stopping for a rest and groaning every few metres because it was so heavy, and the heavy stuff in it was tools from the old building site in Lobeda, or a whole sack of cement, as if he were planning to build something up there in his room.

When he was seen eating in the restaurant in the evening on those three days he looked done in but content, like a man who's been hard at work, and he always sat there at his ease reading *Neues Deutschland*, or watching the young woman from Dresden behind the bar, or just looking out of the window and shaking his head now and then as if amazed by the people he saw walking past, but it was never his Rosa or the children or anyone like Gisela.

In the end he left without paying his bill, and he got in the train to Gera without buying a ticket, and sat down in a compartment with a woman who looked a little like young Dora back in the grounds of the Dornburg Castles, except that she was twenty-five years older and more embittered, and was travelling with two baskets of apples, which she planned to preserve with water and cinnamon, for making enough puddings for Sunday lunch to last until spring. Is it you, Dora, he asked, or rather whispered, although she was someone quite different, but she frowned like Dora and went on talking about her apples, asking if he was from Gera too, yes, well no, from Jena, he was only going to Gera on business.

Train's running late again, said the woman from Gera, and Heinrich said: Yes, we live in a state run by amateurs, that's what it is, and she suddenly took fright and lowered her voice, the gentleman from Jena ought please to be careful and think what he was saying, he ought to watch his words, did he want to go to jail for a careless remark like that, you can easily get put away for a few years.

The name's Hampel, Heinrich Hampel, he said shortly before they reached Gera, just in case, and he got out at Gera and went the way Rosa had known so well years ago, the way to the remand prison in Rudolstädter Strasse, where he knocked at the door, or rather rang the bell, introduced himself, began by mentioning a few names and numbers and incidents, whereupon the people inside had to think it over and said no, and then perhaps, looked him up in the files which said three and a half years without probation, Herr Hampel who had come from the West and was now turning himself in for fraud, they didn't think he looked like a fraudster, well, he knew better, oh, very well then, come on in, welcome back.

10

Russia, then. The years in the Soviet Union, almost exactly four and a half of them when he was between fifteen and nineteen, those years stayed in the mind. The first winter in particular was bad, the great famine with which they made atonement, but that passed with time, and there were many fine summers in Russia, and his first girl friend Lyusya, the love she felt, you wouldn't believe it: her crooked thumbs, the way she squinted, looking beyond you at time past and time to come, the lakes where we swam, afternoons in the June grass, the dramatic sky above the rolling countryside, that beautiful, ill-used country, and always there was Lyusya the Comsomol girl, not forgetting the dead now at rest, killed by Stalin and Hitler.

In the first week after their arrival early in November, mid-winter it was, Mother said: We're not so badly off here with our Russian enemies, it could have been worse, we have three rooms with kitchen and bathroom, and our old beds and furniture from Jena, and we owe this place to the German POWs who built it all for us. There was no running water in the two blocks of flats built by the German POWs, but you could pump water from a well in the yard and carry it up to the fourth floor in two buckets, along with bread and sausage and cheese from the little shop opposite, stowed in Father's rucksack.

It was all right for two weeks, but after two weeks there wasn't so much as a bar of soap to be bought in the military store, and the men just arrived from Germany had to fend for themselves with their families and their ration cards, which were of various different kinds, and anyone who, like Herr Hampel, wasn't in work for one reason or another was in the lowest category. Let me explain, said the commandant of the building, a retired Red Army captain who spoke fluent German, and he started straight in with points one, two, three: Hitler's Fascists left our country in rubble and ashes in 1941; Hitler's Fascists have half the Russian people on their conscience; Hitler's Fascists should therefore be grateful to be alive, because they don't deserve it.

We're not Fascists, said Heinrich's father, we're glass-makers from Jena and we've come here to help you, children, bag and baggage and all.

Oh really, help us, said the commandant, adding that it was also German Fascists who left the Klin glassworks in ruins in forty-one, and I'm afraid there won't be any work for Herr Matthias Hampel until we've finished rebuilding the Klin glassworks, so consequently he won't be getting the ration cards for skilled specialists, that was the bitter truth of it.

So the Hampels went hungry, since they had no work and couldn't very well ask to be given food for work they hadn't done, they just had to wait and beg and fill their empty stomachs with a sip of water, while their better-off compatriots who had salaries and sent remittances to families who had stayed at home lived high on the hog, and would rather throw their stale bread and mouldy jam away than give it to the Hampels, who did they think they were, sitting around idle with their five children.

This bloody Soviet paradise, said the Germans, and Father and Theodor said: These bloody Germans, that's how they behave abroad. Mother had never been heard to swear in all these years, but after visiting any of their German compatriots she did, or she would send one of the younger children to steal a slice of bread here and a piece of smoked fish there, or her no-good son Heinrich, who almost always came away with something, even if it was only a handful of frozen vegetables, or a few rotten potatoes or tomatoes which he had swapped for a couple of dresses or some shoes, or which he had been given in return for a promise or a lie, I don't want to know the details, not in the least.

Sometimes she was surprised by Heinrich and the way he took everything so lightly, always out and about from the very first day, coming back with his first few words of Russian, and stories of Russian children in the street calling him a Fascist and throwing stones at him, and then suddenly they made friends and showed him the skinny calf they kept in their tiny flat, or came pulling kilos of frozen sauerkraut along Heinrich's street on a sledge at minus twenty degrees, with the snow up to their shoulders, that was his life in the first few weeks and months, and apart from the hunger it wasn't a bad life for a boy of fifteen.

They had arrived on a working day at the end of October, they were suddenly there at the door at five in the morning wanting to come in, a Soviet major with two armed soldiers and a young woman interpreter who translated a decree issued by Marshal Zhukov, to come into force immediately, Herr Matthias Hampel must go to do war reparations work in the great Soviet Union, there were two lorries outside the door, and he must decide whether to go alone or take his family, a glassworks had been destroyed by the German Fascists in the town of Klin near Moscow and he was to help get it going again, he'd be back in three to five years at the latest.

We'll all go, said Mother, making up her mind at once, so they all immediately began packing and deciding what to take, and the two Russian soldiers carried it out to the lorries: beds, bed-linen and mattresses, plenty of warm clothes and underclothes for the winter, the new living-room cupboard, the couch and all the most important furniture right down to the kitchen utensils, as well as Mother's work-box and Heinrich's little book in its brown cover, *Basic Facts of Love and Sex*, that was the great dream, the adventure for which he was preparing, and Russia might be a yet greater adventure, they'd see.

My God, what are they doing to us, said Mother, and later they sent a man from Schott who said: Yes, it's just terrible, we can't take it in, thirteen of our best employees, and almost three hundred from Zeiss, and who knows how many more all over the country.

There was not much time for goodbyes, their father was hit hardest because of the house, and around noon they clambered into one of the two army lorries and were driven to the Saalbahnhof, where they joined the other people from Zeiss and Schott in a train standing ready for them, and then waited, they were still waiting two hours later, it was late in the evening before the Russians had finally loaded everything up.

The Hampels were in two fourth-class compartments with freshly painted wooden seats and luggage nets which were much too small, sharing them with the Bergers and Hofmanns, who had three children each and, like the Hampels, were talking agitatedly all at once, except when the train left around ten in the evening, when all was perfectly still for a while and everyone listened to young Dr Berger playing a tune on his flute: *Adieu, adieu, oh fairest native land.*

For young Heinrich it was the journey of his life, almost every glance out of the window was an adventure, look, here we are in Leipzig already, and this is Warsaw the capital of Poland, and it was an adventure when they changed tracks in Brest-Litovsk, and there was a great banquet there on Brest-Litovsk station in honour of the skilled German specialists, white damask tablecloths and vodka and cognac flowing like water, their first zakuski as a taste of Russian life, and tables groaning with salmon and caviar.

After that almost sleepless first night spent on the hard benches, every adult had been given a selection of books, a volume of speeches by Lenin and Stalin, a dictionary and an illustrated history of the Great Patriotic War, and everyone got a parcel originally packed for soldiers from the German Eastern Front going on leave, containing cigarettes, biscuits, a tin each of butter and condensed milk, coffee and sugar, so the Hampel family had seven of these parcels. There was always something to talk about day and night, what on earth would it be like in Russia, they wondered, and Heinrich's father smoked his pipe and cut up the cigarettes with a razor blade, they were fed on millet and gruel and pea soup, and the rumour of a field kitchen in one of the goods wagons was only a rumour.

To German-Soviet friendship, said the general in Brest-Litovsk where they had to identify all their possessions after changing trains, and they went on to just outside Moscow in three Russian carriages open to the sky, arriving early in the morning. Once again lorries were waiting, and once again it took for ever to get everything loaded up, and the great city of Moscow through which they drove was a city of a thousand lights, with sausages and ham in the shop windows, it didn't look so bad after all in the Soviet paradise, and even this dump in the middle of nowhere wasn't so bad when they arrived early in the evening of the tenth day. A small café and some shops were still open for the ceremonial arrival of the Germans, and yet again the shelves were stocked with vodka and cognac and champagne as well as real coffee and everything the heart could desire, oh children.

So now let's celebrate, said Mother when they had been allotted their living quarters, three large rooms with kitchen and bathroom and a stove built of bricks and mud to keep them from freezing, all rather primitive but very nice, even the wood and shavings and paper were laid ready to light the fire, and a match was left half out of its box, they wouldn't forget that. Well, let's drink to us, said Mother, opening the first bottle of Crimean sparkling wine before they all went to sleep in their German beds, Heinrich playing with himself a little and dreaming of faceless girls.

The first winter was bitterly cold in this little place Lytkarino, with its two blocks of flats built by German POWs and the surrounding potato fields stretching as far as the eye could see, the glassworks to the north, old wooden Russian houses to the south near the market where they sold jars of grain spirit and chopped pigs' trotters and ears and innards, heavens above. The famine lasted some ten months, and that first winter lasted an eternity, and the one loaf the family got a day lasted only a few seconds if you didn't control yourself and make little pellets out of it, keeping some for eating at mid-day or in the evening under the thin blankets, when Heinrich experimented with Russian girls in his head, ignoring his rumbling stomach, which was another reason why he never saved any of their scanty meals for later.

Just before Christmas the commandant of the building announced: We're putting the Hampel and Berger families together, seven and five make twelve, four adults and eight children in two rooms, after all, the Russians have no more space to live in themselves, four square metres per person is all they have, even our two Stalin prize-winners on the second floor have to make do with that and sleep on mattresses or the floor like you. Heinrich was the only one allowed to stay on in the same flat, because he didn't mind living with Russian strangers and sharing the bathroom with them, but he could sleep alone on the sofa-bed at night thinking of the new Russian words he had learnt, the first sentences, swear-words, questions in this sea of incomprehensible sounds, the singsong language of the street, the snow-covered fields in the eternally dazzling winter light, it'll send us all blind one of these days.

Father and Mother had refused to learn the language of their new masters, but the children had to and became strange to their parents, and stranger still when they brought home the new words they had learned from their young woman schoolteacher; and talked about the last war and the triumph of the renowned Soviet Union under its leader Josef

Vissarionovich Stalin who hated Fascists but loved the German people.

When the conversation turned to Stalin Mother changed the subject, and Father said nothing, but walked over the snow and ice almost every morning to the glassworks, where he stood in the red gateway and asked how the work was getting along, and what news there was from Klin, perhaps he could go there some time and get an idea for himself, yes, he could have permission to go for a couple of days at the end of the month, travelling by train through Moscow, that was a glimmer of hope anyway.

Father went to Klin at the end of February, and Heinrich would have liked to go too, so envious was he of Father's day in the glittering city of Moscow with its brightly lit streets, its display windows full of hams and sausages and cans of caviar piled high into pyramids, but Father said it was all just for show, the hams and sausages were made of plaster, the cans of caviar were empty, the goods in the shops were prohibitively expensive, and unfortunately, he said, nothing was going to come of Klin yet, not till summer at the earliest.

I'd like to go to Moscow some time, said Heinrich, to which Mother said briefly and firmly, oh no you don't, so he hesitated for a couple of days, then stood in the street up by the works entrance one morning and hitched a lift to Lubercie with a couple of soldiers in an open platform truck, caught the suburban train to Moscow, it was freezing, but he was fascinated by the city, with delicatessen shops as big as cathedrals or old opera houses, heavy chandeliers hanging from the ceilings, and window displays of wine and liqueurs and vodka from all parts of the Soviet Union, enough for a hundred weddings, and more fresh salmon and caviar than you could have driven away in a couple of lorries: this was his Moscow, Maxim-Gorki Street, the GUM department store close by, the dead Lenin's mausoleum, the famous cathedral, none of them far away.

Moscow was bright and friendly and freezing cold, and

Heinrich in his patched anti-aircraftman's trousers and hobnailed shoes couldn't get enough of the city even at minus twenty degrees, people let him jump the queue because he was a foreigner, and if you wanted to drink a hot cup of tea in a café you had to be wearing stout shoes or the doormen wouldn't let you in.

Heinrich went to Moscow three times in March and April, the second time he had a long shopping list with him and bought tobacco and vodka for the skilled German specialists, and a great many brightly coloured chewy sweets for the family, and the third time he was picked up by a police patrol in the middle of Red Square, but he spent only a couple of hours in one of the thousand cells in the big police jail, and after that they took him out and taught him how to drink.

The high-ranking officer who questioned him had to repeat his questions a couple of times before Heinrich understood him, but he realized that they no longer thought he was a POW and nodded, took one of the two tooth-glasses and drank with the officer, toasting friendship and girls, the fine city of Moscow and life as a real man. They took him home in their American jeep, and when he was picked up again a few weeks later they greeted him as an old acquaintance, a lad like Heinrich wasn't really supposed to leave the place where he was billeted, his visits to Moscow were strictly forbidden, but life is short and agreeable, and Siberian vodka is the very best of all.

So Heinrich learned how to drink in Russia, that cold country, and then there were weeks and months when it kept raining and thawing and freezing again, and you hardly dared venture out in the streets, after which it turned very hot overnight, and on one of the first hot days a delivery of meat and fish arrived for the Hampel family: five kilos of salmon and about ten roast chickens, Mother had no idea where they came from. I'm taking it as a good omen, she said, preserving the chickens in jars and putting the salmon in the bathtub to keep cool, they ate every variety of salmon dish from morning to evening three days running, and very early in the morning of the fourth day she sat down at the entrance of the building and refused to budge until she, her children and her husband and all their household equipment had finally been taken to that bloody place Klin, she was sick of this. Heinrich's father said: You can't do that, they haven't finished building our flat or the factory yet, but his mother said: We'll see if I can do it or not, I can and so can they, and she was right too.

So in the summer of forty-seven they ended up in Klin, district town in the administrative district of Moscow, 8720 inhabitants in the year 1931, said Father's encyclopaedia; situated on the Sestra (tributary of the Volga) and the Leningrad–Moscow railway line; industries, textiles and metal goods, peat, bricks, timber; near the Tchaikovsky Museum, former hereditary seat of the Romanov family; glassmaking. Occupied by the Germans in 1941 on their way to Moscow, liberated and pacified by the glorious Red Army the same year, not that the 1931 encyclopaedia knew about that, of course, or that the German occupying forces got their shirts ironed in the town of Klin, and when they had gone anyone who had ironed a shirt for them was considered a traitor.

The manager of the Klin glassworks clasped his hands in the air above his head when he saw the three lorries and twelve Germans arrive on the works site, you've obviously dropped from heaven but I can't say heaven means well by us, because we don't have anywhere for you to live and there's no work for you until the beginning of September. Well, here we are, said Mother, making no move at all to back down, and the manager made no move to back down either, but whatever way you looked at it he was landed with the Germans, so he got a couple of German POWs to move the chairs out of the firm's clubhouse and had the three lorries unloaded; they simply dumped everything in the yard except for the twelve beds and a few clothes and under-clothes.

We'll see what next, said the manager, and now began two strange weeks for the Hampel and Berger families, living in the clubhouse of the state glassworks in Klin, for this was something quite new to the sleepy town of Klin: twelve men, women and children from Germany who had their own beds and mattresses even though they were the defeated enemy and had to make reparations by working in the ravaged land of the Russians, who didn't have a separate bed for every member of their own families while these glassmakers from Hitler's country did.

It didn't take a couple of hours for news of the Germans and their beds to spread through town, and all the locals came thronging up to flatten their noses against the clubhouse windows, a crowd of children from nearby and further away as well as the factory workers, and next morning their wives and their sisters-in-law turned up too, there was constant coming and going. They gaped and marvelled until late in the evening, and if anyone shooed them away they would retreat briefly, laughing, and then come back. I simply don't believe it, said Theodor, and for the first few days he kept going back and forth shouting angrily and gesturing, for they would run after you even on Sunday in the church opposite, or in the red-painted market halls in the middle of town on weekdays, shouting: Fascists, Fascists, how long are you staying, what's your home town called, come on, tell us, hey, you with the fine hair and the eyes as blue as our river the Sestra, what's your name, where are you going to work, what a funny name: Geinrich Gampel, we've got proper names, Tanya and Natasha and Sonya, and Heinrich had made his first Russian girlfriends, so to speak.

Sometimes he thought they'd be standing at the window all night, and on those nights he secretly read his little brown book about girls, how they bled every four weeks, and how a man's juices penetrated a woman during love-making, for the juices came out of a man, and if their love-making had been enjoyable for both parties the woman would inhale the odour of the male juices a while longer.

After a week the minister responsible for the works turned up. This is a fine sort of camp you have here, she said, they're talking about it as far away as Moscow, but that's all over now, the day after tomorrow at the latest, or maybe in three or four days, everything will be ready, and so it was. The new block was one of the few stone buildings in Klin, with three doors in front and at the back and some twenty tenants on three floors, the Hampels were third floor on the right, the Bergers opposite on the left, you could look out over gardens and meadows and fields from the kitchen window and see all the way to the river. Paradise in the Russian paradise, Mother called it, how happy I am, children, given the circumstances, I mean, and now we'll start hoping and praying for all we're worth again, your father will soon have work, yes, he'll have work from August the first.

It was early July, and the children were soon bathing in the river every afternoon and making their first new friends, and although they were still a little hungry and had numbers marked on their lower arms in copying pencil when they stood in queues for food, at least they were living in a proper town with a big market and a small one, a school and a church and a pharmacy, and a little way outside town was the famous composer's summer residence, where the youngest Hampel boy and his two sisters were being prepared to start school in autumn, a Ukrainian Jew was teaching them: his whole family had been taken away and murdered by the Germans, your fathers and sons, barbarians, criminals, a nation of poets and philosophers.

After the first day at the works his father said: My God, these Russians, we'll never get anywhere in a thousand years, half the roof's fallen in right in the middle of the works where the big tank is supposed to stand, it's like a bomb crater, could be quite serious. Theodor will have to make Russian versions of all our designs, and then engineering drawings for the machine parts we still don't have, and they can use Heinrich for this and that with the electrics and then fetching coal for the big furnace, so that was the beginning of it, the beginning of good times in the middle of the bad ones.

The Hampels, father and sons, were bringing a few thousand roubles a month home now, and they had the best ration cards, reserved for skilled specialists, and enough food and drink for them all to feel well fed, and every few days there was meat for supper something no Russian had, but why let that bother us? They wouldn't have accepted so much as a crust of bread from the Russians, they'd sooner die, said Mother and Father, who still didn't speak a word of the new language except to the political official from the second floor when he suddenly appeared to check up on them, a word of greeting and another of farewell, which at least meant they were soon rid of him again.

Heinrich turned seventeen in the summer, gangling Heinrich, Heinrich the dreamer and theoretical expert on women, he wasn't at home much, spent most of his time down by the big river looking at the girls, seeing who already had breasts under their thin blouses and who were still waiting for them, and he knew what it was like to be waiting, and watching himself, and wanting he didn't know what, the moodiness, the wishing, the knowing or guessing, that was the worst of it.

Sometimes he asked one of them if she'd like to go to the cinema right outside her home with him, so there he would sit in the tenth row of the cinema, which was just a hut, in a seat about a hundred years old with a girl beside him, eating salted pumpkin seeds from a jar, spitting the shells out on the floor to join the thousand other shells, and it might be *Battleship Potemkin* showing, or a comedy from bombed-out Germany, but those comedies, sad to say, never mentioned the city of Jena.

Sometimes he didn't even know the name of the girl sitting beside him in the dark cinema, nibbling nuts and sometimes her nails too, and usually it was all perfectly innocent, or a pair of damp hands might make an exploration, but it was only a rehearsal, so that you'd know something when you really started, because one day it would be for real, very delightful and very important, as delightful and important as only that first and awkward occasion could be, he believed.

Now a wonderful, exciting time began, and the only person in whom he sometimes confided was the son of the Ukrainian Jew Eugen Yevgenovich Budde, whose whole family had been taken away and murdered, but the two boys were still far too young to spend much time thinking about the sorrow and grief of Eugen Yevgenovich Budde from Minsk, seeing in every girl the girl from the camp, his cousin from Minsk with the two pigtails and crooked teeth now in Canada, but the rest had been burned to ashes and ground up to sprinkle on the frozen roads and paths of Auschwitz-Birkenau.

So what exactly is a Jew, asked Heinrich.

Ask me another.

Well, a Jew likes girls with plaits and girls with big breasts, I hope we're not going to quarrel with each other.

There ought to be enough for two.

Or we'll share them between us.

Or fight each other for them.

On the morning of New Year's Eve 1947 Heinrich's father said: Well, this will be the year of decision for our poor Germany, as he knew because he switched the radio on every evening and let BBC London explain the situation to him, and it was to be a year of decision for Heinrich too, they had a bet on it. Shall we bet? young Budde had asked at the beginning of January, and Heinrich said: All right, let's have a bet that this year, 1948, is going to be our year, and whichever of us gets furthest must help the other and produce evidence of each success. They were going to report to one another every Friday evening at the bar in the second street along in the market halls, confining themselves to the vital details, everything that happened first time, and they must do more than just wishing (take fright as you might), for instance you had to be entirely naked, no clothes on, a bit shy, how else would you imagine it?

Nothing at all happened for the first few weeks. Yevgeny just kept saying: I'm making progress, I'm working on someone, and Heinrich replied: I'm working on someone too, wait another few days and I'll have more to tell you. Of course it would be easier if it were summer, he said, and didn't tell his friend how he had taken a look at his sister one night, or about the two Berger girls, and nothing else really meant anything, either the girls didn't understand him or he didn't think much of them, there was nothing in his head but the bet, and he was probably lagging hopelessly behind by now.

After a while it was quite reassuring to think that he couldn't win the bet, for now he could see things more clearly the way they were, he noticed a pair of dark eyes waiting in the queue for flour and sugar, made his first jokes, his first admiring comments on a dress or a mouth, noticed doors opening or closing again, went to the movies once a week, invited a girl, took liberties, waited to tell Yevgeny about their first kisses, tales as long and complicated as fairytales, and full of repetitions, for those were the best sort.

One of the first was called Larissa, she liked him, and kissed him, and missed half the film, preferring his kisses which went on and on and became slightly boring in the long run. Then he would take a girl home, and they would kiss again outside the door, just for practice, or kiss again another day. Sometimes one of them said: But I don't want anyone to see us, because my mother and father say you're a German and you'll bring us bad luck, and then Heinrich could always tell whether she was going to the movies with him out of curiosity or because of Heinrich himself, or because he paid for the tickets and did a couple of little tap-dances in the middle of the street, for they almost all knew his reputation as a tap-dancer from defeated Germany. But you're not like other Germans, said Tatyana, and her friend Svetlana, the one with the blonde pigtails, said: My father was in Leningrad in 1941, the whole sky was full of white balloons, and down on the ground people were starving and ate dead bodies.

No thanks, she said, refusing the invitation.

That's okay, you don't have to, said Heinrich, and missed her for a few days, mulling over what she had said and the looks she had given him, which always slipped past him into space, down there by the river, where Budde paraded his voluptuous Sonya past them as if in a triumphal procession, or in the square outside the bar where they all regularly saw each other. Clever Tatyana said: I think you're quite different, you belong in the big cities, Moscow or Leningrad or Kiev would suit you, or further east, our cities of Novosibirsk or Sverdlovsk or Chelyabinsk, they'd suit you too, for she herself came from those parts beyond the great mountains, and like Heinrich had landed up in this little place. My father was in Berlin, she said, but a lot of the girls said their fathers had been in Berlin, and many might have stayed, standing up to the Americans in the capital of the future Soviet state, that was what they dreamed of, and Marx and Engels had dreamed of the same thing: a new homeland for our friend Heinrich.

The spring of 1948 came, and Heinrich had still not got anywhere, but his brother Theodor had, which cost their mother her first sleepless nights. She still scarcely ever left the flat, and made soup twice a week for the German POWs at Father's glassworks who were faint with hunger, and had the wrong sort of ration cards, no rights, and no contract like the Hampels, who had at the most another three years here. Paul and the girls dutifully attended school, recited poems and the dates of battles and Party conferences, the victories of the Great Soviet Union and its triumph in the worst year of all, 1941, a triumph due to our hero Stalin.

That summer Father said: I'm counting the days now. Less than a thousand left, you hear that, I'm counting the days now.

But I don't want to go, said Heinrich, so did Paul, and Theodor did not disagree with them, but Mother tore her hair and took to spending half the afternoon in a darkened room, just as she did in the old days, her heart ached with longing but they had nothing to help her in the pharmacy.

Heinrich's mother had first sent him to the pharmacy in the main square at the beginning of May 1948, and they were all very friendly there, didn't know straight off what would be best for his mother, but she might try this or that, and she ought to go for a walk in the fresh air now and then, that was the old pharmacist's advice. Lyusya had put in an appearance only at the last moment, hurrying back and forth a couple of times and looking at him, eyes shining, but only in passing, or perhaps she was dazzled by the first January sunlight or the prospect of the evening to come.

Lyusya could be said to have a few flaws, she was a tall girl who often squinted and smelled of penicillin, and from a distance she smelled slightly of camphor too, and she had a number of little scratches and marks and scars on her face, and her thumbs were crooked, but how delicately and firmly she picked things up with those crooked thumbs, oh Lyusya, your thumbs.

The first thing she said was: Oh, it's young Herr Hampel, nice to see you, so she seemed to know him, or else a woman friend of hers knew him, and she was saying something with her pale blue eyes, squinting at him with eyes which said: Yes, watch out, I know you, I don't mind your questions, so now go home and try the drops, and if they don't help come back, or come back anyway, but don't stumble over the doorstep, look at you walking backwards and staring and stumbling, this is only the beginning, but a beginning it certainly is.

Mother said: Heinrich, these drops are useless, get me something different or my heart will break, they don't even have proper drops for us Germans in this dreadful country where my husband and sons are each doing two men's work. She said this three or four times before the end of May, with the result that they didn't forget each other, he and his Lyusya, and now Heinrich was going to see her even without an excuse, thinking up reasons for himself and her, or standing outside one of the two shop windows, looking at her standing in the shop in her white coat, mixing up ointments and writing things down, making calculations, waiting until she saw him, when she would wave, knowing, hoping she would keep him. He even showed her off to Yevgeny and his pale Sonya, who shook their heads and said: Well, I don't know, and Budde said, but to himself: Not my sort, I wouldn't fancy her myself, there's nothing special about her, and then all those scratches and marks and scars on her face, well, I don't know.

In July she took to handing him little notes she had written, notes which said: What about it? Or she might write: It's all right by me, yes and yes again, with the result that he lost his nerve and didn't see her for a few days, he found it all so difficult, wondering what the best reply would be, and what exactly she meant by that yes, it probably wasn't that she wanted to go to the movies.

She lived in a timber-built house painted green, halfway to the Tchaikovsky Museum, she was just eighteen, and her father, who was a surgeon in Moscow, had seldom been home since his wife's death a few years earlier, so she lived alone for most of the year, put a couple of wooden logs in the old stove early in the morning from late August onwards, drank a cup of tea for breakfast, and worked very long hours in the pharmacy.

Come another time, she said, shaking hands when he first took her home in autumn, and then for quite a while he was afraid of doing something wrong, or boring her with his stories and their first kisses down under the big willow by the river, she liked it out of doors, loved long walks, or strapping her old skis on and skiing for a long way until she was exhausted, and then she was quiet and tractable with weariness, lit a fire in the kitchen of her green timber house, now put your arms round your tired Lyusya, go on, don't be afraid, I'm enjoying it, yes, it was lovely yesterday, wait there, get to know me there, but go carefully, be thorough, we've got plenty of time.

She collected pebbles all the year round, and chestnuts and acorns and empty snail shells, she would send her hands exploring the many pockets of her old trousers, finding him a shell from the Black Sea here, a dried flower from the grounds of the museum there, and her hands with their crooked thumbs left their first traces on him, like fidgety little animals, he hoped they'd be back again soon. She and he knew every centimetre of skin under each other's clothes, they knew the effect their hands had on the skin under their clothes, and said not a word as they caressed each other and waited and knew: it would happen one day here in her little green house, it would be wonderful, like a great celebration, I'm inviting you, I'm happy, I'm ashamed.

On the day his mother found the photograph and tore it into shreds in the kitchen in front of his father and his brothers and sisters, he had known her for six months, and his mother threw it into the rubbish bin, the shredded photograph of his Lyusya standing in the grounds of the Tchaikovsky Museum in her warm winter coat, unable to produce a smile for Budde and his camera, it had been taken just before Christmas 1948 as a surprise for Heinrich, but Mother was terrified, terrified of losing her sons who might not want to go back to Germany one day because of these girls, they would stay and call it a great love, oh God, there were only two winters and a summer yet to go, and everything was getting on so well at the glassworks, they could hope to be home in the autumn of 1950 at the latest.

It wasn't right for her to tear up my picture, said Lyusya, but she's your mother, mothers get funny ideas, and you won't stay with me, tell her I know better, you won't stay with me, I'll send you off, I'll chase you away.

But suppose I do stay? Heinrich asked, and Budde said: I wish I had your worries, I've already done it, why are you waiting, it's perfectly easy, may not be worth all the fuss really, and look, here's her blood on my finger as proof, because the fact is you've lost our bet.

Yes, said Heinrich, and Lyusya said: Yes, soon, darling, we're not ready yet, and I'm expecting my father home for a few days, and then it'll be spring, and we'll make a great celebration of it in May, when we've known each other a year.

All right, said Heinrich, and he grew bolder every day with his Lyusya his first lover from the little Russian town of Klin, or perhaps it was her hands fidgeting in his pockets that made him bold, the carnation scent of her armpits, her mossiness, the soft hills beneath his fingertips, he got to know her juices, her fragrance, the stains that were left, their desire, and sometimes they went too far and had to go all the long, delicious way back, her eyes wide as she insisted on waiting for her celebration and on the pleasure of looking forward to it, for they had decided it would be like that, and no other way.

She had opened all the windows in May when the great day came, there was a pan of soup on the stove for later, and she greeted him as formally and circumspectly as if they had met again after a long separation, now, take your coat off and make yourself at home, have a glass of tea, I'm here. She had a basin of warm water ready, undressed and washed, put a few drops of lemon balm oil in the water and washed in front of him as if she were his sister, helped him out of his clothes and showed herself, guided him round her for a while, let him thrust into the scent of lemon balm, clenching her teeth just in case, but she knew what she was doing. Are you still there, he said, and remembered the open window and laughed, and yes, Lyusya was still there, amazed and happy, knowing they would get more used to each other in time, it was like a new language you had to learn, just a few words at the start, so they asked each other no questions and needed no comfort from one another.

He told Budde days later, when they met at the market: You may not believe it but we're a couple now, I feel as if I could uproot trees, but his friend Budde didn't want to know, since his Sonya had left him for someone else a couple of weeks ago.

Of course Heinrich's mother guessed at once, she guessed from the lemon balm and the smells of Lyusya on him, and she said Heinrich was a mere child, as for that girl, she didn't want to say what kind of a girl she was, she'd like to forbid him the house and the girl too, that Lyusya.

I'll be eighteen in the summer and then I'm leaving, said Heinrich, I'll be off on my eighteenth birthday at the latest and I'll take the bed with me, just letting you know. At this she turned pale, feeling helpless fury, for she had aged a great deal in these Russian years, what with the hunger and all the worry about her sons and their floozies, yet she wouldn't be fifty until August, it was a few days before Heinrich's own birthday, his eighteenth, that she woke up feeling happy and then was taken aback, because there was nothing at all for her: no flowers, no presents, not a word, no birthday wishes. They had forgotten her so completely that they actually forgot her fiftieth birthday, she still could hardly believe it, such ungratefulness and lack of consideration, they were always taking and taking and sucking her dry, her sons, her daughters, her husband, that ever punctual and conscientious man who hardly knew her, how could he do this to her?

Heinrich was the only one who had remembered his mother's birthday that year, but then the Lyusya affair came along, and Mother still couldn't think of a term bad enough for that slut, the tart who was sleeping with her son, her no-good son who gave her such trouble, so he kept his mouth shut about it all day and was pleased to see that his father and brothers and sisters had really forgotten and were acting as if it were any ordinary working day, walking the same way as usual to work or school or the illegal market near the station, where fresh calves' heads went on sale every few weeks, heads with horrible big eyes, but they made excellent soup, cooked without those horrible big eyes, would you cut them out for me, please, yes, there where I'm pointing, and the butcher went and packed the horrible big eyes up for her specially, what a gourmet she must be, the eyes were the very best bit of a calf's head.

All I want for my birthday is you, said Heinrich, and Lyusya said: Well, you can have me, but I've got a birthday surprise for you, I've thought of something, and once we have the bed you can stay overnight, that's what I dream of. I don't want you getting into quarrels over me, she said, dreaming of his bed and their first night together, because then they would have each other every evening and could take their time getting accustomed to one another, they'd never have too much love or not enough, it would be like one long party, and she would hear the breath of her boyfriend from Germany in his sleep and feel his cold, scratchy feet on her feet, his skin against hers. I could stay and apply for a Soviet passport, said Heinrich, oh, Heinrich.

On the morning of his eighteenth birthday it was his father who wished him many happy returns, he did seem to be getting rather forgetful these days, he said, but at least I'll wish my son a happy birthday, at eighteen he wasn't really grown up, but here in Russia the law regards you as an adult, fair enough.

I'm leaving, said Heinrich, seeing Mother and Father go pale, and they shook their heads and said: You wouldn't dare.

Oh yes, he would, and by the way he was taking his bed with him too.

Go on, then, said Mother, and don't let me set eyes on you again, but the bed stays here, it belongs to your father and wasn't made for the likes of that Lyusya.

We'll see, said Heinrich, and he went, and slept on the old straw mattress at Lyusya's, and three days later he turned up with the militia and a document in Russian requiring the Hampel parents to hand over a bedstead to their son Heinrich, who by the law of the Soviet Union had come of age on 27 August 1949, and consequently was independent and responsible for his actions, and if necessary they would take it by force.

So Heinrich had the bed removed from his mother's flat by two Soviet militiamen in broad daylight, and it was a little piece of her native land they were taking away from her, it was her last love, oh, the shame, the lack of consideration for her these days, the old bonds between them.

Of course the two militiamen laughed as they carried the bed into Lyusya's house, putting it down in the middle of the small living-room with its open windows, and they were given a glass of vodka by way of thanks and went off and left the couple alone. Now make me feel all soft, it's me, I'm yours, I'm waiting, said Lyusya, and it was a pretty language she spoke, like the language of the childhood in which she moved and danced and feared nothing, nothing at all.

She liked hiding various objects about her person so that he could search for them and find them, and find them he did: bright glass marbles here and here, a little pickled gherkin in her mouth, a piece of caramel cut up with a knife hidden between her breasts. She wrapped marinated salmon and smoked ham round his prick, drank brandy and vodka out of his mouth, washed his hair and feet, had a miraculous little surprise for every day.

This was happiness, the criterion of happiness, and so it remained.

One day in September she showed him some things to do, saying: You're a Russian, you're my husband, you know that, but you want to think of your Lyusya there, and there, and I can think of something else there, you'll learn.

I'm very strong.

With you, I'm very weak.

What was it like before, before our time?

I'll show you.

So she showed him, and he saw what she meant, and decided to stay and apply for Soviet citizenship, oh, Heinrich.

They had spent three years in Russia, and he was only just beginning with his Lyusya, they lived as if they were on the outer edge of time and never tired of one another, went to the ballet in Moscow a couple of times, and to the big parade at the beginning of November, caught the last unheated train in the evening and froze, were struck dumb by all the noise and the banners and the weaponry. When he wanted to give her pleasure he bought her a new pair of stockings from the undercover market, or a pair of wickedly expensive Czech shoes, or some white cabbage and beetroot and a bit of meat and sour cream to make bortsch in the evening. You don't have to do that, she would say, and then surprised him with a new recipe, and the latest edition of *Pravda*, or a volume of Soviet love stories: So you won't forget your country or your Lyusya overnight one of these days.

Ulbricht, she said, oh, I'm so pleased for you. To which Heinrich asked: What Ulbricht, never heard of him, and she liked the way he simply asked, What Ulbricht, she liked other things about him too: his firm, rounded buttocks, his sturdy calves, the little tower of his prick as he came erect, the dry heat there, the first fine droplets, the clear, soft water from his mouth. The way he touched her, knew her, covered her, explored ways around her, left her her freedom. The way he slept the sleep of the just. The Moscow accent with which he spoke, the little mistakes that gave him away.

She liked eating with him, often went shopping with him, liked the way he inspected everything and weighed it up in his hand before buying, and the way he knew the names of all the ingredients as if he were a native of the place. People gossiped about her and the boy from Germany, she liked that too, and she liked it when he spilled his sperm on her belly in the light of the oil lamp so that there wouldn't be any baby, oh, the baby, the baby.

He never thought: this is a Russian girl. His Lyusya, he called her.

He didn't know much about her; or maybe he knew almost everything. Her first years of childhood, the two hundred days of winter every year, her father far away, her mother who had those two crooked thumbs as well, who simply disappeared one day and was found a week later down by the bend in the river, drowned, the water wasn't even particularly deep there. She didn't like talking about her past, and spoke as if she were still angry with her mother, but life went on, life changed every few years when you lived close to the mighty metropolis of Moscow, there were the arrests of the thirties, the war against the Soviet's ally Germany, the spotty boy next door with his professions of love hidden in snowballs, the great famine, the quiet days in the pharmacy until one day Heinrich brought a bright light into them, in just a few sentences she raced through the story of her life.

She was counting the hours with her Heinrich.

Just before Christmas he stayed away for a couple of nights, so she had some practice in doing without him, for there had been an accident at the works, a sudden leak in the big tank for the glass, and they needed every man. Theodor and his father had merely nodded briefly when they saw him, but on the morning of the third day, after the damage was repaired, they all shook hands feeling tired and proud and well disposed to each other, for they were a family, they came from the lovely city on the Saale among its many hills, and they would all be going back there some day.

For Mother's sake, said Theodor, think of Mother, she's grieving, you've no idea how much she's grieving.

Exactly, said Heinrich, shaking his head over his mother and his brother, Theodor the favourite child, the gift of God, was he seriously expected to visit and talk about their divided country over coffee and cakes, and wonder whether the Third World War or peace was closer, but none of you will say a word to my Lyusya.

Your Lyusya isn't part of the family.

She's part of my life.

You're as heartless as ever, Heinrich.

I'm only happy here in Klin, though you may see it as a prison. What else matters?.

You've got your first girlfriend, that's what it is.

And so have you, Nadya or some such name.

That's different.

Very likely it is when you're screwing her, said Heinrich, intending to sound coarse, and Theodor turned surly and said he wasn't going to discuss it.

Out of the frying pan into the fire, that's what it's going to be, he said. They've called it the German Democratic Republic.

That's what they've called it, yes. So what?

Well, it can't be worse than here, said Heinrich, and if it turns out better than here, then that's all to the good.

(But he was going to stay and have children with his Lyusya, wasn't he, and become a Russian?)

It'll break Mother's heart, said Theodor.

I can't help that.

At the end of February, in the middle of their second winter, Lyusya's father came home and got a surprise. There he stood in the doorway around ten on a Sunday morning, looking at the bed, and his daughter, and this young man, and was surprised. Lyusya's father looked worn to the bone, dead tired in his crumpled suit and slightly intoxicated, he was also curious about all this, the bed in particular seemed to occupy his mind, and his daughter in that bed and the young man in pyjamas, they weren't even really awake. All right, he said, and he lit the stove first and then made fresh tea in the samovar and gave the pair of them time to wash, the idea was to let them get over the first shock, and quite a shock it had been.

This is Heinrich, said Lyusya, and her father said: Yes, right, Heinrich, now suppose your Heinrich leaves us alone for half an hour and goes for a walk, your father has something to say to you, and when I've finished you can wave from the window. It was exactly half an hour before Lyusya waved to him, and after that she was rather embarrassed, and seemed very young and shy, not the way he knew her. She sat there perfectly quiet as her father talked, all about her and what she had been like as a child and a young girl, when she was as tall as a boy and fought like a boy, liked to sleep out in the fields in summer, was remarkably affectionate and sensitive, and she'd always been a loner until now, until this Heinrich came along, well, it seems you're looking after her, glad to hear it. People are meant to live together, he said, he'd probably forgotten how himself, working as he so often did until late in the night, getting up early in the morning, cutting open soldiers' heads and counting the splinters, the scars, the old wounds of the fighting men who were his patients, and their stories kept him awake at nights. Stories from the war, said Lyusya's father, the defeats of 1941, our persistence and the price of it, the burden of our victories. For a few years everything might be peaceful, there might seem to be no threat, but then all of a sudden the splinters would move, marching through blood and tissue and into a man's vital organs or his head, he knew

318

every centimetre of the head, for he was a brain specialist, born 1905 near the dawn of the Revolution, a Party member since 1924, Lenin's death in January that year was a great catastrophe.

Well, I have to catch my train, Lyusya's father said at last, Heinrich must take good care of his Lyusya, mind he didn't beat her, oh, really, Father. We'll take you to the station, said Lyusya, and she was a different person already as they went to the station, and in the following days when she was thinking everything over again, weighing it up, assessing it, she wasn't his girl any more. You might do better to move to the city when all this is over, her father had told her as he left, and Heinrich took it personally, right, so now he was definitely staying, he'd that moment made up his mind to stay, but her father had not been pleased, appearing to feel that it was a betrayal of his native land, a man of Heinrich's age ought to be working, and as he would soon see you could work well only for your own country.

That last spring came and went, and Lyusya was her old self again, sowing lettuce and vegetables in the garden and planting potatoes for the winter, she was often quiet now, and slow and exploratory and hesitant in their love-making, as she was when she didn't know what would happen next, or as if she had to steel herself against something. When they had been together exactly a year, in May 1950, she said: Now everything is going to repeat itself, and she gave him a notebook for later, so that you'll remember it all, a little grey book of about a hundred octavo pages, your Lyusya is only one girl, you see, look what I've written in it for you: Lyusya Stepanovich, 23 May 1949 to autumn 1950, my first girlfriend who was never ashamed and was happy, she had two crooked thumbs and she held things firmly with them.

We've a lot yet to do before autumn, said Lyusya.

For instance, he had never danced with her.

Then let's go dancing.

And we haven't eaten out with your friends, or had our first quarrel.

Then let's quarrel. About who'll have it easier.

The one who's going will have it easier. Staying is difficult.

Then because I know I'm the one staying, I'll go, said Lyusya, and she still didn't believe it herself, or she protected herself from it, thinking she would only need a few months to pass and then she'd be back, and as the one who was staying she would have her things still there, things slowly ageing, and places, and memories: you are never rid of memories.

One Saturday in August Paul was suddenly there at the door with the latest news, he wouldn't come in but he had the latest news to pass on, the Berger family had permission to go home and were already packing, selling up their furniture and household equipment, absolutely delighted. He said it first in German and then in Russian, and Lyusya nodded and went back into the house, for this meant, surely, it would soon be over. Paul said no, it was only the Bergers going, the work to be done at the factory was finished now but only the Bergers could go, a letter from Moscow said so in black and white, but unfortunately no letter from Moscow had yet come for the Hampels.

Heinrich said: We don't have it in writing yet, but Lyusya shook her head: You're saying We, though, and what's the difference whether it's September or January?

She gave herself and him just three days, she was in such a hurry, she was going to join her father on Monday, she had told Heinrich it would be Monday, and now she had all the time in the world again, so listen: It was down here by the river they found my mother, I slept under the trees here, and here in the market there was kvass or fresh milk from the little cart with its churn, sweets for a few kopecks, or ice-cream when it was available in the windy summers, that was your Lyusya's life. You see, it isn't difficult, she said on

Saturday, and they still had a few hours left on Sunday, and don't forget your little book, you must say goodbye to my mouth, it's not so difficult after all, you go to work on Monday, I'll leave the key in the window and then I'll be gone.

They didn't talk about it any more on the last night, only where he would find the key, and when she had gone he stayed on for a few days, as if she were still living there herself, at least in what she left behind, in the scents she left for him, which dispersed, and soon even the bed and the room said nothing more to him; then he went home.

Years later, Constanze said: I knew straightaway it was you, only Heinrich could turn up so promptly for Sunday lunch without a word of warning, dancing his way up four flights of steps up to our flat nearly at the top of the building, just like Fred Astaire, and there he is, says Hello, here I am, hope I'm not late, I know it's a bit late now but I could smell the dumplings and cabbage and roast meat all over the building.

You look like a Russian, said Constanze, or maybe it was Sibylle, and he looked like a grown-up man too, amazing.

As if he'd never been away.

His father said: You're welcome, and his mother said nothing at first, just put an extra plate on the table, now let's say grace, *bon appétit*, Father, and all you children, we're a family again now, we'll have to work out where Heinrich sleeps instead of in his old bed.

As if there had never been any Lyusya.

Paul was the only one to ask after her and where she was now, Lyusya who was in possession of his bed, should he go and fetch it some day with a truck from the factory, no, I don't think so. You must have been very fond of her, said Paul, who was now the same age as Heinrich on the day he first went to the pharmacy, but Paul wasn't emulating him, he was still the same silly little Paul he'd always been, asking silly little questions, no idea about anything.

Heinrich's evenings and nights were now the way he hadn't known them for a long time, it was like those dreams where you have to go back to school, but you know you're too old and too stupid for geometry or Latin grammar or speaking the foreign languages that you've forgotten, but now all that was to be your life again, together with your anxiety and your delight when the anxiety passed off. He spent his days as if he were in a great hurry, very impatiently, thinking of Lyusya and driving the thought away, unable to shake it off, thinking he saw her almost daily on some street corner, sometimes standing there and smiling, guess what, I've got a couple of days off and I wanted to see you, I love you.

On coming home every evening Heinrich's father would say: Still nothing from Moscow? And nothing had yet come from Moscow, though the Bergers had gone home long ago, and wrote to say that when they came back the whole town was there at the station to welcome them, so hurry up the rest of you.

I'm so tired of all this, Matthias, said Heinrich's mother, still wearing the grey costume from that golden age in Jena, its fifth winter here, and her old glen check coat, and she was indeed tired of it all, didn't want to sit out a fifth endless winter, the sky, the light, living without her own language, with the foreignness she felt and couldn't shake off, the anxiety about her children and her husband and their house in the hilly surroundings of home, the life that was passing her by, life that never happened, everything held in suspension and transitory, like the hands of her husband who didn't want her any more, although when she could conceive and bore him five healthy if useless children he had wanted her at every opportunity.

She didn't say: I've suffered enough. She said: When we're back in my beloved Jena you can buy me a dress in a nice bright colour.

The letter reached them at the end of the first week of Advent, and Lyusya came back at around the same time too and served in the pharmacy as if nothing had happened, and she looked out of the window as she had before and saw him, smiling her subtle Lyusya smile, but as if she had to work out who it was she'd seen, what was his name, how did they know each other, oh yes, that young man from Germany, Heinrich, so he's still in this country, I remember, and what I remember is very pleasant, for instance his dirty hands after work at the factory, coal-dust even under his clothes, the skin of my black Heinrich who explored me.

The short letter from Moscow said: You will stay till the end of the year, and in early January we will drive the Hampel family to the airport in Moscow and send them away from this country and home to East Germany, they could take such and such an amount of luggage each, half that amount for children under sixteen.

So now there was much selling and haggling over prices and the recipients of their beds and the crockery and almost everything they owned, and the glassworks manager had first choice and was glad of it, he was glad for the Hampels too, after all, people belong in their own countries, and the glassworks manager and his wife lay on every bed to try them out, and decided that the brightly coloured Armenian shawl would look good on their shabby old couch. In the end the glassworks manager and his wife left only a little crockery and table linen and a few pots and pans for the neighbours, and the very last things of all were given as a present to the fat lady who sold ice-cream, to whom the Hampels' mother owed eternal gratitude, because in a real emergency she had taken something out of the till and given it to her, the German woman, and saved her life, and now she was quite embarrassed about accepting the old pots and pans and the soup ladle with its worn places, oh, Frau Hampel, what can I say?

At Christmas Father stood them a bottle of red pepper

vodka, and at New Year there was a bottle of Crimean sparkling wine, never available at any other time, and then they said their goodbyes. Constanze and Sibylle went to school for the last time and brought home photographs of all their friends, and Paul brought some photographs too, and Theodor was pale after saying goodbye to Nadya, who couldn't believe it and hid her tears in the steam of the big laundry where she worked near the station, who'd have thought it. Now you know what it's like, said Heinrich, and he walked the familiar way again, stood for a while in front of the green-painted timber house where she had explored him, walked in the snow-covered grounds of the Tchaikovsky Museum, took a few cautious steps out on the metre-thick ice of the frozen river.

Now then, children, said their mother at the beginning of January, putting their linen on big sheets and tying up the seven sheets full of linen and books with large knots, so that they could easily sling them over their shoulders, that was all they had left, all that they were taking away with them to make a fresh start, and finally each of them clambered up on the big lorry with a bundle, and they drove past the markets again and on towards the glassworks, past the illegal market where the first people were bustling about, past the station, the last houses in town, the bumpy road along which they had come, and now they were going back in their fifth year, and maybe they were not the same people they once had been, they saw Moscow for the last time, Moscow where the stores were as big as cathedrals or old opera houses, with heavy chandeliers hanging from the ceilings, and window displays of wine and liqueurs and vodka from all parts of the Soviet Union, enough for a hundred weddings, and more fresh salmon and caviar than you could have driven away in a couple of lorries: so much of it there was.

They kept the Hampels waiting at the airport for half a day before they were finally summoned to climb a wobbly ladder into an American DC-3 provisioned with liqueur chocolates and ham. There was a Russian general with countless orders and decorations on board, a Stalin Prize winner in a dark suit, a diplomatic courier of His Majesty the King of England with a mailbag chained to his left wrist, and a Russian air stewardess who laughed a lot and showed her bad teeth when she laughed.

He lost Lyusya somewhere over the Oder and the Neisse. The general was saying: You'll all be amazed at the country now, and at that moment he no longer remembered her mouth, her forehead wrinkling as she thought, the dimples in her cheeks, he didn't know her perfume, but the Germans who were now much like Russians would be amazed, and his Lyusya, back at home in Klin, was just heating up the samovar and thinking: He ought to be landing soon, the German boy I liked so much, good luck to him.

11

Even in his early fifties, after his first spell in Bautzen, Heinrich had something expectant in his eyes, as if he had a right to keep expecting something for himself to the very last, he looked defeated but resilient, the citizen of a defeated but resilient state, in which he had recently taken to entering strangers' homes by night, morally and psychologically disrupting the lives of their owners, and Rosa and his sons were applying for cancellation of their citizenship and refused to be held responsible for damages in connection with their former husband and father.

In his latest photographs Heinrich looked like a con-man or bigamist on the point of discovery, but he still wore a suit and tie, a man in the prime of life, an advanced diabetic, a wreck turning the scales at over ninety kilos, not always the most reliable of lovers now, always short of funds and unable to pay his old debts. He had once told Constanze all about his debts, like everything else it had all begun in the West, and then he had nothing when he got to the East and ran up debts there, but I was only acting the way states act, running up debts for the future of my Rosa and the three children, and they punished me as if I were a criminal, I paid for it by spending my best years in Gera, Leipzig and Bautzen, but what exactly was the crime, do you think, I mean, states can pay off their debts by running up more and more of them, but a poor bastard like me gets put in jail to improve his character.

He never had an answer to this letter; either the authorities had intercepted it and blacked out those passages in felt pen, or Constanze thought: Surely he'll be all right in the GDR, or why does he himself write: It began in the West with our uncle's two houses, so she supposed they'd have their reasons in the East for what they did with the feckless brother to whom she'd been sending parcels for years, and who never even said a proper thank-you, and now they'd see, they'd treat him firmly, as their mother once did, he probably exaggerated now and then, Mother herself had exaggerated now and then, but he'd survived the three years in Bautzen and had a new woman in his life, a woman who always wanted the latest fashion in shoes.

The name of this last woman of his was Emilia, she was always nicely made up, she was strong, wore half a dozen rings on her fingers, and had been born and brought up in old Winzerla, which was now full of high-rise buildings like everywhere else. She was approaching sixty and regarded love as a garden late in the season, when you must still rake up the last of the leaves and cut a few withered flowers, but the ground is already cold and resting, waiting for the first snow. Come along, let's make ourselves comfy, she would say whenever she ate a cold supper with him in his flat, and they watched those nice placid wildlife films on either Eastern or Western TV, or a political programme. What a comfortable country we live in, she often said, meaning her job at the cash-desk of the Planetarium, evenings chatting in the Magnus Poser People's Solidarity Club, or the dances at the Carl Zeiss Socialist People's Collective Clubhouse to which he escorted her, he had such a way with him when he was dancing that she sometimes forgot herself and failed to remember the boundaries she didn't mean to cross and her good resolutions.

Particularly in the first weeks she was slightly shocked by her friend Heinrich and his eventful life, the way his hands strayed under her new blouse, the compliments he paid, whispering them in her ear as if she weren't approaching sixty, what a strange man he was. The first time she had said: Oh, all that was over and done with long ago, don't trouble yourself, I won't be able to give you any pleasure, but then they did get together after all, and he would sit on her lap and talk about Lyusya's crooked thumbs, that was what he liked best. Sometimes she said: She must have been a nice girl, your Lyusya with her crooked thumbs, and so saying she pressed and caressed and kneaded his prick as Lyusya herself might have done, or that man Karl in prison.

Of his years in prison (his first sentence) he always said: Things are the same in prison as everywhere else, only a hundred times worse than anywhere else, one can't really describe it. She would never kiss him before or afterwards, but when he said: Well, it'll soon be over, they'll be coming to take me away again at the end of the year at the latest, she soothed him, said he was a pessimist, and now do be quiet, dear heart, I'm going to sleep.

All spring he had feared they would come and take him away again, because of the same old deals and debts, the latter never growing any less in spite of the deals, but he continued going to work at the Thüringer Hof every morning, and nothing happened, and Priem kept quiet too and didn't suspect, acting as if there had never been a second IOU. At the end of March, in the Cosmetika, Priem mentioned almost casually that the bastards had broken into his place, just wait till he caught them, he could name this man and that man straight out, but Heinrich did not feature on his long list.

It had all been very quick and easy, Priem hadn't even locked his door, he was so careless and took things so lightly, or perhaps he didn't mind, or perhaps he was ashamed of living in such a dump without heating or a lavatory. Heinrich felt extremely uncomfortable in that flat from the first, and uneasy at the way he was rummaging about, smearing the walls, taking photographs with the knowledge of the authorities and on their behalf, taking a few things away with him, removing a few of Priem's extensive collection of gramophone records to flog them.

This is the kind of case in which you could prove your value to us, Harms had said at their last meeting, and Heinrich had said: I owe him money, he's pressurizing me, he can get me a second term in Bautzen if he likes. Ah, good, Harms had said, it's about time we get something definite on this man Priem with his dubious connections and his deals prejudicial to Socialist property, he makes no secret of his hostile and negative attitude to Socialism, the GDR and the other Socialist countries.

When, then? Heinrich had asked, and Harms suggested Friday, because that Friday all firms were closing in order to send their staff to the big peace demonstration in the market-place, fifteen thousand citizens of all social classes and walks of life protesting against the stationing of nuclear rockets in the West, Herr Hampel would have all the time in the world.

Yes, all right, Heinrich had said, imagining that it would all be much more difficult, but now here he was in the flat, looking around and finding things, sweeping some of the books off shelves, scattering paper from the drawers, and he wrote his report the same evening. Jena, 19 March 1983, for the record: On Friday afternoon P. left his workplace in Dornburger Strasse (tram depot) and went to the mass rally on the occasion of the 38th anniversary of the Anglo-American air raid on the city of Jena in 1945. On the subsequent investigation of his flat in Gartenstrasse, the following items were found and photographed:

1   account of the events of June 1953 (in the West)
2   handbills of the Jena *Junge Gemeinde*
1   DEFA special illustrated book *Erotica* in colour, red and white
1   portable typewriter robotron, brand
23 letters from Uelzen (Federal Republic), sender Hilde-gard Weber

1   picture postcard from Venice (Italy), sender as above
9   new radio sets akkord, brand
     Federal German cash in notes: 4 × DM 50 (total DM
     200)
     USA cash in notes: 10 × 5 US dollars (total $50).

P. lives in primitive conditions in a two-room flat without
WC (probably uses communal WC in the yard), eats mainly
out of cans, drinks beer. Colour TV set, record player, poster
of rock group Puhdies on wall in the hall, underneath, on the
wallpaper, the saying: State property cannot be treated as you
treat it. Lenin, *Telegrams* (1918).

Harms hadn't really understood the point of the Lenin
reference either, but it was obvious that Priem meant to
express his contempt for Socialism, and the two telephone
numbers on the leaflets were those of known dissidents in
Jena, we'll pick them up the next chance we get. For a brief
moment Heinrich had thought: suppose Emilia's name had
been on one of those two leaflets, what then, and he
preferred not to imagine what then, but he did like imagining
her warm and crumpled body, in his thoughts he was almost
home already.

His old friend Harms said: There's something I have to say
about your wife, adding that she had greatly disappointed him
with her application to leave along with their sons Konrad
and Walter, all of them wanting to get out of the Republic
now, at the hour of our greatest triumphs, what a disappointment.

There had been incidents at the mass rally on the occasion
of the 38th anniversary of the Anglo-American air raid on the
city of Jena in 1945, minor scuffling on the outskirts of the
crowd, the destruction – it was to be hoped in good time – of
banners and billboards bearing slogans hostile to the Party,
but Harms said nothing about that, it was all under control.
The newspapers said: The fate of Jena and Dresden,
Leningrad and Stalingrad, Hiroshima and Nagasaki, Coventry

and Lidice must never be repeated, and the people read the papers, but it was the incidents they talked about. Weird, said Emilia, and she knew some people who had talked about the incidents, but, fortunately she had named no names that he would then have had to quote.

He had heard about those applications to emigrate in November when Eva came to see him for a few days, sleeping on the couch in his living-room, and it was a long time before she got around to the subject. She looked tired and strained, his Eva, with her freckles and her coppery red hair, for the place where she lived in some dump in Mecklenburg was still like a building site even after seven years, and her marriage to her Rainer was like a building site too, or as Eva put it: We simply can't get the material we need together, and she talked about the nature of men, she didn't even know the name of Rainer's new woman.

Heinrich would have preferred her not to talk about that, for her unhappiness made him feel ashamed, and the way life repeated itself made him feel ashamed, so he quickly changed the subject and asked about her brothers and her mother, well, yes, they were going, giving everything up here. She didn't know about Konrad, but Walter was hoping to make good money in the West, and with Rosa it was homesickness, she was sick of the East after twenty years, and of course she had lost her good job.

Nothing but bad news, said Heinrich, and Eva agreed: Yes, nothing but bad news, and how were his legs, she asked, and the diabetes and his job as a waiter, and the wedding plans. We'll see, said Heinrich, and did Rosa ever ask about him, she was always so distant on the telephone, how different everything would be if she finally found another man, why doesn't she ever let anyone get close to her? Eva laughed at her father for asking such questions, and he couldn't even make a decent cup of coffee to go with the cake he had bought, so she laughed and ate and drank and went back to her wreck of a home and wreck of a marriage in that dump in Mecklenburg late that evening, kissed him on the mouth as they parted, loyal Eva, his oldest child who he hoped would be staying here near him, he hadn't even asked.

Emilia found him curiously exhausted and low-key in the evening, and the next Saturday they celebrated her fifty-seventh birthday with plenty of wine and vodka and cold cuts, and on Sunday evening Heinrich said: I think I'll have to lie down, I feel rather faint after all that wine and vodka and the fatty cold cuts, and he didn't get up again and had a kind of blackout, the doctors said his system had gone off the rails, and it could easily be several weeks before he was really better again.

This had been the first time he took Priem home with him, just so that he could show his Emilia off to someone, and they got on very well indeed. Priem had even brought her some roses, and Heinrich thought it was almost as if she were particularly pleased with the three roses and the box of chocolates, and they talked about the old times and the new as if they were well acquainted. Even soon after midnight Heinrich was thinking: I ought to be pleased they're getting on so well, both of them shaking their heads over the people fleeing the Republic, throwing everything away for a bit of freedom and foreign travel in the West, but the bread and butter won't taste any better there, and who knows if they'll earn it so easily.

It was not until long after midnight that Priem mentioned the money to him, on the way to the lavatory: Don't get your hopes up, I'm rather meticulous about money matters and you aren't exactly reliable, and although no more was said he wrote a letter to his sisters in the West that same night: I feel really embarrassed about this, but could you please send the rest of my money to the State Bank in Jena, then they'll let me have it in Forum cheques, and I can buy some things I need.

A nice man, your friend Priem, said Emilia, when she

visited him in hospital a few days later, bringing some clean things to wear and his post, and asking how he was feeling, and no, Herr Priem had not called, why should he, well, why indeed?

It was like the time back then in Leipzig, when they said: Don't run away from us, Herr Hampel, will you, it'll only make trouble, but they said it in jest, since Heinrich had been sentenced to five years in Bautzen and couldn't work because of an encysted joint in his left elbow. He had been only three months in Bautzen when they operated on him in Leipzig, and botched it badly, he wasn't up and about for six months, but the children had kept writing, and Eva found time to visit every few weeks.

You and Eva must meet next time, said Heinrich, and Emilia said: Get better for me first, how else will you be able to ask if I'll marry you, wasn't that what you were asking recently?

It was in the summer of 1982, on their first and last trip together, that he had asked her, and Emilia had said: Ask me again in six months' time, I'll think about it, we're on holiday now and thinking only of the present. She would have liked to go to the Black Sea, or for a walking trip in the High Tatra, but Heinrich had said: I can't afford the High Tatra or the Black Sea, but I know a lake-side cottage in Mecklenburg with a rowing boat, we could laze about on the quiet lake, I'd only have to ask. He didn't say: I went there years ago with Rosa and the children, I hope that doesn't bother you, instead he invented some acquaintances whom he would have to ask, and they were going to set off on a Monday in June.

The train was almost two hours late that Monday in June, and when it finally came in Emilia was just drying the last of her tears, but after that she was very brave, stood patiently in the badly overcrowded corridors, unpacked some sandwiches and put the Black Sea and the High Tatra out of her mind,

333

she had even brought tea with milk and sugar, so they stood in the rocking train as they went almost all across the country, changed trains and arrived, oh Heinrich, I'm so excited.

The owners of the cottage had brought a can of milk and a bowl of strawberries to welcome them, and wished them a pleasant few days, and please would they not light fires, and be patient if the water didn't run first thing in the morning, it would come through eventually. Lovely, said Emilia, I wish we could stay all summer, and Heinrich said: Yes, it's a nice place, except that the blankets are a bit dusty, and there are only two hotplates for cooking in the kitchen: it was just as it used to be.

At supper in the café he nearly told her that he knew this place, and what Rosa had said about it, how they lay side by side under the dusty blankets at night, not touching, but Emilia was so happy with her plans, looking forward to lazy afternoons in the boat, all of it just for him and her, like paradise, so quiet and warm and fragrant, that he kept his mouth shut. As usual, they didn't get a table at once and stood waiting for half an hour before one of the two waitresses showed them in and brought them the menus over as if they were a couple of unwelcome intruders, you might as well know straight away that the knuckle of pork's off, so's the pork shoulder. This was one of those moments when he still didn't feel at home in the GDR with its Socialism and unfriendly waiters and operative measures taken to consolidate the class viewpoint, it was all rather miserable. Come on, this is our first evening, said Emilia, see how they envy us, let's just laugh at them and the dusty blankets in our cottage, now do be a kind good man and get me something nice to drink, I'll have the herring and fried potatoes. Or do you want to kiss me tonight, by any chance, she asked, for at this time she did still let him kiss her sometimes, for instance on that first evening in Mirow, which turned out the best.

As always on the now rare occasions when he did it, it took him some time to find his way around his Emilia, but that was what he liked, the way everything about her was a little confusing, and the way she let herself drop into the water from the boat just as the good Lord made her, he liked that, there have to be some fat ladies in the world, or don't you think your fat naked Emilia is pretty?

Wonderfully pretty, said Heinrich, and watched her sparkling with happiness right into the third and fourth days as she swam a couple of times round the boat, or let it tow her along for a while, she didn't feel the cold. What are you dreaming about, she sometimes asked, and made him tell her what he was dreaming about immediately: He wanted to be perfectly healthy again, he said, and a head waiter at the International, because no one much but a few actors made their way to the Thüringer Hof, the VIPs went to the International on the Ernst-Thälmann-Ring, high-ranking delegations from the fraternal countries and Western businessmen who ordered lobster *au naturel*, or the seafood platter, and could identify such unusual items of cutlery as a caviar knife, snail pincers and lobster forks.

I think you're crazy, said Emilia, but not until their last evening but one, adding that this was the best time she'd had for ages, and many thanks, let's do it again.

Do you think I'm difficult? You know what I mean.

You'll learn yet, he said.

It's all kind of hidden away inside me.

Well, he who seeks will find.

In retrospect, of course he couldn't afford that holiday, nor could he afford all the presents, the little marks of regard he brought when he visited her in her room in Grete-Unrat-Strasse, although she preferred visiting him, because she had only a narrow couch to sleep on and no kitchen, a basin for both washing and cooking, and she didn't like it when he lay in bed watching her wash and dress in the morning, almost always in the freezing cold because of the wretched stove. Sometimes he knocked on her door late in the evening, gave her a bottle of Yvette Intim lotion, a dozen new Jana Special hair curlers, or a blue and green striped heating pad for her cold feet in the never-ending winter of eighty-one to eighty-two, when he had known her just nine months.

When the first IOU fell due at the end of March he had a hundred marks in his pocket, but then they met in the Cosmetika as usual, and Priem was in a better temper than he'd felt for years, his business was going extremely well, so what was the sum again? Two thousand, Heinrich had said, and Priem replied, as if it were a trifle: well, obviously Heinrich was in difficulties at the moment, and he knew what it was like when you're in difficulties, but you still want to enjoy your supper in the evening, and if you're a lucky fellow like Heinrich you have a girlfriend, but girlfriends cost money. So let's come to an agreement, he said, the money wasn't the point in itself, we all have money, the trouble is we can't buy anything here with all our money, how can I help?

In the end what it came to was another IOU for fifteen hundred, and he would take five hundred as a down payment on the first, leaving obligations to the amount of three thousand. Could he live with that? Yes, he could live with that, and we'll meet again in six months' time, so now let's not talk business any more, business has to be done but no need to make a great fuss and bother about it, and finally they got back to Bautzen, a subject they had in common, for Priem personally it was quite a while ago, but he had learnt lessons enough for his whole life in Bautzen, for instance those cells where you could only stand, they wore anyone down.

My daughter used to send me a jar of lard with apples and onions in it every few weeks, said Heinrich, saying nothing about his letters to his sister in the West and the parcels she packed up from his wish-lists, including among other things diabetic sweetener, tobacco and loose filters, a long-life dried sausage, long-life cheese, diabetic chocolate and sweets, but no kind word ever came with them, all he got from the West was the things themselves and silence and contempt, the family there didn't seem to think anything of him any more, well, he could understand that. Only Eva ever visited him during the first year, when he was in hospital most of the time, and she always hated to see how quickly people deteriorated and fell into decline behind these walls, decided that her stories of life outside and at home were unsuitable, but her father lived for such stories, memories, plans for the future, painful they might be, but they gave him pleasure.

I didn't count the deaths in Bautzen, said Priem, but they'll have records for sure, those book-keepers with their five-year plans, the quota on the left, set higher every few years, dead souls on the right accepting it all meekly, that's what they like, the peace of a graveyard in this country where at least half the people are informers, though when they come trying to recruit you it's just to entertain themselves a bit. Priem didn't say: You could be one of them yourself, I almost think you are, I'm sure of it, but Heinrich could see from looking at him that he was thinking it, or else Priem saw it all as a game or was an informer too, in which case they'd write reports on each other that evening, giving and taking the same money, and sitting together in the large, cosy trap of which this country, this wonderful country consisted.

Only hours later did Heinrich realize that he was afraid of Priem as both a creditor and an informer, or as Emilia put it: I think you're getting mixed up in something, my dear, only if you don't tell me about it I can't be much help. Oh, it's old history, said Heinrich, and wrote a few lines to Constanze: Dear Constanze, please send the rest of my funds to Herr Rainer Priem, Strasse des 7. Oktober, in dollars; Herr Priem has been very helpful to me and I owe him 3000 marks. I'd be very grateful if you could do that for me, kind regards, your brother Heinrich.

The answer was not long in coming and was unfriendly in tone, they were getting fed up with their brother, always the same old story for years on end, when was he ever going to grow up, when would there finally be an end to all this, they hoped it would be soon, better today than tomorrow.

It was a good two years ago that they had released him from Bautzen, and he had known his Emilia for a couple of months, the job as a waiter at the boring Thüringer Hof was only a stone's throw from his flat, the first flat where he'd lived on his own, and he had a few aches and pains from his time in jail, he injected himself with insulin three or four times a day and sometimes had trouble with standing and walking, but he did stand and walk, and he drank only what was absolutely necessary, or a glass with Harms every few weeks, for that was still the way they began, or they might begin with one of those jokes about life and the wounds it inflicts, the injuries and scars written on human faces as if you could read them like a book, that was the kind of face Heinrich had.

Harms was still a mystery to Heinrich after nearly twenty years, he must be well over sixty, now and then he mentioned his wife and children, and like his country itself he was weary but tough and inflexible, called his work a struggle and a task, just as he had seen it over three decades ago in bombed-out Thuringia, and the struggle had taken its toll of him too over the years, as it had taken its toll of the land and the people, the defeats from which you learn, making victories of them at the last moment, the rehearsal for revolution in sleepy Jena, of all places, that was what always amazed him.

There had even been a death at the beginning of the year in the remand prison in Gera, and many writers had been arrested, and everyone claiming to be in the know had heard about it, and talked about it, and hadn't always doubted the tale, the tale of a man found hanged in his cell one morning, dead, and nobody owning to the responsibility, well, such were the rumours, the whispered propaganda of imperialism and its accomplices, inventing deaths in prison, stirring up unrest among the population of the administrative district of Gera and far beyond, as far as Berlin.

But there are only a few like that, said Heinrich, who knew of no case of anyone's mentioning the alleged incident in Gera. He sometimes felt these days now as if he had to comfort Harms with his reports, pointing out that there was a majority in the country and there was a minority, but the vast majority consisted of two point one seven million members of the Socialist Unity Party, with the members of the coalition parties, the trades unionists, the FDJ, the People's Solidarity organization, was there anything he had forgotten? This was all very cheering, thought Heinrich, and he said so, just to comfort the old Stasi man whom he still saw, and perhaps the old Stasi man liked him, or felt some obligation to him, or was superstitious and thought: If I lose this man Hampel then other things can also be lost here in our beautiful country, and that must not be.

They still used the flat near the Westbahnhof as a safe house for their meetings, but sometimes they went to the Grüner Kranz or the Kosmos café, watched and listened and fell silent, or talked about the latest news of Priem, the suspicion he had expressed to Heinrich, the way Heinrich had reassured him with a private request, a copy of the IOU dated 7 October 1981 was attached. Two thousand marks was the sum on which they had agreed, and a term of six months, so Priem, having him where he wanted him, might stop going on about his suspicions.

That would be something for a start, said Harms, and as usual he had a few questions about the reports, he supposed he hadn't gone any further with that lonely hearts ad. No, Heinrich hadn't gone any further with the lonely hearts ad, but I did get to know someone under the stars of the Planetarium, and the old Stasi man was pleased for his friend Hampel, after all that had happened, really pleased. Yes, said Heinrich, and waited to hear the farewell formula featuring

Rosa and the children, even now, after all these years, he asked after Rosa and the children, a question never omitted.

She ignores me when we run into each other, Heinrich had said, but she looks cheerful and healthy, she's put on a few kilos, why not, I don't mind, so long as she's happy with herself and the mess that was left of our marriage, let her have another husband, I say, and a quick and easy death when it comes to that point, and then if not before we'll all be good to one another and think of each other as former friends.

He had seen Rosa the summer when he was fifty, and she did indeed looked distinctly stout in the summer of 1981, and there was a stranger with his arm around stout Rosa, right at the entrance to the Magnet State Retail Store it had been that she suddenly spotted him and looked surprised, turned away after five and a half years and quickened her pace, but she had turned away from him as if caught in the act of something, or as if she were still ashamed of all that had happened.

The stranger had occupied his mind for a while, and he wondered what it was like when he slipped inside her, and perhaps she still sighed and thought of her Heinrich, although she had simply turned away from him in the street, or perhaps it was because she didn't recognize him with all the damage he'd suffered, that could never be her Heinrich with all those nicks and scratches and cracks, yes, it was him, but what did it matter?

At the time he was out and about in the streets of the city of Jena a good deal at the weekends, but out and about professionally, so to speak, in the service of the state, enquiring into the way Rainer P., employee of the tram depot, spent his days, preserving a distance of a careful few metres when he was following him, tinkered away almost every evening at his list of the names of Rainer P.'s relations, friends and acquaintances, compiled and supplemented weekly by code name 'Rosa' (real name Hampel) in working through the 'Depot' operative process, pp. 43 to 45, and at

340

the bottom, in handwriting, the name of Emilia N., member of staff at the Zeiss Planetarium, born in Jena 9 November 1925, resident of Jena, Greta-Unrat-Strasse, single; no children.

She had shaken hands with Priem after a church service, and was nice and round and soft like Rosa, and then Heinrich had followed her and didn't take his eyes off her, bought himself a ticket to the Planetarium every other day and got to know her voice greeting noisy classes of schoolchildren under the high dome, or the motley delegations from all over the world who came and gazed in astonishment, voyaging through the galaxies in the deepest darkness and listening to one of the thirteen different lectures taped in German and in Russian. Heinrich soon knew every one of them: the four seasons, the solar system, the apparent and real course of the sun, the phases and the orbit of the moon, the ebb and flow of tides, the nature of planets, comets, meteors and shooting stars, the division of time, the calendar in ancient and modern times, orientation by the stars, astronomy and astrology, the star of Bethlehem, arguments about the astronomical concept of the universe from antiquity to the present, and the aspects ascribed in those arguments to hours, days and weeks, he knew the way she tore tickets off the block and made a mark for every visitor, he knew her stern but friendly look when it was crowded and not everyone could get in, except for Heinrich, who could always get in, she made sure of that.

You again? she asked at the end of the second week, and at the end of the third week: Was he thinking of coming to work here, because he kept watching the same programmes, or was there something else? Well, yes.

I hope you're not going to make any difficulties for me, she said, when everything was more or less clear between them over their second glass of peppermint tea in the Prague Café, and as he talked she never took her eyes off him, because you never knew, more particularly you never knew with men, well, that was how it was for her.

Nice job you have here, said Heinrich, and he brought up a few political points, but Emilia thought there were no politics in heaven, and it must be pleasing to the Lord when human beings let their eyes roam the skies above, but he would not see any difference between an imperialist rocket and a Communist rocket.

I really like you, said Heinrich, and didn't know exactly what to do about his reports, but he wrote a letter to his sister Constanze: I have everything I need myself, but I can get hardly anything here for Emilia. If you only knew how important it is to me to give her pleasure! Emilia's fixed up almost my entire flat, I owe it all to her that I've found the courage to carry on. So please take my request seriously. She doesn't ask for anything herself, but I know from talking to her so much what she dreams of having. I'd really like some face powder and face cream for her, and a pair of jeans or a costume, whichever you like, and one or two gentlemen's shirts for me.

Emilia had given him a Golf razor and a tube of Myldeen shaving cream for his fiftieth birthday, and Constanze sent him a wonderful big parcel with all the things he wanted, and he hadn't even asked for at least a quarter of what it contained. Dear Heinrich, his sister Constanze had written, I send you both my very best wishes, I do hope it all works out well for you and Emilia. I wish you health and happiness, as you said yourself some years ago, writing from Bautzen: It's not the first time I've had to begin all over again, luckily I have a good healthy sense of optimism, Bautzen, February 1977.

Those first few weeks with Emilia passed in a flash, he was so happy to have found a woman again, a curvy, reliable, comfortable woman who asked no more of their new life than a few evenings in front of the television together, a few salty sticks to nibble, feet keeping nice and warm under blankets and cushions, and this was quite different from spending identical evenings month after month at the Thüringer Hof, drinking a last brandy in a bar on the corner on his days off, or thinking up walks to take to a stranger's door at weekends: the whole boring life of informers and those on whom they inform, warming up canned food, trotting out Socialist sayings in his reports, dreaming the bad dreams you gave yourself that way, feeling self-disgust.

The winter before he met Emilia had been bleak and desolate, a winter when even Eva didn't visit him, and since even Eva didn't visit him he took to doing deals again, sat up late at night in his armchair studying the naked girls from the latest *Magazin*, read the occasional ad which might prove interesting, but looked for them and found them only to pass the time, read about the people in different seasons of life advertising in the lonely hearts columns and decided it ought to be a woman in her late summer, mid-thirties, no older, and a few lines cost only a few marks.

His ad had appeared in the April number: Respectable gentleman around fifty seeks lady who enjoys life, both parties wishing to make a new start, and then he waited, hurried to his letter-box every evening, was pleased when the first reply came, and by the end of the month there were exactly thirteen letters from all over East Germany. Almost all had enclosed photographs, and they looked at him out of these photographs as if they were not quite sure of themselves but were anxious to enjoy life for Heinrich's benefit and make a new start after the blows inflicted upon them by bloody life, wonderful life, how did he see it developing?

At first Heinrich had intended to reply only to a widow from Apolda who resembled Rosa, but then he suddenly felt suspicious about her resemblance to Rosa and decided to reply to a blonde from Weimar as well, and then he wrote to a lady from Dresden, and in the end he wrote to all thirteen. You are the first woman with whom I've ever tried to make affectionate contact in this way, he wrote, describing himself to some of them as shy and to others as a man of experience, either a widower or disappointed in his great love, with three grown-up daughters abroad, or a son from his first marriage now in the National People's Army, he invented himself various professions and was by turns a laundry worker, a milling-machine operator in the nationalized firm of Carl Zeiss, a lighting technician at the city theatre, and an engineer at the Jena South thermal power station, but he always had a nearly new Trabant and wrote enthusiastically about the prospect of expeditions to the Baltic coast together, that way we could get to know one another other a bit without actually noticing how we're slowly coming to know and value each other, maybe for life.

Seven of the thirteen women answered, so he had to dream up a variety of projects for the warm days to come, inventing remote villages and lakes and meadows, sometimes stopping the car on their imaginary expeditions, taking out a basket filled to the brim with strawberries and black bread and cold asparagus with ham, and he dreamed up a large rug to sit on and eat and drink and who knows what else, well, I suppose we all have our desires.

What a one you are, wrote the widow from Apolda who resembled Rosa, the first to reply, and she suggested meeting on the first weekend in May, while the blonde from Weimar asked for a few weeks to think about it, but many thanks anyway for all your trouble and the bunch of carnations on my birthday, what a surprise. On the first weekend in May he met the widow from Apolda who resembled Rosa and had never been out of Apolda in her life, and it was to her of all people, the widow resembling Rosa, that he found himself talking about Rosa herself almost at once, just to give her some idea about him straightaway, he said nice things and nasty things about Rosa, calling her the biggest mistake of his life, and the widow suddenly turned all silent and cross, did he think he was at confession or what?

Oh, I see, sorry, said Heinrich, and paid her a compliment on her check costume and her brooch, and it suddenly struck him that she had cheated a bit over her age, she must be in her mid-fifties.

I spent three years in Bautzen, Heinrich had said, and then she had looked at him in great surprise, oh dear, you poor thing, three years, that's a long time. That wouldn't matter to me, she had said, did he want to talk about those three years in Bautzen, but there wasn't a lot to talk about, Heinrich thought, only that in Bautzen you get worn to a thread and malice enters your heart.

Perhaps I ought to have talked about it, thought Heinrich later, when he had given up on lonely hearts ads, for in all these years he had never told a woman about his time in jail, only swapped the occasional anecdote with Priem in the Cosmetika. Priem said Bautzen had been his college, you grew up there and learned enough prudence and caution to last you at least two lives, but then one day you were outside again and realized, to your surprise: They don't want us to be grown up and prudent and cautious enough to last us at least two lives, because practically all the people outside are like children, and the Party and its organs are stern but kind, looking after us all, keeping an eye on us in case we burn our fingers by mistake, or run out into the street between two parked cars, because they still need us and everyone needs them, that's to say everyone of good will does, says so and swears it at every opportunity, and repeats it up to three times over in those little talks that make everything clear.

Our country is a country for children, Priem had said on one of their first Tuesdays, when they were already meeting in the Cosmetika and swapping anecdotes about Bautzen, and it was remarkable that he should say this without any fear of Hampel just because they'd both been in jail in Bautzen, yet it made no difference whether you were there in the Yellow Misery with the political prisoners like Priem or among the criminals like Heinrich, with men who had committed murder and manslaughter, the habitual offenders with their tattoos and their identical fiancées, of whom they dreamed and for whom they sought substitutes both with and without force.

For Priem, the years in Bautzen consisted solely of certain isolated events: the first rape in the slanting light of a February morning, the wedding ring lost in the soup, the inevitable floozie and his photos of his mother which the others tore up, dead Fritz and Martin and Otto, the suicides, of whom they thought and whom they then forgot, the black eye they had given one of the screws, paying dearly for it in the pens: that was what Bautzen meant to him.

This was the Bautzen Heinrich knew too, although he always thought: What do I really know about Bautzen, just three years there and three six-month stays in the hospital, so I was only a kind of guest in the cells, though when Eva or his sons visited him he was a real inmate of Bautzen for a few hours, but you could count it in days.

From Jena to Dresden by train is six hours, then you change and it's another two hours to Bautzen: that was the way his two sons came when, in the second year, they once graciously visited with a box of diabetic chocolates, into which they dipped themselves soon after leaving Jena, feeling cold and hungry, they hated him so much, and they hated the place where he was incarcerated behind the yellow brick masonry, the big gateway and the barbed wire, the freshly raked path and the dogs between the first wall and the second wall, the three doors through which they had to go before finally reaching their father.

The inmates sweeping the streets outside had worn brown prison clothing with wide yellow stripes on the back and sleeves, but their father, sitting at one of the seven tables in the visiting room, was in his dressing-gown, he stood up and sat down again, took the presents from Rosa and the neighbours and the now almost empty box of chocolates, and for almost the entire half hour they were very ill at ease, merely exchanging desultory remarks about the family or school which none of them remembered later, and that was the worst of it, the fact that none of them remembered it later, a little time had passed, that was all, it was an onerous duty performed for their mother's sake, and because after all he was their father, or had once been their father, stupid Ede with his bottle who didn't know the way to his own flat.

They had visited him in Bautzen only that one time, and even later all they knew about their father was that he was working as a waiter near the Westbahnhof and had a flat near the Westbahnhof too, but unfortunately they seldom went that way. Heinrich always sent them good wishes by way of Eva, and asked them to look in at the Thüringer Hof some time, bring a good appetite along, I'll be happy to stand you a meal.

It was very odd when they did come in one day, without so much as glancing at their father, but stout Walter snapped his fingers and ordered the most expensive dish on the menu, very much the man of the world, and Konrad was home on leave for a few days, telling his spotty girlfriend about the National People's Army. Enjoy your meal, Heinrich had said, sitting down at the table with them and asking this or that, amazed and incredulous to encounter such silence and contempt, while stout Walter kept calling him Ede and hardly touched his food.

It wasn't right of your sons to act like that, said Elli the second waitress, as a father he ought not to put up with it or where would we all be, no one likes to see that kind of thing. It's just their way, Heinrich had said, and added: Oh well, we must get to know each other better, then you'll understand.

Elli had taken the waitressing job in May, the radio was just broadcasting news of the death of the Yugoslavian head of state when she came in and introduced herself, she could have been in her mid-thirties and came from the north.

At first it had looked as if he might get somewhere with this Elli, but then she didn't like the way he eavesdropped while he was working, with a certain look in his eyes which she thought peculiar while he was eavesdropping. You're not one of them, are you, she had said early on, thinking there must be a reason why someone kept eavesdropping, with a look as if he were one of the firm, but Heinrich only said he really hadn't noticed any eavesdropping or any particular look, it was pure curiosity, and he got along well with people, so what are you complaining about.

She had a room above the café on the first floor, and sometimes let him visit her up there in the afternoon when they were closed, or sometimes late at night when she had finished cashing up, and then she would talk about why she had such terrible luck with men, she had just broken, so to speak, with someone called Dietmar. I could be your daughter, she said, and thought it an amusing idea: Heinrich the waiter and Elli as father and daughter, she hoped he wouldn't give her any grief as a father figure and possible informer, or she was sorry to say she wouldn't be able to respect him.

Elli liked the hours between eleven and two in the restaurant most because she nearly always had regular customers then, and lunch menus were almost always the same, a great deal of cabbage and dumplings and a small amount of meat in dark gravy, a dish for which they were famous. I always feel I'd like to be a guest myself in the evenings, said Elli, and generally she didn't spare the evening customers a glance, she just spared a glance for Heinrich sometimes, still suspicious and on her guard, and letting him notice her doubts.

At lunch-time and after six in the evening the two dining-rooms were nearly always full, and the customers sat together talking about their travels past and future, or some item of equipment their firms had needed for weeks, or women or men, but seldom about politics. Generally Heinrich picked up only a brief remark that could be used now and then, or perhaps one table would become very noisy or fall very quiet for a while, which usually meant the guests there had something to hide. Sometimes just a sentence or a word was enough to make him prick up his ears and look more closely at such people, but alternatively everything was perfectly harmless all along because the people themselves were perfectly harmless, you could almost always tell by looking at them.

Once there was a big wedding party with guests from the other side of the border, which was very interesting, since you could recognize the Westerners at once by their clothes and by their ease of manner, and the fact that they weren't afraid, made jokes and laughed, and above all they were completely unsuspecting and thought a waiter was just a waiter, gave generous tips, handed out Western cigarettes, were ready to smoke one with you on the way to the Gents, and really had not the faintest idea what was what. Even before the soup was served Heinrich saw the bridegroom's mother pointing him out once or twice, knowing what he was, or at least guessing what he was or thinking that he might be, but the Westerners didn't believe a word of it and were as innocent and cheerful as ever, saying exactly what they liked, and when it came to the speeches they spoke of two German states but the single language of love, the best language of all, love knows no borders the world over and will always prevail, let's drink to that.

Heinrich described these speeches as a relic of the past in his report, adding that two young citizens of the GDR were celebrating their wedding on the territory of the German Democratic Republic, but their parents' old friends from the West had been sounding off about unification in language that was hardly even guarded, it had all been rather embarrassing, he had felt particularly sorry for the young bridal couple, he could hardly describe the way they both rolled their eyes during these speeches.

A lovely wedding, said Elli, thinking in particular of a quiet young man from Augsburg whom she had liked, and she had let him see how much she liked him, but when he finally took notice of her she was too cautious to give him so much as a glance.

So silly of me.

Very wise, if you ask me.

I could have given him my address.

Much better not.

In retrospect, it had seemed to Heinrich as if the idea of the job as a waiter was his own, but yet again it was good old Harms who had come up with it, speaking of the future of Socialist café society and how well everything fitted together: there was Heinrich's poor health to be considered, the difficult operative situation in the city of Jena, the combining of economic and social policy and the higher standard of living thus achieved, which meant that more and more citizens were relaxing in restaurants, cafés and bars and satisfying their material needs in company, new times were here now.

Well, why not, Heinrich had said, and Harms was quite definite: You're the very man for it, he said, so in the third week after his release Heinrich had looked around a bit, had lunch in various cafés, drank a beer at the Thüringer Hof in the evenings and talked to the people there, you soon fell into conversation. I made a bad mistake years ago, said Heinrich, and the people in the Thüringer Hof liked him for saying he had made a bad mistake years ago, a mistake he would never repeat, he was cured once and for all of that place Bautzen. Oh, I see, Bautzen, the manageress had said, and hesitated, but she hesitated only briefly, and then she consulted the chef and fat Pauline, who was the waitress then, and Edwin the chef and fat Pauline were immediately of the same opinion and said: At last, we've been looking for another waiter for ages, give him a try, let anyone who's never made a mistake in his life cast the first stone. Very well, I'm Hedwig, the manageress said, and Heinrich said:

Heinrich, and had it all explained to him, about the vouchers and where the glasses and crockery were kept, about pulling the beer and serving juices and schnapps. You can begin straightaway if you like, said Hedwig, the work isn't easy but we've all got used to it, no drinking or chatting during working hours, but you get one hot meal a day and a large beer at midnight.

So Heinrich became a waiter, and of course he got a few things wrong at the start, but he was always friendly and patient, looked customers in the face when they were ordering and couldn't make up their minds and had a long day at work behind them, he always found the right thing to say, liked the children best, and next to the children he liked those tired, depressed women who were glad of a kind word and noticed everything.

One of them had spoken to him in the second week, and he hadn't taken much notice of her there at the bar, ordering brandy after brandy as she waited, and in the end she simply sat there and asked if he had a moment for a word with her, it was a private matter, yes, by all means, but he was sorry to say she'd have to wait.

She lived two streets away in a ground-floor flat, and suddenly seemed almost sober, they'd cashed up quite quickly, she remarked, and could she offer him a little something at home, she'd liked the look of him as both a man and a waiter, she couldn't help saying so. Which of course a woman isn't supposed to do, she said, but she repeated it, and then they went to her home, where they didn't even have time to exchange names, she wanted it so much, she told him how much she wanted it at once, she was certainly rather drunk, and bold and unsteady, with a tendency to lengthy confessions, which in turn led to procrastination, and then she said: Come on, be nice to me, I'm nice too, don't you think it's nice of me taking you home and getting my clothes all creased for you, or don't you want to do it?

In the end he still hadn't learnt her name, which didn't

really matter, but in retrospect it did matter because it was the last time, he wondered what he would have thought about it if he'd known it was the last time a woman would let him come in and feel good after letting him come in, he wondered all that. Her mouth was dry when she came, and he hadn't often known a woman to come so quickly, he was just on the point of it himself and she encouraged him impatiently, as if she didn't really believe this kind of thing any more.

Two years, she said, meaning the years since she last had a man, and Heinrich said: Yes, I know about that kind of thing. Tell me, she said, but Heinrich didn't really want to, and he didn't want to stay there. I don't suppose I'll ever see you again, she had said when he got dressed in the dark, sad that he was simply leaving and felt too old for such nights, for that was indeed what he was thinking: I'm too old, I don't enjoy it, better to keep ourselves to ourselves.

The Republic had been in existence for thirty years in October 1979, and since the whole country was in festive mood they released a few hundred small fry from the jails, people who had a record of good conduct or those who just couldn't take life behind bars, like Herr Hampel from Jena, almost a third of whose sentence they remitted.

This had been in early September, but unlike that first time in Leipzig there wasn't even anyone like Harms to meet him, and no Rosa and no children to shake their heads over him and say welcome back. He didn't even know when there was a train leaving, but he began to feel happier in the train to Dresden, thinking about the little flat near the Schott works, Eva had got some pieces of old furniture in and something to eat and drink for the first few days, you can pick up the key from Anneliese and Friedhelm.

Oh Heinrich, all the best, we really do wish you all the best, Anneliese had said as she handed over the key, but she kept him standing on the doorstep all the time as if he had some infectious illness, and he could hear Friedhelm, who didn't even want to say hello, moving about back in the living-room. He has a nasty cold, said Anneliese, we'll be seeing you, and here's the key in this envelope, and there may be a letter from Eva in the flat.

He almost passed the new flat, he was thinking so much of Eva and her letter of welcome, and then he unlocked the door and saw how shabby and dark and uncomfortable it all was, and there was no letter and only wrapped bread and a jar of gherkins in the fridge, he'd been looking forward to a can of blood sausage, but what else could he expect.

For the first few hours he sat in the big armchair which had once stood in the children's room and stared at nothing, switched the radio on after a while, found a couple of bottles of beer under the sink and tried to get used to things. It took him exactly two days and two nights to get used to things, remembering how a night passes and then the early morning, the long hours until the late afternoon, and on the morning of the third day he set out to visit his old haunts, he had to see the places where he had lived with Rosa again, and when she came out of the factory gate in the evening he had to see her and remember, and realize it was over. He had not said a word to Rosa, and he wasn't even sure whether she recognized him, but she still looked like his Rosa of the old days, and was plump and looked kindly and the sort of woman to be longed for from afar.

In his first letter to Constanze he wrote: I hope you don't mind me writing to you again, I saw Rosa yesterday and the memories came back. They remitted 1 year 5 months and 9 days of my sentence, I'm on probation, and I arrived here in Jena on Wednesday the fifth of September. I have a two-room flat with its own lavatory, gas central heating and tiled stove in Jena South, in a side street on the Magdelstieg, I had 271 marks when I was released. The question is, do I still have any credit with you, I could do with sweetener and soups and some canned meals, soap and toothpaste and toilet things, tobacco and cigarette papers, a couple of disposable lighters, a packet of black tea, maybe some coffee. I can't hope for anything from Rosa, of course, she kept taking my money while I was in custody and now she won't even hand over my books and tobacco tin and my old barometer, well, there we are, here I go complaining again.

He had even complained of Rosa to Harms, but only because Harms kept asking after her, as usual, and now it turned out that his Rosa and Harms had been in touch all these years and knew almost everything about each other. Good heavens, Hampel, Harms had said on meeting him, and it was like the old days to hear his friend Harms saying: Good heavens, Hampel, you're a hard case, even the most generous of states must despair of the likes of you, I'm afraid its prisons will never be empty what with all our Hampels, well, we were here first, said his old friend Harms, but then along come people like you, and some of our most gifted writers with their political fancies, and what are we to do: throw them all out of the country?

Times have changed, added Harms.

So you don't need me any more, said Heinrich.

Do we still trust you, that's the question.

And what's the answer?

This would be the last time, the third since Eisenach and then since Leipzig and Bautzen.

Like in a fairy-tale, said Heinrich.

Our fairy-tale has lasted thirty years, said Harms.

Congratulations.

He had never told Emilia about their meetings, because she wouldn't have understood why he had been writing reports for over twenty years in return for a few paltry banknotes, and she wouldn't have understood about the bad dreams he had recently taken to dreaming by her side, or she would have said it served him right, that was the price to be paid.

Heinrich had dreams almost every other night now, and in

one of the most recent Emilia herself had featured, and had been all gentle and yielding, the way he seldom saw her. Come along, I've been thinking about it and I want you to give me a baby, she had said, and giving her a baby was very nice, but the night it was to be born Priem suddenly stormed into the flat with two Volkspolizei officers demanding his money at once. The money's in her belly, he cried, you must look there and there, cut open the cushions, spill the sugar and salt and flour from their cans, turn the whole place upside down until you find it. But Emilia knew where the money was, and laughed because they couldn't find it, and since they couldn't find it they took him off without more ado. Will you wait for me, he just had time to ask, and Emilia said: Yes, if I live I'll wait, but they were already dragging him off, and they read out the charges to him down in the cellar in front of all his creditors. Harms had turned up too, and suddenly looked like Priem, and Rosa and the children had come and were sitting on narrow wooden benches, applauding at the end of every sentence of the charge sheet. He was sentenced to thirteen years in the uranium mines, and they gave him a battered pan and a hammer and sickle, and there in the mines he was to fill a great wooden tub every day, full measure, which they called his well-deserved punishment. But he's just become the father of twins, said Harms before they led him away, and sure enough the judge had the two new-born babies and their mother brought into court, straight past Rosa and the children, and then everyone suddenly began to laugh and grin because the twins were two monstrosities, freaks, and Heinrich was horrified to see the two freaks, and horrified to see how happy Emilia was, and saw that she didn't notice, she just whispered: Aren't they sweet, our two little ones, I wish them long life.

At that moment Heinrich woke up, and there was Emilia soothing him with her hands, calling him a silly boy, come on, tell me about it, silly boy, get it off your chest, tell me about it and then it won't come true, or laugh at it, whichever you like. Just my stupid dreams, said Heinrich, not believing what he said, and he lay awake a little while longer beside plump Emilia, knowing he was living on borrowed time, and his love for Emilia was only borrowed and wouldn't be his for long, because one day they would come for him, and so they did, they came for him over his petty little debts to Priem and a small transaction involving some second-hand Wartburgs, they were sick of Citizen Hampel and they finally taught him the meaning of fear in their prison in Bautzen with its yellow masonry and damp, dark, cramped cells, that was what finished him.

Just after he had been sentenced to yet another three years they gave Hampel a going over, deprived him of sleep for a while, the way they had deprived thousands of others before him of sleep, depriving people of sleep for a few days worked wonders, or they might take them off to be interrogated in the middle of the night, always beginning at the beginning with questions about profession, age, what people did Heinrich know whom he would have done better not to know, his deals, his debts, the same old ploys he used to cheat his way through life, the same old lies, excuses and promises that they knew from his files, and they also knew from his files how he'd been at the end of his tether after three years in Bautzen the first time, but this second time he was at the end of his tether right at the start. Hampel was going to feel like shit this second time in Bautzen, his teeth were going to chatter, Hampel whose family had gone off to the West, only his eldest daughter was left, living in a run-down place in Schwerin with her second husband.

It was right at the beginning of his second time in Bautzen that almost his whole family went off to the West, and no one shed a tear for him, so he was soon forgotten in the city or, as rumour had it, dead. Rumour said he had died in his fifty-fourth year, worn to nothing, a derisory figure, exhausted, so they had cremated him and didn't know of any family to be informed, life could be so cruel if you didn't take great care, for the penalties imposed by our Socialist state are harsh but just, but we still regard those who incur them as our own.

He wrote to his sister Constanze later: It wasn't me whose neck they broke that second time in Bautzen, it was somebody else, the Heinrich you know and maybe don't always like was at home in his flat at the time, wondering why you never wrote.

12

He always saw her dancing in those years, he saw men's hands on her slender back beneath her shoulder-blade in dance halls, and he saw her learning to fly in her dreams and whistling the latest hit song as she flew, that was his mother. At twenty-five she wasn't in her first youth any more, but all she knew about men was their hands on her slender back, or the little notes they passed her, and sometimes she said: Yes, maybe, why not, but much more often she said: Oh no, not you and me, certainly not, thank you for the flowers but she'd rather wait, unfortunately Mr Right hadn't come along yet, but she'd know him when he did turn up some day.

You're too choosy, her women friends said, you make life difficult for yourself, you make life difficult for men too, but his mother, who loved to dance the Charleston and the tango and the waltz, said: What do I care about men, who cares if they get ideas while we're dancing, I want to have fun, I like whirling through the high-ceilinged dance halls, it's almost flying like in my dreams, until he comes along one day and makes me take life seriously, and the man who came along and made her take life seriously was his father, who turned up at Carnival time in the year 1926.

She realized what had happened because she suddenly felt all warm low down in her belly, and she had not previously happened to feel warm down there at the sight of a man whose full mouth she studied as she whirled past, noticing how young he looked with his sad cardboard carnival nose, his hair already thinning like the hair of a man of forty. She exchanged a glance with her cousin behind the Sekt buffet, telling her, with her eyes: I think that's him, look, sitting over there, he's noticed me, so she kept taking a rest between each dancing partner, waiting, said yes to one of them for the last time, and then waited almost all evening in vain, because he didn't dare ask her to dance. Years later she was still saying: You scoundrel, oh, how you made me wait back then, I wanted to dance with you just once, I knew if he dances with me just once I shall be his wife, and I'll never whisk through these dance halls again, I took it so seriously, Matthias, so seriously.

He was not quite two years older than she was, and thought it a miracle when she herself asked him to dance, and being the woman she could choose whether it would be a Charleston or a tango or their first waltz together, a slow waltz. She nodded when he put his hand between her shoulder-blades and touched her, took her hand, and proved a very stiff dancer, didn't lead her properly and hardly looked into her face, he was so shy and clumsy, not having much experience of women.

Now you must tell me about yourself, she said when she had danced him off his feet, and persuaded him to drink a glass of Sekt at the buffet, look, it's my cousin Lily and her mother, my aunt, pouring the wine, that's how they make their living. What do you want me to tell you, said Father, embarrassed because he kept thinking of her shoulder-blades, and she smelled of primroses in the middle of winter and wanted to know all about him, she even wanted to know about his birthday in May, the job as a metalworker that he had had to give up, and the how and why of it all.

I did something very silly a few years ago, said Heinrich's father, and he told the tale of the two French soldiers who pursued him all round occupied Aachen one evening because in defiance of the curfew he was still out and about, he ran for his life all over town, and suddenly they were gone, or they didn't want to pursue him any more, he'd won. Good, said Mother, who liked the way he talked, thinking of her while talking, it was her shoulder-blades he was thinking of, he let his eyes wander over her as if unintentionally, but very delicately and carefully, he breathed her in with great delicacy and care.

The price I paid was a fissured lung, said Father, adding that he hadn't been able to do any metalwork since, he hadn't been out of doors for almost a year and a half, and he still remembered how breathless he was after climbing a flight of stairs.

Well, we can live with that, said his mother, not even surprised to find herself saying We, and feeling her belly still warm because of this man who lived a few streets away in the beautiful old city of Aachen, which she never wanted to leave in her life, yet she would probably go to the ends of the earth with this man Hampel.

But his father said: I'm only an unskilled worker now I've had to give up as a metalworker, and I've no idea what will become of me or where I'll end up. Why don't we go for a walk some time, said Mother, who was a cook in the French officers' mess, and was already planning the first meal she would cook for him, only it would probably be quite a while, and it was another year before she did cook that first meal for him and he finally realized and said yes to himself and to her.

So Heinrich's father kept his mother waiting a very long time, and got to know her hair, which she curled with hot tongs, learned to know her eyes and mouth and the wild girl she was, his girl, his Elisabeth, he usually saw her only after Sunday lunch, or after Mass in the cathedral, or in the afternoon in the Rote Erde in Aachen, when they would eat *pommes frites* somewhere and address each other by the formal *Sie* pronoun, not sure how to move on from *Sie* to the informal *du*.

They did not get much further than first names all spring and half the summer, told each other about their families and their jobs, and they talked about the Great War; as for the other girls whom he scarcely knew, and the men whose hands rested on her slender back below her shoulder-blade, they never mentioned them. I knew straight away I loved you for life, said Heinrich's father, at the register office ceremony in February 1927. It's taken long enough, she said, and on the morning of the church wedding in April she said: Sometimes I feel quite afraid of you, but I have enough love for two lives.

I'm looking forward to it, said Mother, meaning the wedding night of which she knew very little, but the night would come, and it might be a terrible sort of miracle but a miracle all the same. Even during her last dance with her father in his lieutenant's uniform, she couldn't help thinking that she didn't even know how long it took when a man went to his wife and lay with her and they became one flesh. In fact it was all over very quickly, passing in a swift blur like a dream, it was something to be feared but survived, and it was very dark in their room that first night, which she hardly remembered later, but she hoped at least that she was pregnant from those clumsy embraces, the sharp clear pain he had given her, not knowing what else he could give her, what else but pain.

When she woke first next morning she listened to her own body for a while, wondering if something was already stirring and growing within her, thinking that as a woman one would probably notice, but there was only a slight dragging sensation and the aftermath of the pain, and she knew she must move to their new flat in Wuppertal with this man the very next week, leaving her beloved Aachen for him and living on his money for the rest of her life.

It was only because he must no longer be a metalworker that Heinrich's father moved to Wuppertal in the spring of 1927, to join a firm making technical and medical glass, where he earned almost twice as much as before, and tired as he was after work, he gave her two babies all the same.

It was the second week of May 1927 when the Communists were demonstrating against the Stahlhelm ex-servicemen's association in distant Berlin, that she got pregnant, or perhaps three days later on his twenty-sixth birthday, when she was wearing her new nightdress for him, and trying out a new word now and then. When no period showed up for the third month running she told him very gently and quietly, and they marvelled and rejoiced, counted the days back and the weeks and months forward, got into the New Year and came back to this one, and Mother's belly swelled and swelled, so that she couldn't sleep but heard Father sleeping, he hadn't touched her for months. It could be twins, said the doctor, decreasing but at the same time increasing her happiness, and it was indeed two babies she conceived that May, but sad to say the twins didn't live, dying a few hours after their birth at the end of February 1928. Neither Father nor Mother wanted to see them again before they were buried in the Wuppertal-Elberfeld cemetery, but Mother said: Let's not grieve too long, after all, I'm in my late twenties, but if we hurry up we could easily have half a dozen, where shall we begin?

So they began with Theodor, conceived in the golden September of 1928, born next July, in the Weimar Republic's last good year, a gift of God after a difficult time, they would be grateful and confident that all would go well with them and their children, and it was to be hoped with their bruised and battered country too, the outlook didn't seem too bad. It was only three weeks before their first-born was sleeping through the nights, that first son was always good and well behaved and a joy to his mother, he was soon sitting up and standing up and walking and talking, and then the years in Wuppertal were over and they had to move further east. I'm sorry, said the children's father, but the firm of Schott had paid good money for him and a few others and tools and equipment, and the city of Jena, to which they must now move, lay on a river called the Saale somewhere in the middle of the shrunken Reich, dear heavens, what a long way off.

She disliked the city from the first day. Just because she thought it pleasant, she disliked it, the mountains, hills and valleys around it, the river winding its way more or less from south to north, and people called the centre of town, with the moorings for boats and later the new café, the Paradies. She was so homesick at first for familiar Aachen and her parents and brothers and sisters, and fresh *pommes frites* eaten in the Rote Erde in Aachen, that her head was sometimes nearly bursting with exhaustion, and the long afternoons with Theodor were too much for her now, the evenings in their quiet, unassuming flat on Wöllnitzer Platz when she cooked Father all kinds of French dishes, and he was always tired but interested in her, he wanted her almost every night.

One Saturday in early December she said: Matthias, I think it's happened again, the Lord has blessed us, I'm pregnant, but this time it's not at all the way it was with Theodor, I feel so sick with this new baby, I can't tell you how sick I feel. Her husband didn't say much, he never said much, but he called the second child a blessing, said it would surely be a blessing and grow to be big and strong like Theodor, they must think what to call it if it was another son, but Mother secretly wanted a little girl, and called her Henriette when Father wasn't around, or at night when she lay awake because it was kicking. Keep still, little girl, she said, your mother's tired and would like to sleep, and sometimes she sang little Henriette a lullaby, because the baby gave her no peace at night, what a girl she must be.

That Brüning's a good man, but maybe the Austrian would have been all right too, said Father, knowing that his wife called the baby Henriette, but if it turned out to be a Heinrich then Theodor would have someone to play with. Be careful what you wish for, he said, meaning to warn her ahead of the day when they would know, and everything went smoothly enough with Henriette, who did turn out to be Heinrich, thus disappointing Mother. She saw how he screamed and stared at her, he had pale blue eyes and was bloodstained and greasy at birth, he brought up her milk and proved to be a strange, contrary little creature who deprived her of sleep at night, and by day was touching and exploring everything, particularly beds. Her years with her first-born Theodor now seemed to her like child's play, but it was hard work with his brother Heinrich, you had to be strict with Heinrich or he would get out of hand. She sometimes had to go and sit with Theodor these days, feeling glad he was no trouble, but she would shut Heinrich in a room for several hours, lost her temper with the one-year-old who wanted everything repeated five times over, who was so cheeky by nature that he put his tongue out at her, and sometimes she smacked his bottom or his delicate little face, and then he always seemed to feel the world was out of joint for a while.

When Father came home in the evening supper wasn't always ready yet, she was so tired and worn down by the sleepless nights and her constant struggles with their Heinrich, and she would complain to Father, wanting him to punish the child, or at other times she said nothing but forgave him and kissed him and was at her wits' end. She felt torn apart, just like the country itself, and in her heart she hoped Father would give her a break, she didn't want him sleeping with her and another blessing from the Lord, but what a sin it was for her to think like that and reject her husband in her thoughts, explaining to herself why she couldn't help feeling like that, why the children were the way they were, it was all because of the times, or it was all because of her, the yearning she couldn't shake off and which was tearing her apart, Lord God forgive me.

Have a rest, said Father, everything passes over, we mustn't be ungrateful, we have work and food and two healthy children even though the times are hard, there are several thousand out of work in our city alone, it's about six million in the whole country.

I don't even have time to read the paper, said Mother, feeling glad he had reminded her of the country and its troubles, for the difficult year of 1932 saw a new Chancellor and two elections, with strikes and fighting in the streets of towns and cities, bloody Sundays with dead and injured among the SA and the Communists, there wasn't much difference between them.

I know how it's going to end, said Mother as they drank to the coming year on New Year's Eve, referring to the new baby kicking inside her, their third, but Father thought she meant politically, he was pinning his hopes on old Hindenburg again, but if it was this man Hitler he wouldn't mind, nothing much could happen to them, they were good folk and Hitler didn't have it in for good folk, only the Jews and Communists, who were justified in feeling some alarm now and then.

The first thing they noticed about the changed times was that the main streets and squares had new names, and now they were suddenly living in Adolf-Hitler-Platz as they awaited the birth of their third son, it took them a while to get used to it. As if we'd moved already, said Father, who dreamed of having a house of his own for the three of them and his tired wife, his Elisabeth, who had grown portly and grey fulfilling the demands of her two sons and her husband, and very grave. Just shopping often took her two hours with the boys, and there were all the things they wanted to know and the questions they asked her, why wasn't little Paul or Pauline here yet, how exactly had they got out of her tummy, she felt uncomfortable with such questions and they were far too young to ask them, oh, do be quiet.

She was thirty-two in the first summer under the new government, and the days when she danced with men almost every weekend might never have been, she wasn't slender any more after giving birth three times, and out in the street the SA were guarding the entrances to Jewish shops where she had gone for years, too bad, that was over now. It's no laughing matter for the Jews under our Herr Hitler and his SA, said Father on 1 April 1933, I can't even buy my cigars from them any more: it was as if he held it against the Jews personally.

Another three months, said Mother, not wanting to discuss the Jews, clutching her stomach in her hands as she often did when she had backache, and she was counting the days left, marvelled yet again at the miracle of it, and the fact that her husband was afraid of her when she was pregnant, or afraid of the inhabitant of her body, and so he didn't touch her then.

Heinrich in particular was looking forward to his new brother or sister, planning to talk to the baby every day and tell it all about the world as he knew it. He liked all the banners and pennants in town, and he watched the men in uniform marching, stared at the VIPs' shiny cars in the streets, collected leaves and snails and other little creatures, and was hurt when his mother had no time to look at his treasures, or raised her voice or her arm to hit him, when he would duck away, feeling angry, go into the kitchen, find the knives, and chop up all the fruit in the fruit bowl.

Just before Paul's birth his mother told them: I'm going away for a little while now, so you two must be good children, and then it was another boy, but this one slipped out of her easily and quickly, and it was a long time before he opened his eyes, as if he wanted to go on dreaming a little longer, he was so quiet, it was to be hoped this would be the last of their sons. You've done very well, said Father when she was home, and lying on the living-room sofa, and he added that they were a real family now, and when there are six of us, if not before, I'm going to buy us a house with a garden.

Oh, Matthias, said their mother, not sure whether to be afraid or glad, she gave herself a few months off to get her breath back, thinking up excuses for her husband and the nights she endured as if under threat, praying and imploring God not to let Matthias come to her, or if he did she hoped it would always be on the wrong day, but she prayed and implored very quietly, very softly, and didn't get pregnant again until the spring of thirty-four.

She lost the baby in the twelfth week, it was as if it had heard its mother cursing its father, cursing the half life in her swelling belly, and the child fell out of her, giving no trouble, she was just peeling potatoes for the mid-day meal when it began, there were murderers roaming the whole country, liquidating the top brass of the SA.

She didn't say: If this goes on it'll be the end of me, but the children's father understood anyway, and gave her a year's respite out of love for her, didn't touch her for a whole year, and for her sake alone endured not being able to touch her for a whole year, but she grew a little plumper and calmer again, gathering strength for the daughter she wanted, and the new Reich was gathering strength too for what was to come, building streets as beautiful as paintings or symphonies, giving the German workers low taxes and nice holidays at home and abroad, the Saarland was German again too, and they could all look forward to getting the Sudetenland back.

It's been a year now, said Father in the summer of 1935, and Mother nodded and was prepared, and knew it would be a daughter, quick on her feet and pretty and a little like her, they were just discussing the German-British naval treaty on the radio when she gave herself to him after a year, all the time thinking of her little girl, little Constanze, for that was to be her name.

Constanze, said Father, she'll be here in spring.

I'm expecting her some time in March, said Mother, and the German army marched west that spring, taking and occupying her beloved Aachen and all the land on the west bank of the Rhine, what good news.

So what's Aachen like now that it's German again, she asked when her sister came to stay in May 1936, but her sister couldn't see any difference straight off, except that the Reich was a little bigger, and its appetite probably wasn't satisfied yet, why didn't they finally buy themselves a house now they had six mouths to feed, this flat had been much too small for ages.

Father had been looking for the right house for his family for almost a year, and one Sunday in March 1937 he took his Elisabeth and his three sons and little Constanze up to the Wilhelmshöhe to admire it. Well, what do you think, he asked, pointing to the last house in the street, that is to say, he pointed at its left-hand side, this was a big housing estate with newly made-up roads, and there were privet hedges along the front fences, and plenty of room in the garden behind the house for vegetable and flower beds and a swing for the children.

Mother was still out of breath from climbing so far, and said: Yes, very nice, but it's a long way into town.

You'll get used to it, said Father.

And we'll be in debt for the rest of our lives.

Twelve thousand Reichsmarks for 382 square metres, said Father, who already had the sales contract, five rooms with kitchen, bathroom and lavatory, it looked very big when they saw round the house, but with all their furniture and net curtains at the windows it would be more of a doll's house really.

The children felt it was like a holiday when they moved in, in July, measuring up and taking possession of their little domains, the long way and the short way up the hills from the house, the steep Burgweg into town which Mother never did get used to, the gentle wind up there, the view over the beautiful old city which she didn't like, and although she tried for her husband's sake she did not get far over all those years.

They had been in their new house two months when

Heinrich joined Theodor at school in September, and now surely little Heinrich would improve, he could already count and knew the alphabet except for the difference between B and D, but alas, the pleasure gained from her children was soon over, like her pride in Heinrich's early successes, and the fact that he could soon write his name, and could also draw the swastika on his lower arm in copying pen, the harmless pranks of a boy of six which she punished by beating him, those were their early days up on the Wilhelmshöhe.

Father now had to leave the house half an hour earlier every day, and from Monday to noon on Saturday he was away for over sixty hours in all. Sometimes they didn't even have time to exchange a word with each other, so endlessly did the days drag out with the children, the washing to be done in the big tub, meals to prepare at mid-day and in the evening, the trials and tribulations of shopping which even featured in her prayers, and their new neighbours Anneliese and Friedhelm, who kept talking about a second Great War.

Dear Lord, help me bear it, dear Lord, make the children sleep through the nights, and send my Heinrich a better nature, he's the worst of them, O Lord, make me quiet and patient, and make the country and its Führer quiet and patient, and protect us from our enemies who mean us ill, convert their hearts, be gracious, oh Lord, amen.

Anneliese and Friedhelm were probably Communists or Social Democrats, because they started talking about war straight away, and spoke slightingly of Hitler's party as Nazis, calling them Germany's misfortune. You're exaggerating, said Father in the autumn of 1937, when they were spending an evening together, and in March 1938, after the annexation of Austria, he said: What Hitler and Goebbels are saying is all just bluster, the land will be calm again once we have the Sudetenland. I wouldn't like to be a Jew, said their father in the autumn of 1937, and after the fires in the autumn of 1938: I can't understand why they don't pack their bags and go abroad.

The children, said Mother, talking about the children to change the subject, but unfortunately Anneliese and Friedhelm had none, so they didn't understand what it was like when you hit your little boy and he just laughed at you, or went perfectly quiet and silent, as if a storm were passing over fields and meadows, but when it dies down everything springs up again, and as usual it's made no difference. Heinrich was so obstinate and uncontrollable at the age of seven or eight that he didn't even hide or try to run away, just put his hands over his head and crouched on the floor like an animal, sometimes moderating the force of her blows, but sometimes, on the contrary, making her furious and unpredictable, and she almost always hated herself for feeling like that, sometimes she hated the child too, as if he wasn't really hers at all.

He'll survive it, said Father.

I notice you don't get your own hands dirty.

I'm very proud of you.

Oh, Matthias.

In all these years he had never before said he was proud of her, or really noticed and valued her and said so, in broad daylight when she was feeling very ugly, and she contradicted him. But I've grown old, said Mother, thinking that only Father was still handsome, what a fine man he looked in his new uniform, with his shiny polished boots and the ceremonial dagger marking him out as a Civil Defence district leader in his belt, how proud he was of wearing that uniform, people suddenly addressed him in quite a different way, or was she just imagining it?

He had never told her that they had been on at him for quite some time at Schott, why wasn't a man like him in the Party, they asked, praising his industry and punctuality and saying he was an example to one and all, and since he was an example they would very much like him to be in the National Socialist German Workers' Party. Yes, why not, one of these days, said the children's father, but for the moment he'd rather do something practical, he wasn't a born speaker, and the war being waged in the country was still a war of words, but just in case he'd be happy to join the Civil Defence straightaway.

Even his two eldest sons felt they had to tell their father how handsome he looked in his new uniform when he went to a meeting in the evening after work, or walked out with them on Sunday on their expeditions, which were always the same, up to the Fuchsturm or into the Kernberge, and they, his sons, had to go round delivering the Reich Civil Defence magazine in Jena East once a month, which they found a terrible bore. You too, said Anneliese and Friedhelm, taking it as a bad omen, and the occupation of what remained of Czechoslovakia was a bad omen too, and when the German Wehrmacht marched into the Memel region they prophesied that it was the bad beginning to an even worse end.

There's nothing we can do about it anyway, said Mother, inviting them both to her birthday party, which was four days before the great campaign against Poland, but they had wonderful weather. Some twenty guests had come, and over sausages and beer in the garden they talked of nothing but the coming war, and Mother's new grey costume, and the new washing machine, what a practical device, which they all envied her and which had been Father's present. It was only a week ago that she had passed a great clot of blood in the lavatory, she knew it was Father who made her pass a great clot of blood every few years, only she couldn't tell him so, because after all she was happy with her husband and his birthday present and the long, peaceful afternoon in the garden, which they had all earned, hadn't they? She didn't say: Just *one* more baby, Matthias, no more, that's what I would like. But she said: It's all lovely, thank you, I'm not even scared by the idea of the war now, if it has to come we'll survive it, and Father thought so too, and bought a bottle of Sekt to celebrate the victory in Poland, just a little stroll it had been, that's how they kept describing it on the radio.

It became his custom to sit in his big armchair in the evening and listen to the radio bringing news of the latest victories, nodding and feeling pleased, but quietly, without talking about it a lot, he didn't want to back the Party in front of friends and acquaintances. We're making progress, he would say, or: All Europe is falling into our lap, and since Mother saw it pleased him she cooked a special meal for each victory. After all, we're not barbarians, said Mother, who was a trained cook, and after the victory in Poland she made *Bigos Polski* with sauerkraut and mushrooms, and thick barley soup to start with, she knew a Danish recipe for plaice fillet with *sauce remoulade*, and she cooked Norwegian fish *frikadeller*, and the delicious pea soup with bacon and celeriac was from Holland; the braised ox cheek with potato purée was Belgian and almost like a recipe from her own home, and in the summer of 1940, after the successful conclusion of the Western offensive, they had *coq au vin* simmered in cognac and red burgundy. But unfortunately we haven't got anywhere yet with England, said Father, dreaming of the promised Beef Wellington, always supposing the beef could still be bought in town, or of a Scottish hotpot, but instead he got first a Yugoslav potato and rice soufflé, and then in the spring of 1941 a Greek rabbit stew with onions, they reared the rabbits themselves in two sheds in the garden to kill and eat them.

Let's hope this goes on, said Father.

But it won't.

So long as I still have you, that's what matters, the war is coming to an end and golden times lie ahead.

Another little girl would be nice.

All right, a little girl.

This frightens me, said Mother, when they heard of the attack on the Soviet Union in June, keep quiet so we don't wake the children, this was to be the one last time, and it was, Father gave her Sibylle and heard nothing, not the distant war in Russia, not his son Heinrich suddenly there in the doorway, watching, and then going away again, he was just nine and hadn't understood much about what his mother and father were doing, except that they were whispering and embracing and moving, and their whispers and embraces and movements drove him away, which was perhaps the strangest thing about it.

When he was ten he got a uniform, and like his brother Theodor he sang in the choir on the parade ground to celebrate the great victories of the years thirty-nine to forty-one, he learned to march and exercise and fight for the flag, scuffled with the others and made it up, and in play with his comrades of the Jena Group he won the battles which had already been won long ago, at Easter and Whitsun and in the summer holidays he went to the big tent camps in Dresden or the Riesengebirge, and he particularly liked the huge bonfire around which they all sat in the evening singing songs and never thinking of their parents, as if there were no such people in the world.

One day he found the first hairs growing between his legs, and since there were now big air-raid practices every few weeks they all spent a lot of time down in the cellar, waiting for the all clear between the two sets of bunk beds, and Heinrich was the only one who sometimes lingered down there a little longer, thinking about all sorts of things when he was there on his own, lying on one of the two top bunks, why did his member sometimes get quite big now, and what exactly did you do to make it feel really nice, that was what he thought about at these times. The older boys said: It's dead easy, you just do this and that, and it's a bit naughty because of the stains, and then Heinrich remembered how his mother had once slapped Theodor in the face, both cheeks, just because of the stains, he was to remember that for the rest of his life.

This was the time when the Sixth Army was still victorious in the east on its way along the Volga to the city of that barbarian Stalin, but then suddenly the German Wehrmacht was no longer making progress, had got bogged down or was surrounded, and in fear of the Russian winter. Father was now listening to the radio even early in the morning before he went to work, drawing his cautious conclusions from what few announcements were broadcast, for the war must surely be decided there in Stalingrad on the rivers Volga and Don. Mother said: Don't, the things you hear scare me, or she said: The price of meat and butter has gone up again, and even if we do beat Russia there won't be a special meal to celebrate this time. But she wanted to make brawn with fried potatoes for Christmas, as usual, and she cooked some beef as she did every year, and half a pig's head and bones for the gelatine, putting the big pan on the stove the day before, and in the evening she poured the finished brawn into seven dishes and put them under the cellar steps to set.

They listened to the great round-the-world broadcast at Christmas, and Father became very serious and impatient if anyone disturbed him, and he felt some hope again on hearing the voices of German soldiers from all over the world, and the beautiful German songs, so full of comfort and sadness and strength. Only a miracle can save us now, said Father, but he wanted to believe in that miracle, one evening in January he was seen wearing the badge with the Party swastika on his lapel, calling it his sacrifice, saying that the German people must rouse themselves in the times ahead to keep their enemies from triumphing, they had enemies almost everywhere in the world in the fourth year of the war.

He wept when news came of the lost battle on the Volga, and could not stop for a long time, sitting in his big armchair and listening to the military marches. Decades later Heinrich still remembered Father weeping for the dead German soldiers at Stalingrad in February 1943, because none of them had ever seen their father weep before, and also because it was at this time that something happened when he took his penis in his hand and touched it in the right places, it looked a bit like liquid soap and smelled like he didn't know what. He always took a large handkerchief with him and put it on the sheet when he taught his hands new ways of touching on one of the mattresses down in the air-raid shelter, and every few days he went into the garden and washed out the handkerchief in Father's large water butt. You look as if you'd been up to something again, said Mother, wondering what he could have to do down in the cellar, but when she appeared in the doorway expecting to take him by surprise he was simply lying there dreaming, or reading something for school, he was obviously sufficient unto himself these days.

At the end of May 1943 the first bombs fell down in town, leaving a great many fires and a lot of dust and ruins behind them, and the first dead, but everything was still quiet and peaceful up on the Wilhelmshöhe, and when the enemy bombers had gone again it was a fine summer.

That summer, when Wanda started working for them, Heinrich was twelve, and was gradually getting to know himself under the bedclothes, and although Wanda was much too old for his twelve years, who cared? She came from a village near Bürgel and was doing her year's national service with the Hampels, keeping an eye on the baby and hanging out the washing every Friday, going up and down the hill to do the shopping and hauling it home, her cheeks red with the effort of carrying it. She looked fifteen at the most, a beanpole of a girl with two long dark plaits, and she slept in the room next to Heinrich and Theodor which had room only for a bed, a scratched chest of drawers, and the scent of new-mown hay which she gave off as she worked.

He bathed all summer in that scent of hay, which brought him to the door of her bedroom a few times at night, for it was hot, and the bedroom had no window and only a standard lamp by which she could change her clothes or read before going to sleep. She was still so naive that she would undress with the door open, putting her clothes neatly on the chair, and it was the first time Heinrich had ever seen a girl like that, she was naked and very slim, with barely perceptible breasts: beautiful and strange.

He had seen her one night soon after she came, and afterwards he felt as if he were unwell, or out of sorts, and although he was almost sure she hadn't noticed anything he avoided her for the next few days, just saw her now and then in the kitchen peeling potatoes, or standing in the garden behind the house by the washing lines, she called him a silly boy when he spilled milk in the morning, or was cross when he got his trousers dirty, and he didn't mind at all, he liked her so much. He never imagined actually doing anything with her, but in the last week before the summer holidays, when everyone was talking about going to camp, he would have liked to stay, then he'd discover what it was all about, and whether it was love that made him secretly breathe in her scent up in her room, and rummage around in her things, not knowing what he was looking for or what he found. He would have liked to know words for all these new, strange things, but when he tried talking to his friends Emil and Kurt one day he didn't have much to tell them except her name. This was after a few days in the big tent camp, where they all talked a lot about girls and sometimes about their own willies, or the Allied landing in treacherous Italy, and he forgot his Wanda for a while and how she didn't wear a nightie and called him a silly boy, it was suddenly very far away.

He was happy all autumn hearing her turn the pages on the other side of the closed door of her bedroom, or at weekends when he and Paul and Constanze went with her to visit her parents in the country, where they had cake warm from the oven and home-pressed apple juice better than any they had ever drunk before. Wanda herself became a child again when she was at home, she could ride a horse, she knew how to milk the cows, she knew about the corn in the fields, the hay in the loft where the cats had their kittens, and alas, there was no one to pick the blades of grass out of her long black plaits. Sometimes he thought: I'm almost a man, why doesn't she take any notice of me, but if she did look at him, not exactly meaning to, he found her glance alarming, refused his supper in the evening, or left the house on some pretext, he hardly knew himself these days.

For Christmas he carved the five letters of her name in wood, threaded them on a piece of string and put them under her pillow without saying a word, the first A was rather larger than the second, but each letter was no bigger than her thumbnail. I thought it was from you, she said, when she was back with them in early January, but without a word of thanks and without telling him off for visiting her secretly by night, standing by her bed, almost forgetting to breathe with simply looking at her, and she still didn't see what it was about, that bad girl, the sleeping girl who wasn't going to wake up in a hurry for someone like Heinrich, and if he did wake her one day she'd tell him what a nice, silly boy he is, but he mustn't be in her bedroom by night or by day either. Three nights in a row Heinrich stood in her bedroom looking, and the fourth night she woke up and said nothing at all for a while, and then whispered just one sentence. I feel honoured, she whispered, stroking his head like a sister, but now go away, I'm not blind, and I don't want to learn about love with a big little boy like you.

Do you like my necklace, he asked. And she nodded, yes, of course I like it, it's the prettiest necklace in the world, but did you hear what I said? Yes, he had heard it.

For several days after that Heinrich felt as if he had been doing hard work, the wrong sort of hard work, but he was quite relieved, as if he and she shared a secret. He could even look into Wanda's eyes again at meal-times, looked into her eyes and saw Mother noticing too, after a few days she had had enough of it and planted herself in front of him in the porch, where she slapped his face and said he deserved it for the looks he was giving Wanda at table, and here's another for anything which fortunately I don't know about.

Wanda stayed until the end of April 1944, when more and more bad news began to come in, and meat and vegetables were scarce in town, they would have to wait and scrimp and save and hope, dear Wanda brought them something back from her village even though her own family had only the bare essentials.

When she left in spring she gave him a book, and he was the only one who had a present from her, nearly thirteen as he was now, with the secret wishes he had tried out on her without getting far, a little brown book with a long, complicated title it was, a soldier she was fond of had given it to her, he had fallen in the East at the beginning of March, Army Group Centre, on the northern approaches of the Pripyet Marches, I think that's their name.

For Heinrich who doesn't know everything yet, she had written on a postcard which he tore up for safety's sake, and he spent a long time looking for a safe place for the little book, tried among the books in his satchel, or in Father's shed between a couple of logs, read only a few pages at a time, and halfway up to the Fuchsturm he sat down in a sheltered little meadow and read about love and marriage in the new Germany, the sexual organs of men and women, masturbation and its dangers, the pleasurable sensations almost to the point of intoxicated oblivion felt at the moment of ejaculation, as the Berlin neurologist called it, and why knowledge of the physical tools of your love-life does you no harm.

There were days now when, up in his meadow, he felt he had won a victory over his friends and his elder brother, because they didn't know about all this, or they knew only the half of it, or the old wisdom which was now superseded, and like Theodor none of them had even looked at a girl like Wanda yet, perhaps she was too thin for Theodor, or he thought himself too good for her because she was from the country whereas the great Theodor was from town, had good reports at school, and was now going to the Schott works with his father every morning as an apprentice, cleaning the machinery.

Heinrich's brother had first gone to the factory with their father at the beginning of April, and the new girl arrived at the beginning of April too. Her parents kept a shop down near the station, the Saalbahnhof, so she too could bring the Hampels something now and then when the situation was desperate; Franziska was in her early twenties, with her golden hair brushed severely back, and she looked much more like Heinrich's stern mother than the gentle Wanda.

Heaven has sent her, said Mother, as she had already said of Wanda, but Franziska said: The Party has sent me, as a mother of five you have a right to domestic help, nothing comes from heaven these days except the bombs of our Allied enemies. Theodor always liked to hear her talking like that, saying victory in the West and the East was only a matter of time and determination, but Mother became more silent every week, because Father became more silent every week too, sometimes didn't even switch the radio on and then felt guilty for not even switching it on, so after that he would often leave it running until late at night.

At the end of May news reached them that the city of Aachen had been the target of a terror raid by the British, and three days later there were British bombers over Aachen again, and there had been losses and injuries among the population, no figures given. Mother trembled, and waited for a letter from her family, she waited for seven days and seven nights, and the news arrived one day in June. None of us can find words for what has happened, wrote Mother's mother, who was still alive, and so were Father's parents, who still had their house, and Mother's sister with her husband Sebastian, they had survived, but the Lord God had raised his hand against the family of her brother Peter, missing in Russia, striking down his wife and daughter, smothered under the ruins of the shattered bunker.

Only his son Thomas is still alive, and can't make out what's going on, wrote Mother's mother, and those of us who got off this time live in fear and trembling, waiting for the next bomb to fall, eating and living and praying as if everything was still the same as before, but we deceive ourselves.

They waited all summer for more bad news from the west, but the letters from Aachen sounded reassuring for the moment, people were taking great care, listening to the Wehrmacht report on the radio every day, making calculations, soothing themselves, for instance Normandy was a long way off. Even Mother sometimes switched on the radio and listened, as she worked, to the names of distant battles, cities won and lost again, and she prayed in the evenings for the cities of Aachen and Jena, preserve our dear children and give us strength to bear it, we hope to endure the hour of trial when it comes. She did not say: If you must take someone, then take my second son, but she prayed: Watch over Theodor, he's such a joy to me, and reliable Constanze is a joy to me, and quiet Paul and shy Sibylle, it's hard to say how she's going to turn out yet, and there was always Heinrich left over, she never knew if he understood her when she spoke angrily to him and counted the blows as she hit him with a stick because he didn't come home at the appointed time in the evening, or because of the stains on his sheet, the handkerchiefs he left lying around, so little fear did he have of her, she imagined the worst for this boy of fourteen, dear Lord God, what am I to do with this child? She didn't really know much about her children, she thought most about her eldest son, now doing well in his father's department at Schott, and her big girl Constanze, who always helped her industriously in the house, and went down to the lake, the Schleichersee, at every opportunity with her girl friend from opposite, she nearly drowned there one day. We have nothing to complain of, said Father, and he spent his weekends in the garden as usual, praying for the Führer, on whose life it was to be hoped no one else would make an attempt, Father was growing all kinds of vegetables and herbs, they would soon be able to pick the apples and pears from the fruit trees, and then news came in September that the Americans were on German soil to the west, moving towards Aachen.

My God, this is the end, said Mother, meaning her mother, her brother-in-law and sister and their children in the Rote Erde of Aachen, where you could get the best *pommes frites* in the world, and where she had met a man called Matthias, and now all the people of Aachen had to be evacuated and boarded trains going east, where they were to stay with friends and family and wait and hope, both yesterday and today the watchword had run: Not an ear of German corn shall feed the enemy, no German mouth shall give information, no German hand shall offer help, the enemy shall meet with nothing but death, destruction and hatred, he shall bleed to death in fear and trembling on every metre of German soil of which he means to rob us.

Yes, that was in our paper the other day, said Heinrich's aunt, when they all arrived in Jena at the end of September, wanting something to eat, and beds, and a welcome for who knew how long. Heinrich's aunt and uncle and poor Thomas stayed with neighbours over the road, but room had to be found in Windbergstrasse for Father's parents, and Mother's mother, and the Hampels' house in Windbergstrasse was very crowded, there was a great deal of grumbling and getting used to things. Thirteen people needed to be fed at lunch and supper, sitting round two tables in the kitchen and dining-room, so they had their work cut out for them, put the coupons from their ration cards together, always ate the same thing, mashed potatoes with beans and a bit of beef, and didn't go to bed until they had heard the last news on the radio, Traudchen's husband knew how to tune into a London frequency too.

The battle for Aachen has begun, said the radio at the beginning of October 1944, and they could imagine the Americans destroying their city, surrounding it and its defenders like the Russians in Stalingrad, and after fifteen days of bloodshed and fighting it was over. House after house was defended against the enemy attacking from north, east and south, and the German Wehrmacht fought bitterly, man to man, until 21 October, when the brave but now few defenders of Aachen were defeated.

We've lost the war now, said Mother, when none of the others made any comment on the news, and she said so to anyone who would listen over the next few days, even the woman next door over the fence, or standing in a queue shopping when people said that the Red hordes were already outside Königsberg to the east.

Now listen, Frau Hampel, said the Gestapo man when they questioned Mother a few days later, telling her why a mother of five ought not to talk that way, the people and the Reich and the Führer are united and won't knuckle under so easily, not if we all firmly believe in it and do our duty. We don't make any exceptions, said the Gestapo man, knowing that this woman held the Golden Cross for mothers, so she could just be cautioned on this occasion, but next time we shall take a different tone, Heil Hitler.

Heinrich didn't think it so bad that the Americans had destroyed his parents' native city, but he didn't like sharing a room with Paul and Theodor again, since Paul still had no idea about anything, and Theodor liked to rehearse speeches in the evenings, talking a lot about iron wills and holding out, and threatening to denounce his father and uncle on account of that London radio station. I'm warning you for the last time, Theodor had said one evening in December, but his mother happened to hear him and just looked at him, and her mere glance made Theodor look small and fall silent, and he stayed in his room until next morning.

I don't know what's come over that boy, said Mother, and when, early in January, call-up papers for Theodor arrived, ordering him to Jena West for pre-military training, she wept for two days and railed against the Lord her God for taking him, and Theodor learned to fire anti-tank rocket launchers, volunteered for service, and saw the Russian POWs in a village in Thuringia digging tunnels for an underground factory in a hillside, dying of hunger, and they were sick and wretched and would not live to see the production of the new bombers.

Theodor was not there when the Lord God turned his wrath on the city of Jena, and sent a host of dark angels raining down from several hundred aircraft on its people and its buildings in February 1945, striking down and burning twelve times twelve human beings in broad daylight as a punishment and a warning to the living, what a noise there was, and how afraid they all were sitting in their cellars and praying, it was indescribable. What kind of people can they be, said Mother, when no one could count the hits any more, and the Lord God, not to be pacified, sent one of the angels right above the house of Matthias Hampel and his wife Elisabeth, for lo, I am strong enough to strike fear into you but I will spare you if it pleases me, and it does please me.

The bomb dropped in the garden a couple of metres away from the house, and down in the city those who had escaped were lamenting the dead and guarding the ruins to keep looters away, too angry and ashamed to look up at the sky from which disaster had fallen on them, it had come from distant America, from every corner of the world, to crush the German people. Heinrich said: Let's go and see what the Americans have done to our city, but his cousin Thomas hesitated, for he had seen the ruins and rubble of Aachen, and knew how traces of the old life sometimes stuck out of the ruins, or the hand of a dead girl, but don't be alarmed, she's from this town. Heinrich's cousin Thomas screamed when he saw the dead girl's hand, but Heinrich said: She's from this town, we can easily find something else, we don't want to have come all this way for nothing, but his cousin Thomas didn't want to take dead people's treasures, and preferred to collect the splinters of American shells.

Heinrich took to spending a couple of hours almost every day walking along the streets of the ruined city of Jena, looking for anything that could be re-used, picking up a bit of scorched leather here, a piece of glass or aluminium there, an old pan here, a few old books there, putting them all in his rucksack; he had a hiding place behind Father's shed, and further uphill, in the sheltered meadow, he dug a hole with sticks and his bare hands and stored things in it.

He didn't want the bombs to come, but he knew the Americans weren't through with a city that quickly, there were many cities on their maps, and the faster they dealt with them the sooner the German enemy would be done for. There was more bombing in February, and then on the first and second of March, and on the tenth and eleventh, then again on the fifteenth and sixteenth, always two days running so that the German people gradually got used to it; there were no more deaths. Theodor was home again by now and had something the matter with his knee, he would need an operation in four weeks' time, and he had seen the mortally exhausted Russians in the dump where he had been sent, he talked about that, and Heinrich told him about his dead girl, so they could compare notes.

By March Heinrich had collected three rucksacks full of bits and pieces, and another whole bagful after the ninth of April down by the ruins of the Saalbahnhof, which looked like the end of the world, with over a hundred more dead, and a few dozen heavily guarded Russian POWs in rags were looking for unexploded shells. The Russians, said Heinrich, adding that a train had gone through the city full of dirty, ragged figures, it was said they were Jews. Jews, what nonsense, said his father, but he wasn't quite sure, no Jews had been seen for a long time, he thought they had all left, gone abroad for good, so now it seemed they were back again.

The Americans moved into the city on the thirteenth, and the first of the family to come face to face with them was Theodor, who was down in the Paradies district and was to go back on active service, but he never did, and two days later Heinrich himself saw the Americans patrolling the occupied city, setting up a huge field laundry in the Paradies district, the first black men he had ever seen in his life were washing and ironing their uniforms as if they planned to stay for ever. The Americans had a huge tent with its own electricity supply and portable steam turbines, at which the Germans stared, they gave the children a taste of freshly baked cornbread in the field bakery, handed out the first chewing gum in their faultlessly ironed uniforms and polished boots, and they were always sitting in jeeps or cars of some kind, obviously they felt they were too good to walk.

Those were strange days and weeks, for while Father still listened daily to news of the latest defeats on the radio, everything outside was quiet and peaceful and uncertain, and the ruined buildings in the city lay quiet and peaceful too, hoping for someone to come and do something about them, you only had to go out and pick up the treasures they contained. That April Heinrich had shown his friends Emil and Kurt and a few others what he was collecting and putting in the hole he had dug in the meadow, and said he needed people to help him search and then sell or barter their finds, four packets of chewing gum for a cigarette, and the cigarette plus a young woman's photograph for a little coconut oil.

They called themselves the Greyhounds, because Emil thought they ought to have a name and someone to be in charge, and they all agreed on Heinrich, since he knew where to go, dared to approach the black soldiers and got good ideas, and they agreed that for the time being they must never use anything themselves, just hoard it and wait for a good opportunity, sell the stolen bread instead of eating it, even if your stomach was sticking to your ribs you must just keep selling and bartering everything, and good meals would come of their own accord in the end.

Your Heinrich will go far, said Uncle Sebastian when Heinrich brought an extra ration of meat or vegetables home yet again, and he called the report of the Führer's death good news, and when peace was made at last in May they all agreed that it was indeed good news, and it was better to have the Americans there than the Russians anyway. Very well, we'll call it peace, said Father, burying his little Party badge under the apple tree in the garden, and Mother said: I wish it was just us again, Matthias, that would be peace, I dream of it, but except for Grandmother they all wanted to stay for the time being.

At the beginning of June Heinrich sold the black soldiers his father's expensive telescope, and a little later did his first deal with the bottles of coloured water, he had brought a bottle of red wine for tasting and let them all have a taste in turn, what they bought afterwards was a fake and only looked real, but how would black soldiers from the big country of America know that? They brought off the fake-wine ploy some ten times over the summer, but then the Americans got wise to Heinrich and his red wine, and took him in and taught him a lesson, but the lesson taught by the black soldiers from America was only a couple of slaps with the flat of the hand, and the palms of their hands were all pale and rosy.

I was away on business, said Heinrich when he was home again after three days, and they didn't ask many questions, they all had their lives to live. Theodor and Father went to the works the same as usual every morning, gradually replacing broken window panes, and Mother struggled to keep the household going, much too large as it still was, every few weeks she spent a day lying down in her darkened room feeling that her head might burst apart, her mind on her duty and determination and her love for her husband and children, in the end she would always endure it.

The Americans were in Jena for a good two months, but they didn't stay, they exchanged beautiful Thuringia for part of the bombed capital Berlin, went to Father's works and packed everything into large crates, which they put on their trucks, the best machinery and the patented methods and the most experienced forty glassmakers as well as young Theodor, they were going west and didn't ask for Father, who had the house and wouldn't have gone in any case.

Soon after that the Russians came. The Russians are here, said Heinrich at the beginning of July, and there was Theodor back again, standing down in town with his brother watching the Russians in their wooden carts, and the Russians looked all ragged and dirty, they hoisted the red flag over the Zeiss works, and from now on they were kings in this new beggar state.

The Hampels despised the Russians because they drove into the city in horse-drawn carts, and didn't iron their uniforms or hand out chewing gum, but they spread fear and terror, and shot the fathers of two families on the Hampels' housing estate alone because they didn't open their doors and hand over their old badges or uniforms, or bring out their wives and grown-up daughters, you heard terrible tales. Father had even handed in his expensive boots, and Mother said: You're crazy, they cost so much, you don't give that sort of thing to the Russians even if they issue a thousand orders, but Father didn't want to queer his pitch with the new masters, because offending the new masters was no laughing matter. We'll survive it, said Father, meaning the boots, and Mother was glad they finally had the house to themselves again, and a room for the girls, a room for their sons, and one for the two of them on the rare occasions when he still wanted her.

She was now at the age when periods gradually cease, she

was irritable and restless, had a hot flush now and then and often couldn't sleep at night, and in addition she was still angry with her beloved relations from the West, not that she missed them, but they might at least have said thank you for a year spent with the Hampels, two hot meals a day and clean sheets every other Monday.

Well, we won't be a burden to you any longer, said Uncle Sebastian, calling the coming Russian occupation a passing phase, and in addition you have your Heinrich, and the house, and almost five hundred Reichsmarks a month from Schott, we wouldn't mind being in your situation. Mother had hoped they would say: If it gets very bad of course you'll be welcome with us, and if you have to stay longer than a year at least it'll be peace-time, but instead they were very busy and had no time to write letters to the Hampels in Jena.

Nothing was available yet except on ration, and some things were not available at all, or only from the farmers in the villages, which meant going to the station very early and travelling through the countryside on the roofs of the badly overcrowded trains, hoping and begging and bartering. Mother liked taking Constanze with her best, or she went with Paul and Heinrich, for the schools had been closed for months, while Theodor and Father went to the factory to work as usual, saw the new red and blue flags, and the men put in charge by the new masters, Communists or Social Democrats both old and new who had gone abroad for a few years like the Jews, and now they were back, relishing the work that lay ahead, the ruined bridges, squares, buildings, the wrong ideas circulating in town, the weary, disappointed human souls, how did you know where to begin?

Emil's father was one of those who didn't know where to begin, for the benefit of his son's friends he would take off his shirt and undershirt and show the scars from Buchenwald like little craters on his back, and they all stood there and stared and put their fingers in the scars to learn something from them. He, like Father, had been a man of the centre before

Hitler, and Hitler meant war and the Gestapo and their cellars, and the beatings in those cellars, and now those men were back, writing articles in the Social Democrat newspaper on the idea of a united Labour Party, what else was the lesson to be learnt from the figure of eight hundred dead in the city of Jena alone, what else?

Never mind the dead, said Heinrich, preferring to walk with Emil round the recently reopened market, where he saw Wanda one day, and almost failed to recognize her behind her two crates of vegetables, she wore her dark hair very short and was two years older, a woman now. She was only there on Saturdays, had little time to spare, or let him think she had little time to spare, but by persistently asking questions he discovered after a while that she was going out with a Communist from Jena West, who didn't like her plaits, so she had cut them off for love of the Communist, and because a new age was dawning, it was to be hoped that a new age was dawning for the whole country, what do you think? She never said more than a few sentences, throwing them to him as if he must live on them for a while, and asked what he was planning to do after he finished school in the summer, oh, no idea.

Father and above all Mother had their own ideas, saw him settled with Schott, or if they wouldn't take him there then learning some other trade, but Heinrich himself thought he'd like a career in sales, wines and spirits or cigarettes, or he could imagine a lingerie shop with nightdresses for his Wanda, just to keep her from freezing at night, and thick feather beds, and mattresses so narrow there wouldn't be room on them for a Communist when she fell into bed in the evening and wondered what would become of Heinrich: Oh, don't you worry, something will come of him, he'll make his way, he has no special opinions but he'll make his way, something will come of Heinrich yet.

13

He had been slightly smelly over the last few days, he ate only every other meal and kept thinking about his women, drinking the juices from their orifices once again in his foolish brain, which had been struck as if by lightning in February and didn't always remember faces, but did remember the names of his mistresses who, in alphabetical order, were Anna, Bella, Dora, Emilia, Gerda, Gisela, Jana, Lyusya, Marga, Rita, Rosa, Vera and Wanda. He told them apart by the songs they sang, and the birthmarks he saw on them in various places when they were lying beside him.

And how's Herr Hampel today, asked the nurses when they looked in on him early in the morning and washed him, bringing him out of his thoughts or his dozing, and he was always surprised to find how fast the nights passed, how tired he was after these nights, he didn't want to think about dying.

He did sometimes think of Rosa and the children, but Rosa and the children had long ago gone away to the West, and the only person who still wrote was the faithful Constanze, his sister, whose last letter had been in August. Even Harms and Gisela had visited him, but there wasn't much to be done now for Citizen Hampel, whose flesh was rotting beneath the covers, he probably hadn't even recognized them. He sometimes remembered his mother, and what a hard time she had of it dying, and then he lay back and smiled, thinking of his mother, and died on a Wednesday at six in the morning four weeks after his fifty-seventh birthday, just when the nurses were changing shifts, so he had to lie and wait for a little while until they found him around mid-day, when he would have been eating lunch but didn't, all of a sudden they had one lunch too many.

Oh dear, poor Herr Hampel, said the nurses, saying how terribly sorry they were about Herr Hampel, who had no relations left, not now his fine family thought itself too good for a life in the East, and what a shame that even the famous Martina from Frankfurt an der Oder thought herself too good for him in the end, or perhaps he had simply invented her, who knew?

Then they washed him, put a shirt on him, tied a tag with his name to his toe, and searched his clothes and the locker and drawer by the bed for personal possessions, but what they found would fit into a single box and didn't amount to much: a purse containing small change and four creased little photographs of his lost family, a gentleman's wristwatch, in addition a handkerchief with the initials HH, his papers, a notebook with Cyrillic lettering on the cover and the names and descriptions of various women inside, intimate details, better not touch it; no addresses.

Only the quiet grey gentleman in the suit who had come to visit a few days ago had left an address and phone number, just in case, and he came to the phone at once and said: Yes, sorry to hear it, Herr Hampel, only to be expected, we knew each other, we've known each other for a long time, they should cremate him and do everything that was necessary, he'd see to it and pick up the box, or we'll send someone over for it in the next few days, goodbye.

They did not cremate him at once, because first they wanted to see if he was still of any use, so they put him down in their cold mortuary and they did find some small useful parts of him here and there, he went into the fire on the third day, and they tipped what the furnace had left into an urn and had it buried in the North Cemetery, with no name over it, but there was an inscription carved on a stone for those who had died in the years 1985 to 1988: It was all worth it in the end.

The funeral was in mid-October, and Comrade Major Harms came to it, and Comrade Gisela with her Bulgarian perfumes, and at the back his parents' old friends Anneliese and Friedhelm, who had read a death notice in the paper and identified their acquaintance Heinrich from the past. They all stood there for a few minutes, watching in silence as two workmen dug a little earth out of the place where those who had died in the year 1988 were buried, put the urn into the shoe-box-sized hole, and bowed in silence, it was almost one o'clock

Twenty-six years ago last April, said Harms, and Gisela said he used to write her a lot of letters years ago, the nicest letters she ever had, she was re-reading them only yesterday. Yes, he liked writing, said Harms, and would she care to come to the Paradise Café where they had sometimes met over the years, and Gisela had been to the Paradise Café herself years ago, so let's remember him and drink a toast to Hampel, he'd have liked that.

You knew him professionally, did you, said Gisela, and Harms said: Professionally, well, I kept an eye on him now and then, but hardly at all these last few years, I haven't heard much of him recently.

Didn't he have a wife, mother of that fine lady Eva?

Yes, Rosa, said Harms, told her about Rosa and her daughter Eva, and mentioned his sister in the West, the letters which kept Heinrich going, the parcels he begged for, neither of them knew very much about it.

Enough to make you weep, she said, not wanting to cry in front of Harms, and Harms asked if he could give her a lift in his car, which she thought very good of him.

February 1988
Dear Constanze, you will be surprised to see strange handwriting, but I'm afraid I can't write myself any more. I

had a stroke early in the morning of the seventh of this month, my right side is paralysed, I can talk all right. It was twelve hours before they found me, I was lying helpless on the carpet all that time. I wonder if you could help me in this situation and send a few things, particularly soap, toothpaste, after-shave and razor blades (Wilkinson), moist wipes, 1 can of Aldi coffee, perhaps some black tea. That would do for now. They have been treating the paralysis for the last few days, but they can't yet say for certain what will come of it. Will you tell our brothers and sister? Very best wishes to all of you. With love from Heinrich.

April 1988
Many thanks for your letter and the parcel. Please don't be too hard on me. I know I've not been in your good books for a long time, but how am I to live? I just hope I shall see you all again some day, because as it turns out I shan't be in much of a situation to pass my last days unaided. So much in answer to your letter. The trainers have arrived and the tea and the soap, but I'm afraid the shoes are a size too small. Like life.

May 1988
I'm wearing the trainers anyway. The leather stretches and your feet get used to them, they were only uncomfortable for the first few days. I'm doing reasonably well. Of course I can't write, but my neighbour in the next bed is kind enough to do it for me. I'm afraid there are some more things I'd like: 2 cans of Aldi coffee, Ceylon or Assam tea, canned milk, 1 corduroy leisure suit, 1 motorway map of the Federal Republic. Did Rosa come through her abdominal operation all right? What do you hear about them? Not much, I expect.

June 1988
Many thanks for your letter and the parcel of things. I'm gradually improving. I can use a crutch now, and I've taken my first steps with a walking frame. They'll probably transfer

393

me to a nursing home in August. It's got modern furnishings and they've promised me a bed. Have any of you heard anything about Rosa yet? I don't often think of her, and when I do I realize how seldom it is. She probably wouldn't be very pleased to see me, but now she has worries of a very different kind, she's welcome.

July 1988

In the circumstances I'm fairly well. I'm managing with a crutch as best I can, and enjoying the food. I'll be moved as soon as there's a place free in the nursing home. Can I remind you what I wanted again, it isn't so very much this time: 1 corduroy leisure suit, 2 cans Aldi coffee, a few cans of salmon and mussels. I had a visitor for the first time yesterday, someone I know from Frankfurt an der Oder, but unfortunately she didn't have time to stay long. My old friends don't come either. If only Emilia were still alive I'd have nothing to complain of there, she was always so reliable and supportive. Sometimes my door opens and I think it's her, or I think it's you and the others. But sad to say I know that isn't possible.

August 1988

Did I say before that sometimes the door opens here and I think it's you? I sometimes get such silly thoughts. I'm afraid I'm not very well, who knows how often I'll be writing to you again. An acquaintance asked me the other day if you could help him. He's put in an emigration application for himself and his family and would like to go to Bavaria. I said I'd ask you, although I can't understand the people who are bent on becoming West German citizens. I had a postcard from Konrad in the Pfalz weeks ago, nothing since. Not so much as a sign of life from Walter. Could you send me some underclothes when it's convenient, and a pair of socks, and twenty marks in an envelope for a present I'd like to give my friend from Frankfurt an der Oder? As ever I feel very embarrassed about this. But would we still be in touch at all but for my begging?

In the last few weeks before the great storm, and before the storm broke in his sick brain too with thunder and lightning in the middle of winter, Heinrich was glad to see the days pass by, wrote a great many letters to his sister Constanze and to Martina, and apart from his letters had nothing much to do, had difficulty with his tablets in their little jars and boxes and bags, went for long walks through the streets nearby or drank a cup of tea in the Thüringer Hof with Elli, who was sorry for him, took the tram to the cemetery and talked to dead Emilia about his monotonous days, her feet so often felt cold, poor thing, and now there she lay in her grave and would never be warm again.

He spent half December waiting for his friend from Frankfurt an der Oder, imagining her perhaps staying with him and becoming another Emilia, and when she finally did come she stayed for just one afternoon, used the formal *Sie* pronoun to him at first, and could hardly believe the state he was in after all those letters and entreaties and hopes, how shabby it all was, what a wretched life he led.

You smell, you ought to wash more, she said, and you shouldn't eat just bread and cheap soups and canned food, hasn't anyone told you? Much valuable time was lost by her admonitions, she even cleaned the lavatory for him and carried the old potatoes down to the dustbin as if she were his mother or his cleaning lady, this poor old fellow with the bad leg didn't even run to toilet paper. But that's not what I want, Heinrich had said, still wishing she would stay and go over the reasons why she couldn't stand it at home any more, say she just wanted to be with her Heinrich, and would fetch her children and a suitcase in a few days' time, would wear her old clothes for his sake, could breathe freely again here after all those terrible years, that was what he dreamed of.

She did not actually say: Herr Hampel, you can forget the

idea of me moving in here, doing your housework or whatever, my marriage isn't in such a bad way that I'd change it for a miserable life like this, she didn't say that, but she did speak of a bad misunderstanding, strictly speaking they didn't know each other at all, so what did he expect.

I shall go to the West, she said, perhaps I really will go to the West.

She said: I'm here because you paid me a few nice compliments in the summer, but I'm afraid I can't live on a few nice compliments.

When she had left he was glad that she had sat in his armchair, and he went over what she had said again, thought she looked tired and thoughtful, thought she liked him or why would she bother to tell him off, if she didn't like him at all then she would be completely indifferent to him. On Christmas Eve he washed himself for her, and sent a telegram of good wishes, saying he was thinking of her and waiting, her visit had encouraged him a lot, so he kept sitting in his armchair and thinking about her, she ought to think hard before going to the West, he said.

All January Heinrich waited for an answer, and none came, but something did come at the beginning of February, when she typed him a few lines telling him the truth, she typed her name too, and said she had to ask him please not to pester her any more, she really would be very glad if he stopped it.

At first he couldn't believe that was what she wanted, he put the letter aside and went to sleep, even undressing properly, and he slept and woke, read it again and nodded and wept for himself and her, Martina, and this horrible bloody life, the wretched, wonderful, good life he had lived and was still living, and after all it was something to be still alive and able to look back, receiving the blows of fate and parrying them or handing them out himself, who could he complain to when he ended just lying there, unable to get up again, because he wasn't expecting that blow, one of the last, his stroke. It hit him like a thunderstorm that Saturday in

February 1988, when he fell to the floor, tearing the curtains down from the windows as he fell, which was how some passers by came to notice him hours later, lying struck down in his room, and rescued him, informed the community policeman, broke the window pane with the community policeman's permission, and saved Heinrich Hampel's life, what was left of it.

He was babbling nonsense when they took him away, gave names and mixed them up, had medical files with various doctors, and a special registration among his papers, he was on his feet again comparatively quickly.

He liked to eat soup at first.

Hampel, that's a funny name.

He had experience of being ill. His sister Constanze's letters were few and far between, but when she did remember him he was the happiest man on earth.

November 1987

My dear, kind Constanze, I haven't had a chance to write to you for a long time, because I did some silly things and wasn't in town. It started in October at the hospital, when I suddenly had large gaps in my memory and forgot to keep several appointments, I think it was three or four times. The doctor treating me was very cross, she told me off, wondered if I was suitable for therapy, and one day she called a taxi for me and threw me out. I felt so shaken that I got the taxi driver to take me to the station and bought a ticket to Frankfurt an der Oder, I didn't know where to go. I know someone there, she's a good deal younger than me but we'd come to an agreement. I reached Frankfurt about two-thirty on the 23rd, took a taxi to her flat, and then I had a severe disappointment. In short, I was going up to see her but there was another man there already. She didn't even open the door to me, but we talked it over next day. I took a room, and two days later a doctor sent me to the psychiatric hospital. I had to go and see him because I'd run right out of my pills. It was necessary, since I couldn't talk straight and I'd had a shock. I spent three weeks in Frankfurt an der Oder, they didn't discharge me and let me go back to Jena until the 13th. It was horrible, I can tell you, but instructive as well. The treatment did me good too, even my memory is better again now, I probably prevented worse damage just in time. What I really miss is your letters. Don't you have any time to write? We've had very stormy weather here recently, it did quite a lot of damage. The roofs blew off any number of buildings, chimneys fell to the ground, people were injured. And we've had rain and thunder and storms. I sit here waiting for visitors, drinking your tea and thinking to myself. Yesterday I cleaned the windows and then did my washing. The windy weather was just right for drying the washing. Now I must do the ironing and tidy up. I don't get bored. Only I don't read nearly enough these days. And by the way, I wasn't drinking while I had these adventures. I haven't drunk at all since the 15th of August. I didn't touch a drop during those two days in Frankfurt either. The doctor treating me was very surprised, she hadn't expected it. Sometimes I've felt like a drink, but fear of the consequences stopped me. I remember what it was like. In the end it was just horrible. I didn't know myself, the people I was fond of didn't know their Heinrich either. Hugs and kisses. I suppose I can send you hugs and kisses, seeing I'm your brother? I don't have much chance to hug and kiss anyone these days.

November 1987

I've got over the Frankfurt business. My leg gives me trouble, and the way it's refused to heal up for weeks now, it's what they call diabetic gangrene, I think. Yesterday my annual electricity bill for over 545 Eastern marks arrived by post, and now I don't know what to do, because they're threatening to cut me off. Is there any way you could help me out? I know someone here who'd be very interested in Western money. Could you send me DM 150? I know you've already done far too much for me. But the prison system didn't pay my rent for me all those years, so I've pawned everything I have. I just don't know what else to do. For instance I can't very well ask this person I know in Frankfurt. And I don't have anyone else, or I don't want to ask them. It's still cold and windy in Jena. It was always like mid-winter around this time of year when we were in Russia. Would you like to see all that again? I've had the chance to go any number of times, but I'm afraid I never took it. I don't suppose the others ever went there again either, or did they? Will you write and tell me? I always look forward to your letters, I can't tell you how much. Do you remember the river where we used to go bathing in Russia? We had a good time there, really. The Saale here almost always has little white horses on the surface, and now, in winter, the city is usually full of smoke. I must go out and do some shopping, my fridge is almost empty. Will you remember to send the things? Thank you.

He had simply risen and gone out through the door, there was the taxi waiting, and it drove him to the station. We have no faith in you any more, Herr Hampel, the doctor had said, experience tells us that nothing will come of you, and our country and its people can't afford for us to act as if it would. We have serious cases and we have less serious cases, she had said, but the worst of all are the touchy sort who never get a proper grip on life and just have wishes and demands, as if Socialism were a chance to lounge about or provided everything like the magic table in the fairy-tale, but in that, she said, unfortunately Herr Hampel was wrong.

In the train he couldn't help going over and over what the doctor had said to him, and he couldn't help going over and over what his Martina had said to him, could he really just take her by surprise, turn up at her door without a room or anywhere to stay, but since he was in such need he hoped he could, in his needy state he tottered all through the city to her flat, hoping she was at home and would take him in, but once again everything turned out differently.

He hadn't seen the other man, but he felt sure there was another man in the flat with her, watching her, not letting her go out, making her go to the second floor window to send that man Hampel packing, and what on earth was he doing there, what did he want at this hour of the day, turning up without warning, what a cheek. Tomorrow morning? Yes, maybe tomorrow morning, she told him from her window, or rather her nod said so, but now it's evening, we'll see what next, you go and find a room, and better get something to eat, or was he going to wait here till morning?

He did briefly consider waiting there, spending the night under her window, pacing up and down and keeping warm and passing the hours with pacing, but then he was glad to be in his hotel room and not stirring up any trouble, it was warm there and he could go to bed early and sleep. Next morning he just drank a cup of coffee for breakfast, cleaned his teeth and persuaded her to come and talk to him, rang the bell and greeted her and suggested walking a little way towards the border. It's not what you think, she said, not immediately noticing the state he was in, and when she did notice she was alarmed. You look terrible, she said, what's happened, and she repeated: It's not what you think, that was my husband, and he wanted to talk things over just like you.

I didn't know what else to do, said Heinrich, and asked her what had happened between them in that café on Carl-Zeiss-Platz in the summer, because recently the tablets he was taking had left his memory full of holes.

I can tell you what happened, she said, we drank tea every afternoon, and you paid some very nice compliments while we were drinking tea every afternoon in the café on Carl-Zeiss-Platz, after a few days we knew the story of each other's lives.

Did we touch each other?

No, we didn't touch each other. You said: I'd like to. But

I said: I can't imagine it, not now, perhaps never, because my husband has left me, or maybe I was the one who left him not so long ago, what was the difference after all.

Yes, that was it, said Heinrich.

But I hesitated over saying *du* to you.

And we always ordered streusel cake.

It was almost a beginning.

But you don't believe it really was.

No, I'm afraid not, she said, saw that he was not happy about her just saying No and not wanting him to touch her, because that was what he probably did want, and he was saying so by not reverting to the subject, she felt all this was very awkward. I'll take you to a doctor, she said, seeing that he was losing his self-control because of the way she looked at him and what she said, and he didn't want her to take him to a doctor and then go away, but she persuaded him and went with him, she knew a neurologist quite close, she took Heinrich to hospital after he'd seen the neurologist and promised to visit him next day, said she'd visit as often as she could while he was there if her husband would let her, and Heinrich had asked no more about him.

At the hospital they let him sleep for a while at first, and when Martina came to ask how he was they sent her away, or was she by any chance his wife or a close relation, well no, not exactly, though he'd been describing her as his fiancée recently. Sorry, said the doctors, and let her write a postcard down in reception, she really didn't know what to put, or how you could tell a lie for someone else's sake, saying: You'll be all right, you'll pull through, I'll wait for you, and I won't find the waiting long because I'm your fiancée.

October 1987

Please don't worry, but I've been going rapidly downhill these last three weeks. I'm in the early stages of dementia now. Dear Constanze, do you remember our paternal grandfather? Before we went to Russia he once tried walking from Jena to Aachen, he went to what was the zonal border at that time, in Hesse, and was picked up by the police and sent back. Our father always wanted to go off to other cities too when he got demented, and now it seems I've inherited the condition. I've had no short-term memory for three weeks now, but the doctors and nurses wouldn't believe me, for a long time they thought I was pretending. But sometimes I don't know the nurses' names, I get the male nurses and the visitors mixed up, I go to lunch twice running or stay in my room till evening and don't even notice feeling hungry. Yesterday I was in such a strange way I made one of the nurses a proposal of marriage. But I'm Sister So-and-so, Herr Hampel, she said, laughing, because she could be my daughter, she took my temperature and went away and came back, and soon after that I started asking her again: hadn't she had my letter, I still hadn't had an answer, I'd like to marry her, and so on. It was very embarrassing, I can tell you, but after that they all agreed that there really was something wrong with me. I had to go to the hospital manager and tell him everything I'd noticed about myself, and yesterday they gave me an enema. The damage ought to be all dealt with in a couple of weeks' time. I can thank God that I'm only in my mid-fifties, because otherwise I'd be done for this year or next year. It seems I've been ill for 25 years, but I've only found out now, when it's almost too late.

But now for the good news. I haven't had a drink for over two months, and I'll be setting up house with a new girlfriend next year. A lady I know in Frankfurt an der Oder is going to move in with me in Jena when I'm out of here, and I hope that won't be too long. I've even bought a few household things, and the hospital will find me a flat. I might need to ask you to send some wallpaper. I can see it all in my mind's eye, looking lovely: four rooms and a big kitchen for sitting and eating and talking in, like at home in our Windbergstrasse house, what a dream that would be. Wasn't it you who always used to run down to the cellar as soon as the air-raid warning went in the last months of the war? My dear, brave little sister, I was always very fond of you. Or wouldn't you have thought so? In the photographs you sent you look lovely, by the way. I know I'd have liked you. I mean, I'm sure lots of people say they like you, not just your black sheep of a brother from the Socialist city of Jena who's making a fresh start for the hundredth time. What a fool he is. I'm afraid there are some more things he wants, too, the following, please, by the end of the year: for my fiancée a pair of dark-red trousers size 36, and for me a new training suit (blue), Süssli sweetener, diabetic chocolate and other sweets for Christmas, and things to eat, long-life ready-to-serve dishes with noodles, Pfanni dumplings, dried potato, 1 can Aldi coffee, perhaps some cosmetics for my fiancée. Her name is Martina, she's very pretty, and she has a girl and a boy, aged ten and fourteen. You're all warmly invited to the wedding here in Jena. Will you come and celebrate with us? I'm counting on seeing you. Our father married again very late in life too, but I hope I'll be a bit luckier with my fiancée than he was. There won't be many guests, not a huge party, but we'll have a good meal in a restaurant. As you can see, I'll pull through. Once I'm completely better I'd like to go back to work in my old job and earn enough so that I'd have to bother you only with very special requests. I owe my new start to you and the family. My life has been hell these last ten years. But now I'm a different man. I'll have turned the corner in every respect by 1989. There, this is the letter I promised, I hope you like it. It's two in the morning now, and I'm writing letters to everyone: you, Sibylle, Paul, Eva, and who knows who else. I'm glad my life has been saved yet again. Your loving brother Heinrich.

He had been drinking all summer, waiting for them to take him in and put a stop to his bottle of brandy in the morning, his Polish vodka on Saturday and his Russian vodka on Sunday, the bottle of methylated spirits which burned his inside like fire when he had nothing else. They summoned him on his fifty-sixth birthday, wished him many happy returns, gave him high doses of that useful drug Distraneurin to help with his detoxification, after a few weeks he must pull himself together like everyone else and answer a few awkward questions, why was it he couldn't stop drinking all those years? I wish I knew, said Heinrich, mentioning his marriage and the foreign country and the three prison sentences of three years each or more, but they didn't want to hear any of that, they talked about his character, had anyone or anything actually forced him to drink: his wife, the country, the attempts on the part of the state to educate him, the good will of the firms where he had found work but always went wrong, Herr Hampel might like to take a look at himself and ask himself whose fault it was if not his own, Herr Hampel's, like the others whose names we know, our drunks from the administrative district of Gera and far beyond, they're the worst cases.

Bed at ten, no complaints, stick it out, said the doctors and nurses, and they only ever called him Hampel, but Herr Hampel painted nice bright watercolour pictures in the short hours in the morning, learned to exercise and throw a heavy ball in the big hall during gymnastics every Tuesday, or do fretsaw work between two-thirty and four on Wednesdays, he was successful there, but unfortunately the hours after that dragged on.

At first it wasn't easy for him to get used to it all, but what did he expect? He was in a ward with six beds, and not a single snorer among them, because all the tablets made them sleep like logs, they were woken at seven by the loud bell, the nurse's voice in the ward or shouted in their ears if they failed to hear it: Get up and wash, get dressed, it's another day, gentlemen, breakfast won't wait, the doctors are beginning their rounds, and later they all sat in a circle and told each other stories of their miserable lives and their stupidity, my word, were we ever stupid, stupid enough for two at least, because we weren't really living and it didn't make us feel good, in retrospect feeling good seemed almost possible.

Heinrich sometimes talked about Rosa when they were sitting in a circle exchanging confessions, or waiting in silence for someone else to come up with a confession, and they didn't like to hear that Rosa had gone to the West and persuaded their two sons to go with her, it was Hampel here himself who didn't deserve her and drove her out of the country, so what are you complaining about? Some of them envied Heinrich for having had a woman like Rosa, and Heinrich envied them for having visitors who were soon coming to see them every other afternoon, but no sister from the West came to see him, no girlfriend from Frankfurt an der Oder, no Gisela and no Harms, yet he wrote them letters asking them to visit or hiding his request between the lines, describing the psychiatric hospital as if it were a sanatorium in the mountains or a grand hotel, there was nothing to fear, everyone was perfectly harmless, they were all human beings like you and me.

His first outing was at the beginning of October, they let him out for a few hours to mix with other people and test himself in a bar, order a glass of water when his friends had a beer or a shot of spirits after a meal, it was to be hoped he'd had enough of that for ever. So now Heinrich went out for a walk two or three times a week, was glad to be away from the others for a few hours, was relieved to be back with those others a few hours later, and alas, there was no letter for him, no answer from his sister Constanze, or from Martina, who was horrified by the way he kept writing to her about getting married, saying that she was more precious to him than anything else in the world.

Rosa has a flat and a job, Constanze wrote in October, a good position as a secretary with the Caritas welfare organization, she hasn't asked after you. He had no idea why that should hit him hard, but it did, as if it were bad news, and he sometimes tore up his pictures in the art classes. He said: No news is bad news, so what do I expect, not much except a reply from Frankfurt an der Oder. Perhaps the word precious troubled her, he thought, or she wanted to make perfectly sure, perhaps she walked round the neighbourhood every day with his letter in her pocket thinking it over, and he hoped she'd finally be there in the doorway some day with a bunch of flowers, looking at him with sparkling eyes, saying: Yes, I see you're surprised, I've thought it over for a long time, and after long and mature consideration I've decided it shall be as you wish.

June 1987

I've been in bed again for three weeks. I'm getting worse and worse. Since I can hardly walk now I shall have to go into a nursing home this year, I'll be lucky if I can do some kind of work now and then. Tomorrow I'm going to see a lady I know in Frankfurt an der Oder, I shall stay there for a week. I try not to think about Rosa and the children. Financially I'm at rock bottom now. If you could add a few things to the parcel to help me survive, I'd be glad. They, didn't even give me two hundred marks last pay-day. I'm living on what you send at the moment. Luckily I've hoarded up your presents, knowing they'd help me to survive some day. I don't know what I'd do without you, because I still have possessions which are impounded because of my old debt. Very good wishes to you all. Your brother Heinrich.

July 1987

I'm writing this letter feeling desperate. I don't know how I'm going to manage. Next pay-day I can expect only three hundred marks, and how I'm to get through the month on that is a mystery to me. Dear all of you, please help me again. By now I can hardly walk, and unfortunately I don't have the strength left to earn anything. I'm going into hospital in August if there's a bed for me. I wish that time had come. I haven't heard anything from Sibylle and Paul for a long time. How are Theodor and Ilse? It's been raining since yesterday, after a hot, stormy week. It's quite cool. What else can I tell you? I just keep thinking of Tuesday, because it will be decided then. How will the doctor assess the situation? My pills don't work nearly as well now. Will any of you be coming to Jena some time? What are the prospects of that? There's just been a heavy storm here. The streets have turned to rivers, and poor me, I don't even have an umbrella. It's all so depressing. Your loving brother Heinrich.

August 1987

Dear Constanze, here I am still at home, waiting for a bed to be free in hospital for the drying-out cure. I've tried it a couple of times on my own; it was hell. I couldn't stand it by the second day at the latest. You don't need to do anything about my flat for the moment, because it could well be I'll have to go into a home after I've dried out successfully. I can't manage on my own any more. Who'd have thought it: ready for the scrap-heap at not quite 56. I'd rather forget about my birthday this year. It's raining again at the moment. It's still cold too. Nothing like summer. Very bleak. Did I tell you when I wrote before that I met our Wanda again after all these years? It was quite by chance, when I was shopping, there we suddenly were standing in a shop side by side, looking and wondering. It can't be you, she says. Wanda? I say. And it really is our Wanda. She's manager of a collective farm somewhere nearby, has three grown-up children, she's happily married to the Communist from back then. How we talked. Remember that bedroom? I say, and she says yes, she does, but she's heard bad things about me. Yes, Bautzen, I say, but all the same she asks me to have a cup of coffee and a little brandy with it in honour of the day, and we had so much to talk about. Our Wanda. Wasn't it Wanda who once slapped Theodor's face for calling her a Communist? I don't ask after Theodor any more. Of course he'd have done everything much better in my place, and he did do much better too: he has a house and a wife and children whose names I hardly know, life certainly saw him all right in the end. But is it really always the efficient people who are lucky? Is a lucky person always efficient, or is he just lucky? That's the question. I've had plenty of luck in my own life. But in my case, unfortunately not for free.

He had found her in the Kosmos café and thought: How can I venture to look at her at all, and on the second or third day: This is the last one, this is the very last time. Later he found out she wanted to think her marriage over, was staying with a woman friend round the corner and only saw the friend in the evenings, so she had plenty of thinking time. She was almost on the point of leaving when he saw her and thought: How can I possibly look at her, I'm too old for her, or perhaps I'm not too old for a woman in her mid-forties, for that was where he put her age. She was reading the last few pages of her book, sipped her tea now and then, leafed through the pages again a few times, sighed when she had finished, and saw Heinrich at one of the tables looking at her, which did her good.

They didn't speak to each other, but next day they saw one another again and felt as if they were already acquainted. She liked him looking at her, his eyes saying as he looked: I wasn't expecting you any more, I didn't foresee you, and you're not really my sort with your bitten fingernails and your wrinkles from smoking cigarettes and from the bottles you've drunk while smoking those cigarettes, for he knew that was the case. His eyes said: I know all about you, I know the dark rings under your eyes, your shame at the first shot early in the morning, the nausea, the disgust, you don't have to explain any of that to me, your eyes and the water in your eyes and the water under your skin give you away, they give you away to the bone, to the bottom of your heart, they endear you to me. I'll come and sit beside you, said his eyes, if not today then tomorrow, you decide, and she decided it might as well be today, and was surprised, but had no objection.

You're a funny one, she had said, introducing herself at once by name: Martina Drosch, seamstress in a state-owned factory, two children, what else should she say, she'd come away for a few days to visit a woman friend, taking flight, not a word about the reasons. Change of scene, said Heinrich, treading very carefully because she was treading very carefully too and only ordered tea, didn't pour her heart out straightaway, it wasn't the thing to do to invite a complete stranger over to your table with a couple of glances and pour your heart out in the first few sentences, although she could have done it. I like streusel cake best, said Martina Drosch, whose face was all lined and wrinkled, and who had a bad, habitual cough after every other sentence, so they ate streusel cake together, and knew all about each other straightaway, but unfortunately after a couple of hours she had to leave to go and eat with her friend, see you tomorrow.

We could call each other *du*, she said on the third day, and she felt like taking a little walk after their second cup of tea and the streusel cake in the Kosmos café, and why not have a bit of fun, let's buy a bottle of schnapps in the Co-op and find somewhere nice to sit and talk, where did he suggest, she hardly knew the place at all. I could show you my father's house, said Heinrich, and took her the old way up to the Wilhelmshöhe, showed her the house and garden and up above them the meadow where he had once devoured the little book by the professor from Berlin, acquainting himself with the mysteries of love, learning what foreplay and afterplay meant, how to adapt to each other in love-play, learning that love took practice, and making your partner happy was the guiding principle.

Oh, you're terrible, said Martina, drinking and getting merry, wanting to go further up to the Fuchsturm, and I'll tell you the story of my own life up there, it won't take long.

She had been popular with men, had her first drink at thirteen out of pure high spirits, it wasn't because of a boy. Married in her mid-twenties, three lovers on the side, so to speak, she didn't want to give them up just yet. She had found bed fun for a long while, but as time went on she needed something to warm her up, make her feel like doing it and opening up to the man, she needed a little drink afterwards to help her get off to sleep, she couldn't sleep without it. Her husband: well, a good man really, Hungarian. Cooked a meal for the family every Saturday, could read what she wanted from her lips even after all these years, didn't count the bottles, so what was the matter then?

Easy to see through me, isn't it, she said, and Heinrich nodded and took her back to the city and her woman friend, and then they had only another two days left and had to hurry up a bit with their stories, the bottles they drank on their walks and the questions they still had to ask, there were only a few. We'll see, said Martina Drosch from Frankfurt an der Oder, his last woman of all, and Heinrich said: You go home for now, and if he needed her he'd just get on the next train and visit her and her husband and the children, it wouldn't bother him.

Yes, see you soon, yes, what a shame, she said, hugging him like a good friend, her friend Heinrich from Jena on the Saale who saw through her so easily, not that it was unpleasant to have him see through her so easily, and when he drank he took very small sips, just as she did, that was something she'd noticed about him at once.

January 1987

It's been snowing here for two days, we have the first complete covering of snow. I really am very grateful to you for the parka and all the other things, or I'd probably have frozen. What are the children doing? What have you heard about Theodor? I've just replied to a lonely hearts ad. You might not believe it, but sometimes I get so fed up that I have

410

all kinds of silly ideas, so why not this one? I've heard nothing from you for over a month now. There was an incident last Friday, it affected me very much, I was picked up unconscious in the street in broad daylight after collapsing, it was my circulation. The job's all right. Theodor would laugh his head off if he knew: Heinrich Hampel, lift operator at the University Gynaecological Hospital. But at least you get to mix with people, you see so much misery and learn to what to think of your own. Much love from Jena. Your brother Heinrich.

February 1987
    I'm still in Jena, they've put off the operation, they can't carry it out, not the way my circulation is at present. I was very glad to get the sheets, and I'm very glad of the quilt too, it's wonderfully warm. Dear Constanze, I'll leave it to you to decide what you can send, because you've never sent me anything I couldn't use. Only no textiles for the moment, let's wait for the operation first. Please can you understand that? A parcel like the first you sent would be very welcome just now. Many thanks and very good wishes, love from Heinrich.

March 1987
    The latest news is that I'm a bit better again, and working. I hope I'll be all right for a few weeks, as for the operation, I'm hoping to have it in April, but the circulation in my leg is a disaster. How are the boys? I hope we aren't writing to each other just because poor old Heinrich in the East couldn't manage without the parcels you send. I'd really like to hear how you all are. I'd like to hear from Theodor too, I mean, he's more or less the head of the family now. I really am so grateful to you. There were fifty items on your list with the last parcel, and I can assure you that I'm delighted to have every last one of them. So long, good luck. Your brother Heinrich.

April 1987

I've been working for the last three weeks. My blood pressure has stabilized. I take so many medicaments I can hardly count them. If I had to pay for them I'd have nothing at all left to live on. I've lost almost ten kilos since September. But that's not enough, the doctors want me to weigh less than ninety or they won't operate. Will I ever see you again? The canned food and the cosmetics arrived safely. As ever, thank you very much. Could you by any chance send me a sheet to Jena? Please don't think I'm only glad of the parcels, I look forward to your letters, sometimes they're the only entertainment I get. I enclose a recent photograph of me. I hardly recognized myself. To think a man can change so much if he doesn't change his ways. Gratefully, your brother H.

May 1987

Your parcel saved my life. My neighbour took it in for me, and just as I was fetching it I felt my heart giving way and dropped at her feet. So it's got me again. But look on the bright side, at just the right moment. Please give your boys my love. It's a pity we've lost sight of each other so completely. It's been raining here since yesterday. I'm sitting at the hospital window, there's a view of the Lobdeburg, but you can hardly make it out for the mist. The hospital is a huge complex. They go to a lot of trouble, though. I can't remember anything of the week in intensive care. When were you last in Jena? It must be ages ago. Or did I miss your visits, or have I forgotten them?

June 1987

Many thanks for your parcel, which I nearly didn't get this time, because as an ex-convict I have only a provisional pass, the one for GDR citizens whose personal passes have been confiscated and they're not supposed to get parcels any more. You sent 2 pullovers and 2 shirts, various foods, the Bac roll-on, 1 can olives, mushroom soup, canned ready-to-eat dishes. I'm all right yet again. The clothes fit perfectly. I'm amazed the way you always know my size and my tastes. But now I have my work cut out to bring everything into the open. I was recently in a café talking to a very nice woman from Frankfurt, and now I'm out of action as of yesterday. My family in the West. No trace of my old friends. I'm writing this at ten in the evening. I've just scrambled up on my bed on all fours because I fell over all of a sudden, just like that. Well, all the best. Many, many thanks. Love, Heinrich.

He had Anneliese and Friedhelm to thank for his getting a job again in autumn 1986, earning the last money he would earn in his life as a lift operator at the University Gynaecological Hospital, because Anneliese and Friedhelm knew one of the doctors, and didn't want to see Heinrich Hampel looking so wretched any longer, or have him standing at their door every few days, undeterred when they told him he was a nuisance, and why for heaven's sake wouldn't he finally come to his senses, he'd always disappointed everyone, that's what it amounted to.

Come to his senses, Heinrich had said, thank you very much, he had said, for saying thank you after asking favours was now, you might say, his main calling in life, so he thanked the doctor they knew and later the woman in the administration office who hired him, with some doubts, for 493 marks a month, the work wasn't hard in itself. Yes, thanks, no, said Heinrich, and had it all explained to him, pushed the buttons every day, opening and closing the doors for patients and nursing auxiliaries and visitors, taking dead bodies down to the basement and post-operative patients up to the wards, seeing and hearing nothing when the surgeons cracked jokes about women's sexual parts, wasn't there at all, stood in his corner feeling apprehensive about the people, new people every day, who sometimes looked at him, and then he was just standing around again, waiting in his lift for the next journey, feeling his bad leg as he waited and crouching down to spare it, he had no chair to sit on, cursing the hours that still lay ahead of him.

That was another reason why he would rather have been a doorman, so that he could sit down again now and then while he was working, but they hadn't wanted to take him on as a doorman and they hired him as a lift operator only out of pity, or because they didn't trust him as a doorman, it would be because of Bautzen that they didn't trust him, but anyone who said so openly was breaking the law in the Republic where Bautzen stood.

Not even a doorman, his old friend Harms had said, letting the remark escape him when they met again, and they both enjoyed meeting again and chatting about old times in the Forelle café, but they met for a chat only as private persons, so to speak, and to Heinrich it sounded like: We cannot and will not rely on this Herr Hampel again, not even as an unofficial colleague, we're here to say goodbye and because we're fond of Herr Hampel, we'll thank him for his faithful services and disappear, or we'll be acquaintances who may not, perhaps, recognize each other in the street.

Harms had said a lot about the new strong man of the Soviet Union, and about everything that had recently become possible in the great Soviet Union, it was a miracle and offered hopes which might not apply to the German Democratic Republic. If it was up to me, why not, said Harms, who had been a major, and as a major and a private individual he had an opinion, or sometimes, unfortunately, two opinions. Well, I don't know, said Harms, and of course one can't say anything yet, but of course the West is instantly rejoicing at the top of its voice and coming up with hopes and doing its old calculations, which makes us suspicious and watchful, because I am sorry to say we're miles away from the end of our struggles.

He didn't ask after Rosa this last time, he paid the bill as usual, wondered what Heinrich was waiting for, couldn't work it out, shook hands as if they would be sitting opposite each other again some day soon, clapped him on the shoulder in leaving, didn't turn round as he left, and hoped it was all over now: the case of Hampel over and done with, nothing left for them there, and as for the rest of it, unfortunately they weren't responsible for that.

It had been in November that his old friend Harms took leave of him, and Heinrich already knew where they had buried his Emilia nearly two years ago, Emilia who was going to wait for him, and one day got so tired of waiting that she took her own life with a handful of tablets, which made Heinrich very cross with her, he told her so on every visit, stood by her grave and said angry things to her, but very quietly and carefully so as not to alarm her. It could have been different for us, he said, and told her about his lift, and that one occasion of his farewell meal with Harms, she knew for herself what it was like saying goodbye, it was almost always rather difficult.

I'm still practising, he said, and gave himself another few years, but when he tried picturing them they seemed very pitiable, not worth mentioning.

September 1986

You'll have been expecting mail from me, but I couldn't write for a long time, because I was in Bautzen for another three years, three years to the day. And now I'm so ill that I can't even think of working. I've settled a large part of my debts, but the sword of Damocles is still hovering over me. I got home around eight in the evening on 1 September. My flat had been raided, anything of any value was gone, the lavatory was full of shit. The only comforting thing was a letter from Eva, she married again a little while ago and is living a long way off in Schwerin now, with a husband who's older than she is, Rosa and my sons are over with you in the West, that's life. Can I still count on you at all? Here I am in my flat, with thirty marks in my pocket, doing my sums and not getting very far with them. They paid me 430 marks as wages for the last three years, which is just enough for electricity and gas and to get the flat clean again, only the bare necessities. And I can't ask anyone I know for help, because I'd be accused of attempted fraud if I tried any financial approach, and then I'd be put away for another two and a half years, which would certainly be the death of me. The authorities say I ought to earn my living as a concrete worker, but the doctors won't hear of it. I've been diabetic for years, in addition I have arteriosclerosis, angina pectoris, water in the legs, problems with my circulation, a stiff left hand, a half-paralysed right hand, trouble with my hip joints, all the aches and pains of old age, that's the bill I have to pay for Bautzen. They tipped up to six hundred tablets a month down me in bloody Bautzen, I'm scarcely capable of anything, I'm afraid to face every new day. Do I still have any credit with you? Letters enclosing dollars would be best, and parcels of any kind. I'm sorry to say there's bad news of my Emilia too. Do you remember about her? She was going to wait, but unfortunately she changed her mind. But more of that later. It's too sad. Please write.

October 1986

You say I can still count on your help but not your understanding. Isn't that a bit too glib? Have you any idea what's been going on here? I don't mean to justify myself, but there are some things you just can't know. I hope we'll all be able to talk it over calmly one day, and then I'm sure you'll think differently. Meanwhile I was handed an unstamped envelope yesterday containing 440 Eastern marks, I suppose it's from you. What can I say? Very many thanks, anyway. You sent the money at just the right time. You'd hardly be able to imagine it, but my present life doesn't even satisfy the most primitive requirements, with just 220 marks sick benefit for rent, electricity, gas, insurance and food it isn't even enough for the bare essentials. I'm still being penalized for financial obligations I can't meet, and if it goes on like this, well, it won't have been for the last time. People are very hard here, they don't ask how a man can get back on his feet again after years in prison. I could reconcile myself to that. Only I find it difficult to reconcile myself to your condemnations. I hope you all keep well, and very good wishes for today, from your brother Heinrich.

November 1986

Dear Constanze, many thanks for your letter and the parcel with the food, the pullover and the socks. I can really do with them. Otherwise nothing's changed. I've been trying to get work for weeks, but everywhere I go I fail the medical examination. No firm will venture to employ me in my state of health. It's nothing to do with previous convictions, they don't matter here, far from it, by law I'm guaranteed a job. So I'll end up being classed an invalid, and that's where the bad part really begins. Dear Constanze, if I may be honest, it was only your letter gave me fresh heart. At first sight I've hardly changed in twenty years, I even still have all my hair, grey now, but otherwise I look fine. And so they always ask: You? But you're so healthy, we suppose you just don't want to work. Did I tell you Emilia committed suicide while I was in prison? It was terrible for me. They told me she took an overdose of tablets. No letter, no explanation, just like that. Her family put the key through my letter-box, with the death notice and a few lines. She had the key to my flat, you see. And now here I am again, begging. I'll be grateful for anything you can spare. I've hardly bought myself anything for years. This is what I'd like: 1 anorak size 54, 1 pair of winter trousers, underwear size 7 if possible. And please write to me. You've no idea much how good it does me if you think of me now and then.

They had written to each other a few times, from Bautzen to Jena and back from Jena to Bautzen, short letters saying almost nothing except that they were thinking of each other, and then one day Emilia simply didn't reply, or perhaps she couldn't think of anything to say to him, for he kept writing the same things from Bautzen all the time, saying he was still alive, and thinking of this and that when he thought of her, she just had to keep waiting for him, there were so-and-so many days to go, she was probably getting a bit tired of his letters in the long run.

Everything repeats itself, wrote Heinrich, and for a long time he didn't think ill of her for not writing, and then he did take it ill but forgave her, knew she had her reasons, she'd be out in the yard one day when they let him go, and in the end it was exactly three years to the day they released him, but she wasn't waiting for him, his plump Emilia, she was lying in her cold grave up in the North Cemetery, passing the time away there.

Then Heinrich wept because Emilia had forgotten him, and was lying in her cold grave up in the North Cemetery, passing the time away, and he wept over his looted flat and went round to Anneliese and Friedhelm, who gave him a few old curtains and a couple of pans and a cast-off pair of trousers just to start him off, they were sorry but that was all they had, or perhaps they thought it was more than enough for an ex-convict.

He had been quite busy for the first few days. He put the flat in order, wrote his first letters to Constanze and Eva who, he hoped, had not forgotten him entirely, went to look for Emilia's grave and found it, which took him almost half an hour, and he wept and spoke angrily to her as if she had betrayed him. He went on foot from the North Cemetery down the long curving road to Dornburger Strasse, already feeling rather shaky, glanced briefly across the street at the Cosmetika where he always used to meet Priem, he didn't know just what it was he owed to Priem but certainly a good part of the last three years.

He knew he would have to find work again as soon as

possible, but when he thought of work he felt heavy and clumsy and incapable of any great effort. The doctors said: Definitely not on a building site, at most a few hours waiting tables, so Heinrich had gone round to the Thüringer Hof, where they were very friendly at first, appalled to see what Bautzen had made of their friend Heinrich. What a shame, they said, but now he must get better after that place Bautzen, we don't want hear a lot about it, but you couldn't help wondering whether it wasn't all just a tiny little bit Heinrich's own fault, I mean, here in the GDR they don't put you in Bautzen for no reason at all.

It had been Elli who thought there must be some reason for sending people like Hampel and the rest of them to Bautzen, but how were things going at the Thüringer Hof otherwise, well, we can't complain. I hope you're not going to collapse on me, said Elli, and offered him a cup of tea so that he wouldn't collapse on her, for which he was grateful. They've looted my flat, said the grateful Heinrich, feeling weak, and Elli said: Yes, misfortunes seldom come singly, but life balances out in the end, or then again maybe it doesn't.

Eva too was shocked by the new Heinrich, she took the last train from Schwerin one Friday and said she was so glad they could meet once again, which meant, good heavens, that she already thought of him almost as a dead man. She still had the lovely long red hair she'd had as a girl, and for quite a time she talked of nothing but her Thomas and his high-up position on the district planning commission, and how these days there was all sorts of talk about the friendly Soviet Union, and the curious mark on the forehead of its new Party leader and head of state, it looked like a map or a threat, or like a promise of travel to lands largely unknown.

And how are you, asked Eva, calling him Father, and it touched him that she still called him Father, well, her father had dreams at night and dreamed of the great golden moon falling to earth from the sky one night in the middle of the German Democratic Republic, but luckily there was almost nobody at home. It was on a Thursday at six in the evening that he dreamed of the golden moon falling from the sky and smashing the factories all over the land, and in his dream you could hear loud music, a few deep notes, and when he woke up he was at peace with himself and the world again.

I'm sorry you're not happy, said Heinrich, and then Eva laughed and kissed him, because he was her father, and her father, who had the worst yet to come, was a terrible scoundrel, but she had to kiss him now if only for that reason, and she asked him out for a meal, I hope you'll enjoy coming out for a meal again.

A meal tastes good, and so does life when it's feeling kind, he said.

People ought to be able to begin from the beginning again, she said.

Yes, let's begin again from the beginning.

Starting tomorrow, she said.

Yes, starting tomorrow would be fine by him.